# THE WEDDING NIGHT

## BOOKS BY CLARE BOYD

*Little Liar*

*Three Secrets*

*Her Closest Friend*

*My Perfect Wife*

*The Pretty One*

*The Villa*

# THE WEDDING NIGHT

CLARE BOYD

bookouture

Published by Bookouture in 2023

An imprint of Storyfire Ltd.
Carmelite House
50 Victoria Embankment
London EC4Y 0DZ

www.bookouture.com



ISBN: 978-1-83790-136-4
eBook ISBN: 978-1-83790-135-7

*For Tilda and Joni*

# PROLOGUE

## SATURDAY 27 APRIL 2024

A lone bluebell was snagged in the white lace trim of her wedding dress as she hiked its heavy skirts and ran the wrong way up the aisle. The embellished train rustled behind her. In a silvery streak, she left the love of her life and their astonished guests in her wake. Their eyes bored holes in her back. They'd be milling and muttering and speculating in the sun-dappled clearing, unable to believe that the bride was not doing as she should. Each would have their own theory as to why. Her heart seized at the thought of William's dismay.

The material of her veil fluttered lightly over her features. Through it, the woodland was gauzy, filtered by an apricot glow and more beautiful than ever. It was a relief for her to meet the path where the trees closed in and obscured her from their judging eyes. Her body seemed to liquefy, to dissolve and spread through the undergrowth as though she had never existed there at all. But as she darted through the branches, her veil caught and dragged her head back, perhaps having a final go at holding her there. She yanked it free and let it flutter behind her, abandoning it along with the bricks and mortar of Summerfield House.

By the time she'd reached the field where their guests had parked their cars, her feet ached in her delicate shoes. Her dress restricted her like a straitjacket. Frantically she surveyed the rows to look for a car she recognised.

She moved from one vehicle to another, peering in, hoping someone had mistakenly left a key inside. In nice areas like this, people often got careless. Herself included. But it was hard to see anything in the gloaming. The sun had fallen quickly.

There had to be one damn car in this field she could borrow.

She came across her friend's gold Ford. Like a gift, the door had been left open. She rummaged amongst the sweet wrappers and old tissues for the electric clicker, feeling increasingly desperate. No doubt it would be stuffed into her friend's red clutch bag or her husband's jacket pocket.

She ploughed on. There wouldn't be a lot of time before her scandalised guests would be tramping along the path from the house to retrieve their cars – cheated out of a wedding. The boned bodice dug in under her armpits. She rolled her shoulders to see if she could break the seams for more movement. The garment was too well made, no give whatsoever. Its stitching was designed to hold for a lifetime, to be passed down to the next generation. Her daughter would have been the next victim of its constrictions, she thought with a shudder.

When she came to the final row, her ankle rolled over. The ground was sunken. She gathered the material into her lap and crouched down, running her hands along the dip. It was a circular tyre mark. A car must have U-turned at high speed. She stood up to think through the chain of events that had led to this moment. Something told her it wasn't right. An urgency to locate her daughter came over her in a wave. A gut instinct. The sense of knowing her baby from the womb was all she could go on. Nothing more. She was finally listening to this interior voice. No longer could she ignore her misgivings about her life with William.

She stumbled back from the markings to get a better look and stepped on something in the longer grass. It shone at her feet. Her throat closed up. She lunged down to pick it up, clutched it to her chest and moaned. It was a pink satin shoe. It was Tess's pink satin shoe.

# ONE

## AUGUST 2023

### Amy

There wasn't a trace of them left. Cleared of their stuff, the dank little flat was completely empty and colourless. The walls of the narrow front room were cream. The gloomy kitchenette units were cream. The staticky carpets were cream. Not even the dusty markings of a colourful poster or an ill-advised feature wall remained. The decor was exactly as the previous owner had left it six years ago.

'Let me check my room one more time,' Tess said again.

Amy guessed that her daughter had missed nothing. She had spent the last two hours forensically cleaning, vacuuming and dusting her tiny bedroom for the next owners.

Closing the front door with the metal plaque '7' – lucky 7 – for the last time, Amy simply said, 'Right then.'

Nostalgia flooded her. She knew that if she spoke about the day she had first put her key in the lock all those years ago as a newly single mum, she'd cry. She had never felt more unsure of herself.

'You okay?' Tess asked.

'Yup, totally. I'm ready.' Amy nodded, and then spotted the hole she'd drilled in the wrong place. 'Remember how this fell off?' she said, pointing at the number 7 plaque. It had been wonky for a while.

Tess chuckled, a little sheepishly. 'It was already loose!'

She'd slammed the door with such force after an argument about pocket money – Amy never had enough to give her – that the plaque had clattered off. Amy had used a drill for the first time ever. Before the divorce, Nick had done that kind of power tool stuff, in a stand-aside-little-lady kind of way. Yet she had found it surprisingly easy to plug it in and point it straight – men were so full of drama! – and her argument with Tess had been forgotten.

'We've had some good times here, haven't we?' she said, inhaling. She would not cry on a happy day.

Tess threw her arms in the air and projected her voice into the hall jokily. 'It was the best of times, it was the worst of times!'

'Cheeky. Less of the worst, thank you,' Amy retorted, linking arms with her. 'Seriously, though, Tess, you've been the best flatmate I could've wished for.'

She gave her daughter a super-tight, slightly clingy hug. For a long time she hadn't pictured anything more than it being just the two of them. They had been a team, navigating a brand-new set-up without Tess's dad around, going it alone, skint mostly, cold a lot, hungry occasionally, but becoming the greatest of friends in the process. Never happier than when snuggled for warmth under the same blanket, eating reduced own-brand ham and pineapple pizza and chortling at an episode of something they'd seen a hundred times before.

Then, last year, William had come along. They'd met online. His low-key, unpretentious photograph had stood out from the others on the dating website. He had been comically far away from the camera, standing in a confident pose: hands in jeans pockets, elbows out and lanky legs spread wide. He'd worn an unfashionable sweater, and his blond hair had been flattened to the side by the wind. She'd had to zoom in on his face to get a proper look. His understated good looks were the kind that might go unnoticed in a crowd: his hair was too fine and the green of his eyes too pale. It was his bold, purposeful smile that suggested he was sure of himself in every way, and it gave her heart a jump-start after six years of it flatlining. Her divorce had knocked the confidence right out of her. She'd given up on finding love again.

'Bye-bye, number 7!' Tess said, before popping up the hood of her grey sweatshirt and loping out through the door. Her lightness dispelled some of Amy's niggling concerns over the last few months about her reluctance to move. She was sometimes hard to read.

In the car park, blinking into the sunlight, they climbed into the front of the hire van.

It was the last week of August, but there was an autumn chill in the air, hinting at the end of summer. Tess wiped the screen of the sat nav with the sleeve of her jumper and typed in their new postcode. Immediately a yellow road popped up on the map. As they trundled off, their worldly possessions stacked in an orderly fashion in the back, she sang woefully out of tune to Tammy Wynette on the radio, with that all-important country twang, window wound down, her lovely face catching the breeze.

At a traffic light, a large bald man in another white van pulled up beside them and joined in, surprising Tess with his booming operatic rendition and making her raise her game. Delightedly she duetted with him until the lights changed. When he bipped his horn and drove off, she grinned at Amy as if to say: 'See? Tone-deaf and proud!' and tugged her centre-parted dark hair tightly behind her ears.

Amy glanced over at her. Her skin had a city pallor, like

milky tea. The way she slowly blinked her round black eyes and her bee-stung top lip, which jutted out assertively over the bottom one, gave the impression she was considering something deep. Tess didn't sweat the small stuff, like the adolescent spray of spots on her forehead or how not-at-all-on-trend her purple glasses were. But her city peers had. She was young for her age and under pressure to grow up too soon. Amy had it in her mind that country kids were innocent and wholesome, more like Tess, and she imagined her fitting right in and becoming rosy-cheeked and countrified. The timing of their escape couldn't have been better.

They stopped-and-started their way through the congested grey streets of Purley, crawling south to meet the A3. Here, like the seas parting, they were able to whizz down an empty motorway towards the Surrey Hills, where they were going to start their new lives.

Along the B roads towards Haslemere, their surroundings bloomed into technicolour: pink dahlias held their heads up high above flint walls; luscious green hedgerows protected the fields and houses behind them; sunny yellow roses bounced from beamed cottages; the purple of bougainvillea spilled enticingly over Tudor shopfronts. All the prettiest shades in existence were swirling past them and through Amy's mind, daubing over the hardships and bad choices of the past, painting a beautiful new future.

'Sheez, look at that house. It's so pretty, it doesn't even look real,' Tess said, putting down the book she'd been reading.

'It looks a bit like William's house, don't you think?'

'*Our* house, you mean!'

Amy laughed. 'Yeah, sorry, our house. Weird.'

Summerfield House was going to become home. It *was* real. Dreams really did come true.

# TWO

## William

'They'll be here in less than an hour!' William said, throwing his long arms in the air. He had spent much of his time as a single dad trying not to lose his temper with Hal. In the past, he'd left all that aggravation to his ex-wife.

'It's not that big of a deal, Dad,' Hal said, slouching against the kitchen island in his black running shorts, topless, hair flopping over his green eyes. The boy was doing nothing about the explosion of brown gloopy power-smoothie oozing across the porous marble worktop.

'How hard is it to remember to put the lid on a blender?' William smeared a smelly dishcloth into the mess, failing to catch a dribble that slid down the cupboards and in through the draughty gaps of the floorboards. He must not lose his temper, he told himself, noticing that some of the smoothie had reached as far as the bright blue songbird on the curtains. Admittedly, they had seen better days. And worse ones. Depending on how you looked at it. He began dabbing at the bird, partly now hoping the material was ruined, giving them an excuse to get rid of the heavy old things. He chased away thoughts of why he couldn't.

Hal dipped a finger into the smoothie mixture. 'Ames is such a clean freak. She's so fucking weird about hoovering before Mercy comes.'

William ground his teeth, chomping down on his defence of Amy. He knew he was asking a lot of Hal to accept Amy and Tess into their home with open arms. He was used to rattling around the place like a prince, often with his friend Rory, who was like the brother he'd never had: playing hockey in the vast hallway in their underpants; hitting balls into the broken net of the tennis court to make bigger holes; lounging about in the dinghy on the pond smoking cigarettes – like he didn't know! – the two of them answering to nobody.

'And what's with Tess?' Hal continued.

'What do you mean, what's with her? You two get on brilliantly.' It was a slight exaggeration. She'd only stayed at Summerfield House a handful of times.

'She's not gonna fit in at Heathside. Not gonna lie.'

'Well, you and Rory can help her to fit in, can't you?'

'She'd better not use any of those alternative swear words, like "shiitake mushrooms" or "frickin' this" or "friggin' that". What's wrong with good old fuck and shit?' He rubbed a hand across his lean, tanned torso.

'Some of them are quite funny, I think.'

'She's so *naff*.' Hal jammed his hands in his shorts pockets and glared at his dad through his hair.

With an electric bang, William's rage flared, and before he could stop himself, he had yelled, 'Don't be such a bloody snob!'

Only a slight twitch in Hal's eyebrow suggested he had been shocked by his dad's outburst. He guffawed. 'Chill, Dad. I'm going for a run.'

'Just make sure you're back in time to greet them.' William sighed, letting Hal go.

Up until now, Hal had seemed indifferent to both Tess and Amy and hadn't once complained about the idea of blending their two families. Having said that, William wasn't the best judge. He found it impossible to tell what was bottled up inside his son's head. Hal was sulky and suspicious and beautiful and utterly unreadable. He drove William mad. Those *eyes* of his. They were not windows to his soul; they were green iron-clad shields. Behind them was so much that William didn't understand, wanted to understand, and sometimes feared.

For a minute, he stopped wiping up, let the rag fall to his side and looked over at the huge round oak breakfast table clustered with chairs. The table had been the only furniture in the house that he had put his foot down about. Eleanor had wanted an oblong glass table-and-chair set like her friend Olivia's. Glass had not said 'family' to William. The homely old oak thing, found in a restoration yard, had held all his dreams of family life. He had pictured them eating hearty meals around it, having heated debates and laughing with one another.

It had been miserably underused. Family meals had not been a ritual Eleanor had gone in for. And William had been single-mindedly setting up his business and chasing the next big deal to keep the roof of Summerfield House watertight over their heads. This was his role as Hal's father. Summerfield House was all his son had ever known. Keeping it for him consumed his every waking moment. It was why he got up in the mornings and why he worked tirelessly every hour of every day. If only Hal could understand that this house was his way of showing him how much he loved him.

After he'd finished cleaning up, he checked his watch again. Fifteen minutes before they'd be here. It still gave him time to retrieve something he'd hidden in Hal's room. His armpits tingled at the thought.

He took the stairs two at a time, losing his footing on some worn sisal – stupid bloody sisal – up to a narrow landing that brought him level with the dusty tentacles of the modern light fixture. When he reached the third floor, up the smaller, steeper staircase to the top rooms of the annexe, he was out of breath and his knees hurt, like they needed oiling. Along the corridor to Hal's room, he popped into what would be Tess's room to check it was still tidy. Mercy had arranged the new cushions on the bed and had even put William's mother's old water jug and glass next to it. The duvet cover was a bright bohemian print. The faux fern plants on the windowsill and the new desk made it look homey.

Quickly he looked in on the bathroom that Tess and Hal would share to check for unpleasant boy things: wee on the loo seat, or squeezed-out hair gel, or a sodden, mouldy bath mat. The chain to the Victorian cistern had broken off, as it had a habit of doing. He hooked it back on and then hurried to Hal's bedroom.

Kneeling amongst the piles of clothes in front of Hal's open wardrobe, he stuck his hand deep inside a brand-new pair of Jordans. Then another pair, before eventually remembering he'd shoved it in the old red and black Nike. A stinky trainer was an unusual place to hide such a precious secret, but this room was the only one in the house that was off limits to Amy and her tidying, and Hal never wore his old trainers.

The velvet box sat in William's palm. As he opened it up, it creaked like a stiff joint. The sapphire ring shone from its bed. Love and hope rushed at him when he imagined slipping it onto Amy's finger. He pictured her smiley freckled face, her muddy hazel eyes and her shoulder-length blonde curls, hazy and static. Her freckles weren't the cute pinpricks that younger girls might draw on, but delightfully big. All these details about her he loved.

He neatened the row of trainers. As he did so, one shoe toppled to the side and something fell out. When he saw it, the hairs on the back of his neck prickled. Hal often hid his cigarettes in here, but this wasn't a packet of Marlboro Lights. It was a yellow egg-shaped container, like the ones in the Kinder chocolate eggs he used to give to Hal as a treat when he was little. He cracked it open. There was no plastic toy inside. He supposed he recognised what he saw, but in the context of Hal, his sixteen-year-old son, he couldn't fathom it. Every inch of his skin broke into a cold sweat.

He stuffed the yellow container into his pocket, wondering what he would do with it, reluctant to confront Hal today. Hurriedly he closed the wardrobe and put the ring box in his other pocket. The plastic egg was lighter and smaller than the box, but it felt disproportionately huge at his thigh, and a sinister foreboding landed inside him with a thud. He clutched the ring box for reassurance, ever determined to give Amy the fairy tale.

# THREE

## FEBRUARY 1990

### Me

'It's freezing, stop it,' she said, pulling up her knickers.

Losing her virginity on the fire escape balcony with the bitter February wind zipping up from the cliffs was less romantic than it had sounded.

'Let's go inside.' Her friends would be waiting up for her, eager to hear how it had gone.

'Is that a good idea?' he asked.

'Stop being a wuss.'

They both clambered head first through the small leaded window.

'Shh,' she said. 'I think I hear someone.' It could have been the housemistress stomping to the door to expel them on the spot. The footsteps carried on down the corridor. Or it might have been another girl breaking curfew and going for a smoke.

'I think I should go back,' he said. His breath was hot on her face. She wanted him. Wanted him almost at any cost. It wasn't so much about physical desire. It was about coming top. She'd be the first out of her gang to do it.

The bathroom wasn't the jolliest of settings for such a momentous occasion. The free-standing Victorian tub was crammed into the eaves, the magnolia paint was peeling in the corners and the linoleum was grey and buckled. It was, however, preferable to al fresco on a stone floor in minus 3 degrees. And it was the only room in this whole damned institution that you could lock from the inside.

'We have to be quiet. Okay? No grunting or anything,' she whispered, terrified and turned on all at once.

'Maybe we should wait,' he said, rather pathetically. She forgave him. She thought him terribly heroic for escaping his dorm in the middle of the night, running across the sports pitches and up the fire escape, avoiding the security guard and his Alsatian patrolling the grounds. Doing all this because she'd asked him to. It proved how much he loved her and endorsed her decision to have sex with him.

'Stop heavy-breathing.' She took off her knickers, which she'd bought new for the occasion, and lay down. He positioned himself carefully above her, as though not wanting to hurt her, and pushed it slowly inside. 'Okay?' he asked through a groan.

'I love you so much,' she winced. The sharp pain made her eyes water. She thought she'd burst open and feared that there would be blood everywhere.

But there had not been any blood. Neither then, nor in her knickers later. Nor on her sheets that night. Nor for nine months after that.

Because I came along.

# FOUR

## Amy

Amy pressed the four-digit code into the keypad, which was listing precariously to one side on its wooden post. The five-bar gate was rickety, like an old farm gate, but it swung open for them, automatically and efficiently as ever. The driveway was potholed. They bounced about in the van.

The house couldn't be seen until they swerved around the huge rhododendron bushes. Its splendour never failed to stop Amy's heart. She could not believe that she was going to live in this sprawling 1930s Arts and Crafts mansion. William rather laughingly called it a 'cottage'. The leaded window panes were diamond-shaped, sitting prettily in the white-rendered elevations. The exposed beams holding it all up were wonky and worm-holed. Past generations seemed to be spying on her, weighing up her suitability, questioning her decision to sell number 7, up sticks from Purley and move forty-odd miles away into the depths of Surrey. It had seemed like a crazy idea at the time, too soon in their relationship, and even crazier as she approached it. Staying here every other weekend, or over half-term, or when Tess was at her dad's wasn't the same as calling it home.

'Flying effing flip, I always forget how big it is,' Tess said under her breath, fanning herself with the paperback she'd now finished.

Amy could almost feel her mother sitting next to them now, with her teased blonde bob and her jumper dress and her small eyes surveying the place, warning her not to get above herself like Lady Muck. While she'd be sniffing at the weeds along the driveway and tutting about the eight-foot rhododendrons that needed cutting back, she'd be secretly proud of her daughter and dying to show the Rotary Club ladies the photos. None of that was why Amy's tummy was doing somersaults. Amy would have moved into a garden shed with William if he'd asked her. So long as Tess had okayed it.

William's long, lanky form appeared through the arched studded-oak front door. His big square smile, with that one front tooth crossed over the other, filled her with renewed confidence.

He strode over to the van, grinning and waving, sweeping his blond hair to the side, leaving it thick around his temples. He had a stiff gait, as though he were mentally overriding his self-consciousness to appear more manly and purposeful. It made her want to shake his arms like yoga teachers did to release tension in the limbs.

'Welcome home!' he said generously, kissing her on the lips and looping a long daisy chain over her head.

Home, she thought, looking around her. That was what it was supposed to feel like, and it would in time, she was sure.

With typical old-fashioned chivalry, he helped Tess down from the van with one hand. Then he positioned her square in front of him and put a chain of flowers on the crown of her head.

'It was meant to be a necklace, like your mum's, but I ran out of time. What are those Hawaiian garlands called, the ones they welcome their guests with?'

Tess and Amy laughed. 'Haven't the foggiest,' Amy said.

Hal appeared in the shadows of the doorway. He was wearing running shorts and a tank and was flanked by his white, shaggy lion of a dog, Hamish.

'Leis,' he said laconically.

'That's it! Well done, Hal.'

William was eternally proud of his son's intelligence, but there was an arrogance about the boy that Amy was watchful of. Her mum's favourite phrase came to mind: *Confidence is good, but overconfidence always sinks the ship*. Her mum had trotted it out in a perky, know-it-all way when she thought someone was getting above themselves.

'I'm a real princess now,' Tess grinned, tongue-in-cheek. 'It's lovely, thank you.' She fingered her new headdress and glanced over at Hal, as though seeking his approval.

He returned her gaze steadily. 'Very Joni Mitchell.'

On cue, Tess sang about angel hair and ice cream castles before adding a series of feisty TikTok dance moves, and Hal put his hands to his ears. Poking fun at her tone-deaf singing had been their first family in-joke. 'They don't appreciate my talents,' Tess said, holding Hamish's lion-like front paws and giving him a kiss on his nose. He began howling in a singing way. Hal grinned, watching them guardedly.

'Come on,' William said. 'Let's have a cup of tea before we lug those boxes inside.'

On the wide fitted doormat, flush to the panelled walls of a small atrium, Tess automatically took her trainers off and placed them under the narrow console table laden with wicker baskets and a vase packed tight with lilac hydrangeas.

'You don't need to take them off,' Hal scoffed.

William quickly clarified. 'Keep them on! The floor's rather cold and draughty.'

Amy had trained Tess to take her shoes off before entering someone's home, thinking it was the polite thing to do. 'I'll get her slippers out in a bit,' she said, as a compromise, taking off her own slightly grey trainers.

William hesitated before booming, 'Slippers, yes, marvellous! Hal, why don't you take Tess up to her new room.'

'New?' Tess said, pushing her purple glasses up her nose and blinking her big eyes furiously as she hugged her book to her chest like a comfort blanket.

'Don't get too excited,' Hal said. He bowled around the hall table, brushing past the roses, stocks and asters arranged in a porcelain jug at its centre. She followed him, but backwards, moonwalking in her socks over the chilly hallway tiles, saluting the oil paintings of various ancestors on the walls. Hal glanced back at her. His amusement never quite made it to his lips, but Amy could see it in his eyes.

'It's only a little revamp of her existing room. Mercy did it mostly,' William said to Amy under his breath, winking.

Seeing them head upstairs together made Amy feel unexpectedly uneasy. It was all very well her falling in love with William, but if the children didn't get along or if Tess was unhappy, it was a deal-breaker.

From the landing upstairs, she heard Tess say, 'I always thought it was rude to keep your shoes on.'

'Grandpa Ru says it's common to take them off,' Hal replied.

'Common?' Tess said quietly.

Common? Amy thought.

William cleared his throat loudly, as though trying to mask what Hal had said. He rubbed his chin awkwardly. Hamish, who wasn't allowed upstairs, had given up on waiting for Hal on the bottom step and now trotted alongside them. Anger flushed through Amy, reddening her cheeks. She thought of how much dirt they *weren't* traipsing onto the floors that poor Mercy would have to clean. If thoughtfulness was common, then Amy was proud of it.

# FIVE

## Tess

'Dad's plotting something,' Hal said.

'Oh yeah?' Tess replied, still hugging her book, interested in the photos pinned behind the gaming screens on his desk.

'Yeah.' He glanced up from his phone. He was lying on his king-size bed, tanned ankles crossed, unbothered by her nosing around. His room was painted in a handsome grey and was bigger than the flat she'd grown up in. Usually nobody was allowed in, and she wondered why she had privileged access today. She stepped over puddles of hoodies and T-shirts, lone trainers, cans of Lynx, sticky-looking cereal bowls, two iPads and a laptop sticking out from a jumble of exercise books under his bed.

'Are they from school?' she asked, pointing to the Polaroids. Good-looking boys were brandishing bottles of beer. Girls with clear golden skin and deep cleavages were cutely sticking their tongues out.

'Yeah.'

'Will she be in our year?' One girl had dark hair like Tess.

She had cut it into a cool shoulder-length bob with a fringe. Instantly Tess wanted to be her.

'No, she left to go to a state sixth form. She wants to go to Oxford.'

'And Heathside Heights won't get her into Oxford?'

'Didn't you know, if you get A stars from a private school, you're stupider than if you get A stars from a state school?' He took a cap emblazoned with a roaring lion from the corner of his headboard, put it on and pulled it right down.

'That means I'm way cleverer than you.'

He flicked the cap up, resting it on the back of his head. 'Believe me, I'm well aware of how exceptionally average I am.'

'Don't you want to go to Oxford too?'

'Dad wants me to.'

She turned back to the photos of the girls she was going to be at school with. She felt her stomach rise and drop. 'The popular girls hated me at my old school. I was "irrelevant".'

Hal looked up from his texting for a second but said nothing.

She went on. 'One of them – the prettiest, actually – had yellow eyes because she drank too much. She was okay, though. Less of a b-word than the others. We were in science together. But she was really messed up and got a reputation for shagging around. Her mum gave her a bottle of vodka in her stocking when she was twelve. Then she failed all her GCSEs. And I'm not friggin' kidding when I say *all* of them. I felt so bad for her.'

'Heathside girls shag around and drink too much but get good grades anyway. Best of all worlds.' Hal snorted.

There was a full-length mirror on the inside of the door of his built-in wardrobe. Tess liked her purple glasses, but she frowned at the face behind them, wishing she had sweeter, smaller features like the girl in the Polaroid. 'This girl Carla would spend literally *hours* putting on make-up in the toilets before lessons started. But she didn't need it. Her skin was amazing.'

'I think it's cool when girls don't wear make-up,' he said absently.

She took her glasses off and fashioned a fringe to cover her spots. Ana, Malena's mum, had a salon on Purley high street. She had always cut Tess's hair for free while gassing in loud, animated Portuguese to the other stylists. Tess would miss Ana and Malena now that they lived so far away. Malena was clever, not in an Oxford way, but in a street-smart way. And she was kind. When Tess was pissed off about life, Malena would secretly slip a Double Decker or some bubble gum into her blazer pocket. They'd scheduled a FaceTime tonight.

'What did you say before about your dad?' she asked.

Hal rolled off his bed and sauntered over to her, then bent down at her feet and rummaged through rows of sneakers. 'He hid something in here, but I found it.'

'What?'

'A ring box.'

'A *ring* box?' Tess said, certain she couldn't have heard right.

'Yup. Wait... Oh, that's weird, it's not there now. But hey, lookie what we have here.' He flapped a pouch of tobacco at her with a grin on his face. 'I forgot I had any.'

'What kind of ring box?'

'The kind that has a ring inside?'

'What, like an *engagement* ring?'

'I guess so,' he said, getting back into position on his bed, reaching into the bedside table for Rizlas and a lighter, using an exercise book as a makeshift table. 'It had diamonds and sapphires and shit.'

'Egad,' she mumbled. Her heart thumped. 'But Mum never said anything to me about getting engaged.'

'Isn't it supposed to be a surprise?'

'You think he might ask her tonight?'

He didn't answer as he expertly rolled a cigarette, then stuck it in his mouth, looking like one of those thin, beautiful, tortured actors in a cool indie movie. He mumbled, 'He might. The ring's suddenly not there now, so... dunno, it might mean something.'

He stood up on his pillows and opened the window. The leather headboard wobbled as he bunny-hopped out onto the ledge. Tentatively Tess peered outside. The drop was life-threatening, but she followed him anyway.

# SIX

## Amy

Amy hurried to the boot room to put away her shoes and gather herself. Hamish followed her in and began sniffing suspiciously at her feet. She took in her new surroundings and felt unexpectedly intimidated by it all.

The built-in benches were painted an expensive green and the cubbyholes were stuffed with elegantly tatty tennis plimsolls that had probably been worn by generations of posh people. The large shiny silver hooks were laden with layers of old-fashioned waxed coats. Rows of every size of welly for every size of guest were tipped upside down on wooden pegs. The tartan dog bed covered in Hamish's blond fur was big enough for Amy to curl up in herself.

She noticed a worn leather umbrella-holder embossed with the initials 'TSG' in gold lettering. It held tennis racquets and 'brollies', as William called them. She guessed it had belonged to his late mother, Tabitha, though she realised she didn't know her maiden name. She patted Hamish's flank and scratched his soft mane. She knew Tabitha had died when William was only ten and that she had loved Patricia Highsmith novels and golden retrievers; that she had, in a flurry of angry tears, sold all her grandmother's fur coats and given every penny to the local dog rescue centre, and that she had a mischievous habit of licking her plate behind Rupert's back when they'd had gravy for Sunday lunch.

Amy hadn't yet met Rupert. William's father was very much alive and lived in the Algarve. A sense of panic was building in her. She had moved into William's house, but she hadn't met his dad and she didn't know his mum's maiden name.

Did she know anything much about him? she fretted, feeling sweaty as she sat amongst all this unfamiliar stuff, all this excess. None of it was ordinary. She was unconfident of it, wary perhaps. The terraced houses that she had grown up in – one in Liverpool, then a very similar one in Purley – had been one hundred per cent ordinary. They'd had one front door, one back door and nowhere to put shoes except the floor. It had never occurred to her that anyone might need more than that.

Hamish whined at the door, wanting to go back through. He was a good-natured dog. Dogs often reflected their owners. She reminded herself that Hal was young, that his snobby comment about being common had come from his grandpa. If Amy was honest with herself, her own grandfather's opinions had been just as outmoded, albeit about other things. Over the years, she and her brother and sister had tried to educate him about what was okay to say and what wasn't. In the same way, perhaps Tess could teach Hal and Grandpa Ru some things as well.

Hal had done his best to welcome them both today. Summerfield House was his whole world, his childhood home; it had been his manor up until now. Before Amy could even add one small photo to the collection of silver-framed Hargreaves portraits, she and Tess had shifted the molecules in the house. It would take time for the household to adjust to their presence there. And she realised it would take even more time before Summerfield House would feel like her real home.

# SEVEN

## Tess

Tess's head spun with an attack of vertigo as she sat down cross-legged on the ledge next to Hal. They were on top of the hexagonal bay windows of the morning room below, looking out on to the garden. To the left of them was her bedroom window, which was flung wide open. Through it she could see her standing mirror. She leant back against the cold bricks.

'What's a morning room for, when you already have a drawing room and a TV den?' she wanted to know.

'No clue. Never go in there. Sure you don't want some?' he asked, proffering his rollie. 'Or I've got a vape somewhere, if you'd prefer?'

She shook her head. They both fell silent for a minute. The greenness of the countryside view was unfamiliar to Tess. She felt she'd stepped into a storybook.

Then, 'Shit.' Hal flinched and flicked his roll-up over the side. 'Shit. Shit. Shit. I can hear them.'

'You sure?' She bent forward to see in through her bedroom

windows. In the mirror, her mum opened her door and then closed it again.

'Fuck,' Hal said. He stepped over her and dived deftly back into his room before offering his hand and lugging her in. They collapsed on the bed in a tangle of limbs. There was a knock on the door of his bedroom. Before they could separate fully, it opened. Both parents were looking at them with the same expression, trying to work out what they were seeing. Hal rolled off the bed and sniggered guiltily. Tess straightened her glasses and yanked down her twisted top.

'Oh, hi! What's going on in here then?' Amy said, falsely upbeat. 'I came up to see your new room.'

'Wow, Hal. It's a pigsty in here,' William said.

Tess dragged her mum away by the arm. Behind them, she could hear William asking Hal lightly, 'Might it be a good idea to have a little tidy in here?'

'Fuck off, Dad,' Hal replied.

'This is nice,' Amy said when they were alone in her room. Tess recognised the flatness of her tone, heard the anxiety in her voice and saw the hotness behind all those freckles.

'Mum, I promise you it wasn't what it looked like in there.'

'Hmm?' Amy said, picking up the natty little spray can and watering the fern.

'Mum! You buckethead! Hal and I weren't fooling around with each other, I promise!'

She looked around with a spark of hope. 'Really?'

'Of course! Jeez, Mum.'

Amy sat down on the bed. 'But why did you both look so guilty?'

Tess knew her mum would worry more about the idea of her shagging Hal than she would about her smoking. 'D'you swear on *all* the alternative swear words in the whole world that you won't mention anything to William if I tell you?'

Her mum grinned. 'Fudge nuggets and all.'

'Hal will get in so much trouble if you say anything, and he'll make my life a misery.'

'Tess, I *swear* on Thomas Shatner and Jiminy Crickets.'

Bravely Tess spilled the beans. 'He was having a smoke on the ledge outside his window. But *I* wasn't. You know I hate smoking.'

Amy blew out her cheeks and slapped her hand across her heart. 'Oh, thank God!'

When they had recovered from a giggling fit, Amy wiped away a tear with the back of her hand and tried to smooth down her puffball curls. Then she looked around, as though seeing the room for the first time, clocking the plants and the desk with solid silver legs and the woven rug with gold flecks and the crisp bed linen. 'This duvet cover is from Urban Outfitters, isn't it? I mean, HOW long have you wanted it for?'

'Like. Frickin' FOR. EV-ER. The only thing this place needs is a bookshelf,' Tess said, realising she had left her book in Hal's room.

'Very sweet of William to do all this for you.'

'Yes, really sweet of him,' Tess said, meaning it, and thinking about the ring. She took her glasses off and gave them a clean with the edge of her T-shirt.

The not-telling her mum about the ring felt unnatural and achy, like the beginnings of a sore throat. But she couldn't be selfish and ruin it for her. After her dad had left them, Amy had thrown all her energies into Tess: taken a second job at Waitrose so that Tess could join the after-school theatre club; turned down nights out for months to save up for the latest Kindle for her; slept next to her on a crappy futon when she'd gone through a stage of having recurring nightmares; got up at four in the morning to queue at Waterstones for a signed copy of Harry Potter for her birthday. Tess knew right to her bones that her mum lived to make her happy. But when William had arrived on the scene, Amy had finally found something of her own. Tess couldn't spoil this for her. In fact, she was going to do everything she could to fit in and make this transition easier for them.

'Where's my box with all my toiletries in?' she asked, forming an idea, putting her glasses on her bedside table.

'No idea, why?'

'Can we get that one out first?'

'Why?'

'Ugh, Mum. I just need to find it, okay?'

'If it's at the back of the van, you'll just have to wait, okay?' Amy said in her firm, no-nonsense voice. 'Come on, let's get started.'

'Fine,' Tess said. If she hadn't packed Malena's hair scissors, then kitchen scissors would do the job almost as well.

# EIGHT

Hal

When Hal saw Tess's hair, he almost dropped his phone. 'Oh shit,' he breathed. There was no way now he could associate with her at school next week.

'Oh! Tess!' Amy cried, clapping her hand over her mouth, eyes popping out. 'What have you done?' Hal noticed her Liverpool accent come through for the first time and it vaguely fascinated him to hear her reveal it. He had become good at watching grown-ups. Better, over the years, at predicting them. Although he didn't know Amy well enough yet. It would be interesting to see what she did now. Interesting in the context of two less-than-interesting people.

'It's that bad?' Tess's eyes filled, and Hal looked away, back to his phone. He couldn't cope with girls crying. It wasn't that he didn't care, he simply didn't know what to say.

A message came in from Rory.

*Need to pick up my stash from yours.*

*What stash?*

*Nike air stash mate*

*WTF is it with my fucking nikes today?*

*???*

*Nothing, I'm bringing jagermeister and beer to the party. Dad finished the vodka. What stash u talking about?*

'Oh love, sorry, I didn't mean to... I just thought... It's just that,' Amy gabbled, rushing over to Tess and taking her in her arms, eventually saying, 'It'll grow back.'

Hamish nuzzled into them, trying to get a hug in too. Seeing them together, Hal didn't think they looked related. Amy had a kind of flyaway, freckly blondeness and self-doubt in her eyes, whereas Tess was more intense with her olive skin and black hair.

'Not by next week!' Tess shot back furiously, pulling away and storming out. Amy followed.

There was some shouting from Tess. Hal comforted Hamish by scratching him in his favourite spot behind his ears. Hamish didn't like it when there was a fight.

'Fuck. Her first day's gonna be brutal,' Hal said.

'Yeah, fuck indeed,' William said vaguely, checking his watch.

Hal scrutinised his dad. He had barely said one word to Hal since Amy and Tess had got here. His hands rested wide apart on the worktop, forefingers tapping alternately, as though poised to play a piano concerto. Hal had an urge to ask him if he was angry with him, sensed he'd done something wrong but couldn't think what. Thinking about it some more, the ring box was the more logical explanation for his mood. Hal wasn't sure he was ready for all that.

'The pizzas will be here in half an hour,' his dad said. 'Will you keep an ear out for the girls? I'm just going to grab the candles from the larder.'

'Sure.' Hal sat next to Hamish on the floor by the Aga, and Hamish rested his big furry head on his knees, occasionally looking up at him with a sad sideways expression, as though saying, 'Life's shit, but what can you do?' Hal loved Hamish with everything he had. Loved him more than he could ever love a human being. Human beings let you down. Hamish was solid. Always there for him.

He zoned out of the fuss his dad was making about the pizzas, diverted by a vaguely entertaining group Snap about the party Rory was throwing this weekend for Hal's seventeenth. He'd re-enter the kitchen drama when there was food on the table.

Rory messaged him again.

*Can I come over tonite?*

*Ok*

*What time?*

*I'll let you know. Gotta have pizza with the fam*

'Listen, they're coming downstairs,' his dad said.

Hal noticed the aroma of warm dough and roused himself. Pizzas from Guido's Italiano were far superior to any other and were only ordered on special occasions.

His dad lit some candles in the middle of the kitchen table they never sat at. 'Alexa, play Best of Piano Dinner Jazz.'

This was over the top for a pizza night. Was he going the second mile in celebration of their first night? Or was he going to bring out the ring? The idea of a proposal gave Hal goose-bumps. But he wasn't sure whether it was excitement or fear for his dad. If it was excitement, he was encouraged he could still feel positive vibes towards his dad, but he didn't want to get ahead of himself.

When Tess returned, Hal was pleasantly surprised. The wonky fringe had been straightened and the length evened out. Much shorter all over. It swung at her shoulders, shinier and darker somehow.

'Better?' she asked shyly.

'Gorgeous, Tessie!' William said. 'Amy, you're wasted in kitchen design!' he added.

Kitchen design? Hardly, Hal wanted to say. By all accounts, she had been an assistant at some showroom in Croydon.

Amy chuckled. 'I can't take full credit. We FaceTimed Malena's mum, who helped us out with a mini tutorial. We'll head up to the salon before school starts and sort it out properly.'

'Lesson learned,' Tess said, pushing up her hideous purple glasses and swinging her new hair. The tip of one of her ears poked through. Quite sweet, Hal thought. He had to admit, Tess was instantly prettier now that her fringe covered her spots. Behind her 'zany' glasses, her eyes were turbulent black pools. They were beguiling, almost hard to look away from. If he could persuade her to put her book down for a second and wear her contact lenses, she might survive Heathside Heights. Then maybe, just maybe, he wouldn't have to ignore her.

'Okay, now that drama's over, is everyone ready?' William said, clapping his hands a little manically.

And Hal decided that he was kind of excited after all.

# NINE

## Amy

'Guido's?' Amy cried, warmed by the effort William was making to settle them in. 'It was where we had our second date! Are they on Deliveroo now?'

William raised an eyebrow enigmatically, saying, 'It was a special delivery,' and started handing out the boxes. 'Tess – a Margherita. Hal, we got you the Calabria, with extra chilli – is that okay?'

Hal nodded, looking pleased that his dad had remembered the extra chilli, which wasn't always the case.

William sat down and opened his own pizza box, humming as he took a huge slice of his sausage-laden 'Britannia' sourdough. Amy didn't appear to have a pizza and raised her eyebrows. She'd be happy to share if he had forgotten hers.

'I don't get one?' she asked, laughing.

'Whoops, sorry,' William said. 'I almost forgot.'

From under some newspapers on the countertop he whipped out the final pizza box, twice the depth of a normal thin-crust. It had a strange bulge in the middle. He put it in front of her, moving aside the cardboard lids of the others to give it room.

'Oh my God, what did you order me? It's huge!' It was then that she knew something was going on.

'The Arrabbiata, with an extra-special topping,' he said, sitting up straight like a schoolboy. He wiped his hands down his thighs as though ready to stand up to perform in front of the class.

When Amy opened the box, her chin crumpled. 'Oh!' she breathed, burying her face in her hands, letting her curls fall around her fingers to hide from it.

William and Tess crowded around behind her chair. The pizza had been cut into an imperfect heart shape. At its centre, on a little white plastic stand, a black velvet box was tied in place by a white ribbon.

'Oh!' She undid the ribbon but whipped her hands away from the box. 'Oh my God. Is this really happening?' she cried in genuine disbelief and utter delight as she looked around at all three faces.

'Open it,' William said, uncharacteristically shy.

Hal too gave her half a smile, as though embarrassed for his dad.

'Go on, Mum!' Tess begged.

When she did, she burst into tears.

William shuffled forward and cupped his hands around hers. 'Will you marry me, Amy?'

For one blissful and intense moment, she felt wholly loved; a lifetime of self-doubt and insecurity flushed away. His faith in her was like a spotlight that shone on her, forcing her to put her chin up and her shoulders back and believe in herself. Without hesitation, she spluttered a slightly snotty, teary, but definite 'Yes!'

'Holy crap, Mum!' Tess cried, wiping her eyes under her

steamed-up glasses, taking them off, patting her face with a napkin. 'I feel a song coming on!'

Hal snorted. 'No!'

William placed the ring on her finger and a kiss on her lips and whispered in her ear, 'I love you, Amy.'

'I love you too,' she replied, pleasure blooming in her heart.

# TEN

Hal

The old bell clanged just as they'd settled again to eat their reheated pizzas. They'd been laughing at Hamish, who was sitting on a chair like a human, waiting for his own celebratory slice. It didn't immediately occur to Hal that it might be Rory at the door. His friend was more likely to bowl in through the boot room as though he lived here. But then his phone vibrated.

*I'm outside the front. Didn't wanna disturb the famalam love-in*

Hal's heart sank. In his earlier funk, he had been keen for Rory to swing by. But he would ruin this. And right now, *this* – whatever it was – was all Hal wanted. Since his mum had left them for *that man*, he missed the feeling of being part of a proper family.

'Who the hell is that?' William said, immediately glaring at him.

Boom. The beautiful family moment was gone.

'It's Rory. I didn't know all this was going to happen, did I?' Hal said accusingly. The jazz music tinkled away.

'This is special *family* time, Hal, it's not—'

'William, it's fine,' Amy said, touching his arm. 'Tell Rory there's loads of pizza left!'

They laughed at the barely touched pizzas abandoned in their boxes.

'Thanks,' Hal mumbled appreciatively.

On his way out, he saw that Tess had left her purple glasses on the kitchen island. While everyone was busy inspecting the sapphires on Amy's hand again, he grabbed the glasses and dropped them in front of Hamish like a dog chew, saying, 'Good boy.' As he walked away, he could hear the cheap plastic cracking in the dog's big jaws. It was best that Rory met Tess without them. He was unforgiving of things like that. And he had clout at Heathside Heights. It was for her own good, even though it might not look that way.

He let Rory in. There were no fist bumps or manly hugs tonight. Rory bolted past him and up the stairs towards Hal's room, and Hal remembered the 'stash' he'd mentioned in his message.

# ELEVEN

## Tess

Tess carried her smashed spectacles upstairs to her new room, trying not to cry. She'd cut her fringe like the girl in Hal's Polaroid because she'd wanted to get her look right so that she'd fit in and make it easier on her mum. Tears of frustration were now getting mashed up with happy tears about the proposal. She couldn't separate the two. She was tired. It had been a long day. She wanted to go home. Home wasn't here, it was there, in Purley, with Malena and her other friends. None of this would ever feel like home. Impostor syndrome would be a luxury right now. Being an actual impostor in what was supposed to be her own life was ten times worse.

She locked the bathroom door, hearing the beat of music and the murmur of Rory and Hal talking. She was intrigued to meet Rory, having heard so much about him.

Should she go in and introduce herself? she wondered, putting her face close up to the mirror, squinting and scowling at her reflection. After Ana's tutorial, her hair looked better. She was pleased that her new fringe hid her spots. As she fiddled around with the contact lens instructions and the solution and the tiny plastic packets, the two boys' voices through the wall grew louder. There was a series of thumps on the floor. It sounded as though an object was being thrown about. Hal and Rory sounded angry.

The process of putting contacts in was so much more of a hassle than putting glasses on her face. Blinking into the mirror, eyes watering, loathing the strange sensation on her eyeballs, she looked at herself again. The effect wasn't all bad. But she needed mascara. She applied some before stuffing her glasses in the bin with a flourish.

'YOU HAVE TO FUCKING FIND IT!' a voice roared. The music cut out. There was some mumbling from Hal.

Tess trotted left out of the bathroom to Hal's room, knocked once and flung the door open. Everywhere she looked, trainers were scattered across the existing mess. The racks they had lived on were empty.

'Holy cow. What's going on in here?'

'Don't you knock?' Hal said.

'I did.'

Rory swivelled round. The blond buzz cut and the hooded blue eyes had the effect of a chop to the back of her knees. His tanned, smooth hip bones showed above the white Calvin Klein logo of his underpants. As he brushed his hand up from the base of his skull to his forehead, she could hardly catch her breath enough to say, 'I just wanted my book.' Dumbly, she pointed to it on Hal's desk.

'I was giving your bro here a hard time for losing my stuff.'

'*Bro*? Fuck's sake,' Hal mumbled, sitting down on the end of his bed, slumping over his phone, pulling his lion logo cap over his eyes.

'Congrats to your mum, by the way,' Rory said, doing that head-brush thing again. From under his brow, he dragged his gaze slowly up Tess's body. Self-consciously she zipped her hoodie up and down at her chin. Their eyes locked. Now she knew what it felt like to have a proper crush. An instant, body-tingling crush.

'Thanks,' she managed to croak.

He turned back to Hal. 'I think your dad must have found it.'

'Don't be dense. If he'd found it, do you think he'd not've gone fucking nuts?'

'Why, what is it?' Tess asked.

'Fuck!' Rory yelled at the ceiling, hand clutching his head. 'Hal, man, you've just got to get it back for me. I'm serious. I'm totally fucked if you don't get it back.'

'It's not my problem that you were too much of a thickhead to mention it was there,' Hal said.

Tess wanted to help. 'What am I looking for?' She began picking up clothes, shaking them out, folding them.

Rory watched her and laughed. Just once. But enough to flip her heart. 'Where have you been hiding *her*?' He directed the question at Hal, who didn't answer. 'Look, I've gotta go. Let me know when you find it.' He grabbed a portable speaker from Hal's desk and put it in his rucksack. As he walked past her, he twisted his chunky silver chain, straightening it over his T-shirt. 'See you at school, Tess.' And he was off with a loose-limbed jog down the stairs.

'What was he looking for?' Tess asked, gathering up a dirty plate encrusted with tomato ketchup. From Hal's open bedroom window, she could hear the skid of Rory's mountain bike wheels out front.

'Happy hour, four for twenty-five,' Hal replied incomprehensibly.

Confused, she laughed. 'What does that mean?'

'Nothing,' he said.

She began folding one of his T-shirts, but he leapt up and snatched it from her violently. 'LEAVE IT ALONE, okay? Just because you have to live here, it doesn't mean *my* business becomes *your* fucking business. *Ever*. Get it?'

It shocked her. Usually he was understated, buttoned up, brooding.

'Whatever. I just wanted to help.' She rubbed at the scratch he'd made on her hand and took a wide step over a pile of shoes towards the door, feeling shaky. The short walk to her own bedroom didn't feel far enough. It was going to be like living with a popular boy at school; those changeable, untrustworthy, cruel types who could be your best friend one minute and then turn a whole group of friends against you with one remark. Now she had a bedroom next to that guy. She suddenly didn't feel so happy for her mum any more.

# TWELVE

## Amy

Amy knocked. There was a delay before Tess answered. While she waited, she thought she heard a baby crying somewhere behind the door. She pressed her ear to the panel, guessing it came from a TikTok reel on Tess's phone. She knocked again, dreamily spreading out the fingers on her left hand, tilting it left and right, watching the ring sparkle under the downlighters: stars in her eyes. She wondered if her heart would ever return to its normal rhythm. William's beautiful and funny proposal played through her mind again and again. It was almost impossible to come down from. But she would have to try. Before she could settle into the idea of getting married, she had to check that her daughter was all right with it.

'Yes?' Tess said. She was lying back against her new fleece cushion. Into her phone, she said, 'Gotta go. Yeah. Bye.'

'Just checking on you,' Amy said.

Tess stared down at her screen saver, clicking it on and off. 'Such exciting news, Mum. You must be so happy.' The laboured quality to her voice was like hearing scratches down a blackboard.

'Everything okay?' Amy asked.

'Yeah, fine.'

'Sure?'

'Why wouldn't it be?' Tess shot back, rubbing at two red marks on her olive skin.

'How did you do that?'

'It was Hamish when he jumped up.'

'I can't believe he ate your new glasses.'

She looked confused for a second. 'Oh right, yeah. Bummer,' as if she'd forgotten.

There was a loud rumble of voices through the wall and Tess flinched, tugging at her top lip.

'You two getting along okay?'

'Yes,' she answered, curling on her side, pulling the blanket up around her chin.

'You can tell me if you had a fight. It's bound to happen.'

There was a pause and then a mumble. 'No. We didn't, Mum. I'm just tired.'

Amy sat down on the bed and jammed her hands between her crossed thighs, feeling the jewel on her finger dig into her flesh. 'If I'd known he was going to propose, I would have told you first, you know, made sure you were okay with it,' she said quietly.

Tess sat up. Her voice was anguished, her black eyes flashing. 'Mum! It's not about that, I swear. Stop overthinking everything. Honestly, I'm so, so happy for you.' She tugged at Amy's hand and held the ring close to her face, inspecting it. 'It's gorgeous. Vintage. And it's so *you*. Isn't it?'

'It is pretty,' Amy said cautiously, suppressing the sharing of her own joy until she could gauge Tess's real mood. 'And you're *sure* you're okay about it? Because if you're not, then...' She stopped. She couldn't say out loud what she couldn't bear to contemplate: that she would sacrifice every happiness in the world for Tess.

Tess struggled upright and patted the covers. 'Mum! Sheez. Shut up already. I'm okay about it. More than okay about it. *Okay*?'

'Okay. But it's a big thing. And if you have any wobbles, you must talk to me. Don't feel it changes anything.'

'I promise to talk to you. Now, let's look up cool wedding venues on Pinterest! What about a crumbling chapel on the edge of a loch? Near Auntie Maggie, maybe.' Tess showed her a magical scene of a small chapel lit up with candles in the pinkish evening light of the Scottish Highlands. Gliding across the glassy loch in a motorboat was the bride in billowing white, trailing her fingertips in the ripples. A small crowd in tartan sashes holding champagne flutes waited for her on a shoreline tangled with seaweed.

'Maggie would love that. And Amy would love that. But it's a bit far for people to come.' Amy swung her legs up and got under the blanket next to Tess, thoroughly relieved that her daughter was on board with the idea of a wedding.

'Maybe clip that for a honeymoon idea then. How about this?'

It was a picturesque church in a village with a couple being showered in confetti.

Amy said firmly, 'No churches this time.'

Her ex-mother-in-law had been half Spanish and whole Roman Catholic, and she had insisted Amy and Nick marry in their local church in West Norwood. It had a bus stop outside it and a huge white statue of the Virgin Mary suspended over the stained-glass windows. Inside, the air had been thick with incense and traffic fumes. The ceremony had been excessively long, and Amy had felt like a non-believing fraud with her lace-covered head and shoulders. During the vows, her legs had ached, and she'd noticed that the priest's lips had been cracked and flaky in the corners.

'Okay,' Tess said. 'No churches. What about a field?' They scrolled through images of sun-blushed, hay-baled, muddy-hemmed bliss.

'Yeah, maybe,' Amy said, hiding that familiar prickle of self-doubt. 'Where would *you* like it to be, Tess?' She wanted to get it right this time but didn't know how.

The angry vibration of music started up through the walls.

'I'm not the one getting married! What do *you* want?'

Thinking beyond what Tess wanted was an alien concept. 'Don't ask me.'

'Let's make a mood board,' Tess suggested.

A sense of inadequacy dropped inside Amy. She stood up and went to the window, looking out on to the dusky, peaceful garden, admiring its established shrubbery and tall poplars tamed by Pete the gardener – two sugars and a digestive! She recalled how in spring the woodland was carpeted in bluebells and the lawn thick with daffodils. *There's nowhere more beautiful than this in the springtime*, William would say. With every change of season, he'd say the same, that there was nowhere more beautiful than Summerfield House. The place was his pride and joy.

What struck her as odd now was the fact that he hadn't mentioned the house on their first date. When she thought about it, she had fallen in love with him almost instantly but had found out few particulars about him that day. More, they'd got a sense of each other and what mattered to them. Like his interest in the obscure cloth-bound books on the café's shelves near his head. And his attentions towards a dog sloshing water from the bowl by the door. When he had hung his jacket on the back of his chair, she had seen it was weighted by a paperback displaying green hills on its cover.

'What are you reading?' she remembered asking him rashly,

before wishing that she hadn't. She had always wanted to read more, and certainly wouldn't be able to hold an intellectual conversation about literature.

'Robert Macfarlane,' he had said. 'It's about walking.'

This had been a relief. She loved to walk. 'I walk across the common to work every day, even though the bus would take me a quarter of the time,' she had admitted.

'Are there some good walks around here?' he had asked, just as a dirty great number 445 trundled past, sending vibrations through the table.

'Really peaceful,' she had said, and they had chuckled.

Having no idea at the time that his garden was the size of a park, she had suggested a walk on Riddlesdown Common, innocently proud of her stamping ground. She had taken him on her well-trodden local loop and pointed out the yew trees and the junipers and the unusualness of the quarry. And she had mentioned the rare orchids that were rumoured to grow in the woodland.

'Rare orchids,' he'd repeated, slowing to a stop beside her, brushing his blond hair confidently to the side and out of his eyes to look right at her. 'Somehow that seems just right,' he had said, and a big, friendly, boxy grin had broken out across his features.

After only a couple of hours of knowing him, her heart had felt less like a fist, and she had dared to hope that her grim swiping left and dodgy dating was at an end.

Now, the reminder of what she had shared with William on their first date grounded her. Their wedding should reflect their love of the outdoors, which gave her an idea.

Tess's voice penetrated her thoughts. 'I just met the infamous Rory, by the way.'

Amy nodded. 'Yup. He spends half his life here.' She sat down on the bed again. 'His mum texted me, actually. Olivia.

She wants to organise a coffee morning at her house with some of the mums from school. You know, welcome me to the area.'

'Aww. That's so sweet of her.'

'I thought so too.' Amy twisted her ring. As much as she was looking forward to making new friends, she couldn't wait to send a group WhatsApp message to her old friends Pip and Joanna to arrange an evening at Pip's on Kenmore Road. She'd tell them in person about getting engaged and ask them for advice about the wedding. How realistic was it to drive over to Purley one evening this week? Tomorrow? Was it too far?

'He's not in any of my classes.'

'Hal or Rory?' Amy asked, confused for a second.

'Rory!' Tess said, sounding frustrated.

Amy eyed her daughter for a second. 'And did you *like* Rory, then?'

'Ugh. No. He's a bit of an idiot, don't you think? His hair's like a loo brush and he wears a *chain*. And he's in the rugby team,' she guffawed. On the whole, Tess tended to be more interested in bookish boys who read modern American literature and didn't wash their faces as often as they should. But Amy guessed that her daughter was lying to her for the second time in the space of an hour.

# THIRTEEN

William

'What was all that shouting about with Rory before?' William asked Hal.

'Nothing,' Hal said.

William closed Hal's door. 'Anything to do with this?' he asked, holding up the yellow container filled with a dozen or so little cling film pouches of white powder. He felt sick about it but was going to give him a chance to explain.

His son visibly blanched. 'It's not mine.'

Keeping his voice down, William asked, 'It's Rory's?'

'He left it here without telling me.'

'What the hell is it?'

'A bit of coke, I guess. No idea.'

'What's he doing with it?'

Hal clicked his tongue. 'I dunno. It's got nothing to do with me.'

'Do you realise how serious this is, Hal?'

'It's not that deep,' he mumbled.

'Excuse me? Are you really trying to tell me this is okay?'

'But you're blaming me for something I didn't do.' There was a catch in his throat.

William squeezed his temples. 'I found drugs in your room! What the hell am I supposed to think?'

Hal glared at him, his jaw pulsing. 'Whatever you usually think, I guess.'

Too many times Hal had used Rory as an excuse for their scrapes. Like when they'd got caught selling football cards for silly prices to the younger kids at prep school. Or when they'd nicked Olivia's housekeeping money, skipped class and caught a train to London to buy trainers in the Nike Town sale. Or when they'd 'borrowed' fifty pounds from William's wallet to buy beer from a local wino on Lion Green to flog to their mates. Since the beginning of their friendship, their get-rich-quick schemes had been ongoing. A familiar weariness seeped in. William's sole aim was for Hal to have everything he wanted, never to feel lacking for a second, but Hal appeared to be a bottomless pit of want.

He supposed there was always a child who had more around here. Heathside Heights was chock-a-block with fathers who spoiled their sons. Sam, who lived down the lane, had hired specialists to dig out a mountain bike course for his son on their land. William had not done that for Hal, who loved his bike. Marte and Miles had spent months working out the shape and lining of a swimming pool for their four boys. William had decided that a pool would be too costly and bothersome to heat. And then there were the holidays. Even Paula and Jared, supposedly broke, had spent their last two Christmases in Dubai. William had instead plumped for the cheaper option of a small apartment in the Austrian Alps, which Hal had been a brat about.

The ludicrous and impossible list of what William hadn't given him went on. He could provide more for him, but Hal already had too much. And William determinedly believed that the magic of Summerfield House was better than any of those things, better than having all the money in the world.

Hal continued nonchalantly, 'Dad, seriously, you're giving me shit over something I haven't done. If you hadn't stuffed that ring in there in the first place, you'd never have known any different.'

'Well, okay, if it's that inconsequential, you won't care if I get rid of it then.' And William began walking out, possibly looking more confident than he felt.

Hal yanked the neck of his jumper and clawed at his hand. 'You can't take that. It's Rory's!'

William experienced a flash of anger that felt more like terror. He grabbed his son's wrist and formed a vice-like fist around the egg. 'Don't you dare!'

'Give it back,' Hal said, but there was a flicker of doubt in his eyes.

William tightened his hold, feeling the rage surge through him. 'I'm warning you, if you want to continue to live under this roof and enjoy all the comforts that I work so bloody hard to provide for you, you have to abide by my rules.'

'You'd... what? Chuck me out?'

'You're almost seventeen years old! If you do anything that could endanger the others, then yes, that's exactly what I'd do!'

The words had come tumbling out. He hadn't meant it to be anything more than a scare tactic, but it had sounded too convincing. The distress was etched on his son's face. William regretted what he had said while holding out some hope that it might jolt Hal into appreciating what he had.

'What the hell? That's fucked up, Dad.'

Amy appeared. And in that second, Hal took full advantage of William's diverted attention, plucking the yellow egg out of his loosened grip and shooting down the stairs.

'What's going on?' she asked.

William tried to find the right words. 'It's complicated.'

From downstairs, he heard the boot room door slam.

'Try me.' She looked at him with her 'let's talk about it' face, which usually led to her asking him how he was feeling – deeply uncomfortable for him, but not always a bad thing. *Talking about how you feel takes practice*, she'd once said to him. *The more you do it, the better you get at it.* He was trying. But he couldn't possibly tell her what he and Hal were really arguing about.

'It's about his school work,' he said, thinking fast. 'He's got so much potential, but his grades are dipping.' This was also the truth.

'How much have they dipped?'

'He's still mostly getting As, but the stars have disappeared.'

The hazel of her eyes swirled with tiny flecks of green. 'Oh blimey, Will. Ha! Since when are As dips?'

He felt foolish. 'I know it shouldn't really matter. But his English teacher wants him to apply to Oxford.'

'Does *Hal* want to apply to Oxford?'

'It would be a shame if he didn't go for it.'

She shoved one side of her hair behind her ear, and a fluffy curl pinged out. 'They're either going to work hard because they want to do well, or they're not, and there's nothing we can do about it.'

He laughed lightly. 'That's not how it worked for me.'

'No?'

'If my parents hadn't literally reminded me every day of my life that the school fees were crippling them, guilting me into working harder – or taken my privileges away if I didn't get good enough marks – I would have pissed about and failed everything. And I certainly wouldn't have been able to afford a home like Summerfield House for my family. People might see all this and think I'm lucky. And I am, of course, but it's hard bloody work to keep it.' He had said more than he had wanted to, and added, 'I just think Hal needs a push sometimes.'

'Nobody pushed me, and look what happened!' Her pretty Northern lilt came through and she flung her arms out as though to say, 'I have nothing!' and all he could see was everything.

'You look okay to me.'

She kissed him. 'Say sorry to him, won't you? You mustn't ever sleep on an argument.' She hummed to herself as she pottered off down the corridor with her golden curls bobbing at her shoulders.

Amy was the most open and forgiving human being he had ever come across, with the sole exception of his mother. Every time she overlooked his flawed behaviour, he fell in love with her even more and wanted to try harder to be a better person. Her presence at Summerfield House had been like throwing the curtains open to let the sun stream in, blanching out its secrets. But now Hal was creating shadows all over the place. However hard William worked to overcome his own shortcomings, his son threatened to spoil it for all of them.

# FOURTEEN

## JUNE 1990

Me

The drawing room was filled with dust motes. My beautiful young mother seemed to be dragging them into her lungs with each sob.

'I want it out of me!' she screamed, clawing at the waist of her jeans.

She was only sixteen. She was much too young to have me inside her. But I wanted her to stop. Her distress was seeping into my bloodstream, sending stress hormones and adrenaline shooting through my tiny form. I would have liked to reassure her, tell her I already loved her more than any living person ever could. I wasn't quite in existence yet; only an embryo of four months.

My survival was in Grandma Annie's hands.

Annie was eyeing my mother's histrionics – for that was how she viewed them – sitting very straight on the armchair with its back to the French windows of the apartment. Sunlight spilled through the wrought-iron balcony, leaving lacy patterns on the carpet at her feet. She wore brown brogues, flesh-coloured tights and a spotted silk shirt with a necktie. Her hair had been curled inwards above her collar, looping around her pearled earrings. The blue shimmer on her lids was subtle but brought out her startling eyes. A stripe of blush emphasised her incredible cheekbones. She had been beautiful enough to be a model or an actress, though she would have considered both those professions beneath her. Only a certain class of person became models and actresses, she'd said to my mother once. Apparently they were barely better than waitresses or prostitutes.

Her faithfulness to society's rules was Annie's religion. Decades of cultural change had passed her by.

This wasn't her fault, I suspected. In the sixties, she had been tapping her courts underneath rigid satin gowns at debutante balls in hotels in Mayfair or Knightsbridge. In the seventies, she had been busy marrying a suitable young man in the Home Office and furnishing a big house in Surrey with her young children biting at her heels. In the eighties, she had hosted nice dinner parties for her balding husband and learned to play tennis exceptionally well. In the nineties, exhausted by all that convention, she was old before her time, well and truly wedged into a fifties time warp of upper-class womanhood. Exactly as her parents would have wanted. And she was screaming inside.

The pied-à-terre in Cadogan Gardens, a few streets from where she'd grown up, had been purchased as an investment with some money from her sizeable but tightly controlled trust fund and had counteracted some of her boredom. A group of wealthy connected socialite wives had rescued her. They spent weekends at their houses in Portofino or Verbier, had girls' lunches at Le Caprice, went to the Tate or the Royal Academy – her favourite – and sometimes even danced at Tramp. She had begun to feel young again, as though she were living her life upside down, old to young.

But then my mother had ruined it by getting pregnant with me, and her sense of duty had kicked in like muscle memory.

'We've been through this. You're not going to get rid of it. It's too late for that, you silly girl.'

'But I can't have it, I just can't!'

Annie lurched from her upright chair and knelt in front of her, grabbing her shoulders. 'Pull yourself together, for Christ's sake!'

My distraught young mother couldn't control her emotions. She let out a series of siren wails, arms flopping, mouth contorted.

In desperation, Annie slapped her cheek, quickly and lightly. 'Listen to me!'

While I flipped about in my mother's womb, her body became still, wide-eyed and attentive, alert to Annie's every move. Annie sat next to her and placed her hands into the dip of her lap, rubbing her palms.

Very calmly she explained the situation. 'Your father and I have considered the options. If you have the baby here, it'll ruin your prospects, not to mention what it'll do to your father's chances of running for Parliament or your brother's future in politics. So you and I are going to pack our things and we're going to drive down to the cottage this weekend, where you'll have the baby. We've found a lovely French lady to help us.'

'But what about my A levels?' Her tone was meek, cowed by that one slap.

'The timing is fortuitous. You can finish the last few weeks of the summer term, but you won't be returning in September. Instead, you'll take a year out. We'll find you a private tutor while you bring up Baby.'

'Will I ever be normal again?' Her chin wobbled and Annie's heart softened a little.

'Oh my darling child, of course you will. You can start your A levels at a lovely new girls' school – I was thinking of

Roedean or Cheltenham. How about that? It'll be as though nothing had happened.' She brushed a hand lightly down her daughter's sleeve, which had ever so slightly grubby cuffs. Underneath the cotton, her arms goosebumped. Annie had never touched her affectionately like that before.

'I'd leave the baby?'

'Avril, the French lady, and I will care for it until you're ready.'

'You'd do that for me?'

'I'm your mother,' Annie said, as though this explained it.

'But what do I tell my friends?'

'That you're taking a year out to learn French fluently for Oxford. It isn't a complete lie – Avril is going to speak only French to you. You've always wanted to do languages there like your father, haven't you?'

'What about...' Then my mother whispered my father's name and Annie stood up, moved to the windows. She straightened the curtains as she looked out to the street below and watched a crocodile of children in mustard jumpers and brown culottes trot past the church opposite. Only yesterday, she thought ruefully, her daughter had been that same sweet age.

'We'll invite him down to meet the child. But he needn't worry himself with the details. Daddy will have his solicitor draw up a contract.'

But I was growing inside her. A contract written by the most eminent solicitor could not control the girl who would give birth to me. The fact of me was enough to wreak its own havoc on such a young mind. Nobody seemed to consider this. Not until much later.

# FIFTEEN

## Tess

'Here we go,' William said, pulling the car up at the train station, where the school bus left from. Hal shot straight out of the back, shouting goodbye. Before Tess opened the passenger door, William stretched over her to the glove box. He said, 'I got you something. For your first day.'

It was a brown paper parcel wrapped in green ribbon from Daunt Books in London. She opened it. Inside was a cloth-bound edition of *Tess of the d'Urbervilles*.

'Oh, it's beautiful! Thank you so much, William,' she said, delighted.

'Look inside the front cover,' he said. 'You said you wanted to be a writer someday.'

She read the inscription: *Dear Tess, You will sing through the words you write. All my love, William.*

She laughed. Their jokes about her off-key singing made her feel accepted. 'Thank you,' she croaked again, slipping it in her bag, knowing she would treasure it for ever.

'Off you go. Have a good day.' He beamed at her. 'Everyone will love you.'

The Shreddies she'd forced down roiled about in her stomach. Hal loped ahead of her in his blue suit, looking like a younger version of the men hurrying past them to catch their trains into London. Tess's stride was restricted by her grey woollen pencil skirt. The lining made a swishing sound as she walked.

As they waited for the bus to arrive, she stood apart from Hal, who focused only on his phone. She messaged Malena, but there was no reply. Right about now, she'd be running freely in her black uniform trousers, faster than the boys, to catch the number 289 on Purley high street. Tess longed to be with her.

A brand-new twenty-seater Heathside Heights bus, with the slogan *We Are Prepared For Greater Things!* painted on its side, pulled up at the stop and opened its electric door.

Hitching her skirt to climb the three carpeted steps inside, she tried not to look at anyone. She chose a window seat behind a red-headed boy with a violin and immediately pulled out her book.

A group of kids from a local school streamed past the bus in their green blazers. Tess stared at them through the blacked-out windows and yearned to be in that crowd instead of this one. Those other kids were more familiar to her: the girls with their way-too-short rolled-up skirts, purposely laddered forty-denier tights and loosened nylon ties; the boys with their skin fades and Nike rucksacks and untucked Aertex. They jostled and shouted, guffawing and swearing, huddled into cliques.

Here in this Heathside Heights vehicle, there would be new rules. Next to her, two blonde girls were muttering together on their phones. Their skin was tanned, their hair slippery clean, their blazer collars popped up at the neck and their fresh blue cotton socks rebelliously pushed down. Cluttering the space between them were sports bags and music cases embroidered with the school crest and motto, *Sapere aude*, which she had looked up. It meant *Dare to know*.

In front of the bus, a Mercedes jeep pulled into the kerb, cutting up a small hatchback behind it. An extremely beautiful blonde woman driving the jeep waved and smiled apologetically. The passenger door opened and Tess recognised Rory. His suited attire was markedly different to the slouchy-cool leisurewear of the other night. His shirt was untucked at least. He joined Hal and they talked head-to-head as they approached the bus. Until they stepped inside, the bus had been quiet in a way she'd sometimes wished the number 289 had been.

'Sorry we're late, Mrs Fox,' Rory said, hiking his belted suit trousers onto his hip bones, seemingly for the sole purpose of showing off his lean body.

The teacher immediately clenched her jaw. 'Sit down, you two.'

Hal mumbled an apology and walked past Tess without a glance. The two boys sat in the back row. Their presence seemed to charge the air. The girls next to Tess began to talk loudly about a pool party they'd been to; a boy in front of them began playing sweary music from his phone, which was then confiscated.

Once that commotion had died down, Tess began to read. After only a few pages, she felt a tap-tap on the top of her head. She had a feeling it was Rory, but she didn't trust herself not to swear at him if she turned around. This was what she had done on the number 289 when Robbie Griffiths or Daniel Hardy had thrown balled-up sweet wrappers or bottles of Lucozade at her. So she decided to sit very still and focus on the reliable sentences in front of her, taking her to another world.

It happened again. This time with an 'Oi!'. She could feel the eyes of the two blondes – one straight, the other curly – on her, but she tried to concentrate on her book. Her heart hammered. Another tap and an 'Oi, Tess!'

She plugged her AirPods into her ears and turned her music up.

What Rory was doing now was what popular, sporty, stupid boys did. They made girls like her suffer. Tess's mum had insisted it was because they had small willies.

'Sit DOWN, Rory Clark, or you'll be in detention!' Mrs Fox hollered.

She was in for it at this new school. Nothing had changed. The boys would still make fun of her for being a 'neek', as they had at Kenley High. A pellet of sweet-wrapper foil hit her neck and landed in her lap. Without looking behind her, she threw it back in Rory's direction. There was a loud guffaw. Her Google Maps search told her to expect six more minutes. Six more minutes of pretending she didn't care about Rory goading her. After *eight* torturous minutes, thanks to a traffic jam, the bus finally swung into a tree-lined tarmac drive.

Tess's breathing stopped. The Victorian gables and multiple chimneys of the country pile in front of her were reminiscent of a stately home. Ancient oak trees dotted the lawns leaving huge shaded areas underneath which picnics might be held on a hot day. On the left, they passed a sprawling modern wing with wood panelling and floor-to-ceiling windows. The bus parked up in front of ten tennis courts laid with fresh red and green asphalt and crisp white lines. For a minute she forgot about Rory and hurried behind the blonde girls towards the arched stone entrance of the main building.

As she fumbled for her timetable, sweaty and frightened, someone tall appeared by her side.

'Were you actually ignoring me back then?' Rory asked.

Thinking quickly, she came back with, 'You were interrupting my favourite song.'

'One Direction?'

'Cigarettes After Sex, if you must know.'

He nodded slowly, and with less bombast said, 'Respect.'

'Now I have your approval, my life is complete.'

He grinned. 'Just wanted to say, if there's any trouble today from anyone, come find me. Okay? Or your bro here. All right?'

She rolled her eyes, unable to suppress a grin. 'I went to a south London comp, remember. I think I can take care of myself, thanks.'

He exaggerated backing off with his hands up in the air, as though surrendering.

'I like your new sister, Hargreaves,' he said to Hal, loudly enough for Tess to hear as he dropped one arm over Hal's shoulders. Hal ducked, undoing himself from Rory, taking out his phone and walking on ahead.

'I'll add you to the group chat for next Saturday,' Rory shouted. 'The theme's Suits and Sluts.'

'So the girls will be in suits and the boys are going as themselves then?' she said.

'Ha! Girls in suits sounds sexy as hell!'

Her heart somersaulted. The two blondes joined her, weighed down by instruments and sports bags. 'Did Rory Clark just ask you to his pool party?'

'No clue. Did he?' Tess said.

'It's Hal's birthday, so I guess that's why.'

'Oh right, yeah.' Tess had not known that Hal's birthday was coming up. Nobody had mentioned it at home, which she found distinctly odd. Her own seventeenth was on 21 December, and she was already thinking about what she wanted to do. She couldn't imagine what a birthday at Summerfield House would look like.

'He's only adding girls he wants there.'

'Who he thinks are fit.'

'That's so superficial,' Tess said, motioning to push up her glasses before realising they were no longer on her face. She straightened her new fringe instead.

'I know, right? He's hot, but not too smart.' The girls both grinned. 'I'm Anoushka and this is Tilly.'

Anoushka was tall and had train tracks on her teeth and perfectly tonged curtain bangs. Tilly was tiny and full-chested, with wavy hair that hung fluffily either side of her cherubic pink face.

'Hi. I'm Tess.'

'We *knooow*,' Tilly laughed. 'The whole bus knows!'

The two of them chuckled, and Tess immediately wanted to be their friend.

'Want to come shopping with us at the weekend to get our outfits? This is what we're going as.' Anoushka showed her a TikTok reel of a girl in a satin bodice with laces.

Tess said, 'I might wear a suit.'

'Coool,' Tilly said.

Anoushka narrowed her eyes and looked Tess up and down. 'Are you sure?'

'Yes, she's *sure*, Noushie. Just because you want to get your tits out and jump Hal's bones doesn't mean the rest of us do. Right, Tess?'

'You want to get with *Hal*?' Tess asked, incredulous.

Anoushka's laugh was tinkly and mischievous. 'I can't lie,' she drawled. 'I like the moody, quiet types.'

'The HH shag hut needs to be prepped!' Tilly squeaked.

'*Shag* hut?' Tess said.

The two blondes linked arms with her. 'We'll show you. *And* the vaping tree,' Tilly added.

'You're kidding, right?'

'Nope. Seven grand a term pays for outstanding facilities,' Anoushka cackled.

Tess stopped dead in her tracks. William was paying seven thousand pounds a term for her to go to this school? She'd had no idea it was that much. The weight of it pressed into her sternum.

'Maybe you'll be hooking up with a certain loo-brush head in the shag hut,' Tilly said, nudging her.

Tess enjoyed a racy thought about Rory, then tried to stop the blush spreading across her cheeks. The heat moved through her hairline and across her whole head. And Tilly and Anoushka spent the rest of the day ribbing her about it and plotting ways she might get with him at his pool party next Saturday.

# SIXTEEN

Amy

Olivia had given Amy directions to her house by text. It was only five minutes away, up the Petworth Road, through Lythe Hill Park and further into Haslemere itself, but she'd already got lost and was driving a little haphazardly.

Olivia had mentioned that three other 'girls', as she called them, would be coming. Amy was keen to make a good impression, wanting to make some new friends. But she felt jittery and clammy, like before a job interview.

She had first met Olivia a few months ago when she'd picked Rory up from Summerfield House. She was a real-life Barbie doll. Her chin and nose and mouth were petite, paling under the shadow of her big blinking blue eyes. She was model height with an enviably tiny waist and long, subtly waved blonde hair. Amy guessed the comparison to the doll would have offended her. Aside from the obvious fake tan, she was very much classier than Barbie. No hot-pink minis or plastic shoes anywhere in sight. She was more about silky shirts and gold chain cross-body bags.

As Amy drove slowly along Scotland Lane, trying to read the house names, she passed by the most beautiful town houses she had ever seen. Acres of garden stretched between them. Some were modern and some traditional, and most of them were much larger even than Summerfield House, which perhaps explained why William called it a cottage.

The sign 'Oak Hills' was outside a dove-grey estate gate. Behind it was an enormous and impressive Georgian house with tall sash windows, a rarity amongst the many traditional Surrey Arts and Crafts houses. The automatic gates stuttered open. Unconfidently, she navigated the car in. She noted that only the front of the house was painted white. The rest had been left as bare sandstone, which she thought was odd. But what did she know? Maybe painting one side of your house was normal around here, like a statement wall was in Purley.

She parked William's second car, the red Mini, next to a white Tesla, a black Mercedes jeep and a wine-red electric Range Rover. Over the brow of the sloping garden, she saw a kidney-shaped pool holding water that looked green. She guessed it was one of those natural, chlorine-free pools she'd read about.

The front door creaked open and two overweight French bulldogs waddled out. Olivia appeared in the narrow opening wearing shiny Lycra leggings and a long cashmere sweater. Her hair was tied back into a gorgeous thick, high ponytail and her face was shiny and pinkish.

'What a beautiful house,' Amy gasped.

Olivia eyed her for a second, and Amy wondered whether it had been the wrong thing to say. 'It could be,' she replied cryptically, and then, pointing to her leggings, 'Sorry I'm still in these. I love your sweater. Such a pretty blue. Where's it from?'

'Umm...' Amy tugged at the neck to find the label. 'Zara.'

'I *love* Zara. You can mix and match it, and nobody would know.'

'I'm not sure how much mixing I do. Most of my clothes seem to be blue and come from Zara.'

Olivia tilted her head to the side and opened the door wider, saying, 'Oh really?'

'Well, not literally *all* of them,' Amy clarified, feeling stupid for the exaggeration. The two dogs snuffled at her legs, saving her. 'Cute. What are their names?'

'They're rescues. Come in. The others are here already,' Olivia said, walking down the corridor. They passed a sitting room. 'Margot wees on that sofa every time she hears a car on the drive.'

'Poor little thing,' Amy said, bending down to scratch the dog's flank.

'I've given up changing the cushion covers,' Olivia sighed. 'Rory calls it the piss sofa.'

'You know you can get one of those sofa covers that are designed especially for mucky pups.'

Olivia threw her head back and laughed. 'Oh, that's hilarious!'

Amy wasn't sure what was so funny.

They continued to the back of the house. Toys that Rory would have grown out of ten years ago were tossed about the floor. Two console tables were piled high with letters and books and the odd shoe. Amy's socks stuck to the limestone floor. There was a slightly sour smell in the air, as if the bin needed to be taken out. The house seemed unloved, where happiness had perhaps once filled its space, long since gone. It was the opposite of how Olivia presented herself.

In the kitchen, blue plastic sheeting was pinned to an opening in the wall where you might expect sliding windows. Some of the cabinets didn't have doors. There was a glass table big enough to fit twenty people comfortably, but it had a dangerous-looking crack in one corner and only two scratched see-through plastic chairs at one end. A woman stood in front of a floor-to-ceiling wine chiller.

'Whoops! Caught red-handed!' she said, brandishing a bottle. She was small, with sloping shoulders and dark hair, and wore a bright red and pink yoke sweater. Her pointy eyebrows gave her a surprised expression. 'Hi, you must be Amy. Lovely to meet you,' she said, putting the bottle down and shaking Amy's hand. 'I'm Paula. Oscar's mum. He's in Rory's year.'

'And this is Marte,' Olivia said. 'Mylo's mum, who's also in Year 12.' Marte was a beautiful, angular woman of roughly Amy's age with white-blonde hair tapered into a strong widow's peak. She was holding the handle of a jug of pulpy orange juice.

Amy handed Olivia a packet of chocolate digestives. 'I brought these.'

'You didn't need to do that.' Olivia put them away in the cupboard, and Amy regretted the offering. In Purley, if she hadn't turned up at Pip's with something with chocolate on it, she would have been shown the door.

Paula laughed mischievously. 'We're going eighties and making Buck's fizz!'

'We don't usually crack out the bubbly this early, but we thought we'd celebrate your news,' Olivia said.

'What news?' Amy was on the back foot.

Olivia's glassy eyes widened. 'Rory told me that William proposed?'

'Oh. Yes.'

'It's beautiful!' Paula cried, pointing at her ring. 'How did you two meet?'

'Online. Which doesn't sound very romantic, does it?'

Olivia smiled sweetly. 'You can meet people from completely different walks of life online, can't you?'

'That's true, I guess.'

It was true that she was from a different walk of life to William. She hadn't imagined it would be that obvious after only five minutes of being here. Maybe the packet of biscuits had given her away.

'I miss wearing a ring,' Olivia said, pouting.

Both her friends gave her a little side hug, jogging her hand as she poured the champagne. 'I separated from Rory's dad, Toby, last year,' she explained to Amy, looking down at the spilled champagne, dabbing her forefinger into it, swirling it into patterns across the worktop.

'I'm so sorry, Olivia. That really sucks.' Amy found a J-cloth in the sink and mopped up the fizz.

Olivia licked some champagne off her finger, watching Amy clean up. 'You're officially divorced from Tess's dad? Or just separated?'

'Signed the papers six years ago.' Amy took a glass, enjoying that first sip. A much-needed boost.

'But aren't you lucky? William's lovely. And rather mysterious. We knew he'd be snapped up,' Paula said.

Marte added, 'In the playground at prep school, he used to be called a DDILF.'

Guessing at the acronym, Amy chuckled shyly, but Paula felt the need to spell it out. 'The *Divorced* Dad I'd Like to F—'

Olivia interrupted. 'He's like, the last proper gentleman left in the world. None of us could believe what Eleanor did to him.'

'She was always a bit of a strange one,' Marte argued, twisting her white hair into a bun and then letting it fall around her face again. 'Kept herself to herself in the playground.'

'Plainly not, considering she was jumping into bed with Mo's husband,' Paula guffawed. 'Although he *was* a dishy BA pilot,' she added. 'We shared a picnic with the four of them at sports day once. It was so obvious that something was going on.'

'He had a tough time of it,' Amy said, feeling uncomfortable that these women were talking glibly about William's heartbreak. He had very reluctantly confessed the whole sorry story to her in bed one night. Embarrassed and apologetic, he'd needed constant cajoling to get through it.

'I've heard she barely even sees Hal,' Olivia said.

Amy felt a draught down her back. 'That's not the whole story,' she said cautiously. 'But he was bloody upset with her for a while. As you can imagine.'

'Sorry, Amy, God, we're sounding bitchy now, aren't we?' Olivia said.

'No, no, don't worry. I would've been just the same.' And this was true. 'There was this time at Tess's primary once, when one of the mums sent a round-robin email to the year group telling us about some yoga classes she was teaching, and we got a return message from this other mum saying, "Thanks so much for letting us know about your yoga classes, but I don't think I'll be able to attend because you're screwing my husband and it might be a tad awkward." We gossiped about it for weeks.'

Paula almost spat out her Buck's fizz.

'Laying my cards on the table, I was good friends with Eleanor,' Olivia said, holding both palms up. 'The three of us were at Manchester together.'

'Oh, right!' Amy exclaimed. She'd known that William and Eleanor had met there. Every time she heard William regale Hal with his antics – freshers' week, halls of residence, graduation – she felt she'd missed out by not going to university. Not necessarily for the qualification but for the self-confidence it instilled in young people. It was a quality she wished she had more of.

'Yes, Will and Ellie met through me, actually.' A gust of wind blew at the plastic sheeting and Amy jumped at the noise. The other two took awkward sips of their champagne. 'But we fell out. She started posting her love affair with the pilot all over Facebook, thirty pics at a time. I mean, who does that? I thought it was time to bow out of the friendship.'

'Let's not give her any more "air time",' Paula said, chuckling, miming quote marks. Everyone groaned and she poured more champagne. 'Amy, we want to know *where* and *when* you're getting married.'

'To be honest, we'll not rush it. Maybe do it next summer or something? I've no idea what sort of wedding we want. The thought of organising it is doing my head in.'

Olivia tilted her head to the side. 'Is it?'

'Not because we want a big bash or anything,' Amy added hastily. 'Maybe something simple at the house.'

'Summerfield House?'

Immediately the atmosphere changed.

'Yes. In the garden, I thought.'

With a sideways glance at Marte, Olivia said, 'Have you asked William about it?'

'No, why? Oh Jesus, he and Eleanor didn't get married there, did they?' Amy was sure they'd married in a registry office. She remembered seeing a photograph of them standing outside on the steps. Eleanor had worn her auburn curls in tight ringlets around her neck and her dress was scooped at the neck to show a muscular décolletage.

'It's not that, it's just...' Olivia hesitated. 'Because he doesn't own Summerfield House?'

Amy's heart thumped as she took in that revelation, but she managed to come back with some kind of reply. 'Oh right, yeah, that! Course, we'd clear it with the landlord.'

Again Olivia looked over at Marte, whose flute hovered at her lips as though she was about to say something. She didn't, and Amy was glad of it. Instead, she swallowed a large gulp of champagne.

# SEVENTEEN

## JULY 1990

Me

Annie drove the green Jaguar, but it wasn't used to the potholes in the country lanes. She made a mental note to purchase a proper country vehicle, like a Land Rover.

In the passenger seat, my mother had her knees up and pressed into her belly. I was squirming about inside her. The stars were in bright clusters above them, and the air smelt of warm tarmac and barbecue smoke.

'I'm glad we're not going all the way to the cabin now, aren't you?' Annie said, tapping her thumb on the stitched steering wheel to the beat of a tune, turning the radio up.

'Which cabin?' my mother replied.

Annie turned it up again. 'Chamonix, darling. That's where we first thought to have it, remember. To which other cabin could I possibly be referring?'

'I thought you meant our cabin in Argyll.' My mother didn't care about which cabin. She just didn't care.

'That's not a cabin. That's a *croft*.'

'Ma, just to let you know, a real croft doesn't have running water or heating. And I definitely remember there was a radiator at the end of my bed when we were there last because it gave me heat lumps.'

'We modernised it, of course, but we still call it a croft,' Annie said. 'When we bought it, it had no windows and an open fire that...'

My mother with me inside her stopped listening and smiled to herself when she remembered that she hadn't changed her knickers in three days. It would have horrified Annie, who kept on talking about nothing.

A voice in my mother's head repeated, *SHUT UP, SHUT UP, SHUT UP!*

The long journey through dry fields had been peppered with bickering between them. Already, my mother with me inside her couldn't imagine spending a day longer with Annie, let alone a year in isolation with her.

The dire contemplation of it prompted her to undo her seat belt, propel herself up and push her top half out of the window. She let the wind blow through her hair. Her T-shirt billowed. One hip dug into the protrusion of the lock. The shouting in her head finally ceased.

'Get inside, this instant! If a car comes past, you'll be decapitated,' Annie yelled.

My mother didn't immediately react, having decided that if her head was knocked off by a passing vehicle, she would not have to hear another annoying syllable uttered from Annie's lips.

Her wish had been the universe's command.

The beams of two headlights swung into the road ahead of them. Two circles of light became larger and larger, brighter and brighter. Her arms juddered underneath her, but she clung on. A smell of gasoline burned the insides of her nose. The rushing air dried out her mouth.

'Oh MY GOD!' Annie shrieked.

She released one hand from the wheel, groping at the back of my mother's jeans, screaming in sheer terror. The car wobbled, out of control, across to the wrong side of the road. The low, deep horn of the truck warned them of its approach.

A few moments more and everything would stop.

Then the sound of brakes vibrated through my mother's head like the high-pitched wail of a baby. She was reminded of me inside her. Without a second's delay, she pulled herself back into the safety of the car's interior. Her chest heaved in exhilaration, and the sheer fright of it, and she rolled up the window and rested her head back onto the soft beige leather of the headrest. The truck rattled past them, oblivious to the near-death experience of her and me.

Both hands went to her belly. She had learned that she wanted to live so that I would survive. It had been a revelation to her that she could care for someone other than herself. It was our first bonding moment as mother and child.

# EIGHTEEN

### Amy

Amy had been snooping about in old drawers and chests. Olivia's comment at the coffee morning had sparked her curiosity about the house and William's connections to it. If it was a rental, had the furniture come with it? She'd always assumed it was filled with William's family heirlooms from his father's house in Dunsfold, where he had grown up. Now, she questioned that assumption, wishing she'd been more curious. She couldn't recall him specifically mentioning buying Summerfield House with Eleanor, or moving in, furnishing it, decorating it for that matter. Had she forgotten? Had she asked? Had she cared?

Some of the random family memorabilia she had stumbled upon certainly proved he'd lived here for decades. She had found a charming painting by Hal at five years old of William standing in the apple orchard holding a rake; and a note from Eleanor's dad dated 2002, tucked into an old chess set, thanking them for having him to stay at 'William's magical Summerfield House'. There had been one other item of interest, which she had brought downstairs to show William.

Now, she prepared a chicken and chorizo traybake for their supper. He was upstairs showering. The wine was open. Candles were flickering on the kitchen table. A bowl was filled with their favourite chilli-flavoured nut mix. Normally these rituals were cues for some relaxed chit-chat. It was her favourite time of the day with him. Tonight, though, she felt a headache coming on. The big questions she had for him were grinding through her thoughts. She hoped the little tissue-paper parcel would ease them into it gently.

When he came in a few minutes later, pink-cheeked from the shower and eager to eat, he didn't notice it.

For the rest of the evening, she put off pointing it out.

Instead, she resorted to a series of deathly dull questions about housekeeping. How much should they increase Mercy's weekly money by? Did they need to keep Hamish's dog walker on while Amy didn't have a job? Did the creaky floorboard on the stairs annoy him as much as it did her? Should they get a carpenter in? And did he know there was a leaky window in the morning room, too? Might Pete fix it?

His replies were vague. He was disengaged. Bored, probably. Then he said, 'I might have to stay late in London tomorrow night.'

'Making excuses to get away from me already?'

He laughed. 'Don't be silly. Not at all. I love our chats,' he said, holding her hand.

She felt a flush of love for him. Should I care who owns this place? she thought. It's just a house with a roof, like any other. If he'd at any point misled her about owning it, it might have been because he was ashamed. Around here, that kind of thing mattered. Everyone had too much time on their hands, including her... which reminded her. 'I meant to tell you,' she said. 'I've applied for an admin role at the kitchen shop on the high street. It's more high-end than Banstead's, but... you know. I can do that. I think.'

'That's fantastic, Amy. They'd be mad not to snap you up. Will it be all right with a wedding to organise?'

'Of course. What do you think of these?' She showed him the floral design versus the gold confetti design for the save-the-date emails. More distraction. 'I can't decide.'

'I like both.'

'Helpful.' She chortled. 'Anyway, I'm jumping the gun. We haven't nailed down the date yet. Have you thought more about next July?'

'That should be okay. I think,' he said. 'I need to double-check one thing work-wise.'

She was learning that his organisational skills were lacking. He was prone to leaving big decisions until the very last minute, hedging his bets. It was bewildering that he'd managed to set up a successful data analytics company. He seemed almost bungling in how he ran his business affairs. At his desk in his garden office, he tapped at his laptop with two forefingers like a toddler playing on a keyboard; he dropped his iPhone so often it was permanently cracked; he tripped up on tree roots while pacing the garden on phone calls with important clients; he knocked over coffees in the middle of Zoom meetings. And so it went on. She shouldn't have been surprised that he was dithering over the date of his own wedding.

The niggle about the house swirled up once again. She swallowed her mouthful of food and then said, 'I was thinking about venues too.'

'Any ideas?' he asked vaguely.

She paused, poised to bring up Summerfield House as a possibility, and then lost her nerve. 'Not really. Do you have any?' Confronting him about it would be too mortifying. If he had lied.

He stopped chewing for a moment, as though contemplating something, then said, 'Hmm. This is the kind of thing my mum would've been good at.'

'Oh, love.' It put a lid on the house issue for now. 'I've been missing my mum, too.' She put her knife and fork together. 'Then again, she would have been very meddling.'

He smiled. 'At least we've got each other.'

Later, she returned the folded tissue-paper parcel to where she'd found it in the mahogany wardrobe in the yellow room. She'd unpack it another day.

Or not.

It was a bright, blustery day. The clouds were white and cottony against the cool blue sky. In the emerging sunshine, Amy could see Olivia's swimming pool more clearly, and noticed that the green water was stagnant with algae. Everything around her had an illusory quality.

She was at another one of these coffee mornings. Her heart wasn't in it. The other three slipped into their usual complaining about Heathside Heights. They were angry about the maths teacher who hadn't recognised Oscar's brilliance and just wasn't up to scratch. And the *nightmare* of getting up early on weekends for Saturday school. And the waning wins at sports fixtures. And the headmaster droning on about God at Speech Day last term – Amy wasn't even sure what a Speech Day was.

They were making up worries. There was nothing real to complain about at Heathside Heights. At Kenley High in Purley, Amy and her fellow parents had to work out a rota to scrub the graffiti from the toilet doors; had to fight for more government funding to keep the school open on Fridays; had to campaign for free school lunches through the summer holidays for the kids who were struggling to eat. Amy couldn't relate to these women's concerns, and she kept wanting to shout, 'Get a life!'

Olivia seemed to have a sixth sense about what was going on in Amy's head. 'First World problems, right?'

Amy blushed, found out. 'No, no. It's all relative,' she said.

This was true in her own case, too. Her thoughts bounced back to William and the house. Did it matter?

'It's a bit of a bubble round here,' Olivia mused. 'I do wonder how Rory will cope in the big bad world.'

'Speaking of the big bad world, I'm nipping up to the Tate Modern today,' Marte said, standing up.

'Nice. Whereas I've got to go to Waitrose. Ugh,' Paula said.

'I should walk the dogs,' Olivia said.

And I've got to get that job, Amy thought.

While Marte and Paula got into their cars, Olivia held Amy back. She said quietly, 'Please let me help you with the wedding. Events are my speciality – it's what I used to do for a living, many moons ago. I could do with something lovely and romantic to think about.'

'That's a very kind offer,' Amy said cautiously, wary of involving someone she hardly knew, who hardly knew her. 'I'm a bit at sea with it all. I'm not even sure what kind of wedding we want, to be honest.'

'We'll find out together.'

'Thanks,' she said. Although Olivia wasn't her usual type of friend, the effort she'd made to welcome her here had been very kind and she appreciated it. And if Amy's personal experience of divorce was anything to go by, Olivia might need her as much as she needed Olivia. She would never forget how she had felt at a similar time in her life. Divorcing Nick had been a living hell. She'd lost all her confidence. Her moods had shifted edgily: one minute she could be wrung out, numb, and the next she would be filled with too much feeling – often with a pure, almost unmanageable rage. What she had thought were whispers amongst the school mums, whether real or imagined, had created endless paranoia. Mostly she had been quite bewildered by what was happening to her and hadn't known who she was without him.

It occurred to her that she'd had to confront Nick's lie about Maxine. Perhaps that was why she was reluctant to broach the subject of the house with William. In Nick's case, challenging him had been the beginning of the end. He still swore he hadn't had an affair with Maxine, and who knows, maybe he hadn't. It didn't matter now. Maxine hadn't really been the problem, only the symptom. Amy could see that now. And a lie about an affair was very different from withholding information about a house. Wasn't it?

'You're welcome, sweetie. Seriously, please don't worry about it, it's not a problem at all,' Olivia said. 'Maybe come in for a drink before you pick Tess up on Saturday night and we can chat through some ideas.'

'Am I picking Tess up?' Amy searched her mind for what was happening on Saturday night.

'She's coming to Rory's pool party, isn't she? I think it's for Hal's seventeenth. Or have I put my foot in it again?' Olivia stretched her pretty lips, revealing her perfect teeth. 'Eek.'

'Umm. Neither of them has mentioned anything. Hal was being funny about his birthday. He said he didn't want any celebration.'

'That's why Rory wanted to do something for him.'

'That's kind. Come to think of it, Tess did say she's going shopping with a couple of girls she seems to have made friends with.'

'Tilly and Anoushka.' Olivia smiled.

'That's it,' Amy said. Olivia seemed to know more about her daughter than she did.

'Yup. Those two are coming over, which means Tess will be too, I'm guessing.'

'Okay, then. If that's all right with you?' Amy said.

'Of course! It's like the local youth club round here at the weekends. I think because we're so close to the station, it makes us an easy target.' Olivia laughed.

'That must be exhausting.'

She laughed again, but there was a dreamy quality to her expression. 'I like having them about, actually. They liven the place up.'

'Well, in that case, I'll see you on Saturday. I really look forward to it.'

'Me too. But be prepared for my Pinterest board of ideas. Summerfield House will be such a beautiful canvas to work with. I'm thinking the orchard?'

Amy hesitated. 'I haven't talked to him about that yet.'

'Oh?' Olivia's head tilted to the side.

Amy glanced down at the dogs sitting at her ankles and scratched behind Margot's greying ear. 'I just haven't got round to it.'

'I would do that soonish, hon. Before we get ahead of ourselves.'

Olivia was right. She couldn't avoid it any longer.

She'd bring out the tissue-paper parcel and show him what she'd found.

# NINETEEN

William

The sun streamed through the diamond panes, bathing Amy in gentle morning light as she dressed. He loved her in this room, with its low, sagging ceilings, delicate lemon wallpaper and old beams. She was like a painting. Her pale, freckled body, with its slender shoulders and broad hips, was more beautiful than any he had seen before. He found it strange that she was shy of it, often changing quickly or complaining about her tummy. She always underplayed herself. Eleanor had been proud of her nakedness, stamping about the house with nothing on except the hairspray in her stiff auburn curls. She made tea naked, slept naked, read the papers in bed naked, covers thrown off, almost as though he wasn't there. It was true her body had been perky and toned, no excess fleshy bits or cellulite anywhere to be seen, and he'd had nothing against it. But there had been too much obvious work in it, too much stress and tension.

Amy closed the wardrobe, turning the little iron key.

'Did you hear that?' she asked, glancing round at him. She had the key in her hand still.

'Hear what?'

She went over to the open window, stuck her head out. 'I heard a baby crying. Do the next-door neighbours have a baby?'

'I'm not sure,' he said, trying to remember more about the family who had moved into the overpriced bungalow last year. All he knew was that they'd applied for planning permission to build a six-bedroom house.

'I often hear it crying.'

'Oh, do you?' He picked up a stray sock, put it in the laundry basket.

'I wanted to show you something,' she said, kneeling at the wardrobe, struggling to open one of the two old drawers at its base. From the back, she pulled out a tissue-paper parcel and undid it. Revealed was a newborn baby sleepsuit with a white collar and a yellow frog pattern on its breast. 'I found this,' she said. Something fell out as she picked it up by its little shoulders. 'Oh, look.' She peered at it. 'Is it a photo of Hal as a baby?'

His temples throbbed. 'Yup. Sweet,' he croaked, briefly resting his eyes on the photo but not long enough for it to come into focus.

'So this was Hal's babygro?'

He answered her mechanically. 'Yes.'

She tilted her head and laid the sleepsuit flat on the floor to do up the poppers on the inside leg. Snap. Snap. Snap. 'At first I thought it must've been yours. It's so old-fashioned. But these aren't yours or Hal's initials.' Her fingers brushed over the yellow embroidered 'SSG' on the tiny breast pocket.

He wondered if he could lose his mind in one split second. 'The brand, maybe? Not sure.' His palms were slick with sweat.

'No. It's by "Thomas".'

Snap. Snap. Snap.

'Must be a hand-me-down from someone in Eleanor's family.'

He watched her carefully refold it and tuck the photo back where it belonged. He shuddered, relieved it was gone.

But she wasn't done. 'Was this wardrobe already here when you moved in?'

'Umm, God, bloody hell. No idea, Miss Marple!'

She flushed under her freckles, and he felt bad. 'I wondered if the previous owners left the babygro in here by mistake,' she said. 'And I was wondering if you knew anything about them.'

'If you like, I'll ask Eleanor about it.'

There was a pause, and he saw doubt in her eyes.

'Don't be daft,' she replied, waving her hand in the air. 'It doesn't really matter. I was just interested to know why it had been so carefully preserved. The rest of Hal's baby clothes are in the Indian chest upstairs, so I thought there'd be a story behind it.'

'No story!'

'You're being a bit defensive,' she said, with a half-laugh.

He scratched at the knotty bits of hair at his nape, felt the fraying collar of his shirt. 'Sorry. Anything to do with Eleanor gets me going.'

'I understand.' She paused to chew at a thumbnail. 'I found an old pair of Nick's socks once and I wanted to cut them up into tiny pieces, like I was Glenn Close.'

He laughed. Her expression remained grisly.

To get them out of here, he said, 'Want to take Hamish out this morning?'

From their very first date, walking had become their thing. One of them might start out in a bad mood, tension in their joints or irritation in their voice. But plodding along, with Hamish bounding through the undergrowth, they talked and worked it out. Thoughts came more easily for William if he was looking ahead, going somewhere, even if that somewhere was back to where he started. And with Amy as his sounding board, the ritual was somewhere near perfection. But this morning, he wanted her to be the one to share her thoughts with him.

Over the last few days, she had been quiet. Fewer dimpled smiles, fewer musings, more of a harried air about her. She'd spent a lot of time bent over a computer, ruffling her blonde curls, fretting about finding a job, even though he'd reminded her they didn't need the second income.

'One of us needs to take Tess to the station at some point,' she said. The station was a ten-minute drive and would not impede a dog walk.

'We could do that together afterwards?'

'It's annoying that we have to ferry them about all the time.' She looked at him directly, buttoning up her jeans, stuffing her blue T-shirt into them. 'I'm not used to it. In London, she'd just walk out of the door shouting "See you later!" and catch the bus.'

'Houses near the station, like Olivia's, cost a small fortune,' he said apologetically. The adjustment to a whole new life in a conservative backwater seemed to be the cause of her dip in mood. The novelty had perhaps worn off already. Imagining that this might be the root of it was not a small relief to him. 'And I don't mind ferrying them to and from Olivia's tonight, if you want a glass of something.'

'No, don't worry. I told her I'd drop in and have a quick drink with her before I take the kids home.'

'Oh God. Really?'

'She was being very sweet, actually, wanting to help me out with the wedding.'

From bitter experience, William wanted Amy to be cautious of any help from Olivia. How much Eleanor had shared with her remained an unknown.

'That's good.'

'What?'

'Hmm?' he said, getting up.

'You said "That's good" in that voice, like it wasn't good at all.'

'I *did* mean it was good.'

'Yes, it is actually. It is *really* good that I've found friends, and it's lovely of Olivia to include me in things. Really, *really* lovely of her. Because I miss my old friends. I miss Jo and Pip. *Really* bloody miss them.' There were tears in her voice and the guilt sliced through him. Bringing her here had been selfish, perhaps. For all its trappings.

'At least you've got me,' he said, crushed by her upset, feeling responsible for it, pulling her rigid body towards him.

'I know,' she conceded, her blonde curls tickling his nose as her head turned into his shoulder. 'I'm okay. I don't mean to sound like I'm feeling sorry for myself. I'm so lucky to be here and to have you. I have nothing to complain about.'

'Let's go on that walk then, hey?' he suggested again, wanting to get them back on track.

'Okay,' she said in a small voice.

Downstairs, they stuffed dog treats into their pockets and found their walking boots – he'd have to find her some better ones – and Hamish flew into the car, knowing what 'walkies' meant.

'Where'd you put his lead, Amy?' William hollered from the boot room.

'It's in your mum's umbrella thingy!'

His mother's? he questioned silently. He found it on the hook under a Barbour and jumped in the car with it.

Suddenly Amy cried, 'Wait! Stop!'

'What?' He pulled the handbrake.

'I've forgotten to give Pete his tea and biscuits!'

'He won't mind.'

'William! Don't be so rubbish,' she admonished, getting out of the car.

She took for ever. He read the newspaper on his phone.

When she returned, she said, 'Sorry. He was telling me all about his two new kittens. So cute.' She smiled to herself.

William felt jealous of Pete and his ability to bring out her smile. He sensed that her suspicions about the babygro and the wardrobe and Eleanor had been stemmed only temporarily. There was more to come. If he was honest with himself, he had noticed a change in her ever since her first coffee morning with Olivia.

They didn't talk about anything in particular as they drove through the sunny tunnel of trees towards Hindhead. The tarmac beneath them was ragged and fragmented after a waterlogged year. He dropped one hand from the wheel and onto his thigh, attempting to give off a relaxed air. What could Eleanor have told Olivia? How much had Eleanor really known? The wheels zigzagged. There was a bang as they went over a pothole.

'I should sue the council for all the money I've spent on new tyres,' he grumbled.

In his rear-view mirror, he could see the pothole had been marked with red paint. How had he not seen it coming? As with Eleanor, he couldn't let that happen again. He couldn't be foolish enough to trust someone that much.

They arrived at the car park, placed their National Trust card on the dash, and with Hamish to heel began their trek down into the heathland and Scotch pine and oak trees of the Punchbowl, weaving along the narrow sandy tracks. There hadn't been a day since he'd moved back here in his early twenties that he had taken it for granted. He loved that he had introduced Amy to its peaceful splendour.

They walked one behind the other: she in front of him. He

noticed her twisting her engagement ring with her thumb and little finger, around and around.

'I've been thinking about where we might want to get married,' she announced suddenly. Hamish shot off into the undergrowth.

'Oh great, where?'

'At the house.'

His step faltered. He hurried to catch her up again, biting at his lip. 'Summerfield House?' The landscape became brittle and hostile around him.

'What other house would I mean?' she laughed, looking over her shoulder briefly. Her profile was backlit by a series of rainbow refractions and his heart shattered.

'Whose idea was that?' he asked suspiciously.

'Mine,' she said, stopping and turning to face him. He wished she would walk on, away from him.

'Not Olivia's?'

'Why does it matter whose idea it was?'

'It doesn't.'

'Well, what do you think? The hallway is as big as a church, and we could have a marquee in the garden. By the pond, maybe? Or in the orchard?'

He walked around her and stalked onwards, checking for Hamish. 'Umm. I'm not sure.' The gorse bushes scratched at his calves, spiteful and stinging, and his back stooped further and ached more with every passing step.

'Is this about Eleanor?' she asked.

'Eleanor? Why would it be anything to do with *her*?'

'William?' she said quietly, and he sensed her pace had slowed. He checked for her. She had stopped dead in the middle of the path.

'Yes?' he asked.

She looked down at her feet, kicked awkwardly at a stone and shoved her hands into the back pockets of her jeans. 'Olivia said something about the house being a rental. I got the vibe that there'd be a problem with the landlord or something?' The intonation from her long-lost Liverpool roots came into the sentence, which he knew meant she was stressed.

'A rental?'

'Yes.'

There was a clanging in his chest, but he kept up his front and forced his brow into a frown. 'She's talking rubbish. The house isn't rented.' Hamish came padding up to them and wove between William's legs, then sat between his feet in his favourite safe place.

'I wouldn't care either way, you do know that, don't you?'

'You mean you're not after me for my money?' He was in a blind panic now, gathering himself, planning his next move, wondering how much more Olivia had said. Was it time to cut his losses and enlighten Amy here and now about the secrets of Summerfield House? Was this how it worked? Did he dare come out with a secret he had kept under lock and key all his adult life? Might he truly, and a little madly, be able to simply swing open the door to this dungeon-like reality of his?

Of course he couldn't. He couldn't do it to her. He loved her too much to foist it upon her and bring her down with it.

'Why would Olivia say something like that if it wasn't true?' she asked. Hot pink circles flashed underneath her freckles, and the dimples in her cheek and chin deepened, like markers of determination and resolve underneath her diffident exterior.

'I've no idea, but it's not true.' He scratched Hamish's shaggy head, anchored himself and breathed. 'Olivia and I have a complicated history. She was good friends with Eleanor, don't forget. They were thick as thieves at Manchester, and then when we moved into Summerfield House they reconnected again. We all grew up around here and moved back as adults.'

'Did you and Eleanor buy the house together?'

'She fell in love with it on sight,' he said, sidestepping the question, moving on as quickly as possible. 'Eleanor has always been good at twisting the truth. Maybe she said something to Olivia to suit her own agenda at the time.'

There was a pause. Long enough to give him hope.

'Toxic divorces can do that to people,' she murmured.

'They can.'

She scratched her cheek. 'I feel bad now. I should've just asked you sooner.'

'It's okay. But from now on, you mustn't believe anything that comes from the general direction of Eleanor. She's a nightmare. The whole thing was a mistake from start to finish.' This much was almost true. There was Hal, of course.

'I know all about marrying the wrong person,' she conceded, adding, 'I only thought of Summerfield House for the wedding because you love it so much, and it keeps it simple, in a way, which is more like us. D'you know what I mean?'

'I do,' he said. He would find a way around the problem. 'Marrying you in Summerfield House would be a dream come true.'

'Are you sure?' Her eyes lit up.

'How about at Christmas?'

'*This* Christmas? Are you mad? That's only three months away.'

'Why not?' If the ceremony was small and soonish, he might be able to carry it off.

'No!' She laughed. 'You crazy man. There's too much to do, and I'd stress out even more than I am already.'

'Okay, what about April, then? When the bluebells are out. How about having the ceremony in the woods, like a couple of old hippies?'

She tucked her hand into his and said, 'That would be perfect.'

'That's settled then.' He closed his eyes, already contemplating the consequences of this decision. 'And we must have rare orchids from Riddlesdown Common.'

She laughed. 'Even if you did find one, you couldn't pick it!'

'I suppose I don't need to. *You're* my rare orchid.'

'Soppy git,' she chuckled, burrowing her head under his arm, which he put over her shoulders. She added, 'I'm sorry I've had such a cob on. Olivia *is* a strange one.'

'No, no, you like her,' he bluffed. 'And you have good instincts about people. Don't listen to me. She's great fun. And she's a useful contact to have at school. The networker extraordinaire!'

He didn't want to rock the boat with Olivia. If she had more secrets of his rattling around in her booze-addled brain, he would need to keep her onside.

'She was an event organiser before she had Rory, which is handy.' Amy grinned, looking lighter, back to her old self.

His palms were still clammy.

'Come on, I want to show you something,' he said.

He led her off the beaten track and into a cluster of tall oaks on the brow of a hill. They sat on a log near the slatted shelter of an old camp built by Hal and Rory years ago. With Hamish's majestic head between them, they looked out across smudgy purples and scrubby browns.

'Look, you can just about see it from here,' he said, pointing to where the gables and chimneys of Summerfield House rose out of the trees in the distance.

'Oh wow, yes!'

He sighed. 'Aren't we lucky?'

'Yes, we are,' she said.

He sought out her hand. It seemed they'd found each other again. He closed the book on his past. For now, at least. His anxiety about gaining permission for the wedding was only a distant murmur in his mind. Amy did that for him. Being with her was like taking something for the pain.

# TWENTY

## Tess

Tess took in her surroundings. The shed-like double doors of Rory's pool house had been opened and hooked back to reveal the pool and the garden beyond it. Two sofas were positioned either side of a black glass coffee table. The low evening sun was fighting its way through the trees and spreading its light like a golden carpet across the lawn, turning the water of the pool mercurial. The air was warm for September. The fire pit leapt and crackled. Fairy lights flickered. She couldn't believe she was here.

She caught Rory staring at her. Her tummy fluttered. She glanced at her phone screen, pressed on a few messages she'd already read and then pretended to fully immerse herself in what Anoushka and Tilly were doing. In fact, they were huddled together around the mirrored drinks trolley, pouring straight gin into two quarter-full litre bottles of Vimto and discussing big news.

'You're not going to believe this, right?' Anoushka said, whispery and wary.

'What?' Tilly asked, gripped.

'Rory's invited... *Logan.*' She was straight-faced, but the glee in her voice was barely contained.

'Oh my God. That's fucked up,' Tilly said.

Tess was not in the loop. 'Who's Logan?'

'He's just this friend of Rory's.'

'But Hal hates him,' Tilly said, bright-eyed.

Anoushka added, 'Because he's a dick.'

'He's not that bad,' Tilly said.

'Just because he gave you free weed.'

'Why doesn't Hal like him?' Tess asked, taking a swig from one of the Vimto bottles.

'I hate to say it,' Anoushka said, pausing, 'but he's a bit of a chav. Sorry. But he just is.'

Tess bit the side of her cheek and said, deliberately dim, 'Is he at Heathside?'

Anoushka paused, as though reading how serious Tess was being, 'Er, no?'

'He comes down from *London*,' Tilly explained, saying 'London' as though it were a dirty place and then realising her mistake. 'But he's nothing like you, Tess. I mean, you fit in around here. He's... you know. He doesn't.'

Tess felt the gulf between them. After a while, she moved off to take a film of the party for Malena, panning her camera around the room. She cringed at their accents. The visuals were as bad. The wealth was in everything: the Urban Outfitters pick-me outfits and their mums' cast-off Chanel handbags; the designer tracksuits, the expensive mullet haircuts, the latest trainers. The Bose portable speakers. Shiny unopened packets of Marlboro Lights and every type of vape available on the internet. Two big bowls of Kettle chips. Four opened bottles of Prosecco. The house, the pool. It was too much. If she sent it, it would be like showing off.

Back home in Purley, Malena and their other mates would

simply have been grateful for some cheap beers and dried-up pouches of tobacco. If one of them had some birthday money or had been paid from their Saturday job, they'd order one medium Domino's Margherita to share between six.

Oak Hills was an alternate universe. Malena would judge it; Tess would have done so in the past, too. The thought of not being in Malena's camp any more while also not being in this new one gave her a hollowed-out feeling.

More people trooped across the lawn. All eyes swivelled to see if it was the infamous Logan. It wasn't. Emily, Jasmine and Lana joined them. They began complaining about how shattered they were by all the homework they'd been given. Tess knew what they meant. The workload was five times that of Kenley High. But she had no interest in talking about it now. Her attention moved to Rory, who was sitting forward on the sofa telling a story to a group of boys. While they joshed and swore at each other, Rory looked over at her, brushing his shorn, bulky, gorgeous head with his hand.

'Hello, birthday boy,' Anoushka said to Hal, who had joined them. She pulled a pout over her braces.

'It's not actually today,' he said rudely, and then, to Tess, 'You okay?'

She nodded. 'Yeah, why?'

They hadn't talked about his outburst on that first night, but they'd been adding a 'hi' here and a 'how's it going?' there and had managed to move slowly out of their funk with each other.

'Did you know Logan's coming tonight?' Anoushka asked him. Her eyes bored holes into his, inhaling, waiting to see his reaction before she breathed again, perhaps.

Hal's green gaze remained impassive. 'Yeah?'

Anoushka side-eyed Tess, then said, 'We couldn't believe it when we heard.'

Hal ignored her and glanced at the Vimto in Tess's hand. 'Go easy on that.'

'I'm okay,' she shot back, embarrassed by his concern.

'So *cute*,' Tilly said. 'Playing big brother!'

Hal pushed his hair down over his eyes before walking off, joining the boys again.

'He's so hot,' Anoushka said. She kept staring at him as she sipped from her plastic cup. 'Imagine if we both got into the same college at Oxford. How funny would that be?' Then she looked Tess up and down. 'You're so brave to wear that. I didn't think you'd actually buy it.'

'Thanks,' Tess said, choosing to take her backhanded compliment as a genuine one. Earlier today, with some money her mum had given her, she'd bought the pinstriped waistcoat and trouser ensemble. She'd teamed it with high-tops and gold jewellery. It was the kind of outfit she would have dreamed about owning last year.

They heard a voice shout, 'Oi!' and a tall streak of a boy with a shifty shadow of hair over his top lip and two razored stripes through one eyebrow slouched past the pool. One hand was thrust into the front of his pants. His brand-new Jordan trainers were undone. Rory greeted him with a handshake. Instantly the atmosphere of the small party changed. The boys inside the pool house became quieter. Their talk about exams switched to a discussion about getting pumped in the gym.

'Turn it down, Hal!' Rory yelled when Oscar turned up the volume on the speaker. He glanced furtively at the house. The table throbbed with drill music. The Prosecco and beer vibrated on the glass surface.

'Olivia won't mind,' Oscar said. Oscar was the tallest of the group. He had a Viking-like jaw and nose, and a slice of golden hair across his forehead.

'Why not bring her down here, mate. Your mum is fit,' Mylo said.

There was a commotion as Rory left Logan's side and

hovered over Mylo. Tess had seen Mylo around. He was a rugby player with oversized shoulders and a dark rust mullet.

'Want to repeat that, Kitteridge?' Rory said, forming a half-cocked smile, managing to sound both flippant and threatening.

'Rory. Chill out,' Hal mumbled.

Rory glared at him.

Under her breath, Tilly asked Tess, 'What's going on with those two these days?'

'Not sure.' Tess recalled Hal's temper on the evening she'd moved into Summerfield House.

Anoushka rolled her eyes. 'They've always got some kind of beef with each other.'

There was a momentary glitch in Rory's show of manhood. As he returned to Logan, he took a look over his shoulder at Tess. She raised an eyebrow at him disapprovingly. He rubbed his head and grinned. A shiver ran across her skin.

Hal turned the music up again. There was an aggression to it, as though he was goading Rory and Logan. This time, Rory didn't complain. He opened another two beers, gave one to Logan. The two boys talked, head-to-head, and the flames of the fire pit licked at their knees.

Tess watched Logan pull what looked like a tin of Smints out of his Gucci manbag, which was slung across the hoodie of a black designer tracksuit. He slipped it into Rory's hand, and Rory zipped it into his pocket. Logan's mobile rang.

While she listened to Anoushka bring the conversation back to the major stress of her life – her art coursework – she saw Hal join them outside. Rory's body language changed. His arms were across his chest, his feet placed wider. As the three of them chatted, they were interrupted every few minutes by Logan answering his phone or texting. The tension between Hal and Rory was palpable. It was more like a noise. Tess's back teeth clenched.

After a brief exchange, both Rory and Logan turned their

heads in her direction. Rory winked. Then Tess was shocked to see Hal jerk towards him and say something angry. Coolly Rory flicked his cigarette into the fire. Before Anoushka could finish her story, Hal had chucked his whole weight at him, sending him careering into the kidney-shaped pool behind him.

'Oh my God!' Tess cried, running over to them and kneeling at the edge, offering her hand to Rory.

'Aw, bruv.' Logan guffawed and slapped his thigh, laughing at Rory spitting and lurching for the surface. 'Not on my Jordans! I'm outta here. Fuck! Dickheads!' He backed off a few steps, then his phone rang and he walked into the night.

A foul smell of stagnant pond filled Tess's nose. Close up, the water was thick with slimy green algae. She twisted around to look at Hal, who appeared almost as shocked as she was at what he'd done. 'Frickin' hell, Hal. What is your problem?'

Rory pulled himself out of the pool in one swift move and fronted up to Hal. His lean muscles showed through his T-shirt. He was a hot screen idol in a commercial. But his laugh was sneering and right into Hal's face. 'You *prick*.'

There was a crowd around them now. Oscar stepped between them. 'Let's cool it down.'

Tess warned, 'Yeah, come on, Hal.'

'I'm going up to the house to change,' Rory said. 'Tess, come with me?'

# TWENTY-ONE

William

William relished his walk to his garden office, particularly in autumn. It was a nifty commute. He simply pottered diagonally across the dewy lawn, through the break in the beech hedge and into the flower garden adjacent to the grass tennis court. The wayward persicarias, Michaelmas daisies and red-hot pokers brushed his trouser legs as he kicked his way through ankle-deep leaves. He felt silly and childlike doing this, but he didn't care. It was helping to lighten his mental load, which felt quite significant right now. Granting Amy her wish to marry here at Summerfield House had posed a problem. If he were to do it the right way, it would require an awkward telephone call at some point. It would invite in trouble.

The low gate at the end of the path was nestled, almost hidden, in the Leylandii hedge, which was full of nesting birds, wasps' nests and the occasional sleeping black cat. He slid the latch and stepped into the expanse of orchard. Its grass corridor stretched all the way through the line of trees to the converted barn. Or Petit Chalet, as it was once known. Its design resembled an Alpine chalet, unusual in a Surrey garden. The spikes and tangles of the woodland behind it threatened to engulf its wooden structure, perhaps sensing it wasn't at home in this environment. Tendrils of ivy and other rampant weeds crept over the frontage of the tall A-frame window like fingers clutching greedily, claiming it as their own. A little to the left of the building, there was a tunnel-like route through the thicket that led eventually to the large clearing, carpeted with bluebells in the spring, where he and Amy hoped to be married. A frisson of excitement and fear shuddered through him.

The door was unlocked. He accepted that this was careless but doubted any thieves would know to venture this far. The air was still inside. A blanket of calm settled over him, physically taking hold of him. His attachment to Summerfield House was as much about this odd building as it was about the house itself. Being alone here was complete and usually uninterrupted.

Rarely would anyone bother walking over from the main house to see him, except Mercy to clean and Tess, who loved to borrow his books. This morning before school, he'd said goodbye to Tess and to Hal and had felt very lucky to have them in his life. He smiled at the memory of Amy fiddling shyly with her gold hoop earring, explaining that she and Olivia were going to a wedding fair near Lewes today and that she vowed not to turn into a bridezilla. They'd all laughed about how unlikely that was.

Now, he made some coffee and sat back into his Eames leather chair. While his two computer screens fired up, he surveyed the tall bookshelves, running his gaze absently along the spines. Company business slowly filtered into his mind, percolating through domestic concerns. Later he would make the call about the wedding, after some more thought about it.

It was during this contemplation that he heard a noise outside. His breath caught as he saw a willowy figure in high black boots stalk past the bank of windows to stand at the

French door. In an ungainly way, he leapt up, sploshing coffee onto one jeans leg. She came straight in.

'William,' she said, as though telling him off for being here.

His heart seized. He decided it couldn't be real, that he had conjured her up after thinking about her so hard.

She slammed the door behind her and smiled, nervously tugging the sleeves of her black jumper over her hands, running her fingers along her centre parting, repositioning her handbag strap on her shoulder. She was as much out of place as she was part of the furniture.

'Hello,' she said, huskier than her younger self.

'What are you doing here?' he asked stupidly, and tried to return her smile, but his lips were gummy against his teeth.

'I was passing.' Her pale, intelligent eyes and red, bitten mouth were staggeringly beautiful. Her low blonde ponytail with the wispy bits playing around her ears and at her nape was a reminder of how she had felt under his fingertips. She had worn her hair like that back then, too. Although when he'd seen her last year, it had been down and somehow it had suited her less, or he hadn't liked the change in her.

'Was Amy...? Has she...?'

She picked at an eyelash. 'Gone. Yes. But I parked in the field anyway and came through the back way like the old days. Can I use the loo?'

'You know where it is.' He nodded to the door in the corner.

The minutes she was in there might as well have been hours. When she returned, she launched into an account of her journey – the roadworks in Woking and the diversions in Guildford – as though her appearance here was quite run-of-the-mill. He pressed his fingers into his sternum. She ran out of steam and trailed off, moving over to the windows to look out at the burnt-amber view. The Lutyens chimneys and gables of Summerfield House poked up above the hedges. 'They did a good job on the roof,' she said.

'No more buckets.'

'That's a bonus.' There was a catch in her throat and her shoulders hiccuped.

'Are you okay?' he asked dumbly.

'I'm fine,' she sniffed, digging a finger into the corner of one eye. 'It's lovely to be here. I always forget how beautiful it is.'

He made a clumsy attempt at consoling her by patting her shoulder, resisting moving his hand down her long, elegant back, remembering its protrusions and contours like it was yesterday. At the leavers' ball, she had worn a backless dress. Her diamanté necklace had slipped and swung across her skin as she had danced. Unforgettably sexy. She was thinner now, too thin, and he noticed how her shoulders seemed to have rounded apologetically and her hair smelt stale.

'I hear the old place is going to have a wedding?'

An instant sweat broke out on his face. 'I was going to call you about it.'

'Were you? I must be telepathic,' she said flatly.

And then he realised that her timely appearance was not a coincidence, and that Eleanor and Olivia's chins had been wagging.

'If it's a problem, we can rethink.' He wasn't sure how the rethinking would go down with Amy, though.

'It's fine, I guess.' One of her shoulders jerked into a shrug. 'Can we just go in?'

His heart palpitated unnaturally. 'Let me just close up the computers.'

While she waited, she hovered at the bookshelves, touched them. 'You left them unpainted?'

'Hmm, yes.' He felt another uncomfortable flutter.

A branch scraped at the roof. She shot a dirty look upwards. Packs of autumnal leaves were wedged into the four skylights. 'Mummy wouldn't have liked those like that. It's rather gloomy in here because of it, don't you think? You should get Pete on to it.'

'I don't need natural daylight in the same way she did.'

'She'd have liked that you're here, though,' she said with a pale, penetrating gaze. The tip of her toe made an arc across the carpet. Then she visibly shivered and rubbed her arms. 'Come on, let's go.'

He shuffled his feet, as though moving towards the door, but went no further. She was almost halfway through the orchard before he lumbered forward to catch her up. Walking towards the house with her like this brought back the echoes and murmurings of a long time ago: someone crying in the yellow room; a scream along the panelled corridor; a crack in a tile in the blue bathroom.

Sophie pushed her way past him and in through the boot room door as though she had never left. It was her house, her right to do so. Her proprietorship here was ingrained, bred into her and undiminished by twenty-four years of absence.

# TWENTY-TWO

Amy

Jo showed Amy a post of a young socialite in a lace fishtail dress. 'What about something like this?' she said through a mouthful of cheese straw. It was a reel, in fact, on her #beautifulbrides feed – they'd already laughed about that hashtag.

'Hmm. Dunno. I'm a bit old for that, aren't I?' Amy handed the phone back.

Pip's blue eyes popped open over her gin glass. 'OLD? You'd knock that contour-cheeked... bum-implanted... dim-fluencer's socks off.'

Amy laughed. 'Nah.'

They were sitting at Pip's kitchen bar after a depressing Saturday spent in a hot, impersonal bridal department on Regent Street. Every dress that Amy had tried on would have put her into the #hideousbrides most-viewed category. But Jo wouldn't give up her search.

'You don't have to wear a dress at all, you know,' she suggested.

Pip cackled. 'Oh blimey. That'll shock all those Surrey housewives!'

'They're not quite ready for that yet, Jo,' Amy spluttered into her drink.

Over her shoulder, Amy watched her type *#maturebrides*. One of the posts that came up was of a 'mature' skin-and-bone woman, aged roughly one hundred and five, sporting a peach lace Miss Havisham-style get-up. Her face was like a bronzed prune and her waist-length, witchy white locks flowed behind her. She brought to mind the spectral image of dead people's hair and nails growing in their coffins.

'What I meant was, you could wear a suit instead of a dress. Like this one.' Jo showed her a photograph of another 'mature' bride in a modest white tuxedo.

'I could, couldn't I?' Amy said, feeling hopeful.

'But it's so *safe*!' Pip cried. 'And you've got such a big chunk of change to play with. And you have such a lovely figure. And by the sounds of the bluebell woods, they're really fairy-tale-like. And William is so posh and handsome. And, I mean, with all those things in mind, don't you think you should be going all out on a jaw-dropping frock? Nicola Peltz and Brooklyn Beckham, eat your heart out!'

'But she has to feel like herself in it,' Jo argued. Amy could always rely on Jo to understand her. The nurse in her had endured long after she'd left the NHS wards.

'Why's that even matter? She's meant to feel like someone else! Someone special – no offence, babe – like she's a famous person, or a princess for a day!'

The two of them continued debating it heatedly for a while, as though Amy were their much-loved problem child. She listened on, increasingly ambivalent. The conversation was giving her a sickly feeling, like when she ate too many mint Matchmakers.

'I might order something online,' she said, to put an end to it.

Jo furrowed her brow, but said, 'That could work.'

They both looked to Pip for her response. Silence reigned. Amy crossed and uncrossed her ankles, hooking her heels onto the bottom rung of the bar stool. Pip took her time retrieving a can of tonic from the fridge and topped up their glasses with an extra splosh in each.

'Do you actually *want* to get married, Amy?' she asked. Her question had the effect of hacking through layers of white satin, slicing right down to the bridal bones of the matter.

'Pip!' Jo said.

But Amy had questioned it herself. 'When he asked, I did. And I still do. But there's a lot I don't know about him. Sometimes I worry we're rushing things.' It was a relief to admit it.

Pip asked, 'Because of what Olivia said about the house?'

'Sort of. But I do believe him.' She thought about the frog-patterned sleepsuit in the tissue paper. Those initials bothered her still.

'Who cares who owns it? It's got a roof and walls and central heating,' Pip said.

Jo wrinkled her nose. 'It's tricky, though. Because lying about it would be a bit weird.'

'Don't underestimate men and their pride,' Pip said.

'He wouldn't lie to me about it, would he?' Amy asked.

Pip put down her half-eaten cheese straw, getting really serious now. 'What do you feel in your gut?'

Amy looked from one friend to the other. Jo was nodding approvingly at Pip's question. These two women were her lifeline. From the moment they'd met at their NCT group and splintered off after two classes, Amy had known she wouldn't need anyone else to get her through motherhood. Since she had moved to Surrey, Pip had neatened her beautiful shock of red hair to a bob, but that was the only change in her. Amy would travel continents to sit at her kitchen bar of an evening and hear her infectious, generous laugh. Her humour had the ability to cut right to the heart of things. And Jo, with her unadorned prettiness and her heart of gold, was her moral compass. Nothing felt real until she had aired it with them.

'I know he's a good man,' she replied solidly. She pictured how his blond hair curled at his temples and the tops of his ears after he'd swept it off his eyes to look at her properly, seeing her, loving her; how his beaming, golden smile could fill her heart. 'I love him. I really do. I can't even put it into words. He's just got this knack of making me feel good about myself, like his confidence rubs off on me or something. Or maybe it's his belief in me. He does the same for Tess, who literally worships him. He's made this extra-special effort with all the book stuff, and they've been bonding over it. It's so amazing. Honestly, he's like a real dad to her.'

'That's really lovely,' Jo said.

'Also, I kind of feel this wedding would be symbolic. I don't know, like this is me moving on from Nick, properly, you know?' A lump formed in her throat. 'Like my second chance. Does that make sense?'

'Oh, love! It makes complete sense,' Pip said, wiping one cheek. 'Bloody hell.'

Jo reached over to hold Amy's hand. 'You really deserve it, Amy.'

Because Amy had never wanted to worry either of them, she hadn't relayed the very worst bits of her marriage to Nick – she and Nick alone knew that side of things – but these two incredible women had read between the lines and she loved them so much for it.

'Cheers to frumpy suits and second chances!' Pip teased, holding her glass up high.

. . .

On the hour-and-a-half drive home to Summerfield House that night, Amy buzzed with ideas for her wedding day. Pip and Jo had swung open the door to her excitement. First thing the next morning, she called Olivia to accept her offer of help. And this time she meant it.

# TWENTY-THREE

## AUTUMN 1990

### Me

My mother settled into the quieting rhythm of her exile. Time seemed suspended. But the months passed and I grew healthily inside her – her sixteen-year-old body took to pregnancy surprisingly well.

During the first half of each day, she would study from carefully selected A level curriculum textbooks. Annie would then encourage her to explore the extensive grounds or play tennis on the grass court or stroll through the woods to the bluebell clearing or pick apples from the orchard. Then they would spend the afternoons reading together in the morning room. My mother liked to lie under a tartan blanket on the Laura Ashley sofa, devouring trashy novels, mostly. Or she could while away an hour watching the sun make patterns across the beams or by plaiting the tassels edging the tapestry footstool. Annie would be more upright on one of the wing-backed chairs newly covered in green velvet, and was partial to browsing through light factual books about the Queen, or travel journals. She enjoyed a small glass of *trou Normand* – introduced to her by Madame Garnier.

Avril Garnier, who had been employed for her expertise in midwifery and for her French, had brought a little bit of Normandy into Surrey. She made them omelettes or cheese salads for lunch, always with vinaigrette and a baguette. In the evenings, she cooked more substantial meals, such as bean cassoulet or salt-meadow lamb or *joues de boeuf*. She'd source good produce from local farmers, who must have wondered who this demanding Frenchwoman was.

It wasn't often that they would go out, but when they did, they took trips to the seaside at Littlehampton or Clymping – early, so that they weren't seen (Annie couldn't risk them bumping into an old acquaintance). These outings were good for my mother, filling her lungs with salty air, getting her feet wet and her hair blown off her face. Walking along the beach, she talked to me. Sometimes about the books she read – *The L-Shaped Room* had been her favourite – or the letters she received from my father every week from his boarding school. They were quite soppy and juvenile, and far, far removed from the reality of me.

You see, I was a handful, or more accurately a bellyful, causing sickness and swollen ankles. As I got bigger, I would press on her bladder, forcing her up in the night every few hours. I was already quite in charge.

When I set off her first contraction, she was watching videos with Annie – in French, of course – in the den. For a while, she controlled her breathing while studying the patterns of the painted tiles that surrounded the fireplace and zoned out of the actors' burbling. Annie complained about this.

'Concentrate, darling. You might as well have *something* worthwhile to show for your time cooped up here,' she snapped.

'Other than a baby, you mean?' my mother retorted, rubbing her belly, trying not to wince. The cramping pain was a private feeling, between her and me. Together we were preparing for our outer-world meeting.

Annie grumbled, 'Only if you do *want* to go to Oxford, darling...'

My mother's womb tightened and relaxed with agonising regularity. Unable to hide it for much longer, she ruched her big blousy house dress up around her waist to cool herself off and staggered upstairs, moaning all the way. Annie followed close behind, shouting for Avril, mildly revolted by the sour odour of her daughter. For days beforehand, my mother had refused to shower or brush her hair and couldn't be bothered to go further than the old barn for their daily walks. Annie had warned her she'd have a terrible time of it trying to lose the baby weight, but my mother was beyond caring about that kind of thing.

In the yellow bedroom, she roamed around, swearing at Annie when she suggested she lie on her back on the plastic sheeting. It was Avril who encouraged her to walk and breathe, or kneel by the bed, or lie in warm water in the bath.

After many hours of this, she finally planted two hands on the large mahogany wardrobe, hung her head between her arms and wailed animalistically. The time had come for me to breathe the fresh air of Summerfield House.

# TWENTY-FOUR

## Tess

It was Monday after school, a couple of weeks since Hal's birthday party at Oak Hills. Rory had asked Tess over to study with him. She had butterflies. Nothing had happened between them yet. On the night of the party, she had sensed he wanted to get with her. But while he had changed out of his pond-stinking clothes upstairs, Olivia had collared her in the kitchen, asking her a thousand questions, and then Amy had arrived shortly afterwards.

His bedroom was the only tidy space Tess had seen in the house so far. The Versace-print duvet was militarily straightened. The leather desk empty of everything except a neat line of gold chains and a closed laptop with a Gucci sticker across its logo. Brand-new trainer boxes were stacked high on one wall and a cluster of logoed leather manbags hung from the back of his chair. The row of books on the one shelf were non-fiction self-help with jazzy titles on how to make money and be a success – quick! – at which she resisted a cartoonish eye-roll.

'Your mum actually bought the whole homework line?' Rory grinned.

'We *are* doing homework together, aren't we?' she said seriously, squeezing her school bag tightly to her side.

'Oh yeah, definitely.' He nodded slowly, taking her in, top to toe.

Nervously she looked away. Drawn across the tall Georgian windows were heavy pink curtains that clashed with the hard edge of the rest of the room. She spotted ivy growing through one of the cracks above the architrave. Rory saw she'd noticed it, but she distracted him by saying, 'Pretty,' brushing her hand over the drapes, teasing him.

'I like pink,' he said absent-mindedly, stepping closer to her.

Spotting a small tin of blue breath mints on his desk, she grabbed it and waggled it at him. 'Can I have one?'

He stared at it as if waiting for it to explode in her hand. 'No.'

She laughed. 'Really? Rory doesn't share food?'

He grabbed the mints off her, chucked them lightly, thoughtfully from one hand to the other, observing her. 'None left.'

Instead of throwing the tin into the waste-paper bin, he put it away in a drawer and then sat on the corner of his desk, beckoning her over, spreading his knees a little so that she could slot between them. Moving on from his weirdness about the mints, her heart flew about her chest. It was going to happen. She was going to kiss him. It was actually going to happen. Her stomach lurched. Her head floated off her body. Everything was haywire as she positioned her hips into the V of his thighs. Nothing on earth could have stopped them from kissing now.

As soon as their lips met, their desire escalated rapidly.

Within minutes, he had loosened her tie and unbuttoned her shirt to reveal her bra. He gazed at her body as though she were a goddess, running his finger gently across the ribboned edge of her underwear. Never before had she felt like this. They were almost breathing through each other, couldn't break away, though she knew she must.

Standing back from him, holding her shirt closed, she whispered, 'What if your mum comes up?'

'Mum wouldn't notice if I had orgies with goats up here.'

She sighed, thinking this was sad, but knew he would be embarrassed if she said so. 'She's good fun.'

He brushed his hand over his blond head. 'She's an arsehole sometimes,' he hissed.

Tess related. Her dad was similar. He wasn't an alcoholic exactly. More, his drinking was part of his socialising, like a hobby. He was a great dad in lots of ways. But she'd just come back from a weekend at his place in Streatham, which had been spoiled by his going out. He'd come home from the pub late, fallen off the sofa and hit his head on the side table. At least he hadn't pissed on the carpet, like a few months ago. Cleaning him up had been embarrassing. She hadn't called her mum to collect her, but probably should have.

A small black phone vibrated on the desk.

'What's that?' she asked.

'Replacement phone,' Rory said. 'Sorry, got to get it.'

Before answering, he went into the en suite and closed the door. All she could hear was mumbling. When he came back out, he said, 'Sorry, babe, I've gotta go.'

'Now?'

'It's Logan. He's down from London.' He kissed her and began rebuttoning the front of her shirt carefully, like she was his doll.

She felt discarded. 'How will I get home?'

'Mum'll take you.' He crouched to adjust the lips of his high-tops.

'Won't she mind?'

He looked at his protruding groin area. 'Better wait for this to go down.'

She stared at the bulge and laughed half-heartedly. While she put on her blazer, he took down one of the shoeboxes, set it on the desk and opened its lid. There were piles of cash inside. Her heart began thumping.

'Whose is all that?'

'Mine.'

'You get pocket money in cash?'

'Paper round. I've been saving.'

'Jeez,' she guffawed. He wasn't laughing as he counted out fifties into a neat pile. 'What are you doing with it?'

He folded the money into his pocket. 'I owe Logan.'

'For *what*?'

'Trainers,' he said. His eyes were bluer than ever, communicating a message, challenging her to question him.

'Right.' She bit her lip.

'Don't look so worried,' he said, and took her hand. Her thoughts were galloping, but she didn't want to let go. Not quite yet.

# TWENTY-FIVE

Amy

Amy had exhausted her search for Tess's AirPods in the main house, so she pulled on a pair of wellies and nipped out to William's office. It was plausible that Tess had left them there while choosing her next book. Either way, it was a good enough excuse to have a snoop around. Like an insecure child in a dysfunctional home, she had begun taking a needy interest in any detail of William's past life at Summerfield House, often looking for clues that gave credence to his ownership of the place. Consciously she trusted in what he'd told her.

William had never said she couldn't go into his office. But strangely, she had never done anything more than stand chatting at the door in her bright pink wellies, peering in or handing him a sandwich.

She placed her boots by the door. The room was like a log cabin in a storybook. It had pine log walls and floor-to-ceiling bookshelves. There was a free-standing wood burner, and sheepskin rugs strewn across the carpet and the sofa. Her eye passed over a small watercolour on the wall depicting the orchard in spring, trees laden with pink blossom.

The desk was placed centrally in front of the main window. She stood behind it and looked out. The glass was spattered with driving rain. It was only midday, but the view out on to the orchard was reminiscent of a wet winter's evening. The banks of fallen leaves under the trees, which had been so pretty a few weeks back, had turned to black mulch.

Amy felt cosy inside and couldn't resist neatening a few piles of papers and clearing the bookshelves of old coffee cups. Then she moved on to some of the documents on his desk, curious about them as she shuffled them around to find the lost earbuds. She tried not to go so far as to read his private papers or open his drawers, or anything like that.

There was a gust of wind and the door flew open with a bang. She jumped out of her skin – a little guiltily. Before she closed it again, properly this time, she heard the baby next door. It was eerie on a day like today, and she wondered how the sound carried through such thick weather. Her cheeks caught a spray of rain before she pulled the door to.

'Right, where was I?' she said aloud, patting her chest after the small fright.

Immediately her eyes were drawn back to the bookshelves. She stood on a chair and skimmed her fingers along the top of the weightier hardbacks. Here she stumbled on something that was not at all like the little AirPods case, but she brought it down anyway. Too nosy to leave it be.

The envelope was cream. The sticky bit had turned brown. Written on the back in William's messy script was the name Sophie. She couldn't resist opening it. Dare to know, she thought to herself, remembering when Tess had translated the school motto for her.

Inside were a series of photographs of William and his friends as teenagers. Glued to him in every shot was a pretty, pale-eyed girl. Her mousy-blonde bob was flicked into a quiff. In many of the shots, they were kissing. They wore the same black blazers and white shirts with starched pointy collars. They appeared to be in love.

Amy was not jealous of her per se – both she and William had had various exes predating their first marriages – but he had not mentioned a serious girlfriend called Sophie.

She went through the photos again.

The two of them were the perfect couple, alike in a way; both fair-haired and tall and clean-skinned. They had summer tans and looked at ease in their formal, faintly ridiculous garb. They strolled through cloisters or smoked on sports fields or cuddled up on fire escape battlements. Amy could not relate to any of it, had no similar references, felt illogically excluded from the privilege they had obviously once shared intimately. But in the last photograph, they were in mufti. Sophie wore yellow slacks and a pink sweater. Amy noticed they were standing in front of the old Indian-style dowry chest that lived on the first-floor landing of Summerfield House.

This would have been impossible.

Forgetting about her spurious search for Tess's AirPods, she charged through the rain to the main house. She shook droplets all over the carpet as she ran upstairs to kneel at the chest and compare the ornate paint markings. It was the exact same piece of furniture. But how could they have been at Summerfield House as teenagers? William had moved here with Eleanor in his early twenties. She looked again at their young faces; they were no older than sixteen. Putting the photograph to her nose, she inspected the wonky plaster and beam behind the chest. She supposed she couldn't pin it to this exact landing. Maybe the chest had once lived at his family home in Dunsfold? Had that house had beams? Had this Sophie visited him in the school holidays?

She stayed on her knees staring at the photo. The girl's presence in this house swirled around her, almost like a visitation.

Even later on, as Amy tidied up in a rough sort of way for Mercy, she could not shake off thoughts of the photo. Like one of those dreams that lingered the following day, she felt she was being followed about by it. By *her*.

When William came home from work, she did not admit to prying into his private things. Olivia, who seemed to know everything, would be the first person she would ask about Sophie.

# TWENTY-SIX

Hal

Under his breath, Rory said, 'Mate, any chance you could get me some photos? I mean, you live with her. You share a bathroom with her. You could get some hot pictures, right?'

'Er? Let me think for a second,' Hal retorted sarcastically, stamping out his cigarette, hoping Rory was kidding. 'That would be a no.'

Rory had sloped back to Tess's side, winking over his shoulder at Hal smugly. The cat that got the cream. Hal was beginning to hate these parties at Rory's. Hate this place. He felt the winter encroaching. Clumps of leaves had made it inside on people's shoes. The sofas were damp, the pool was slimy and the lawn was covered in dried yellow circles of dog piss. The others had taken whatever it was that Logan had supplied. They were getting more adventurous. Perhaps they'd take MDMA, sometimes a few tabs of Xanax, or even ketamine. Tonight it was coke. No more than a few tickets, working out as a couple of bumps each, at most.

Still, they had ripped their tops off and shouted out lyrics to nineties hip-hop until they were hoarse. Muscular fights had broken out. Rory had poured them some lean mixed with Fanta. The codeine-laced cough syrup was strong on their breath afterwards, and they'd slowed down. Finally Hal had had enough and he'd called Amy for a lift. She'd sounded delighted to hear from him, said she could be there in half an hour.

The wait seemed long. As the minutes ticked by, Hal's mind drifted, perhaps a little high on residual smoke, and he watched the party unfold as he might watch a film. He remembered that Oak Hills had once been beautiful. All this had been cared for. A bit like Rory had been. He recalled hot summers of splashing about in the clear heated pool, followed by sips of real lemonade and rub-a-dub-dubs from Olivia. She'd wrap them up in pink fluffy towels and tell them their lips were blue. Or they'd play cricket on the lawn. Or Monopoly in the dining room. Or war games in the woods – Rory would become immersed in the characters he'd play. He sometimes cried. Olivia, with a glass of something in her hand, would soothe him. Hal had envied that he had a mother at home to kiss him whenever he needed it.

A text came through, jolting him out of his nostalgia. *I'm here.*

'Your mum's here,' he said to Tess, who was snuggled into the crook of Rory's arm.

'What the...? But it's only eight thirty and it's half-term!' She had become quite the party animal.

'I was tired.'

'Wow, thanks. You didn't even check with me?'

Hal shrugged.

'Thanks a bunch,' she said, storming off to tell Anoushka and Tilly that she was going.

'Jealous much?' Rory said, sitting forward to crack open another beer.

'Of what?'

'Of me and her.'

'You want to be shoved into that pool again?' Hal said, half joking, half raging at the memory of Rory's sleazy, disrespectful remarks about Tess at his seventeenth. Pushing him in had been the least he deserved.

'I didn't mean anything by it, mate. I like her. You know? Really like her.' Rory spoke out of the side of his mouth, dropping the south London slang he saved for Logan. He was a chameleon, now reverting to his roots to sound like his Etonian-educated father. That was Rory, always lurching from one persona to another.

'Just keep her away from Logan. Okay?'

'Logan knows she's off limits, believe me,' Rory said, sipping from his beer. Then he groaned. 'I mean! Fuck. Look at her. She's so different to the others. She's driving me nuts.'

'She's different, that's for sure,' Hal murmured, glancing over at Tess. She was throwing her arms about the place furiously, her black eyes flashing. One of her ears was poking through her dark hair, as it had the habit of doing. Its goofiness was endearing. He had grown to like her quirky ways: her tone-deaf singing; her ridiculous replacement swear words, like 'balls' and 'crap' and 'flying flip'; her ballroom dancing with Hamish; her unsolicited bear hugs; the fun she injected into their hard-going study schedule.

Rory said, 'Don't forget the photos, will you?'

Every muscle in Hal's body became taut. 'I thought you were kidding?'

'Nah, mate. I'm serious.'

'What is *wrong* with you? I can't do that!'

Rory sat back. 'Trouble is, there're some bags worth a couple of grand at Summerfield that you might not want your dad to find. You see?'

'What the fuck?' Hal hissed.

'Just saying,' Rory said, sticking up his hands in surrender, sidestepping culpability. Rory didn't comprehend guilt. He had a cog missing, an empathy malfunction, a darkness that you couldn't see with the naked eye. 'Your decision.'

'You're sick in the head,' Hal growled, standing up, feeling like spitting at him. He approached Tess, Tilly and Anoushka. 'Ames is waiting.'

All three girls gave him the evil eye. Tess hugged the other two as though it were the last time she'd ever get to see them alive, and stormed off ahead.

Rory shouted at Hal sarcastically, 'I'm glad you enjoyed the party, mate!'

Hal gave him the middle finger.

Tess was a thundery presence by his side, arms locked in front of her, chewing madly at her bottom lip. He could handle it. Anything was better than watching Rory use her. It had been so strange to feel protective towards her. She had stirred him up in some inexplicable way. It had felt good.

Now, he was utterly torn. Rory's request was repugnant, unthinkable. He wouldn't do it. But if he didn't, he risked his dad finding class A drugs in his possession again. He needed to locate them and get rid of them or he would be in line for the kind of trouble that was life-changing, family-ruining. He recalled his dad's words. *If you want to continue to live under this roof... you have to abide by my rules.* His dad had given him a chance, but he might not give him another.

When he and Tess climbed into the back of the car, Hal didn't bother making conversation. Tess was mad as hell, scooched up to the door as far away from him as possible.

Olivia and Amy were standing by the open driver's door discussing a wedding dress shop in Farnham. Finally Tess couldn't hold it in any longer. She found it impossible to keep her feelings bottled up. 'You were totally out of order tonight,' she hissed.

Idly he carried on playing a game on his phone. What could he say to her?

'Are you seriously not going to say sorry?'

He wasn't bloody sorry.

'It's like you want to ruin it for me and Rory,' she continued.

He thumbed the up button on his screen, dodging cars and houses and chickens and children and piles of rubble. Each gold coin he won became in his mind's eye a plastic container of Rory's drugs. The little creature on his screen jumped up and down, up and down, and up again over the obstacles.

'Yeah, that's it,' he said casually.

'You know, I was actually beginning to like the idea of us becoming brother and sister. But I was right before,' she seethed.

Hal crashed into a railway sleeper and lost four gold coins.

He had to find those drugs.

# TWENTY-SEVEN

## Amy

Amy was standing on a pedestal in front of a mirror. She was in a white dress with a long train, swooped elegantly to the left. It was the thirty-first dress she'd tried on, and the fourth dress shop.

Her freckled arms and cleavage were encased in thick lace. Her blonde hair had been neatened into a low bun. Silk buttons ran down her spine, visible to her in the angled mirrors. Two assistants wearing all black had taken fifteen minutes to button her up. Each fiddly fastening had further squeezed her flesh and vital organs upwards into her ribcage and downwards into her hips. Another assistant in black with pins in her mouth fussed at the fishtail hemline.

On first sight, both Olivia and Tess had gasped, while Amy tried to adjust to the image of herself in the floor-to-ceiling mirror. Dresses as beautiful as this weren't designed for ordinary people like her. They were worn by types like Sophie, the girl in the photographs. *Confidence is good, but overconfidence always sinks the ship*, her mother's voice echoed.

'You look absolutely stunning,' Olivia said now.

Tess took a photo with her phone but didn't say anything.

'Whad'ya think, Tess?' Amy asked cartoonishly, hiding her insecurities.

Tess looked up briefly. 'It's beautiful.' Having talked excitedly about this dress appointment all half-term, she was now showing disinterest, at best.

'And the final touch,' the assistant said, draping a veil over Amy's head. 'This one is embellished with a pearl trim and Gutermann seed beads.'

Just like that, Amy's reflection disappeared. Her face became a pretty blur. The organza sucked at her lips as she tried to breathe. She was taken back to 2002, when the heat had built underneath a similar headdress at the altar of St Matthew's. How she had sweated under the full coverage of satin-back dupion; how she had buried herself in what Nick and his mother had wanted; how she had played the fantasy of his perfect wife-to-be rather than the flesh and blood of a real woman. How she had gulped air in relief as he had lifted it from her face. The unveiling of his virgin bride. The virgin bride he'd been sleeping with for two years.

Was she making another mistake now? Her face under the veil was older. The crow's feet around her eyes, her moony cheeks, the pinkening behind the blotches of freckles. She stared at the dress some more, twisting a little this way and that to see whether she could get used to it. There was no doubt it hid her untoned arms and gave her more of a waist. And the low V at the front covered by the gauzy Leavers lace protected her virtue while teasingly hinting at the bare cleavage underneath. It was hard to find fault.

'It's the one,' Olivia said, matter-of-fact, taking a sip of the champagne they'd been handed on arrival. 'Don't you think, Tess?'

Tess replied, 'Yup.'

One of the assistants stepped forward, tugged at the train and proudly surveyed her work with a nod.

'It is lovely,' Amy began doubtfully. The photographs of Sophie came to her once again; her own face seemed to disintegrate behind the spectre of hers. 'But it's quite stiff and uncomfortable.'

'Let's just skip to the bit when you say you don't want it,' Tess said suddenly.

Amy was taken aback by her rudeness. Olivia patted Tess's thigh and gave her a knowing look. Tess had been spending a lot of time at Olivia's, with or without Hal, either studying after school with Rory or hanging out with their friends at his pool house. The fun she had over there seemed to make her crankier at home.

'What's up, Tess?' Amy asked her.

'Nothing,' Tess mumbled.

Standing on this ridiculous plinth waiting for Olivia and Tess's approval, Amy felt not only boring, but also like a third wheel at her own dress fitting. The togetherness of the two of them, sitting thigh to thigh on the curved white sofa, legs crossed in a similarly elegant fashion, was getting up her nose. Perhaps Tess would prefer Olivia as her mum instead, she thought hotly. Let's face it, Olivia had grown up around here and had herself once attended a school just like Heathside Heights, which was just like William's boarding school, where he'd kissed that annoying Sophie girl on the lacrosse pitch. Let's *really* face it, Olivia had the right accent and the right clothes and the uber-confidence. Tess could now relate to her in ways that Amy could not.

She pointed to a dress she'd tried on earlier, which neither of them had liked. 'That one was easier to wear.' It was a satin floor-length shift that had shimmered over her lumps and bumps, highlighting them like jazz hands.

'Uh-huh. Yes. I imagine it was comfortable,' Olivia said,

patiently, before looking across at the assistant. 'It wasn't quite as flattering though, was it?'

The assistant pushed her name badge flat against her bosom – she was called Candace – but it dropped forward again. 'I think they're very different. It depends on what kind of look she's going for,' she replied diplomatically.

'I'll get changed,' Amy said. The bodice was beginning to constrict her like panic. 'Whew. I can hardly breathe in this, to be honest.'

Through the closed curtain of the changing room, she heard Olivia pour herself another glass and say, 'You did warn me, sweetheart.' Her fingernails tinkled a tune on her champagne flute. Amy's ears pricked up. Olivia continued, 'She thinks she's not allowed beautiful things. Like she's not good enough for it or something. When we know she is.'

'I told you,' Tess agreed. So, they *had* talked!

Candace paused her unbuttoning. Amy could almost hear her holding her breath, waiting for her reaction.

'I heard that, you two,' she said, sticking her head out of the curtain.

'Oh, whoops,' Olivia said, unmoved.

'I allow myself lots of beautiful things,' Amy said defensively. Sweaters from Zara and bright pink wellies sprang to mind. 'And I'm not saying no to it quite yet.'

'No?' Olivia said, arching one eyebrow.

'Maybe breathing is overrated,' Amy said, studying Tess, wanting to please her.

Olivia laughed. 'My life's motto, sweetie.'

Bright-eyed, Tess sat straighter on the white sofa and performed some quick claps with her fingertips and little dance steps with her toes. 'Go on, Mum. It's super classy,' she cajoled.

'It's true. It's the classiest dress we've seen, honestly,' Olivia said. 'You'll look totally at home in it at Summerfield House.' Then added quickly, 'If that's where you're having it?'

'I forgot to say, yeah, William's up for it. He suggested we hold the ceremony in the woods. The bluebells will be out.'

Amy imagined herself transformed into a Sophie-like woman: self-assured yet restrained, nodding and smiling gracefully as she floated through a carpet of flowers.

'So he talked to Sophie?' Olivia asked, wide eyes glassy.

*Sophie?* Amy baulked, unable to believe she was hearing that name spoken aloud. 'Why Sophie?' she asked.

'Oh shit,' Olivia said, pressing her red fingernails against her eyes, peering between her fingers. 'You haven't talked to him about her yet?'

Tess asked, 'Who's Sophie?'

Thinking on her feet, Amy shot back with, 'She's an ex-girlfriend of William's,' as though she knew all about her.

Olivia said, 'So you know.'

'Know what?' Tess asked, looking from one woman to the other, sniffing out drama.

Amy hesitated, panicking.

Olivia explained. 'Sophie Sandeman-Gore was William's first love. She owns Summerfield House. She grew up there.'

The dress was a vice clamped around Amy's chest. It was a miracle she remained standing. Sophie Sandeman-Gore. SSG. They were the initials embroidered on the babygro.

Tess was agog. 'William's *ex* owns our house?'

'No, no, not any more,' Amy stammered, and swallowed bravely. 'He bought it off her a few years back.'

Tess snorted. 'Phew. That would've been majorly awks.'

'I didn't know he'd bought it. Although word-of-mouth sales *are* common around here,' Olivia mused. 'What a relief. I've been worrying about it. I didn't want to ask, though. You know.'

Amy's heart battered her ribs. She managed to sound upbeat as she said, 'Right, okay, give me a sec.' When she closed the curtain to dress into her own clothes, her whole body shook convulsively.

Candace said, 'Is this the one, then?'

Amy murmured absently, 'They said I'm good enough for it, so, you know, maybe I'll go with that.' Images of Sophie by the ornate chest strobed across her vision.

Candace grinned. 'Very wise.'

Olivia whipped back the curtain. 'My protégée is ready to go to the ball!'

Amy tried to smile. Tess fist-bumped Olivia and then threw her arms around Amy, who remained motionless and numb. 'Mum! I'm so happy. Sorry I was grumpy before. But it's so annoying when you play yourself down like that, like you don't want to get ideas above your station or something, which is just so *limiting*, you know?' She glanced at Olivia. 'But isn't it just the best dress ever? You look like an actual film star in it.'

Amy was reeling, barely hearing what they were saying as she tapped onto the machine to pay the eye-watering deposit on a dress she now questioned whether she would ever wear.

# TWENTY-EIGHT

Hal

Hal heard Tess come home after Amy's dress fitting. She ran straight upstairs and into the bathroom. The noise of the shower lever made a clanging sound through his bedroom wall. He listened to the running water, waiting for it to stop.

Tensely he tossed his phone from one hand to the other.

The flow stopped. There was the familiar creak of the glass shower partition. Plastic bottles rattled. The mirrored wall cabinet snapped closed. In a few minutes, the click of the lock would be heard. This was the moment she'd leave the bathroom in her dressing gown with a towel turban on her head and pad to her room leaving wet footprints on the carpet.

If he was going to do it, now would be the time.

Rory had been pestering him for weeks now, threatening to tell his dad about the drugs, which were stashed somewhere in the house. Hal had been through every trainer, sock and jacket he owned, searching underneath beds, upending baskets, rifling through sports bags and bedside drawers. There was nowhere new to look. In the end, he had accused Rory of making it up. Rory asked him whether he wanted to take that risk.

One last time, Hal opened his closet and, for the hell of it, shoved his hand deep into each trainer. He knew there'd be nothing, felt desperate about it. He pictured himself carrying out Rory's sordid request: crouching under the windowsill, arm outstretched, his camera phone pointed into her room. Timed right, it would take seconds to capture her changing, or standing in front of her mirror assessing her figure in her new underwear, or whatever girls did before meeting boys.

The process of taking the photographs would not turn Hal on like it might some horrible peeping Tom. If he were to go through with it, he would adopt a professional mindset, stripping out the emotion, doing what he had to do. Tess would remain oblivious. Rory would get his kicks. Hal would stay out of trouble with his dad.

He stood up and looked out of his window at the ledge, mentally preparing for the task ahead. His heartbeat picked up speed. His body was sending him a warning message, but he emptied his mind clinically. Necessity pushed him on.

The moment he opened the window, a dash of shiny blond fur charged across the grass, sniffing at Pete the gardener. Hal hadn't noticed Pete, who had his headphones on as he deadheaded the hydrangeas. Thankfully he had his back turned to the house. He was ignoring Hamish. For a minute, Hal watched the dog perform a little leap backwards, sneeze, stick his nose into a bush, scratch one paw at the soil. A grubby tennis ball rolled out. He barked at it, pushing himself down on his front legs, waiting for the ball to spring to life and play with him. Hal was hit with a stab of love for his dumb dog. The innocence of him; the simple things that made his tail wag. Hamish had blind faith in his ball and in his humans. Especially Hal. He had always trusted that Hal would take care of him. Like Tess, who would stalk around her bedroom half-naked with the curtains open and no lock on the door. Because it wouldn't occur to her that anyone would spy on her.

Remorse and self-hatred flooded him. He slammed the window shut and threw himself on his bed, face down into the pillow, feeling the need to yell. He thumped a fist into the mattress. *Think, Hal, think!* He racked his brains, tracing Rory's movements around the house, knowing he wouldn't dare hide drugs where Mercy or Amy might snoop.

He must have dozed off. The next thing he knew, he had slobber on his cheek. As he stirred, he had a brainwave. A memory, more accurately, of an argument he'd had with Rory years ago. They had been eight years old when Hal's battalion of hand-painted tin soldiers had gone missing from their silk-lined red box. His mum had bought them on a special day out at Harrods after the divorce. Rory had known what they meant to Hal, yet he had stolen them as a joke and concealed their whereabouts for weeks, enjoying Hal's distress. Until, that is, Hal had cut him where it hurt and asked Sammy Whitlock to be his partner on the school coach trip to Calais. Rory hadn't talked to him for weeks after that. But he had eventually told him where he'd hidden the toy soldiers.

Hal shot out of his room and locked himself in the bathroom. The air was still thick with the aroma of Tess's shampoo. He reached up and under the lid of the porcelain cistern. Feeling about a bit, disliking the sensation of the crusty watermark, he found what he was looking for. It was bobbing on the surface of the water – unlike his soldiers, which had sunk to the bottom, rusted and ruined by the time Rory had confessed. On his tiptoes, he untied a plastic bag from the refill tube. Inside this, in an airtight ziplocked bag, were two sausage-shaped packages.

Shaking with rage, he tore into one of the packages, through layers and layers of cling film, finding what must have been as many as a hundred little white rocks, all individually wrapped.

In the other, there were as many similar-sized pouches filled with brown powder. He opened each fiddly damn one of them and emptied the contents into the toilet bowl, pulling at the chain repeatedly until it broke off.

Afterwards he slumped on the floor with his back to the bathtub and stared at the empty wrappings. His fingertips gave off a nasty chemical waft. He realised he was panting, not from the physical exertion, but from the daring act. As he stared down at the detritus in his lap, wondering how he might dispose of all this too, the enormity of what he had done seeped in. There must have been thousands of pounds' worth of drugs in those bags. He might as well have burned that much cash. Rory's cash.

He decided to cut the cling film up with Tess's hair scissors and wrap the pieces in wads of loo paper. Later, he'd bury them in a bin bag in the wheelie bins at the bottom of the drive.

But none of this would save him from Rory. When he imagined telling him what he'd done, and the potential backlash, his throat flooded with dread.

Later, Rory called him on FaceTime. Five times. Six times. Ten times. Hal didn't pick up.

# TWENTY-NINE

## Amy

On the dot of eight, William padded in through the boot room door in his socks with a mild-mannered and jaunty air about him. Amy was in the most opposite of moods. Olivia's eye-opener about Sophie Sandeman-Gore earlier had knocked her sideways.

She turned her back and put away the peanut butter jar left out by Tess with a slam of the cupboard door. In the cavernous silence between them, she heard the faint cries of next door's baby. To drown it out, she clattered about preparing their supper.

'The kids are out, by the way.' She chucked the forks on the table, took out a wine glass for herself but failed to get him one.

'You have a good day?' he asked nervously, straightening the cutlery, pushing his hair off his pinking forehead.

Without answering him, she put a bowl of lentils and brown rice in front of him. It was food he only ever ate reluctantly. Meat and two veg were his staple. Like, she thought, an upper-class fifties child accustomed to being served in a dining room with a gold-rimmed gravy boat on the table. She plonked herself down and took up her fork. Steam rose from the bowl onto her already hot cheeks.

'No, actually,' she said, fixing him with a stiff glare. She got up, rifled in the drawer where she'd put the envelope, and threw it and the loose photographs on the table in front of him. 'When were you going to tell me that we live in your ex-girlfriend's house?'

'Oh.' His expression was pained.

'I had to find out through Olivia.'

'I'm sorry,' he said, putting down his fork.

'I asked you directly about the initials on that baby's sleep-suit and still you said nothing.'

He looked momentarily horror-struck. 'Sorry.'

'It would've been a good time to mention she owned this bloody place, don't you reckon?' she said, raising her voice.

'I... I... didn't know how to tell you,' he stammered.

'I'd get a shift on now, if I were you.'

He rubbed the back of his neck. 'It's all above board. I pay market value, and fork out for its upkeep, which is more than most tenants do. And I've lived here since I was twenty-three. All my adult life. It feels more like my house than Sophie's. But yes, officially she is my landlord.'

'And unofficially?'

'What do you mean?'

'Do you still see her?'

He picked up one of the photographs. 'It's a transactional thing. The money is paid by direct debit into her bank account every month. Occasionally she ups the rent, depending on interest rate rises and so forth, but that's done through solicitors. That's all.'

'But why choose this house, *her* house, of all the houses in the UK to live in?'

'Houses often change hands around here through word of

mouth, sometimes before they've even reached the open market. And my parents and her parents ran in the same circles, so when I got wind of it being available, I jumped at the chance. I'd always loved it.' He slid his hand across the table towards hers. 'I'm so sorry I didn't tell you before. I was embarrassed.' His expression was imploring. Chunks of blond hair curled at his ears. His gentle eyes had filled. They were as familiar to her as her own, more grey than green this evening. The stuffing had been knocked out of her, her anger replaced by a weak, hungry feeling.

'Were you in love with her?'

'I suppose so. When we were going out.'

'When did you split up?'

'God, I can't remember. Must've been before Manchester.'

'What was she like?'

He leant right back in his chair, almost tipping it, and began to spout facts about Sophie's family, while looking at the ceiling and saying 'umm' and 'let me see now' a lot, rambling on about her first in PPE at Oxford and subsequent law degree. How her father, Thomas, had been an MP and her mother, Annie, had inherited vast wealth from her own family. 'He was tipped to be PM, but his heart attack put paid to—'

She stopped him mid-sentence. 'Jesus. You sound like a Wikipedia page. Maybe I don't want to know.'

'Sorry.'

'This is all so surreal.' She trained her eyes on the repeating pattern of diamond glass in the leaded windows. The night was black outside and felt like blindness. Then she remembered the other people in the photographs. She sifted through them again. 'Are you friends with any of this lot still?'

'No.'

'*None* of them?' She wondered if that was unusual.

'Most of them left before sixth form.'

'And Sophie?'

'Yes,' he said. 'Sophie, too.'

'This was taken here, wasn't it?'

He looked closer. 'Must've been in the school holidays.' He shuffled the photographs away.

She remembered her lie to Olivia and admitted shamefacedly, 'I told Olivia you'd bought the house off her.'

'Huh,' he said, half smiling. 'It could've been true. That was always the plan. I was waiting for Hal to get through school. Once the fees are out of the way, my monthly outgoings will be reduced by thousands, which frees me up financially to save for a fifteen per cent deposit. I'd borrow the rest.' There was silence. Then he said, 'Does any of that matter to you?'

'Don't make me sound like some gold-digger.'

He laid the backs of his hands on the table, showing his palms. 'It's just a house, Amy.'

'Just a house,' she echoed, and as she said it, she heard the baby crying from outside again. Or was it the memory of hearing it before?

'Yes, just somewhere nice to live,' he said.

'And somewhere nice to get married?'

'Yes. Of course.'

'She won't have a problem with it?'

'I'll ask her.' He scratched his earlobe.

'Okay. Good.'

'Is it?'

She raised an eyebrow. 'No more secrets, though, okay? This is about the kids, too. We have to be proper grown-ups. And be honest with each other. *Please* let's not repeat all those mistakes from our first marriages. Okay?'

'Okay.' Then he added forlornly, 'My God, I thought you were going to tell me you didn't want to marry me any more.'

She tutted. 'Over a bloody house? You're an idiot, you know that?'

'A total bloody idiot. And I'm going to eat this yellowy gruel that looks like sick to show you how sorry I am and how much I love you.'

A grin twitched on her lips. She would allow him another chance. The honesty she was asking for was in his heart, in his love for her, in his commitment to her. Boiling it down to these core feelings was all she could do right now.

It was only a house.

# THIRTY

Tess

Tess, Rory and Hal stomped along the centre of Scotland Lane, hands dug into their pockets, hoodies up, battling the eye-wateringly cold November wind. Because Olivia had been 'a little over the limit', she hadn't been able to drop them at the station. It was a five-minute drive and a fifteen-minute walk, but they'd left just enough time to catch the 20.10. Rory was meeting someone by the canal at eight thirty, but he was being cagey about whom. Hal was in a bad mood about it. Tess was going with the flow. She was simply happy to be with Rory. Every second she wasn't with him, she yearned to be. When he was in the same space as her, at school or around their parents, it was almost torture not to be able to touch him.

'Did Sammy Whitlock cancel on you tonight?' Rory asked Hal. 'Is that why you changed your mind about coming?'

Hal mock-punched him in the arm. 'Fuck off.'

'Who's Sammy Whitlock?' Tess asked, wanting in on the joke.

'Nobody,' Hal mumbled, ruffling his hair further over his eyes.

'Whenever Hal had beef with me at prep school, he would play chess with Sammy Whitlock in lunch break and leave me out.'

'Awww,' Tess said. 'Poor ickle Rory.'

The three of them laughed, even Hal. Their threesome felt tight, both brand new and unbreakable. They bantered about Sammy Whitlock for a while. Tess half listened, taking in the huge, quiet houses of Scotland Lane nestled amongst the trees, every window lit up; two, sometimes three cars on the drive. Mostly there didn't appear to be any actual people. Except inside one house, where she could see a beautiful woman with soft wavy hair and wide blue jeans. She was in a plant-filled kitchen, reaching up to an open shelf that had been secured to the wall at the perfect height for her to reach. While laughing at something, she took down two long-stemmed wine glasses.

When I grow up, I want her life, Tess thought.

Rory put his arm around her. She appreciated the added warmth of his down jacket.

His replacement phone began ringing. He walked on ahead. They were now cutting through the recreation ground, where a huddle of teens sat on the bench in front of the cricket pavilion. Clouds of vape smoke ballooned from their heads.

'That's the Beechwood lot,' Hal informed Tess.

'That's where Mum wanted me to go, I think,' she said. They carried on walking past the Beechwood kids. Nobody said hi.

Rory turned. 'Hurry up,' he urged, fingers now moving over his iPhone.

'I thought that was broken?' Tess said.

'I've got two now.'

She was confused. 'Why are you using two phones?'

'It's not that deep,' he replied.

The surfaces were icy down Hill Road, and Tess's trainers slipped about. On one patch, she lost her balance entirely. It was Hal who caught her. His reaction had been lightning quick, as though he'd predicted what was about to happen.

By the time they reached Guildford, after a twenty-minute train ride, Tess had drunk two cans of pink gin. She felt giddy and had an uncomfortable feeling in her sternum. The gin tasted better than most alcohol she'd tried. Olivia had once said that everyone needed their signature drink. Tess had decided pink gin would be hers. It was a blessed relief to feel the alcohol slip through her bloodstream, releasing some of the pressures of school.

As they walked through the barriers out of the station and over the bridge, Rory answered a series of calls on his phone. They crossed the road, passed the Electric Cinema and dropped down to the canal. Hal was trailing behind. Along the shady pass they were eyed by a group of four guys. Tess was self-conscious in her short skirt. Up ahead was another huddle of men. She recognised one of them as Logan.

'Wait here,' Rory said, peeling off to greet Logan and the others.

Tess and Hal hovered by an overflowing bin, which stank. Strewn around their feet and up the bank were discarded vapes, syringes, condoms, cigarettes, plastic bags, bottles.

'What the hell are we doing here?' she whispered, stamping her feet to keep her toes warm. 'Who are those guys?' She buried her chin deeper into the neck of her coat, looking furtively over. Something wasn't right. Voices became harsh and aggressive. Fists were pinned at thighs, heads bobbed forward unnaturally. Someone's phone lit up three white, angry faces.

'This isn't good. Let's go,' Hal said.

'We can't just leave Rory!' Her heart started beating out of her chest.

He hesitated, switched back on himself. 'Wanna bet?' he said.

The group broke up. Logan and Rory were jogging away. The three other men were close behind them. Was it a chase, or were they together? There was a flash of something shiny in the mix of hoodies and puffer jackets. A phone? A metal can?

'Fuck, they've got knives,' Hal said, grabbing hold of Tess's coat sleeve.

'Who have?' she yelped, wondering if he meant Rory.

'Just run!' he hissed.

Adrenaline kicked in and she charged along the canal towpath with Hal, faster than she had ever run in her life. The only sounds were their pounding footsteps and their gasping breath. Behind them there was a commotion of male voices, and then she felt a shove in her back. She stumbled, before speeding up, dry-mouthed, petrified, barely daring to look over her shoulder. It had been Rory, sprinting behind her. He dug his knuckles into her back again, spurring her on.

'Hurry, run! They're carrying blades.' His neck was strained, but he was grinning, almost laughing. 'Fuck!' he cried.

Gripped by fear, the four of them careered away from the threat until they were out in the open again, bent double and panting by the busy roundabout. There were cars. They could be seen. They were safe. If need be, Tess would throw herself in front of one. Anything to evade the men who'd chased them.

'FUUUCK!' Logan roared.

Tess shuffled closer to Hal and grabbed his hand. His skin was clammy, like her own. Every muscle in her body quivered.

Visibly hyped up, Rory snorted. 'What the fuck was that about?'

'Beef over turf, bruv.' Logan sucked his teeth. His phone

went, and he answered it curtly. 'Yeah... Lemme call you back.' He looked at Rory. 'I've got some business here.'

Rory rubbed the back of his head, coughing, then gobbed on the pavement.

Tess could feel Hal's fingers squeezing hers, but he remained tight-lipped.

'Jesus, you two look like you've shat your pants!' Rory began laughing, belly-laughing, wiping his cheeks. 'It's okay. We're safe, children. I can deal with those pricks. I've had worse.'

Tess's throat swelled. Biting back the tears, she said to Hal, 'Let's go.'

Avoiding eye contact with Rory, she turned away and Hal followed. They walked quickly over the bridge towards the station. Her legs were like jelly. Rory came up behind her and slipped his arms around her waist, hampering her progress. 'Don't go, Tessie,' he said. 'It got out of hand. Sorry. But they're gone now. It won't happen again. Come on, don't go.' His breath was sweet, strawberry flavour, and her desire for him made her feel angry with herself.

'Get off me,' she said.

He understood she meant it and released her. 'Okay, okay. You go home. We'll speak later, yeah?'

She fell into step next to Hal, but they didn't talk. She was trying to process what had happened. Perhaps he was quiet for the same reason. Or it could be that he was used to situations like this and was too jaded to speak about it. Either way, she was grateful that he was by her side.

By the time they were sitting opposite each other in the empty train carriage, she was calmer and could go over what had been said.

'What was all that about turf?' she whispered urgently.

'Logan's a dealer.'

'Is Rory involved?'

'I guess so, by the looks of it,' he said, typing into his phone.

'You're not mixed up in it, are you?'

'I'm not an idiot.'

She paused to think. Then it hit her. 'You came along tonight because you knew I'd be out of my depth, didn't you?'

He shrugged and stared intently at his screen, saying nothing. Her cheeks burned hot with both shame and affection. 'Thank you, Hal. Seriously.'

Outside the window it was pitch-black. Inside the carriage the lighting was yellow and harsh. Her eyes couldn't adjust to either. In her mind, the memory of Rory's clear blue gaze flashed at her; he'd been thrilled by the chase.

'What did he mean when he said he'd had worse?'

Hal pressed his head back into his seat and stared up at the luggage rack. His jaw jutted out as he exhaled. 'I guess he was talking about his dad.'

'He lives in Notting Hill now, doesn't he? But I don't know much else. What's he like?'

'I witnessed something once. It was years ago. I was meeting Rory at Oak Hills after rugby practice, but nobody came to the front door so I went round the back. Rory was curled up on the kitchen floor at his dad's feet. At first I didn't know what I was looking at – I was only, like, eight or something – but then I realised that his dad was kicking him in the stomach. And Rory's arms were crossed over his face.' He paused, gulping. 'It was fucked up.'

'Jesus,' Tess breathed. 'What did you do?'

'To be honest, I wanted to run, and I almost did, but then the next thing I knew, I was hurtling towards Toby – who's six foot seven, by the way – and screaming my head off, and he just stopped, like he'd come out of a trance or something. He even looked scared – not like *I'd* scared him, but like he was shocked that he'd found himself doing it. He helped Rory up and just walked out. It was so weird.'

'How badly hurt was Rory?'

'Not as bad as you'd think. He had a couple of days off school, I think.'

'What did Olivia do about it?'

'No clue. She didn't leave Toby, obviously.'

'I can't believe she didn't stop that from happening,' Tess breathed in disbelief. She knew with every fibre of her being that her own mum would never have let that happen to her. Never.

'Maybe she didn't know?' Hal suggested. 'Rory never talked about it.'

'Poor, poor Rory. It's so awful.'

'Yes. Poor Rory,' Hal replied flatly.

'What was his dad like around you after that, knowing you'd seen him?'

'He acted like it had never happened.'

'Seriously?'

'Toby was just Toby. He was charming and clever and shit. And he thought you were irrelevant if you couldn't make him more money than he already had,' Hal said, staring out of the window at the blackness speeding past. 'Money's literally all he cares about. And he never thought Rory was clever enough to make as much as he had. It was total bullshit.'

What Rory had put them through tonight by the canal was bad, but the horror of being beaten by your own father was utterly unimaginable. Tess considered the enormity of the pain he carried inside him, and felt burdened with it.

# THIRTY-ONE

Amy

Steam rose enticingly from the surface of the infinity pool. The grounds of the health club stretched out onto the South Downs like a rolled-out carpet. Amy hadn't believed that places like this existed outside of Instagram.

'William had to go to Bristol suddenly this morning. Apparently he'd forgotten about some conference,' she said to Olivia, apropos of nothing. She was weighing up whether to bring up Sophie Sandeman-Gore, needing to talk to someone about her, knowing Olivia would have some juice on her. More than William or Google had offered up.

'Rory's being secretive too,' Olivia declared, dropping her waffle-cotton robe onto the sunlounger. She wore a cut-out white swimsuit, and her long legs were expertly tanned and toned.

Amy peeled off her own robe. Her jaw instantly juddered in response to the cold. Her Speedo sports costume – which had never seen any sport – flattened her boobs into pitta breads, while its edges cut deep into her bottom and underarms.

'William wasn't being secretive, I don't reckon. His head-of-something-or-other sprang it on him last night,' she said. 'What was Rory being secretive about? They're not planning some massive party at Summerfield tonight, are they?' She laughed lightly.

'I hope not! No, it's not that. He said he was looking forward to a chilled Friday night at your place – you know it's his home from home.' Olivia bent one arm down her back, stretching. Then the other, inhaling and exhaling as she dropped forward into a yogic bend. 'It's just he's been cagey lately.' Bony vertebra by bony vertebra, she rolled up to standing, seemingly oblivious to the November chill. 'And a little withdrawn.'

Withdrawn was not the word that sprang to mind when referring to Rory. 'He always seems okay when he comes over to ours.'

'Tess hasn't said anything, has she?' Olivia's big doll eyes flickered over Amy's body.

Amy cringed, wanted to scratch all her freckles off. She hurried into the pool. 'Tess doesn't tell me anything these days.'

Like a swan, Olivia glided through the water towards a metal contraption that resembled sunken conjoined sunloungers. Two middle-aged men lay prone on another one nearby. They eyed her beautiful body before resuming their business chat, a little louder than before.

'They're such a sweet couple, aren't they?' she said, lowering herself in.

Amy was buoyant, bobbing about stupidly above the metal rungs. 'Tess and Rory?'

'Don't worry, I've had the condom chat with them.'

'Oh?' she spluttered, slipping back, almost drowning.

'They *are* almost seventeen.' Olivia pressed a button between them, and jets of water pummelled their backs.

Amy rested her head back on the cushion and closed her

eyes, processing the news that Tess and Rory were more than just friends. 'I'm finding it hard to keep up with all the changes in her.'

'She's such a lovely girl. I wouldn't worry.'

'I just wish I knew what was going on in her head. All she does is shut herself in her room to work. Or go out. I guess I shouldn't complain really. I'm loving how motivated she is on the academic front – she's doing so well. But I feel distant from her. I miss our girly chats, you know?'

Olivia didn't say anything for a minute. Then, 'Do you worry for *your* sake or for hers?'

'Mine *and* hers, I guess.' Amy considered how distant she felt from everyone. Especially William, who had been preoccupied before he left for Bristol. Sophie Sandeman-Gore's name was on the tip of her tongue now.

'Teenagers are almost worse than ex-husbands,' Olivia said.

'Come on now, let's not exaggerate.' Amy chuckled nervously, and her stomach flipped at the thought of her next line of enquiry.

'That's why we need to do this every Friday night!' Olivia said.

Amy exhaled deeply, bracing herself to ask the question. But all that came out of her mouth was, 'Too right. This is so nice.'

'Not a bad spot for the hen do, right?' Olivia said.

'It's definitely a bit different to wearing a pink tutu on Brighton pier like last time. I think that was the best night of my life. We drank bad wine through willy straws and danced to Salt-N-Pepa. Both my big toenails went black and blue from my stupid pointy tight shoes, and the next day my ribcage muscles were agony from all the laughing. I could hardly move!'

Olivia raised her head from the cushion to open one false-lashed eye. 'D'you think all this'll be too sedate for your London friends?'

'Oh my God, no, Pip and Jo would sell their grandmas to come to a place like this.' But Amy couldn't imagine what they'd make of Olivia, Marte and Paula. The six of them would be an odd mix: old and new worlds colliding. The mention of Pip and Jo was an opportunity to segue neatly into a chat about old friends, and perhaps Sophie. 'Who organised *your* hen night?'

Olivia turned on her side to face her and leant her head on her hand, one bony hip above the water. 'Caroline. An old school friend. I don't see her any more, sadly. But she pulled out all the stops to get us a tent at Glastonbury, and we smoked too much pot and danced to Basement Jaxx. And, oh my God, *Bowie* was on the Pyramid Stage! He was incredible – I can't *believe* he's dead. And that other singer I loved at the time. What's his name? Oh, bloody hell. I can't remember any names these days.' She paused. 'Anyway, no matter. It was way more fun than the honeymoon.'

'Why, what happened?' Amy asked, telling herself to give up on her plan to mine Olivia for information and instead enjoy getting to know a new friend.

'Oh God. Toby's contract with this massive chemical waste company fell through while we were out in Sri Lanka. He was a nightmare the whole time, and we had to come home early.'

'That's awful!' *Chemical waste?*

'At least I got a few days out there. I'd always wanted to go.'

Amy paused to reflect on her own honeymoon. 'Nick and I had a shit one too. We went to Turkey. There was a fire at our hotel and we were evacuated in the middle of the night and bussed to the airport hotel. It didn't have a pool, the croissants were plastic and we had to put up with the lovely sound of planes taking off.'

It reminded her of how unhappy she and Nick had been, even in the beginning. She leant back. The wintry freshness on her face contrasted with the warmth of the water massaging her body. Birds chattered in the trees. Above them, the sky was a dome of white, peaceful and calm. Was she going to ruin it by finding out more than she needed to know?

They were silent for a moment or two before Olivia said, 'Where are you and William going for yours?'

'We're thinking of Scotland. Maybe visit my sister. Bag a couple of Munros. I used to go as a kid every summer. It's where I fantasise about retiring one day.'

She wrinkled her nose. 'What about the weather?'

'I don't really mind that.'

'Wherever you go, it'll be so special for William. He didn't have a honeymoon the first time round, did he?'

Amy stole a sideways peek at Olivia. Her eyes were closed. There was a dewy film of sweat like cling film across her skin. 'That's right,' she said, remembering that William had mentioned this. 'Like with Toby, it was because of work, right?'

Olivia tilted her head back into the water, smoothing her hands across her scalp to slick her hair back. 'Eleanor never really got to the bottom of it, but she had her suspicions.'

'Suspicions?' Amy pushed her bottom lip against her teeth.

'I'm sure it was nothing. I don't want to cause any trouble.'

'*Sapere aude*,' Amy said out loud. *Dare to know*.

Olivia laughed at her. 'You're speaking Latin now?'

'You poshies have turned me.' It came out sounding less jokey than she'd meant it.

The bubbles stopped. Olivia sat up. 'Okay. Let's get some juice at the bar. I guess it's best you know the whole story.'

# THIRTY-TWO

William

'The website said it had sea views,' Sophie said, peeking through the net curtains of the bay window.

'It didn't lie,' William said wryly. A bleak churning slate of sea met with doomily black clouds at the horizon. A spray of foam shot up from the sea wall. The sogginess of the scene seemed to seep in through the cracks in the woodchip under the sill. Five hours on the train had brought them to a different universe.

Sophie propped herself up by the handle of her small suitcase. 'Next year, *you* can book it then.'

He paused. 'I'm grateful. Sorry.'

Up the stairs, an institutional fire door led to their rooms, one next to the other.

William opened his door with the plastic card and watched Sophie's repeated attempts to unlock hers. 'Oh, these bloody things,' she said.

As he took the card from her to try it himself, their hands

touched. The damp heat of her seemed to drench the whole of him. Contact like this was enough to weaken him.

Her door opened. The odour of old cigarette butts and boiled bedsheets hit him. There was a stain on the green nylon coverlet. 'I hope mine's the luxury superior penthouse suite,' he said.

'If it is, I'll be knocking on your door tonight.'

'I don't think so,' he blurted. She had been joking, he knew it, and he had overreacted, rendering her remark immediately less jokey.

'This Amy woman has changed you, I see,' she said, winking. 'Where does she think you are tonight?'

'At a conference in Bristol,' he replied miserably. 'What time did you say we'd be there?'

'Visiting hours end at four thirty on Fridays, so we'd better get a move on.'

He checked his phone. It was just after three. 'I'll have a quick shower and see you downstairs in half an hour.'

'I *promise* not to make any jokes about joining you,' she said.

'Ha ha,' he replied, feeling a disconcerting stirring at the thought.

Once he was in his own room, he sat on the bed and exhaled. His bed was identical to hers next door, but it faced the opposite way. Tonight, the tops of their heads would be almost touching through the papery walls. He decided against a shower and instead got out his laptop to whizz through his finances. He scanned his accounts on his banking app and totted up his assets and savings, making calculations with renewed rigour, an idea forming.

# THIRTY-THREE

## Amy

Amy got out of the pool, wrapped herself in her robe and set a speedy pace towards the juice bar, desperate to know more about William's past. Her teeth were chattering, more from apprehension than cold.

Olivia ordered them kale and kiwi smoothies, which came with umbrellas as though they were cocktails. A pink neon sign that said *Juice Bar* in italics flickered behind the waiter, who was wearing a white collarless jacket, more like a doctor than a barman. Amy wished it was a proper bar so that she could ask for a shot of vodka in hers.

'So tell me,' she said.

Olivia took a sip from her straw with a glossy pout before beginning. 'Okay, well, Eleanor had booked this incredible honeymoon on Lake Como for them, but a week before the wedding, he told her that something urgent had come up with the business and they had to cancel the whole thing.'

'You mean the honeymoon?'

'Nope. The whole bloody shebang. The ceremony at

Chelsea registry office, the reception party at Bibendum. The works.'

'But they were definitely married. I saw the photos.'

'They were in the end. Six months later. Though still no honeymoon.'

'But why?' Amy asked impatiently, feeling the cold water from her hair dripping down her back.

'It was a crazy time. He was setting up ExoAnalytics. And with hindsight, you don't set up such a successful company without being a little ruthless, right?'

'I never saw him as ruthless.'

'Ambitious might be a better word. One-track. I mean, he didn't really have many friends of his own. A few colleagues he liked, that was all.'

'He's quite self-sufficient.'

'Men aren't like us. They don't need friends in the same way.' Olivia squeezed Amy's hand.

'They *think* they don't.' Amy smiled.

'For all Eleanor's faults, she was amazing about the whole thing. A real trouper.'

'Definitely more understanding than I would have been.'

Olivia paused and blinked as she took another sip. 'When it happens to you, it's not that easy to take a tough line. Not when you love someone.'

Amy focused on sucking up the dregs of her juice, feeling her cheeks redden, regretting her prying. 'I guess so.'

'The real trouble came later. Eleanor often complained to me about how disconnected he could be at home. He'd go through phases when he'd withdraw from family life completely. She'd try everything to get through to him, but she said he was in his own world. Utterly impenetrable, she said.' Another sip was taken.

'He can be like that,' Amy admitted quietly. 'I'm always trying to tease out how he really feels.'

'Eleanor wasn't exactly your touchy-feely type either. It was more the secrecy that bothered her.'

'Secrecy?'

'Well, that's the point.' Olivia hesitated.

'Go on. *Please*. I'm fine.'

'She thought he was having an affair.'

Amy spluttered. 'Really?'

'I'm afraid so.'

'Why did she think that?'

'The usual clichéd things. Working late in London all the time, sudden work trips at the weekends. One time she found a receipt for a buffet breakfast for two at some hotel in Scarborough – of all places – when he was supposed to be somewhere else.'

'Bristol?'

'It might have been.'

Amy felt sick. 'Did she suspect who it was with?'

'Remember, it was only a hunch. She didn't actually know it was Sophie.'

Her heart lurched. 'Sophie Sandeman-Gore?'

'I'm afraid so. That house has some kind of hold over them both.'

The circular seat pad of Amy's stool wobbled on its pole and twisted underneath her precariously. Her toes couldn't quite reach the floor to balance. She grabbed for the bar to stop herself from falling.

Watching her struggle, Olivia tilted her head to the side. 'Sorry, is this too much?'

'Not at all. I just thought I was going to fall off.' Amy righted herself, blinking away the unwelcome image of Sophie's initials on the tiny sleepsuit. 'Did she never have proof?'

'No. Never.' Olivia stopped to circle ice around her glass with the straw, glancing up at Amy as though Amy had an inkling of what was coming. Amy did not. 'She ended up turning a blind eye. She rather liked the lifestyle, if I'm honest.' She brought out some lip gloss from her robe pocket. 'Want some?'

Amy shook her head. 'I'm okay.'

'Talking to you about it now is slightly déjà vu, I have to admit.' Olivia waved the gloopy pink wand at her. 'They're very dry. Maybe just a little bit?'

Self-consciously Amy dabbed some on and rubbed her lips together quickly to get rid of the sickly taste. A burning sensation circuited the skin around her mouth.

'Ow, shit,' she said. 'What *is* that?'

'Oh, does it hurt? It's a lip plumper! Oh gosh. It's gone all red! I'm so sorry. You must be terribly sensitive!'

The stinging was acute. Amy's eyes watered. 'It's fine, honestly.'

Olivia plunged the corner of a napkin into a jug of iced water and began dabbing at Amy's lips. Amy blinked rapidly, but an inexplicable escapee tear plopped out and rolled down her cheek, followed by another. 'Sorry,' she said.

Olivia caught them with the napkin. 'I'm so sorry. I've upset you.'

'I'm glad I know,' she sniffed.

They were almost close enough for Olivia's lashes to tickle Amy with synthetic butterfly kisses. Her tiny little chin bunched up. 'You've changed him, I promise you.' Pulling back, giving Amy some much-needed space, she added, 'Honestly, he'd never cheat on you. Eleanor was a short, hard-nosed little cow with crispy hair! He loves you much more than he loved her.'

'Just differently, maybe,' Amy said, wiping her nose, unnerved by Olivia's bitchy outburst about her old friend. Her thoughts skimmed over Eleanor and trickled further back into William's past, to the photographs of the long-limbed, pale-eyed beauty of his school days. Perhaps he had loved Sophie differently again. It might explain why keepsakes from her childhood were wrapped up in tissue paper and kept in old drawers.

'Exactly. Differently. Different times. Come on now, lovely, let's get into a hot shower before our treatments. Then we can have some proper bloody cocktails before supper. The restaurant's amazing here.' Olivia plucked the paper umbrellas from their empty glasses and chucked them over the bar, then smacked her hands together as though ridding herself of something bad. 'We can order a cab later.'

Amy was able to laugh. 'Okay. D'you think the kids will be all right at the house on their own for a bit longer?'

Bringing out her phone from her pocket, Olivia said, 'I'll text Rory to make sure.'

'You know, a free house back in my day meant broken picture frames and vomit in the bath.'

Olivia showed Amy Rory's reply:

*We're chill just watching a movie c u later xx*

She slid off her stool and offered Amy a hand to help her down. 'All those fees, and they haven't taught them about grammar and punctuation?'

Amy attempted a chuckle. 'Tess's are the same.'

They shuffled in their towelling sliders along the jasmine-and-sandalwood-scented corridors to the changing rooms.

In the shower, Amy's mind whirred with the new information she had gathered about William's past. Did people change according to whom they fell in love with? She'd never believed that this was possible before, but now she hoped with a heart full of an aching sort of love that William had changed for her. Then the photographs of slender, graceful, pale-eyed Sophie came charging into her thoughts once again.

She shouted over the glass shower divide to Olivia next to her, 'I found some old photos of William and Sophie and some other people I didn't know. Can I show you them when we're back at the house later? You might know some of them.'

'I might do, but it's unlikely. Remember I only knew Sophie vaguely back then. I got to know her properly through Eleanor later on. But what do you hope to find out anyway?'

'Just curious, I guess,' Amy said. More accurately, she was ravenous for knowledge about William's past. The crumbs of information only made her hungrier.

# THIRTY-FOUR

William

There had been a break in the rain, allowing William and Sophie to take Avril on a walk through the marina and along the front before the light faded. Avril's head was covered in an orange fleecy hood that smelt to William like the care home they had collected her from. She had preferred that William take charge of her wheelchair, complaining that Sophie drove it too fast.

Nevertheless, he felt the wheels escape from him as they went down the slope of the little white bridge. Reacting to the speed, Avril clasped the blanket that covered her thighs as though it might fly away. Fondly he remembered when she could walk, and the specific side-to-side rock of her gait as she'd bustled around Summerfield House.

They made it safely onto the flat section of the marina, passing pleasure boats and fishing trawlers. 'How's Lucie, Avril?' William asked, bending towards her ear.

'The baby is always crying!' she said. Her IV-bruised hand swiped the air. Whose baby? he thought. Her daughter Lucie had grown-up sons, but William hadn't heard Avril mention any great-grandchildren.

'Whose baby?' Sophie shouted over the circling seagulls and the frantic clinking of masts.

'Tsk, you know what I'm talking about,' Avril scolded. Despite the fact that she'd lived in England for over thirty-four years, her accent was as strong as ever.

Gingerly William continued pushing, refusing to look at Sophie. They passed the pink shutters of a kiosk selling rock candy. At a seafood bar, two women discussed tide times. Further along, the outdoor tables of a new pizza restaurant were empty.

'Pete's doing wonders in the garden, Avril, although he's getting a little slower,' William said.

'I should say so! He must be as old as me,' she chortled, tickled by the thought. Back then, Pete had only been twenty-five years old to her sixty. He assumed she was getting confused with Pete's father.

'We're hoping for snow this Christmas,' he said.

'You're not going to tell Avril about the new lady of the house?' Sophie asked archly.

'Pah,' Avril cut in. 'Only Annie is the lady of the house!'

William wondered if now was the time to break the news about the wedding. He wasn't sure how Avril would feel about it.

Sophie added sadly, 'Mummy was an impossible act to follow.'

'Annie wanted you to bring your children up there,' Avril said, wagging a finger at her.

Abruptly the conversation stopped. William held his breath, didn't trust himself to speak, would not bring the wedding up now. He looked out, past the stacks of lobster pots that reeked of salt and rotten fish, to the suspension of clouds.

Avril broke the silence. 'You see, I hear him crying still, *vous comprenez?*'

Sophie let out a small gasp. Her haughty beauty was stripped from her. Her pale, dusty eyes became empty holes and her mouth a thin line. William felt sick, could only manage a shake of his head. His hands tightened around the rubber handles of the wheelchair. 'I'm sorry to hear that,' he said formally. The cold became a shooting pain in his knuckles. The noises around them grew loud. He struggled to push Avril on towards the lifeboat station, where the promenade ended. The sandy beach stretched ahead, the waves charging up and down, frothing at the mouth.

Avril continued. 'He is unsettled. As I get closer to our meeting,' she paused to cross herself, 'I hear him more often. He cries out, always needing more.'

Sophie crouched down to the old lady and held her knees. 'What does he need, Avril?' she rasped.

Avril tugged down the hood of her coat. Her bony head with its sparse covering of downy white hair was exposed. Her wide back was hunched forward. 'He tells me he wants you to be together again. He feels he is to blame. He can't leave until this is fixed.' She cleared her throat and shifted in her chair to look at William. There were pouches under her rheumy blue eyes. Tears blew in horizontal rivulets towards her hairline. 'It's up to you now, William, *mon fils*.'

Fear detonated inside him.

# THIRTY-FIVE

Tess

Rory was knee-deep in the pond at Summerfield House, staggering and spitting as he waded out of the water, jeans sodden. He pulled the wooden dingy onto the bank. Four of the other boys were stranded on the central island, where he and Hal had apparently spent half their childhood building a *Swallows and Amazons*-style camp. Anoushka and Tilly, in their identical bodycon minis and down jackets, were safe and dry on shore, laughing hysterically at the spectacle.

'He capsized us! You dick, Rory!' Mylo bellowed. With every bottle of vodka, whisky, schnapps, Jägermeister, the boys were getting rowdier. At least there had been no drugs. Taking Tess's advice, Rory had stopped all contact with Logan and had promised never to see him again. It was the only reason he had been allowed over tonight.

'It's getting a little out of hand,' Tess said worriedly.

Her phone alarm buzzed and vibrated, reminding her again that her mum was due back from the spa in an hour. It was meant to have been a chilled Friday-night gathering after school rather than a full-blown party. If her mum saw the mess in the house, let alone how drunk everyone was, she would lose her shit. Summerfield House was sacred ground to William, and her mum would never let Tess forget it.

'I told you not to invite that lot,' Hal mumbled. He was stone-cold sober. 'To be honest, I wouldn't be surprised if Logan pitches up.'

'Rory wouldn't do that,' Tess said.

'Yeah. Lighten up, Hal,' Tilly said.

There was a collective roar and kaboom-splosh as the other boys dived in. They swam over and pulled Rory under, play-fighting.

'I'm going back to the house to make sure everything's okay,' Hal said.

'Come on, guys! Can we all go back to the house!' Tess hollered uselessly.

Rory was the only one to get out. His T-shirt clung to his muscles.

'Any excuse to show off your pecs,' Tess said, twisting away from his freezing-cold advances, bullishly maintaining their friend-zoned status. His lapse of judgement in Guildford had ruined what they'd had, although she had already quite recovered from the experience itself. Giving up on him completely would have been a predictable response; would be letting him down. Just like his parents had. She would not be like them.

Rory flexed his bicep. 'Tell me that bulking at the gym isn't worth it.'

Anoushka downed the last of her can of porn star martini and said a little loopily, 'I want some more. I'm going back to the house.'

Tess and the others went with her, hurrying through the cold night, leaving the other boys thrashing about in the icy water.

. . .

A crowd was ambling and lurching around the garden; dark, unidentifiable figures, white phone lights zigzagging. Above their heads, plumes of vape and breath rose against the black sky. At Tess's last count, there had been twenty-six kids, mostly from Heathside Heights, though others from Priory House and Beechwood had got in on the group chat. She didn't know half of them. At least there was no sign of Logan.

Hal had lit some logs in the fire pit, brought out Doritos, marshmallows and a speaker. Begrudgingly, Tess thought him clever to have drawn as many of their guests as possible outside. Nevertheless, he was poking at the embers as though the world's problems were on his shoulders. Anoushka was trying to get his attention by eating a marshmallow in a sexy way. Sadly, it was this very marshmallow that sent her running inside to chuck up in the blue bathroom.

'There you go, well done, get it all out,' Tess soothed, holding back her sticky blonde blow-out and kneeling next to the two puddles of vomit she had failed to get into the toilet bowl. The clock was ticking away towards 11.30. Her mum could not see Anoushka like this.

'We need Rory,' she declared, remembering that the only adult who wouldn't judge was Olivia.

'Nooo,' murmured Anoushka, barely coherent, with a lump of sick stuck in her braces. 'You don't need him. He's a bashtard. You don't desherve him... I mean, he doesn't desherve you, Tessie.' And then she burst into tears.

'Don't be a buckethead, Anoushka. Shh. Shh. I'll go get Tilly so she can stay with you while I find him. I was thinking that Olivia could take you home for a sleepover, then your mum will never know.'

'Okay,' Anoushka groaned, clinging to the toilet bowl, girding herself for another round of vomiting.

Tess found Tilly to take over, then searched the ground floor of the house, sweeping up empty bottles and crisp packets along the way. The drawing room was empty and as formal as it had been this morning. The worn, dusty, mismatched furniture was like ancient relatives. The smallest room, the TV den, was stuffed with boys vying for the PlayStation.

William's office was next. Unseen, she shot out through the back and jogged across the orchard to the strange chalet-style outbuilding. Inside, the rows of glossy spines on the bookshelves glinted in the half-light. The full moon hung centrally in the apex of the windows. Every day after school, William would encourage her to have a browse here. She'd amble along the shelves, reading through the names of the authors, intrigued by the eclectic mix of titles, sliding some out to read the opening paragraph, imagining how her own opener might compare one day. There was a book on the side with a Post-it note: *Tessie – your next read. It's marvellous. William.*

But there was no Rory, so she closed the door and retraced her steps to the house, across the lawn and towards the kitchen French windows. She was thinking mostly about the book William had left her and when she'd have time to read it.

It was why she was caught off guard. She stopped dead in her tracks, aghast to see the emaciated streak of Logan standing on the grass of Summerfield House. His bony face and tired, slothful eyes sent a shiver down her spine. There was someone else with him. As she drew closer, she could see it was a man in his twenties. He had a five o'clock shadow, metal Versace glasses and a slight paunch. As he flipped up his black sweater to retrieve his phone from his pocket, she saw the handle of a knife tucked into the waistband of his jeans.

Backtracking, panic-stricken, she swerved the crowd unseen.

Her breath came out in white puffs as she sprinted through the shadows along the side of the house and behind the garages, passing a black hatchback on the drive. She didn't stop; continued through the spiky trees to the pond, which was the only place she hadn't yet looked. If she found him there, she'd yell at him and beg him to get Logan off their property.

And there he was. Shivering and smoking, hunched with his arms folded across his chest, inches away from Hal. Two halos of moonlight circled their crowns. Something stopped her from racing over. She crept closer, trying to catch what they were saying. She wasn't sure what to make of their body language. Hal seemed to be touching Rory's eye, and Rory flinched, flicked his cigarette. Oblivious to her presence, they began walking back along the path.

She crept behind a cluster of trees.

As they passed by, she heard Rory say through chattering teeth, 'Maybe he'll be gone by now anyway.'

'You hang back and I'll check.'

Hal went on ahead while Rory shuffled about nearby.

Tess waited, unsure of what to do. A few minutes later, Hal returned. 'His car's still there.' There was a pause.

'Can't you bloody drive me home?'

'I've only had four lessons, Rory.'

'Don't worry about it,' Rory grunted.

'Mate, I'll fix this,' Hal said.

Their footsteps started up again. Tess followed at a safe distance.

At the house, Hal peeled off around the back. Rory grabbed his bike from the drive. She jogged over. 'You're leaving?'

'I've got to get home.' His foot rested on the gravel. The outdoor security light struck his face for a second before it timed out, long enough for her to see that one of his eyes was red and swollen.

'What happened? Why is Logan here?' she whispered urgently.

'It's Hal's fault.'

'I don't believe that.'

'Seriously,' he said, looking nervously over her shoulder.

'Hal got involved in something he doesn't know shit about and landed me right fucking in it, and now those dickheads want something I don't have. Best that you and your bro stay out of his way. I've gotta go.'

Before she could ask more, he had swerved and pedalled away.

'He's not my *bro*,' she mumbled to herself angrily, trying to cover up her fear.

Logan and his friend were lurking near the French windows. Vape smoke mushroomed from their heads. The thought of that slim-handled blade set her teeth on edge. Soon the driveway would be swarming with four-by-fours, their engines running, tired-looking parents behind the wheels. Tess remembered Anoushka, drunk somewhere.

'Where have you been?' Hal asked. Hamish nuzzled her hand as she walked on. 'You're not going over to them, are you?' He pulled her back.

'Get off me.'

As she drew nearer to Logan, the smell of weed could have knocked her over. Blood rushed into her head.

Boldly she said to him, 'Better get out of here. This place is going to be swarming with uptight mums any minute now.' She dared to glance in the direction of the man with the knife. His eyes were magnified by his glasses. He had a lipless hole of a mouth.

'But Tessie, babe, me and Ralph just got here,' Logan said. 'Come all the way down from London town.' As he tipped his head back to take a slug of beer, his Adam's apple poked prominently above his zipper. She thought of the Bible story of the apple stuck in Adam's throat, symbolic of the forbidden fruit.

'Gutted you've come all this way, mate,' she said, trying to keep her voice steady.

Hal approached with Hamish, who sniffed intensely at Ralph's black jeans. Ralph bent down to scratch the animal's head. 'Hello, dog,' he said. Hamish growled.

'Logan, seriously,' Hal said, self-assured, unruffled, pulling at Hamish's collar. 'I've just told everyone to go. This isn't personal.'

Logan took a languid step forward. Tess could smell washing powder on his clothes. 'Where's Rory, bruv?'

'No idea. He was out with the Guildford group tonight.' Hal's lie was cool and convincing.

At that moment, Tilly bundled over. 'Noushie's still locked in the loo!' There was a snort from Ralph, who mimicked her accent. The Purley part of Tess didn't blame him.

A call vibrated from Logan's pocket. He answered it under his breath, 'ACE,' and turned away.

With Tilly in tow, Tess headed to the downstairs bathroom, annoyed that Tilly had abandoned her friend. Malena would never have done that to Tess, and vice versa.

'Who was that old guy with Logan?' Tilly asked.

Tess didn't answer her. They banged on the bathroom door. 'Anoushka!' she yelled. 'Open up!'

The door lock clicked open. Anoushka was in a state. 'Shi-ii... znit, Anoushka. We'd better sort you out before your mum sees you,' Tess said, blowing her cheeks out, feeling frantic and pulled in all directions.

While Tilly sat on the loo and scrolled through TikTok, Tess got to work on Anoushka's appearance. Rage for Hal and Rory and all their secrets rose inside her.

'There,' she said to Anoushka. 'You're good to go. Just leave Tilly to do the talking in the car with your mum. Say you're too tired.'

Anoushka hugged her hard. 'I love you so much,' she slurred.

As Tess hugged her back, she heard the revving of Logan's

car engine. It accelerated away. She held her breath, hardly able to believe her luck. Even when the noise grew faint, her heartbeat ran away with itself.

They had half an hour to get rid of the last few stragglers and sort out the house before her mum's return. She stuffed bin bags with rubbish and swooped a cloth over the surfaces. Hal guided clusters of teenagers to their parents' waiting vehicles. It took only twenty minutes for the final group to leave.

Hal came in and plonked himself down at the kitchen table. 'That was a close one.'

She reached for two cans of Coke from the fridge and handed him one. He put it straight onto his cheek, which she could see was red like Rory's eye.

'You guys had a fight?' she said, toying with the ring pull of her own can.

Another of Rory's Snapchat messages pinged through. She left it unopened along with the rest of his messages, including some funny photos of his two French bulldogs, but couldn't resist checking his location. His avatar hovered over his home address.

'Not really.' Hal opened his Coke and drank thirstily.

'Rory said you stuck your nose into something and got him in trouble,' she said, feeling the heat in her cheeks. Before she had a chance to go on, they heard a car outside. 'Who's that?' she said, peering out of the window, on high alert again. 'It's a cab... but Mum took the Mini. Wait a minute... What's Olivia doing here?'

Seconds later, Amy and Olivia burst in through the boot room door.

'Hello, darlings!' Olivia cried, showering them with wine kisses.

'Did you have a nice evening?' Amy asked Tess. She had swirly eyes and a moony smile. Her hair was wilder than usual.

'Yeah, it was chilled but fun,' Tess said, trying to seem relaxed and cheery. 'Rory's gone home, I'm afraid, Olivia.'

'I'm only stopping by for a second. The cab's waiting. Your mum's just showing me something quickly in William's office.'

'We'll just be a minute,' Amy said, putting her finger to her lips, then tripping up and grabbing Olivia's arm as they left, giggling. Tess heard her say, 'I hope they're still there.'

Hal crunched his Coke can into the bin. 'What's all that about?'

'Who cares,' she said, yawning so wide her jaw clicked. 'Best to stay out of other people's business,' she added pointedly.

'Best to get your facts straight,' Hal retorted.

As she walked away, her phone buzzed. It was her mum calling.

'What the...?' she said, picking up.

Amy's voice reverberated through her head. 'You and Hal better get out to William's office this instant.'

# THIRTY-SIX

## Rory

Rory rolled a spliff in the pool house. But he shouldn't have let his guard down, for as soon as he leant his head back, the doors banged open and two men barged in wearing balaclavas.

Before he could react, they had knocked him to the floor.

Their trainers seemed to be made of iron, hard and deep and reckless in his gut, though they were no worse than his father's hand-stitched leather brogues bruising his young ribs as a boy. The familiarity of the pain reminded him that he deserved it. He was aware of his worthlessness. Nobody needed to remind him of his deficiencies as a human being. Not these two thugs, not his dad. But in the same breath, ragged though it was, he knew with a resolute and defiant certainty that he could survive anything they threw at him. He had spent his whole boyhood fearing beatings from his father, and when they came, it was almost a relief. A release of something truly terrible.

Margot and Mabel barked from the main house. Voices shouted at him through the fug. Listening to them was like looking down the wrong end of a telescope. They should have been loud, but they were quiet and small. His father had often complained about his rudeness, disrespect and laziness, that he was a waste of space and a waste of money. Yeah, yeah. These younger voices penetrating him now had a similarly tired message: he had wasted their fucking time and money, shown disrespect by losing the bags, broken their trust, underestimated their dominance.

Another, keener foot soldier could be recruited to 'go country', didn't he know?

Didn't he know he was an acceptable loss? He knew all right.

His father had once told him that Hal was the son he wished he'd had. A son who might warrant the sacrifices he made to pay the school fees. A son who might show his gratitude by working hard for good grades and a high-salaried career. A son who wasn't surplus to requirements, who earned his place in the family. A son who showed some fucking respect. Rory would have done anything to bow out and give him Hal.

These guys wanted his fucking money.

With a mouth full of blood, he came back with a simple, gargled one-liner. 'Fuck you.' He'd given them all he had.

*Man needs t'show some fucking respect.* Their boots rained down on his head with a savagery his weak, angry father had never had. They didn't care about visible injuries.

One final blow shut it all down.

Losing the connection between his beleaguered brain and his bruised, bleeding body was utter bliss. At last it was over.

# THIRTY-SEVEN

## Amy

As Amy had shoved at the door to open it wider, William's desk chair had toppled over to crash-land on a sea of books, setting off a cascade of them. She hadn't been able to believe what she was seeing, had to blink a few times to check she wasn't imagining things.

'You've been burgled!' Olivia had exclaimed, stating the obvious, standing just behind her in the doorway.

Everything was in disarray. The shelves were emptied. The metal cabinets were scratched where they had been prised open. Papers and files were scattered everywhere. Two desk drawers had been flung on the floor, upended. The room was freezing due to the open door. Amy closed and locked it, shuddering as she peered outside into the dark, hoping the intruder was long gone. In all the years she had lived in London, she had never experienced a break-in.

'But they left the computers?' Olivia noted, picking up the chair and putting it upright on a small patch of carpet.

Two Strongbow cans had toppled over on the desk, leaking

cider onto some of William's documents. Lost for words, Amy picked them up and was holding one in each hand dumbly when Hal and Tess knocked on the glass. She let them in.

'Oh shit,' Hal breathed.

Tess slapped her hand flat across her fringe, pressed into it as though she had a headache. No words came out of her mouth. She hid behind Hal.

'Who could have done this?' Amy knew she needed to call William and the police. Then she noticed Hal had a red cheek. 'What happened to your face?'

'Oh, this! We were mucking about in the woods and a branch bit me.'

She turned back to the mess.

'Has anything been taken?' Olivia asked.

Amy shook her head back and forth. 'I don't know.'

The envelope she'd come in here for was at her feet, lying on top of a hardback of *Mao: The Unknown Story*. She picked it up. 'They didn't take these, at least,' she laughed feebly.

Olivia took the envelope and shuffled through the snaps inside, saying nothing.

Amy had stopped caring about the photos. 'I'd better ring the police.'

Hal said, 'The police? Is that really necessary?'

Olivia and Amy glanced warily at each other, before Olivia said, 'Hal, darling, if you know who did this, you need to say now. We don't want to get anyone in trouble, not if it was just a silly prank or something.'

'For fuck's sake. I don't, okay?' he snapped, collecting up a few books, stuffing them on a shelf randomly, his back turned.

Amy waggled her phone at Hal and Tess. 'Hal? Tess? It's now or never. If you know anything...'

Hal looked at Tess, who nodded. 'Okay,' he said. 'I know who did it, but I really don't want to get him in trouble. *Please* don't call the police, Amy.'

Amy could see genuine vulnerability in his eyes, stripped now of their indolent glaze. She said gently, 'I won't, Hal, don't worry. Not if you just tell us the truth.'

A shy, unlikely hint of gratitude shot through his expression. He turned to Olivia. 'It was Rory. But please don't tell him we told you. He and Logan were drunk and they got it into their heads that William had some weed in here and so they went mad looking for it. I think it started out as a laugh and then it got out of hand. I was going to clear it up. Tess knew nothing about it.' He glanced at Amy. 'I'm so sorry, Amy.'

'Weed?'

'Sorry, yeah.'

She couldn't judge. She'd been a kid herself once. Deciding to give him the benefit of the doubt, she said, 'It's okay, Hal. It wasn't your fault by the sounds of it.'

Olivia's blue eyes darkened. 'That Logan boy is trouble. I *knew* I could smell something on Rory the other day,' she hissed. 'I'm mortified, Amy. I'll get Rory to come over and clean it up first thing tomorrow morning.'

'No, no, don't do that,' Amy said, dazed. At least she was released from the burden of making calls to the authorities.

She would tell William when he got home tomorrow. The room would be back in order by then and the incident would have less of an impact on him, meaning he would go easier on Hal. 'Look, we're all exhausted. You two go up to bed, we'll deal with all this in the morning. Olivia, you *must* get home.' Then she remembered. 'Oh shit, your cab is still waiting!'

Olivia kicked into action, repeating her apologies, gathering up her things.

On the driveway, she hugged Amy goodbye and whispered into her ear, 'I didn't recognise anyone in those photos. Sorry.'

'Not one familiar face?'

'No. Sorry. None of them live around here anyway.'

'So I'm guessing they won't still know William then.'

Amy was disappointed, but appreciated she'd been clutching at straws. Realistically, she wasn't going to stalk them on Facebook, ask them over for dinner under false pretences and probe them for information about an affair William may or may not have had with Sophie Sandeman-Gore over ten years ago. No, the screwball idea hadn't even crossed her mind. Not for a second.

With that ever-present name rolling through her mind, Amy got to work on the mess. She preferred to do it herself, rather than have Rory rifling through William's papers.

With methodical care, she started by sorting through the books, taking the opportunity to put them in rainbow order. Alphabetical seemed boring. She supposed she was still a little drunk and didn't mind the task as much as she might have done sober. It was cathartic to tidy the place while she processed what had happened. Hal and Rory's friendship group had become Tess's by default, but Amy didn't like their influence on her. Anyone capable of doing this to someone's things – sober or drunk – had a shocking disregard for other people's feelings. William had never liked Rory, and now she was beginning to understand why.

As she sorted both the books and her thoughts, deliberating on solutions to rein Tess in, she was pleasantly diverted by a kind inscription from a friend inside the front cover of a paperback, then in another one a birthday wish from a relative, then a cloth-bound hardback with a signature from the author. Too few of the books she had read herself. She kept an eye out for the Robert Macfarlane volume he'd brought to their first date, remembering that he'd said it was about walking. She'd been taking Hamish on long walks through the woods every day, but she was less confident of the routes without William. She'd missed his companionship while he'd been in Bristol. She hoped he'd missed her as much, but she shuddered at what she'd learned from Olivia. It couldn't be true that he had cheated on Eleanor with Sophie Sandeman-Gore. Could it?

It was one in the morning by the time she had finished the shelves. The rest could wait until tomorrow. She slipped the Macfarlane paperback into her handbag and picked her way through the eruption of paperwork. Another can of Strongbow was hiding under William's tapestry seat cushion. As she reached for it, sighing heavily, she noticed, amongst other documents dotted around it, a letter on watermarked cream paper. It was bent out of shape and half trampled. Even rumpled, though, its smartness stood out from the others and caught her attention. When she smoothed it out, she saw that it was headed with the embossed name and SW3 address of 'Sophie M. Sandeman-Gore'. Instantly wide awake, she took it up and read through its two sheets.

*2 September 1997*

*Dear William,*

*I won't bother asking how you are or how this letter finds you or anything stuffy like that. We are quite beyond that. The reason I'm writing is a sad one. Having seen you last year at my father's funeral, the next time we'll see each other will be at my mother's. She was diagnosed six months ago with pancreatic cancer and last week lost her struggle with it. She died in the morning room, with Avril by her side – she came to stay in those later months. (One of her cups of coffee probably sent Mummy over the edge!)*

*I would have called, but I couldn't because I might cry, and I'm rather attached to how dignified and self-contained I have become. Mummy would approve. While the nation is sobbing over Princess Diana, I am dry-eyed over my very own mother. Does that make me a bad person? How ghastly it must be for those two beautiful princes. But how strange it is for me to walk past hundreds of bouquets at Kensington Palace, knowing that Mummy will have only a couple of old carnations. As you're probably aware, she became quite the recluse at the cottage after my father died.*

*I'm ashamed to admit I didn't see her for a whole year. We fell out (again); I can't even remember what it was about. Avril won't tell me, which probably means it was my fault. I was horrible during my finals and quite cross with her for being ill. When she telephoned me, she would insist I carry on with my studies, said she was feeling better. If she'd told me she was dying, I would have obviously made the trip from Oxford. Apparently she hadn't wanted me to be distracted, so obsessed was she with my achievement. By the way, I got a first. What a thrill! Mummy was very proud of me. Another first! Perhaps we have maligned Avril's coffee when really what carried Mummy off was the unfamiliar feeling of maternal pride.*

*Aside from all this macabre talk, I was also writing to ask you for a favour. Mummy left her finances in a dreadful mess. In her grief, she sold off most of the properties and donated the proceeds to some of her causes (not quite cat homes, but along those lines). The exception was Summerfield House, which she wanted to keep for me and my children when I had them. Note: 'when' rather than 'if'!*

*Trouble is, since Avril returned up north to be near her daughter, the cottage has fallen into a terrible state of disrepair and it's getting more neglected by the day. I need someone to live there and inject it with some love, and to oversee the renovation work. Someday, as per my mother's wishes, I'll live there myself with my doting husband-to-be and pop out some sweet little sprogs. Do you think that sounds like me? I couldn't think of a lovelier spot to bring up kids, could you? It was where I was happiest.*

*For now, I need to be in London. I'm starting a law conversion course at King's in October. As you can see from the header, I'm living in Mummy's lovely low-maintenance Chelsea flat. (Do you remember how the Tube trains going underneath make the whole place shudder? I find it a comfort.)*

*So I thought you might like the idea of some time in the country while you set up your geeky little computering business. (How's that going, by the way?) I'll have no time for managing Summerfield House. Cleaning the windows alone costs an arm and a leg! And don't even talk to me about the heating costs. Our old gardener died, but he has a son called Pete who has been tending to the borders. All this will be your financial responsibility, rent to be deferred until you're on your feet. Is that okay? Does your father still have his property business? Might he be able to advise me on how to update the place?*

*You know why I must keep it, of course.*

*Might I come down to stay with you one weekend?*

*When Mummy was alive, she mentioned once that we should ask you to stay. But I never did. I wasn't sure I could handle both of us being there together again so soon after it happened. Maybe it's still too soon. Will it ever not be? What do you feel about it? Maybe when I've got used to being an orphan? (Boo-hoo. Poor me.)*

*For what it's worth, Mummy became quite sentimental at the end and was racked with guilt about how she and Daddy cut you off. (Though still furious with you about the broken tile in the blue bathroom!) She wanted us to heal, which sounds as unlike her as the idea of me with sprogs in semi-rural bliss. Ugh. Hell on earth.*

*All these things to discuss! I should have called. But I've enjoyed writing, just like the old days. I found some of your letters from school the other week and they did make me laugh. You were so mushy! Do you still have mine? Anyway, we can discuss it at the funeral, which will be held at the church in Grayswood village. Details to follow.*

*I will call, tomorrow maybe.*

*In the meantime, sending my love.*

*With all my heart,*

*Sophie*

*PS There hasn't been anyone serious since you.*

*PPS Perhaps if everything else goes wrong, you can be that doting husband of mine and we can pop out some bright little sprogs and live in the cottage happily ever after together.*

Amy let the letter fall from her hand. It fluttered to the floor. *You know why I must keep it, of course,* she had written. *After it happened.*

What happened, Sophie? Amy asked herself now. What are the secrets of Summerfield House?

# THIRTY-EIGHT

## NOVEMBER 1990

Me

My mother wasn't giving me what I needed. I was screaming at her, screaming and screaming until I could barely breathe. She talked over me, jiggling me about in her arms. Shoving me into my grandma Annie's arms. I didn't want Annie. Her elbow nook was bony. I needed my mother. Her milk smelt delicious when it leaked.

'He's hungry,' Annie said.

'I've only just fed him!' my mother cried.

'How much did he take?'

'He kept coming off, and it hurts. I can't do it any more.'

I screamed and screamed and screamed. I needed more milk. I needed more.

'How long was he on the breast for?'

'I don't know. Ten minutes or something? I don't bloody know!'

'That's not long enough for the good creamy milk to get to him. He's starving, the poor little mite, try again!'

'I can't!' she wailed. 'It's too painful!'

Annie shoved me back to my mother, and I was relieved. My lips frantically rooted for her nipple. The vibrations of her heartbeat were fast through my body and it distracted me from drinking from her. Was she okay? Was I okay? Was this okay? Was I safe? When I looked up at her face, it didn't look right. Her eyes were telling me something was wrong. What was wrong? *What's wrong, Mummy?* My screams built up and I twisted away from her. By then I was even hungrier, and I tried to get the milk again. Her hands were in the way of where I wanted to suck. She held me too tight and moved her flesh and pushed it too far into my mouth. What's wrong? I fussed. Why can't I get any? I wanted to do it in my own time, in my own way. Petrified that I wouldn't get the chance, I screamed and screamed and screamed.

'You see? He won't latch on! I can't do this!' my mother cried.

'Of course you can!' Annie insisted brusquely. 'It's natural. I breastfed you and my mother breastfed me. Now calm down and try again.'

'No!' My mother put me down on the sheets. 'Maybe he's hot in this old thing. It's too tight.' She unpoppered my romper suit. It had been hers as a baby too. The breast pocket was embroidered in yellow with her initials, SSG, and the collar was tight around my neck. She yanked it too hard over my head. Being naked and away from her wasn't right. It was cold and scary. *Pick me up!* I screamed until I was choking on a dry, red-raw throat. My whole body was taut with rage and fear and hunger. My fists punched out. *I'm hungry! I need my mum!*

Then I heard a voice, a voice I didn't know. A deeper voice. This person picked me up and I liked their steady arms, but when I searched for milk, it wasn't there and I got mad again.

'Avril says we should bottle-feed him,' the voice said.

'No. She just needs to keep trying,' Grandma Annie said, handing me to my mother again.

There was a sensation of my mother's arms flopping and a strange sound coming from her chest. 'Sorry,' she whispered. 'I'm not good enough.' A wet plop from her eyes fell onto my face.

My mother doesn't want me! I thought.

'He doesn't want me,' my mother said and curled up on the bed.

'Mum always said it takes a whole village to bring up a baby,' the deep voice said.

I stopped for a second. Big, clumsy hands grasped me, and my head fell back. Avril's familiar face appeared too. She had helped me to come out into the world and was now making cooing noises at me.

'*Attention, ici, comme ça, oui?* Like this. You hold his head,' she instructed, and the person with the deep voice held me properly.

I could smell milk this time, and a soft teat was in my mouth. I sucked and sucked and felt it run warm right through me, filling my belly, satisfying me. I looked up at this person, and he smiled down at me and said, 'Hello, little man. I'm your dad.' And I felt safe.

# THIRTY-NINE

## Amy

A baby's cry was inside Amy's head. A repetitive mewling call, disturbing her sleep. She was dreaming of the photograph of Hal as a baby in his crib in this very room, the yellow room. He was wearing the initialled sleepsuit belonging to Sophie. She woke with a start, blinking in the dark, breathing rapidly, feeling sweaty. The photograph had fallen out of the sleepsuit as she'd unfolded it for William. At the time, she hadn't known who Sophie was.

Her mobile was ringing from her bedside table. The noise must have disturbed her sleep. She hesitated before reaching for it, assuming it was William. She wasn't eager to have the conversation about Sophie Sandeman-Gore. Not yet, and certainly not after such a dream. It rang off before she got to it, and she was relieved.

It seemed like only yesterday that she and William had strolled across Riddlesdown Common, lost in time together. She remembered the evening he officially called off the search for rare orchids, laughing, 'I've already found mine.' That was when he had kissed her for the first time. Tingles had crossed her skin. Her happiness had filled her up with what had felt like a song ready to burst from her chest.

There had to be a simple explanation for the contents of Sophie's letter, surely. She could rely on William. His solid pragmatism would harness her overthinking, stamp out her paranoia and bring her down to earth with some uncomplicated, assertive reassurance. She clung to the trust she had in him and cracked on with the to-do list in her head: call photographer about albums; send confirmation of menu to caterers; book date for florist consultation; pay the deposit on the cottage on Loch Lomond for the honeymoon; book Lythe Hill Spa for the hen do; and check with William about the stag and his suit. Her stomach somersaulted when she remembered they had a cake-tasting booked for tomorrow afternoon. She was never going to get back to sleep.

The photograph of Hal careered into her mind's eye.

She got up and went straight over to the wardrobe. The musty smell was strong enough to taste. Her fingers met with the tissue-paper parcel that cosseted the sleepsuit. The photo was still inside the garment's soft folds. She shone her phone torch onto it and squinted to find the emblem. There it was, small but clear: SSG. Again the question struck her: why was baby Hal wearing it? If Olivia was to be believed, Eleanor had loathed Sophie. It seemed unlikely that she'd have dressed her son in Sophie's old baby clothes.

More confused than ever, she put it back and climbed into bed. Her heartbeat pounded her eardrums.

Her phone rang again.

She braced herself and fumbled for it in the dark. Maybe the middle of the night was exactly the time to bring up the letter and the photograph.

When she heard Olivia's hysterical voice instead of William's, she sat bolt upright.

. . .

Amy could see Rory through the opened curtain. He was barely recognisable but for his shorn blond head. Blood was caked like a second skin across his bloated face. His eyelids had blown up into balls of purpled flesh. A two-inch gash across his cheek had been pulled back together by strips. As Amy drew nearer to his gurney, her first instinct was to cry, but she kept her composure and tried to settle her churning stomach with practical thoughts of how she might be of help to them.

'Hi, Rory, you poor love,' she murmured, wanting to kiss him better, realising that any kind of touch would hurt. Ever so lightly, she brushed her hand over the very tips of his hair – 'loo-brush head', as Tess called it. Whatever he'd done to William's office didn't seem important.

Olivia was sitting on a chair next to him with her eyes closed. Her head was pressed back into the headrest, her knees were clamped together, and her hands were claws over the ends of the chair's wooden arms.

'Olivia,' Amy whispered, touching the arm of her soft grey sweater, which she wore over her pyjamas.

'Oh. Amy,' Olivia said under her breath, roused from sleep. There was a faint whiff of wine on her breath. 'You're here. Thank you so much for coming. I'm so grateful to you.' Her skin was thin over her cheekbones and blue under her eyes. She looked underweight, malnourished, as though the hours between their spa experience and now had been years.

'My God, of course. How's he doing?'

She fiddled with the white piping on her pyjamas. 'How are Margot and Mabel?'

'They're fine. I gave them cuddles and let them out for a run around,' Amy said. She didn't mention that she'd cleaned up four puddles of wee and one poo from the kitchen floor. 'How is he doing?' she asked again.

They both turned to look at Olivia's battered son, who stirred and groaned but remained asleep.

'He's broken four ribs, but his lungs are okay and there's no internal bleeding. They want to admit him and keep him in for a couple of nights for observation, just as a precaution, but aside from some bad bruising, some cuts and concussion, they think he's going to be okay.' Olivia pressed the space between her eyes and exhaled.

'Poor boy. And poor you.' Amy crouched down to her level and squeezed her knee. 'It must have been terrifying.'

Olivia's eyelids fluttered twitchily, neither closed nor open. 'I can't even begin to describe to you what it was like to see him there on the floor like that. Thank God I stayed up for a bit after I got back from yours, or I wouldn't have seen the light on in the pool house. I only went down there to turn it off.'

'Who would do this to him?' Amy breathed.

'He said he fell off his mountain bike,' Olivia said, and began to cry. 'He's such a kind, lovely boy.'

While Amy rubbed Olivia's back, she was remembering the state of the study. The destruction left behind indicated that Rory was not such a kind, lovely boy. With his smart comebacks and winning grin, she imagined he was the sort of boy who would find enemies as quickly as he found friends. 'Do you think Logan had anything to do with it?'

'I wouldn't put it past him.'

'I wonder how much Hal and Tess know.' She bit her lip. Tess had been shifty earlier. Before she'd let her go to bed, Amy had asked her quietly, out of Hal's earshot, whether there was anything else she wanted to tell her.

'No, Mum! I have never lied to you, have I?' Tess had said. It was true, she hadn't lied to her before they'd come to live at Summerfield House.

'Well, the police are involved now, so they'll find out *exactly* who knew what,' Olivia said.

'The police?'

Olivia eyed her. 'Yes.'

'I really don't think Tess or Hal had anything to do with it.'

'No, I'm sure not,' Olivia replied, too suddenly and too sweetly to be believed.

Amy was reminded that their friendship was flimsy and untested, that there was too much they didn't know about each other. They were both mothers, first and foremost. Their children would always be their priority.

'The police were asking me all these questions about him earlier, like *he* was the criminal or something! It was unbelievable! I told them they needed to go after Logan or some of those dodgy boys from Beechwood who hang around on the rec, not someone like *my son*, for God's sake!'

'Oh dear,' Amy said. 'Was Logan at Beechwood?'

'I don't know. It'd be some school like that, if you know what I mean.'

Amy knew exactly what she meant, but she did not hold the same prejudices. She herself had viewed the Ofsted Outstanding Beechwood before they had moved, and had considered it an option for Tess. William had persuaded her out of it. In the end, the shiny, expensive excellence of Heathside Heights had dazzled her like the bright lights of a big city. It had its own theatre! An Olympic-size swimming pool! A level grades that made the top sixty in the *Sunday Times* league table!

Now, Heathside Heights impressed her far less. Tess had been happier and more amenable at her bog-standard south London comp. She had read more books for fun, and her friendships had seemed easier. She had been quite happy ambling along the grubby pavements of Purley with Malena; queueing in Chickin' Lickin' to buy chips on the way home; stripping their school tights off to tan on the salon's roof terrace; meeting boys for picnics of Doritos and Coke on the common. Why hadn't that been enough? The slogan on the Heathside Heights school bus popped into her head: *We Are Prepared For Greater Things!*

Tonight more than ever, she had an acute longing for fewer so-called greater things, for their old stamping ground. For the streets that Tess had toddled through so blithely as a little girl. For the grit and anonymity of the city, where they could get lost in the crowds, incognito and unnoticed, a small part of the bigger picture.

'What about bullying?' she suggested.

'I don't think so,' Olivia scoffed. 'That kind of thing doesn't happen at Heathside.'

'Could it be something to do with drugs?'

'Just because he might smoke a bit of weed?' Olivia laughed incredulously.

'No, no,' Amy said, backtracking.

Olivia got up and ushered her out of the curtained cubicle. She spoke quietly. 'There was this boy in the news who was attacked on his way home from school because some gang thought he was someone else. Maybe someone followed Rory home, a case of mistaken identity?'

'I don't think kids lurk about on Scotland Lane waiting to jump rival gang members, do they?' Amy said, picturing the electric gates, leafy driveways and dead quiet atmosphere of the neighbourhood. Likewise, Rory didn't fit the typical profile of a troubled kid who'd get beaten up. His attendance at school was excellent. He was in all the sports teams and was playing Scrooge in the Christmas production. Rumour had it he was talented enough to apply to RADA or one of the big drama schools. His grades were decent enough and he had close friends. Yet here he lay in front of them, beaten to a pulp shortly after ransacking his best mate's house for weed. Could the two incidents really be unconnected?

Olivia offered a small smile. 'Unlikely, sure.'

Rory's wounds were raw and vivid, and they had a violent story behind them. Amy felt scared for Tess. Fresh doubts about bringing her to live here growled in her mind. Nothing was as it had first appeared. The letter. Oh God, that letter. *You know why I must keep it, of course,* Sophie had written about the house. It seemed Amy had been hypnotised by the loveliness of the life William had offered her and had blithely stepped across the threshold of Summerfield House, draped in daisies, feeling as lucky as a princess. It had been too good to be true. And now her daughter was entangled in sinister goings-on and she didn't know how to fix it.

# FORTY

Tess

'I didn't know I had it in me,' Hal said, deadpan.

Rory tried to smile, but it was plain that it hurt. 'Your fairy punch wasn't even a good warm-up act,' he croaked back.

'I can't keep up with you two,' Tess said lightly, trying not to show her shock at his appearance. She perched on the edge of his hospital bed. Their fingertips met and her feelings for him shuddered to the surface. However hard she had tried to put him out of her mind since the incident at the canal, telling herself his mischief-making and risk-taking were bad news, she hadn't been able to shake him off. In a way that many others might not understand, she could see the vulnerability of him, right into his soul, and she wanted to hug that inner part of him better, scrabbling past the layers of trouble.

'Thanks for coming,' Rory said seriously, hitching himself up a little.

She adjusted his pillows. His helplessness and her acceptance of that was strangely intimate. There was a feeling that the small, wordless interchange had shifted the dynamic between them.

From behind the curtain, someone in the next-door bed groaned and then threw up. A waft of sick filled the air. She covered her nose and looked to the boys. Neither of them seemed to have noticed the smell. They were now observing one another. Tension thickened the air of the small space. Hal's almond eyes swirled with suspicion and reproach, but he bent towards Rory and squeezed his hand awkwardly. 'Good to see you, mate.'

'We brought you these.' Tess pulled out a Mars bar, a bottle of Lucozade and an iPad. 'Mum wanted us to bring orange juice and grapes. We laughed in her face, obvs. But I thought you might like this.' Shyly she handed him a book she'd carefully chosen for him.

'Aw. Thanks.' He put it on the side table, face down.

Hal sat down on the blue chair. His lanky thighs jiggled up and down and he blinked rapidly through his flop of hair. 'You're going to miss the exams next week, you lucky fucker.'

'To be honest, I wish I wasn't.'

'Did they knock your two brain cells out or something?' Tess said, feeling her stomach flip at the thought of the week ahead. English lit was first thing Monday morning and she already knew she wasn't going to be able to concentrate. She was too worried about Rory.

'They tried,' Rory said.

There was a pause. Her left leg ached from trying to balance one buttock on the mattress. She wanted to be affectionately near him but was acutely aware she must give his battered body space.

'Who did this to you, Ror?' Hal asked under his breath, leaning forward on his elbows.

'I fell off my bike,' Rory rasped, offering a wincing grin.

'Right, yeah,' Hal laughed.

'That's what I told Mum.'

'Seriously, was it Logan?'

The two boys shared a look that excluded her. There was an obvious twitch in Hal's jaw. Rory said, 'Not Logan. They were wearing balis, so I couldn't see who it was. That guy Ralph, I recognised his voice. The other one I didn't know.'

'Ralph, the creepy guy with the glasses at the party?' Tess whispered.

Rory nodded.

'Why, though?' she asked urgently, keeping her voice low, knowing the answer but wanting to hear it from him.

Rory adjusted his position. 'I missed a deadline.'

'You're dealing *weed*, aren't you?' she whispered, airing her suspicion for the first time.

He snorted, dropped his voice and said almost proudly, 'There's no money in that shit.'

'What, then. Coke?'

Hal answered for him, a little too loudly. 'Crack cocaine and heroin, actually.'

Rory lifted his head slightly, 'Keep your fucking voice down.'

Tess sucked in her breath. '*What*? Is that true?' she asked, incredulous. 'Seriously? Why would you do that?'

'Er, let me think now. Maybe 'cos I'm making loads of money?'

'But how did you even get into it?'

'It just happened. I met Logan at a party in Esher, jumped on his line for a week and it kind of went from there.'

'What's a line?'

'A phone line for drugs. He gave me a burner phone, I took the calls, made some drops. And boom, cash in hand.'

Hal added wryly, 'Amazing how many crackheads there are in Surrey, right?'

'It's a business, that's all. Supply and demand.'

'Tell her how Logan brings it down from London,' Hal said.

Rory tried to laugh. 'Yeah, he banks it, the poor fucker.'

'Banks the money, you mean?' she asked.

Now he did manage to laugh, and then grimaced in pain. Hal replied instead. 'No, he puts the drugs up his bumhole with a nice big scoop of Vaseline and hops on the train.'

Tess gaped at Rory. 'What the hell? Have *you* done that?'

'No fucking way!'

Hal interjected. 'Remember, Tess, any time you fancy a sneaky line of coke at a party, it's probably got traces of faecal matter on it.'

She screwed her face up. 'Ugh. Don't.'

'Whatever,' Rory said. 'Take the piss. But it's good business. ACE is like a brand name, a franchise. Not gonna lie, our product is good shit. Strong. I'm more like an entrepreneur, you know? The profit margins can be insane.'

'ACE,' she repeated.

'Yeah, it's the name of the line. The numbers on our SIM card will be worth thousands if we keep it up.'

Tess made a point of tracing her gaze over his injuries, then said coolly, 'So what went wrong?'

'Everything would've been fine, it's been light work up till now, but...' He paused, shot a dirty look in Hal's direction. 'I'd stashed a couple of G-packs in a safe place—'

She interrupted. 'G-packs?'

'Bags. You know. It's a pack of a hundred pebs – crack and heroin, white and brown. But then someone lost them.' He eyed Hal again. 'And now I owe them.'

'The gang?'

Hal leapt in. 'Is that why this happened? How much do they want?'

'Two grand. And they won't stop until they've got it. They've threatened all sorts. Said they'd hurt Mum.'

Tess sucked in another breath and slipped from her perch.

'Can't you ask your mum for the money?' Hal said, no trace of mockery now.

Rory snorted at his suggestion, flinching in pain as he said, 'Mum? She hasn't got shit. *I'm* the one paying for her champagne habit.'

'You give her money?' Tess was baffled, unable to resettle into a comfortable position on the bed.

'I pay the mortgage now. And buy her clothes,' he mumbled. 'Dad stopped the maintenance. Even though he's minted. Fucker.'

Panic was frothing up inside Tess. She felt hot and irate. 'So what are you going to do now?'

Rory raised a gammy eyebrow at Hal. 'Hal's going to ask his daddy for the money, isn't he?'

'Are you kidding?' Tess guffawed.

'Yeah, he's fucking kidding,' Hal scowled.

Rory looked from Hal to Tess and back again. 'They know where you live.'

'We have to go to the police,' she said, panic-stricken, shooting up from the bed.

His eyes stretched wide and fearful. 'They'd fucking kill me and Mum if I snitched. No joke.'

'Sorry,' she said, remaining standing, crossing her arms over her chest. 'That's ridiculous. You have to tell the police the truth.'

'Right, yeah. "Oh, terribly sorry, Officer, sir, I've been dabbling in a spot of county lines drug running, might you be a good old chap and get those nasty London gangs off my back? I'll give you three-for-two."'

Neither of them laughed.

'I can't ask Dad,' Hal said.

'Eleanor, then?'

He scowled. 'Mum still thinks I read Harry Potter and collect football cards.'

Tess had never properly met Eleanor. She was a distant figure in Hal's life. She FaceTimed him regularly and he visited her in Somerset every two weeks, but he seemed to rely on her for nothing. William had taken on the role of both parents.

'Two grand's small change to your dad,' Rory said.

'I don't want him mixed up in this.'

He shifted on the bed, wincing. 'But he's already mixed up in it. Because it's your fucking fault.'

Hal exhaled, ruffled his hair and put his head back on the blue seat, eyeing Rory, tight-lipped. 'You were the one who hid it all there. How was I to know?'

Tess stepped back into the curtain behind her, feeling crosser with each new revelation. Suddenly the penny dropped. She closed her eyes for a long second, trying to calm the stormy feeling gathering in her chest. 'They were looking for those G-packs or whatever they're called in William's study last night, weren't they?'

'Uh-huh,' Rory grunted. 'And they didn't find them. Because dickhead here flushed them down the loo a few weeks back. So they paid me a friendly little visit instead.'

'Why did you *do* that, Hal?' Tess breathed. She understood that the dealing itself was the bigger issue here, but the disappointment she felt about Hal's involvement was crushing.

He wouldn't look at her and didn't answer, reaching for two paper cups on the bedside table and fiddling with them. They made a clopping sound.

Rory said, 'It doesn't matter why. He's just gonna fix it. Aren't you, Hal?'

Hal began tearing strips off one of the cups. 'If I told Dad, he'd make us go to the police and then he'd put me out on the street. No joke.'

'No parent in their right mind would go to the police and risk their kid getting in trouble and expelled from school.'

Tess tsked. 'And he wouldn't put you on the street.'

Hal rounded on her fiercely. 'You don't know him like I do.'

Taken aback, she was momentarily speechless.

'You need to get that money from him, Hal,' Rory said, becoming less of the victim in bed and more like an aggressor. 'For your own sake. Or you could end up in this state, or worse. They wouldn't think twice about sticking a knife in your face. And they know you and Tess now. And where our families live. If you don't care about yourself, surely you want to keep her out of danger?'

'Don't talk about me as though I'm not bloody here!' she hissed, terrified.

'First one for the swear box there,' Rory said, but the joke had dismal comic timing.

She scowled at him. Her compassion was unravelling. Why had her mum brought her here? How had she become embroiled in this? Back home – yes, *home* – she'd barely been able to tolerate Malena's vaping, but this situation made that small rebellion laughable. She was way out of her depth. She wanted to cry, not pitifully, but angrily. Enraged with Rory for his stupidity and with herself for having stupid feelings for him. And furious with her stupid self for taking her old, happy, stupid life in Purley completely and stupidly for granted.

Hal said quietly, 'I'll talk to Dad, okay? Don't worry, Tess, I'll sort it out.'

And a stupid tear escaped from her eye and rolled down her cheek. Stupid, stupid tear.

# FORTY-ONE

William

William dropped his bag and took Amy in his arms, overwhelmed by how much he had missed her after only one night away, exhausted by the journey. The Saturday-morning train had been packed with day trippers. He and Sophie had been lucky to get seats.

He rested his chin on her head for a second, enjoying how comfortably she slotted there, like her body was designed for that space. Her hair smelt like home. Hamish's nose nudged between them, trying to get in on the hug. His whole backside was wagging with joy, reflecting William's own feelings about their reunion.

'Good to be home.' He sighed, adding, 'How's Rory doing?'

'Yes, good,' she said, pulling away. 'He was lucky.'

'Scary, the whole thing,' he said, holding in so much scary stuff of his own it was almost physically painful. What Avril had said about him bringing up a family here with Sophie had rattled him to the core. His own determination to sever ties with Sophie and secure a new future with Amy was stronger than ever. Throughout the journey south, he had wanted the train to speed through stations, hurry him home so that he could run his new idea past her.

'Tiring trip, was it?' Her tone was stiff, with that Liverpool lilt slipping out. 'Faye's here, by the way,' she added.

'Who's Faye?' he whispered back.

'The wedding cake lady. Remember?'

His heart sank. 'On a Saturday afternoon?' How would he get through that? '*Down*, Hamish,' he snapped, but the dog ignored him.

Tersely Amy said, 'Olivia pulled all sorts of strings to get us this appointment. Usually she's booked up years in advance.'

'Oh, right. Good,' he said, following her into the kitchen.

His emotions were so close to the surface, the sight of the miniature cakes topped with flowers dipped in sugar filled his eyes with tears.

'It has to be the lemon drizzle first,' he said, tucking straight in. 'Hmm. It's terribly good. An instant contender.'

'I *knew* you'd say that,' Amy said, with a weary laugh and half an eye-roll.

'Which one is your favourite?'

'The vanilla and peanut butter.'

'Because of Tess?' he asked. Tess's habit of spooning peanut butter directly from the jar drove him mad.

'No,' Amy retorted. But he knew she always put her daughter first.

Faye sipped a glass of water. Two lovely fans of crinkles animated her blue eyes. 'Back in *my* day, us kids never got a say! Every Friday night, my parents would leave my brother and me in sleeping bags in the pub car park while they were inside partying. We'd have a torch and some cheese and onion crisps and just get on with it, no questions asked.'

'You're lucky you got sleeping bags!' Amy chortled.

'I know it's not fashionable to say it, but I think our parents had it right,' Faye went on, adjusting the elasticated waist of her old-fashioned dress. 'I think our darling children have it their own way too often and then we're surprised they can't cope in the real world.' She petted Hamish.

'Maybe,' Amy said, sounding unsure.

Faye eyed them both, then said, 'Which venue have you chosen?'

'We're having it here,' they said in unison.

'Ahh. How marvellous. Well, this is the kind of house that would suit a traditional cake, don't you think?'

'That's a good point,' William said, sinking his fork into the fruit cake. 'Wow. Taste this.'

Amy's fingers touched his briefly as he handed her a piece, but she didn't look up at him.

'Yummy,' she admitted, licking her fingers. 'Actually, fruit cake was my mum's favourite. She'd be up in arms if they didn't have it at a wedding.'

William said, 'My mother saved theirs in a tin for a whole year and then she and my father ate it on their first wedding anniversary on the terrace of a hotel on the Isle of Skye. She told me the whole story before she died, but I was only nine and I just thought it was gross to eat stale cake.'

Faye laughed. 'That's very sweet.'

William caught Amy's eye. There was gentleness there, and, he hoped, love.

'Well, if you go for the fruit cake, I do have a special option for you, though it isn't cheap.' Faye beamed. 'I know a jeweller who makes silver wedding charms, which I'd bury in the cake for your guests to pull out on little ribbons. Or it's lovely if the bridesmaids and the maid of honour do it after the cake cutting, maybe. Have you chosen who you're having yet?'

William, strangely, had thought about this already. 'I was thinking we should ask Tess to be maid of honour and Hal best man? What do you reckon, Amy?'

'That's a nice idea,' Amy said, a little more warmly.

'How much would it set us back?' he asked.

Faye laid out the costs and he had to swallow a few times before he could speak.

'Isn't that a bit too expensive?' Amy asked.

'We'll go for it,' he said. She looked gobsmacked and tried to protest, but he wouldn't let her. He found her hand, and she didn't pull away.

Faye clapped and said, 'Splendid!' then began to describe her ideas for tiers and white roses and sugary columns. William was heartened by their decision to go for the institution of the fruit cake. It reminded him of the power of rituals, how they could bring people together and reinforce positive, happy memories, create a renewed sense of security. These customs were dependable. You could build your feelings around them.

He couldn't wait to be alone with Amy to share his new plan.

# FORTY-TWO

Amy

As Amy and William waved Faye off, William said, 'How about a walk? I've got an idea I want to run past you. Or are we too full to move after all that cake?'

Dropping her hand and the happy couple act, she said, 'I need to show you something.' Nothing was more important than the letter. She took off across the kitchen and out of the French doors to William's chalet office.

'Rainbows!' he exclaimed when he saw his bookshelves.

'What I have to say isn't quite as pretty,' she told him. She went on to explain what had happened in the office before Rory's attack.

His expression clouded over. 'I'm guessing Hal was involved?'

'No, William.' She sighed, shaking her head. 'I really don't think so. But that's not why I brought you in here.' She picked up Sophie's letter from his desk and handed it to him. 'While I was clearing up, I found this.'

He cast his eye over it and chucked it back down. 'Funny to read that again.'

Her voice trembled incredulously. 'Why does she need to keep Summerfield House, William?'

'Because her mother was sentimental about it!' he said, as though it were that simple.

'Was Sophie anything to do with why you cancelled your first wedding?'

His expression sharpened. 'How did you know about that?'

'Olivia.'

'She shouldn't have told you.'

'I think I have a right to know.'

His eye followed the line of apple blossom trees outside. 'I was having doubts.'

'Because of Sophie?'

'No. Because of Eleanor.'

'But Sophie wrote that PS about you being her backup plan if everything went wrong, and having kids together and bringing them up in this house.'

He knocked over the penholder on his desk with his elbow and stuck it upright again. 'Not a chance in hell of that happening. She always said stuff like that. I'm guessing she was feeling maudlin after losing her mother. We had nothing to do with one another.'

Amy had a flash of Hal in Sophie's sleepsuit, but it was almost as unreal as a dream and seemed impossible to bring up. The letter was solid and contained facts. She asked suspiciously, 'Why did her mum want you to visit? To heal after what? What happened?'

'Annie was a tricky character, to say the least. When Sophie and I split up, she was totally vile and our families fell out. So I suppose she felt guilty about how she'd treated everyone. But to be honest, I couldn't tell you what Sophie was going on about there. It was a long time ago and they were a very dysfunctional family. Too much money for their own good.' He picked up the letter and waved it at her. 'There's nothing to worry about here.'

'I thought... It sounded like... I don't know, that there were things that went on here that I don't know about. It freaked me out.'

He stepped forward. 'Look, this is why I wanted to talk to you. I've had an idea. It might solve all this.' His eyes lit up. 'I want to buy Summerfield House from Sophie. Now, rather than waiting for Hal to leave school.'

'But you said you couldn't afford it.'

'I might not be able to.'

'Oh.'

He corrected himself. 'What I mean is, I might. Exo's profits are better than ever. If I juggle things around a bit and do some number-crunching, I think it might be possible to raise the deposit now. And maybe I could try a different lender to get the mortgage payments down. I'm going to have a go. If you're okay with that?'

Getting shot of Sophie sounded too good to be true, felt like an urgent, stabbing need. 'Hell, yes, I'm okay with that.'

He went through more details of the financial logistics, and she thought about how she might be able to help speed things along. There was an obvious solution. 'I've got some savings from the sale of number 7, remember?'

'No. That's your pension pot.'

'What if I invest in property instead?'

'No.'

'Why not?'

'Because it's your money.'

'I didn't do anything clever to get it. Unless you consider divorcing Nick clever?'

'That *was* pretty clever.' He grinned at her.

'And now we're getting married, I guess you and I will be old crusters together one day, right?'

He swept his hair off his forehead. A clump of curls formed a tick shape off the side of his head. 'But it's your security. You told me you barely ate back then to keep that flat. No, no, I couldn't possibly ask—'

'You're not asking. I'm offering. And this house would be an incredible investment opportunity for me,' she added, looking out towards the orchard and the gables of the main house, feeling the excitement building.

'Potentially, yes.'

'And we could draw up proper contracts.' She smiled, not too much, but enough.

'We could?'

She paused for a second. It occurred to her that this was her last chance to ask him one last niggling question about Sophie's monogrammed babygro. It was such a silly thing, really.

'Can I ask you something first?'

'Yes?'

Her heart pounded. Did she really need to know every last detail about his past? Could she not live with it as one of those small unexplained mysteries?

'Nothing. Let's do this, Will. Let's buy this old place off her.'

'You sure?'

She hooked one ankle across the other, wobbling a little. 'Yes. Totally.'

'Oh my God! I never thought I could love you any more than I already did, and then you do something like this!'

She laughed. 'Now you're the one after me for my money.'

'Ha! Yes, I love your money, you clever old thing.' He laughed gleefully.

Buying the house with William was a thrilling idea and put them on more of an equal footing. Amy hadn't previously acknowledged how the financial inequality between them left her with less agency in the relationship. 'But I don't want you seeing her, okay? You can do it through solicitors.'

'Promise,' he said. 'Oh my God, I can't believe it. I'm going to write her an email right this minute.' He kissed her. 'I love you, Amy.'

Her return kiss was tentative, nervous, like a first kiss. 'I love you too. So much.'

# FORTY-THREE

## Tess

Tess was trying to keep up with Hal as he strode across the sports fields to the lunch hall. He was throwing an orange into the air and catching it as though he hadn't a care in the world. From afar, in his red and white sports kit, with mud on his rugby boots, he looked every bit the model Heathside sixth-former.

'Are you going to ask your dad about the money when we get home?' she asked him.

Her English exam had gone better than expected. Last night, after a nightmare about Ralph breaking into the house, she had tried to read her book, but more and more these days she found reading for pleasure a luxury she didn't have time for. Unable to finish even one paragraph, she had padded into Hal's bedroom. He had been up and at his desk, as highly strung as her. To take their minds off Friday night and the pressure of finding the cash for Rory, they'd made coffee and studied next to each other in her bed, laptops on top of the duvet. They'd tested each other on *Macbeth* and Hal had smoked out of the window and she had eaten peanut butter out of the jar. At points, they had stopped revising to go over and over the nightmare predicament they were in. She was delirious with tiredness and anxiety.

'Are you then?'

'What?'

'Are you going to ask your dad when we get home?'

Rory had texted her five times in the last hour, begging her to get the money. Death threats had been streaming into his phone all weekend. Every minute that went by, every moment Hal prevaricated seemed to increase the danger to Rory's life. And to their own.

'I'll do it after my driving lesson. Yup.'

She cracked her knuckles. 'D'you want me with you?'

'Nope.'

'Are you going to word it like we decided?'

'Not sure yet.'

'Make sure you get straight to the point. No wimping out.'

'*Wimping out*?' he snorted, lobbing orange peel into a bin.

'And your dad has to swear he won't tell my mum.'

'I told you, she's the last person he'd want to tell,' he said.

It was true, she thought. If her mum learned the truth, she'd do something crazy like cancel the wedding and go to the police. Literally that was what she'd do. Tess knew it. William would know it. Based on this and on the fact that he had found drugs in Hal's trainers and not told Amy, Hal had predicted his father would keep this far worse situation to himself. The last thing William would want was Amy blaming his son for putting Tess in harm's way and risk shaking the foundations of their blended family only months before the wedding.

All this was what they'd concluded in the early hours before pressing play on *Stranger Things*, which they'd watched a million times over.

'You sure, sure, *sure* you don't want me there?'

He swung around. 'Just trust me, okay?'

She grabbed a large clump of orange segments from him, stuffed them in her mouth and talked through the mouthful. 'I'm going to comfort-eat until it's done.'

He grinned at her and dropped his jaw in mock outrage. It was the first light moment they'd shared since visiting Rory in hospital. Now she just wanted Hal to get it over and done with. Neither of them knew how William would react, but they were desperate to be unburdened of the problem. When weighing up the threat to Hal, throwing two grand at the problem would surely be a no-brainer. She imagined William, who was proud and private, doing everything he could to avoid going to the police and inflaming the situation.

They'd both agreed that nothing could be worse than carrying the secret around. It was all going to be fine.

She cracked her knuckles again.

Another message pinged on her phone from Rory.

*Has Hal asked W yet*

She replied with, *Give him a chance*

*When is he going to do it*

*Later after driving lesson speak then hope you're feeling ok*

# FORTY-FOUR

Hal

'We want to ask you two something,' William said, getting in there before Hal could.

Hal lost his grip on his sports bag as he swung it off his back. It skittled across the kitchen floor. A talk with his dad was the last thing he needed right now. In his driving lesson, he'd almost hit a traffic light. The instructor had used the emergency brake.

'Was your lesson okay?' Amy asked as she picked his bag up and hung it on the back of a chair.

'Yeah. Fine. What did you want to talk about?'

'It won't take long. There's some cake left over from our tasting thing at the weekend. Thought you might like some. Cup of tea to wash it down?'

Wash what down? he thought cynically. The two grown-ups were both grinning and twitching, and William even gave Hal a quick little side hug. Hal and Tess shared a look. Her eyes urged him to say something, to start the conversation about the money. A swoony, woozy feeling came over him, like extreme hunger.

Rory had been messaging him all day. Some of the texts Hal would read, others he left on delivered. The tone was increasingly desperate, and he didn't blame him. While Rory was stuck in bed recuperating, Logan and Ralph had been in the house, introducing themselves to Olivia, helping themselves to food in the kitchen. Asking over and over for the money he owed them. Rory had sounded terrified. Hal had to get it for him.

'Come here, Hamish!' he called, whistling. When the dog came bounding in from the garden, Hal dropped to the floor and allowed him to jump all over him and lick his face off.

'Come on, let's go and get comfy,' Amy said.

They followed her with the tray into the morning room. Hal chose the big green velvet chair and put his legs up over the armrest so that he could lie back and not look at anyone. Hamish flopped nearby. Tess hovered about and then took up position on the edge of the floral sofa opposite their parents.

'Right,' Amy said, clutching at her thighs. William pulled one ankle up onto his knee, adopting what could have been a confident and relaxed pose but appearing the opposite. He was embarrassingly ungainly, like he was still that gawky, gangling kid at school who grew too tall too soon.

Hal inspected his quietly handsome face and noticed how exhausted he looked. His eyes were bloodshot. Dark circles were smeared underneath them. His swept-to-the-side blond hair looked unusually dirty and had less life at its ends. This worried Hal for entirely selfish reasons. If his dad was stressed out about work, he would not listen to him closely enough to realise that none of this had been his fault. Rory had planted the drugs on him without his knowledge, had tried to blackmail him into taking photos of Tess, had told Logan where they lived, had endangered his and Tess's lives. But his dad would only hear 'drugs' and 'money' and lose it.

Tess leant over to him and whispered in his ear, 'I think we're about to find out what morning rooms are for.'

A smile passed behind Hal's eyes.

'Sit up properly, Hal,' William said jauntily, with that edge Hal hated.

Hal dragged himself upright and took a slice of cake. Although it tasted good, he couldn't swallow it. The sponge mushed around his mouth until it dissolved to nothing. He fed a sneaky piece to Hamish, who then sat at his feet and stared longingly for more.

His dad rubbed Amy's back. If Hal had been braver, he would have cut in on their little talk, grimly confident that his news would trump theirs. But every time he momentarily considered bringing it up, the dizzy feeling would come over him and he feared he might black out or projectile-vomit. Scratching behind Hamish's ears was his only comfort.

Amy cradled her mug of tea and leant forward. 'Sooo, we have a proposition. And you can totally say no if you think it's too much. But Tess, I would very much like it if you would consider being my maid of honour, and...'

She turned to William, who took over to say, 'And I'd be honoured if you, Hal, agreed to be my best man.'

'Wow, Mum! That's amazing! Yes! I'd love that so much!' Tess enthused.

'Cool, yeah,' Hal mumbled, and Hamish jumped up onto his lap and put his paws on his shoulders like a hug, blocking his view of the others.

'Hamish approves!' William laughed. 'And I'm very glad to hear it too. Thank you. You are my best man in all senses, and I'd be truly honoured to have you standing by my side in this special place on my wedding day.'

Hal, though he could barely see his dad because of Hamish's big head, detected unshed tears in his voice. For one great moment, as he hugged Hamish's neck, smelling his doggy smell, he let his father's words sink in and his heart swelled. It reminded him of winning the long-distance athletics cup at

Speech Day. His dad had clapped up in the air and given him a bumbling side hug on the way out of the sports hall. He thought of them standing in matching suits next to each other and wanted nothing more than to be a good son to him.

Hamish barked suddenly, jumped off him and charged over to the window seat. He sniffed at the pane, leaving circles of condensation in one of the diamonds. His ears were up and his eyes were trained on something in the garden. He barked, sounding fierce, though if the window were thrown open for him, he would probably cower between Hal's legs. Silly mutt. Hal was the same. The opportunity was right there. All he had to do was ask. Dread swirled up around him, sick-making and surreal. He didn't have the courage to do it. Rory would have to find the money.

It was Rory's bloody problem, not his.

# FORTY-FIVE

## Amy

'It's horrific,' Tess said, sounding every inch the poor little rich girl, screwing her face up at her reflection in the changing room mirrors, round-shouldered in a lilac satin dress.

At this point, Amy couldn't have given a hoot whether she wore a brown sack or an Alexander McQueen gown to the wedding. The changing rooms were hot and stuffy. She longed to be outside in the crisp, cold December sunshine on an invigorating dog walk. After another night of broken sleep, she didn't have the patience for Tess's rudeness.

The dream about Hal as a baby crying in the monogrammed sleepsuit had become recurring. She'd always wake with a start after it, as though his crying were real. Then she'd be unable to get back to sleep. Although the physical presence of the sleepsuit and the photograph in the drawer nearby bothered her, she'd left them be. Looking at them again, moving them or even discarding them had crossed her mind, but the real value of them was still unknown. They weren't hers to tamper with. Her only consolation was that she was going to own Summerfield House soon, and when she did, she'd rid the place of every single reminder of Sophie's presence.

'This one is even worse,' Tess said, whipping back the curtain to reveal a peach dress. Christmas muzak tinkled away in the background.

'You look absolutely stunning in it,' Amy said.

It appeared that Tess was violently disinterested in her choice of maid of honour dress. Normally she'd have thrown herself into finding one. Not necessarily because she loved shopping, but because wearing the right thing for the occasion would have been important to her.

'I hate it.' She stripped it off.

'I hope William and Hal are having more success in London.' Amy sighed, wondering whether it was too late to hop on a train to Waterloo.

'Suits are easier. Men *always* have it easier.'

The decision to go shopping in Guildford rather than tag along with William and Hal had been strategic. She'd wanted more time alone with Tess, fewer distractions, but it was backfiring. Sticking to Plan A, she resolved to ignore the insolence and instead focus on uncovering the root cause of her daughter's mood.

'Come on, we're not getting anywhere. Let's go get a hot choccy at Gail's,' she said.

They handed ten rejected dresses to the assistant on the way out of the changing rooms.

En route to the café, Amy had an urge to confide in Tess about her plans to buy Summerfield House. On a good day, she would be delighted by the news, which might improve her temper. But it felt premature to mention it. Sophie hadn't yet replied to William's email.

Having queued and waited for ever for their order, they sat down with cinnamon buns and gingerbread hot chocolate. The lights from the Christmas tree flashed near Amy's head. She stared across the mistletoe table decoration at her beautiful daughter. Tess's prominent upper lip was diminished somehow, balanced out by a confident stroke of liner on her bottom lip. Her glossy fringe was blunt and a little hard over her eyes. She ruffled it self-consciously, sure of her appeal. She was almost unrecognisable from the girl Amy had brought here a few months ago. It was hard to keep up with all the changes.

'Eugh, it's too milky,' she said sulkily, pushing her cup away.

The couple at the next table glanced over at her and Amy was mortified. A telling-off in full-throttle Scouse, just like one of her mum's tirades, was on the tip of her tongue. It had been building in her all morning: *Good manners cost nothing, you little terror! At your age I'd have killed for a posh frock and a hot choccy out! Show some respect! There are children starving in Africa! You don't even know you're born!* She was ready to unleash all the adages she vowed she'd never repeat, but in the end she bit them back. She had a more pressing agenda. The couple at the next table would just have to judge her for being a typical Surrey mum who indulged her child.

'Oi, you. It's December the first today,' she said, giving Tess a pinch and a punch for the first day of the month.

Tess flinched and forced out a brief fake smile. 'The first was yesterday.'

'Details, details,' Amy continued with sing-song light-heartedness, 'The point is, it's December, and you know what that means?'

'What?'

'Well, firstly, it's Christmas! But more importantly it's—'

'Mum, can we just go? I've got loads of homework to do this weekend. And we're never going to find the right dress anywhere except in London. Guildford is frankly pathetic.'

Tess's haughtiness cut right through Amy, but again she ignored it. 'Oh my goodness, Tess, you can't finally have grown too big to get excited about your birthday, can you?'

'Too *big*? What, are you fat-shaming me now?' But there was a tiny glint of mischief in Tess's eye when she said it.

'Ha, ha,' Amy said, before ploughing on. 'Seriously, though, it's only three weeks until you're *seventeen*! That's nineteen days exactly until you get to open your pressies and start learning how to drive!'

Tess jazz-handed with dead eyes and sneered sarcastically. 'Woo. Yay. Great.' Then she got up and flounced off to the ladies'.

Her behaviour today took 'out of character' to a whole new level. Amy texted William.

*Tess thinks Guildford is pathetic. I think what she means is that I'm pathetic. Miss you. Wish we'd come to London too.*

*Miss you too. Hal has barely spoken to me since we left Haslemere. I'm trying not to take it personally. But maybe I should.*

*Let's elope to Scotland.*

*Don't tempt me.*

*Love you*

*Love you too*

It helped to laugh with William about their temperamental teens, but Amy was fretting that the wedding was too much too soon for Tess. Was it at the heart of her mood, and perhaps Hal's? Had she and William got carried away with the planning and been cavalier with their children's feelings?

When Tess returned from the toilets, Amy said gently, 'Look. Usually you plan your birthday six months ahead and you've bought everyone's Christmas presents by November the first. What's going on?'

Tess uncoiled her cinnamon roll and dug her nails into the brown paste. 'Slight exaggeration, Mum.'

'Tess,' Amy said, leaning forward, 'you're the living incarnation of Pollyanna.'

Tess's reply was glum. 'I used to be.' Amy heard a wobble in her throat.

'Tess, love, you can talk to me,' she coaxed. 'Is it the wedding? If it's making you sad, I'll call the whole thing off. I'm serious.'

Tess shook her head. 'It's not that.'

'Better out than in. However bad it is.'

One glance up was all it took. In that split second of contact, Tess's eyes flooded with tears and Amy's heart pinched. She placed her hand on her daughter's arm and whispered, 'What is it, Tessie?'

Two fat tears plopped onto Tess's plate. 'Not here.'

# FORTY-SIX

William

'Quite rare that the vitals are exactly the same. Almost to the millimetre,' Clive said in his still-strong West Indian accent. 'It doesn't often happen.'

William and Hal were standing on plinths in front of two huge mahogany mirrors wearing grey blanks stitched together in the shape of their suits. They'd chosen a lightweight cotton and wool blend in dark blue with an indigo lining. No waistcoats, and a tapered slim-fit leg, roomy in the thigh with one break on the shoe. Because Hal's back was straight and his chestnut hair was off his face for once, the resemblance between them was more evident. William felt a stab of pride.

They exchanged a look. The green of Hal's eyes whirled with disquiet. William smiled at him reassuringly, wondering what might be wrong, unable to ask in front of Clive. He recalled the light-hearted text exchange that he and Amy had shared earlier. They had joked about eloping, but he recognised her more serious point. The wedding might be bringing up complicated feelings in Tess and Hal, which they had perhaps underestimated. Would it have been kinder to disappear off and tie the knot without involving them? Were they being self-indulgent?

He cleared his throat. 'You know how Grandpa Ru's much smaller than I am?' he said.

Hal nodded.

'I played a trick on him the day I married your mum. We were getting ready in a hotel around the corner from the registry office. While he was in the shower, I decided to put on his suit instead of mine and then I waited for him to come out of the bathroom.' William paused to grin. 'I stood there squeezed into a jacket and trousers three sizes too small, pretending I was ready to go, acting all normal like I hadn't noticed the arms were almost up by my elbows and the trousers were flapping mid-calf. I'll never forget his face.' He chuckled. 'He went puce. Completely hopping mad, thinking Clive had sent the wrong one!'

Clive chortled.

What William did not want to mention was what his father had grumbled under his breath: *My God, your mother would be rolling in her grave.* He liked the edited story, though. How silly he'd been. Now, standing in the fitting room of Powell Brothers of Savile Row, he and Hal laughed. Properly laughed. And William's heart grew a little bigger. He hadn't heard his son's laugh in a long time. It reminded him of how easily Hal had laughed as a toddler.

'How is Mr Hargreaves Senior these days?' Clive asked, picking off a stray thread from William's shoulder. With his razor-sharp afro cut into a neat square at his forehead, he was every bit the cliché of the old-school Savile Row tailor: gentlemanly, dignified and a little bit camp. 'Still in France?'

'The Algarve,' William corrected. Which reminded him, he hadn't put in his duty call to his father this week.

'Oh, that's right. My apologies. A beautiful place to retire, I imagine.'

'It certainly keeps him out of the Garrick,' William said. His father had often followed up his visits to Clive with a trip to the Garrick Club. It had been his happy place. Ironically, it had been Sophie's father, Thomas Sandeman-Gore, who had been responsible for pulling the strings at the members' club, circumventing the five-year waiting list to get William's father membership.

The reason for Thomas turning this high-end favour on behalf of a man he would have considered rather low-end in the social pecking order might have baffled some people. The Garrick's original tenet had been: *It would be better that ten unobjectionable men should be excluded than one terrible bore should be admitted.* Rupert Hargreaves was that one terrible bore. The mental image of him toadying about the club, remarking on the artworks he knew nothing about and garnering business for his dwindling property listings as he lounged in the leather chesterfields provoked in William a cringing to his boots. Because he knew Thomas Sandeman-Gore had had an ulterior motive: a lifetime membership in exchange for a lifetime of silence. It reminded William of the email he had sent about the house, which Sophie had so far completely ignored.

'He'll be coming over for the wedding, I presume?' Clive asked.

'Yes indeed,' William said, trying to sound enthusiastic. His father had received the e-card invitation for 27 April and had passed comment on its modern design. *Rather unconventional*, he'd remarked, signing off *Rupert* rather than *Dad*.

'What shoes are we wearing?' Hal asked.

'A Tricker's Derby?' Clive suggested.

William agreed. 'Spot on, Clive. I think a trip to Jermyn Street is the answer.'

'Can't I wear trainers?' Hal suggested. 'Black would look cool.'

William was about to remonstrate. Then he pictured his father's frown and his late mother's anarchic smile from heaven, and replied, 'Why the hell not?'

He didn't want anything to spoil their day together.

# FORTY-SEVEN

## Amy

Amy and Tess had grabbed their things and bundled themselves out of Gail's. The sun had gone in. Amy led her daughter along the damp cobbled street underneath the Christmas lights to the castle ruins, where they could walk and talk through the gardens. Icy drizzle wetted their noses and shoulders, and tears rolled down Tess's face.

'Oh poppet, what is it?' Amy said.

'I can't say it,' Tess mumbled, swiping her cheeks pointlessly as more tears and raindrops fell.

'You can tell me anything, absolutely anything, you do realise that, don't you?' Amy, while desperate for Tess to unburden herself, was also panicking about what she was about to hear. She wondered how easy it would be to cancel the wedding.

Tess stopped walking and swivelled to face her. 'But I can't tell you! Because you're *so* happy and I don't want to make you unhappy and spoil everything for you and William! And we've got our first Christmas coming up, and your wedding! I can't!'

Amy turned to her and cupped her face. 'Don't be daft. If you're not happy, how can I possibly be happy?' she replied tearfully.

As they stood under a bleak sky on a path in the shadow of the towering walls of William the Conqueror's fort, Tess finally unleashed her long confession. The story spilled out of her like verbal diarrhoea, sometimes incomprehensibly. Occasionally Amy would have to stop the flow, much to Tess's consternation, and ask her to go back and explain some of the points to get it clear in her mind.

At the end, she was unable to speak. Over Tess's shoulder, her gaze traversed the stone walls. She imagined it had once been proud and splendid and strong, yet it was now in ruins, and Amy realised she felt that way too. Ruined. Utterly destroyed by what Tess had told her. She didn't know what to say or do. It disgusted her that Rory should want to deal drugs, that he wanted more than he already had, which was already too much. He took his privilege for granted and thought himself so special he could operate above the law. Then he had the gall to drag Tess into it.

Bringing Tess to Summerfield House should have been a win-win for them both. In reality, she had slotted them into William's ready-made life with too few questions asked. She didn't feel informed or in charge any more. What had seemed like a fresh, breezy start had become thick with the stale air of festering pasts. She had a sudden urge to take Tess away from there, sever ties with the insidious influence of those boys and that school and Sophie Sandeman-Gore's Summerfield bloody House.

*But I could never leave William*, a small voice said inside her head. Abandoning him was inconceivable. There was a gust of wind. Her flesh turned cold as stone. Like the crumbling fortress, she was tempted to let the weather corrode her until she was part of the landscape, no longer burdened by the responsibility of sheltering those under threat.

# FORTY-EIGHT

William

After the fitting, William took Hal for an ice cream at Fortnum & Mason. It was where his own father had taken him as a boy, once a year on the exeat closest to his birthday. The Fountain restaurant downstairs had been different back then, arguably better. William had loved the swivelling stools at the long bar and the tall ice cream glasses and the long silver spoons.

The Hargreaves tradition lived on, though a few things had changed. The bar had gone, the restaurant had been squeezed upstairs into kitchenware, the ice creams had tripled in size, and they didn't have to wait for school exeats. Never would William have put Hal into boarding school. Let alone at seven years old, which had been the age his dad had packed him off to Windlesham House. As a child, he hadn't questioned the fact that the school was only half an hour away from home and had taken day pupils. After his mother died, he remembered angrily counting the exact number of extra hours he would have had with her had he been a day boy.

It wasn't anyone's birthday today, but the occasion had

clearly warranted a special ice cream. Festive garlands twinkled all around them. Hal seemed to be enjoying his Rocky Road. William was basking in their time together. He would never take this for granted. His latest trip to Scarborough had reinforced that. The recollection of Avril's hallucinations came back to him now. *I hear him crying still,* vous comprenez? Her haunting words forced a swill of Darjeeling tea the wrong way up. Again he checked his inbox for Sophie's reply to his email about the house. Nothing.

Putting his phone away, he asked Hal about his driving lessons.

After their ice creams, they trundled southbound from Piccadilly on the Bakerloo line to catch the 14.30 from Waterloo. Finding seats, they retreated to the separate world of their phones.

At one point, when passing through Godalming, Hal murmured, 'Shit' under his breath.

'What's up?' William asked. But Hal hid his screen cagily and his thumbs moved quickly across the keys.

'Everything okay?' William asked.

'Tess said they're picking us up from the station,' Hal muttered, slipping his phone into his pocket.

'Oh? That's good, isn't it?'

'Yeah, sure.' He leant his head against the window and plugged his AirPods into his ears.

William was puzzled for the rest of the journey.

At Haslemere station, they hunched against the cold. Large droplets of rain splatted onto the white paint of the pelican crossing at their feet. Hal appeared pale – sickly, in fact. William's foreboding worsened when he got into the passenger seat next to Amy and kissed her. From the hardness of her lips, he sensed something was up.

'Hello. You all right?'

Amy started the car. 'We'll talk about it when we get home.'

William turned to the back seat. Tess was eyeing Hal.

'I'm scared now,' he joked, trying to gauge how serious it was.

A deep sigh from Amy turned his stomach. She switched off the ignition. In the sudden quiet, the rain sounded like bullets on the roof. She undid her seat belt and twisted to face Hal and Tess. 'On second thoughts, let's get it over and done with. I don't think I'll be able to drive safely until he knows. Sorry.'

The kids' faces were stricken. Both were strapped into their seats as though poised for a ride of terror. Tess shook her head, tears brimming in her eyes. Hal covered his mouth. Through his fingers, his voice was muffled. 'Rory's got us into trouble, Dad. Really big trouble.'

# FORTY-NINE

Amy

Amy's hand was on the dash. William was driving too fast.

'Can you even withdraw that much over the counter without notice?' she asked him.

'Yes. I did it recently,' he replied.

'For what?'

'When I bought Hal's mountain bike off that guy from school.'

'I'm not sure this is the right thing to do, William.'

'We can afford it, so...'

She could almost hear the shared exhale from the pair in the back, but what William was saying didn't feel right.

'And then what?'

'Then we get on with our lives.'

Admittedly, life was good. There was the wedding to look forward to. And the potential purchase of Summerfield House. And Christmas was only a few weeks away. Happy times were ahead. 'But what happens if Rory screws up again?' Amy said, incapable of quelling the panic. 'And his debts are bigger? And the dealers are even more dangerous?'

Tess leant forward between the seats, 'He won't, Mum. He's learned his lesson.'

'How can you be so sure?'

'We can be. Totally. He was properly scared. Don't you think, Hal?'

There was a prolonged delay before Hal answered. 'Yeah, sure.'

'I'll make it clear that this will be the last time I'll ever bail him out,' William said, taking one hand off the wheel to push his hair off his forehead.

It was plain he was decided, confident it was the right way forward, but he was reacting faster than Amy could think. This wasn't a cut-and-dried situation. She needed time to process the facts after the initial shock. She understood William's instinct to throw money at it, and although it felt reassuring to have the luxury to do so, her own thoughts on the matter were more complex. There seemed to be fires everywhere in her head. Here was Tess, who was scared and sorry and still strangely sympathetic towards Rory – wanting to save him? Amy felt they needed to unpack these conflicting feelings first before they made such a big decision. 'We need to talk about this,' she reiterated. 'Can we just go home?'

'I'm worried too, quite honestly,' William said, 'but this really is the best way of dealing with it. We'll drop the cash off at Olivia's on the way home, then it's Rory's business, not ours.' He paused. 'I'm guessing Olivia knows?'

'Yes,' Hal said. 'Rory already asked her for money. And she was okay about asking you.'

'Okay then.'

Amy squeezed her temples. 'Shouldn't we first consider going to the police before we hand over that amount?'

Tess gasped. 'What? Mum! No!'

Simultaneously Hal said, 'Are you *insane*?'

Amy turned to look at them both. 'But if Rory's attackers are arrested, they won't be able to extort money from us, or threaten us again, or harm Rory or anyone else.'

'Good plan. Rory'll then be shanked in the head by someone higher up the chain,' Hal retorted caustically.

'The police would protect him from that,' Amy said.

Tess yelled, 'Don't be so naive, Mum!'

'Your mum isn't being naive, she's just thinking all the options through,' William said firmly.

'But he's been through so much already!' Tess cried, jutting her head forward, grabbing the corner of Amy's seat.

'I'm sure the divorce affected him badly, love,' she conceded. 'But you and Hal have both been through loads too, and you're not dealing drugs, are you?'

'We didn't have abusive dads, though, did we?' Tess threw at her.

Amy was taken aback. 'What do you mean?' She caught William's eye. 'You're talking about Toby? His dad? How?'

'Physically!' Tess shouted, as though it was obvious.

Convinced she would have gleaned something from Olivia if Tess's claim had been true, Amy asked, 'How do you know that?'

'He told me,' Tess said quietly, sitting back, staring out the window, pulling at her top lip.

Amy guessed that her daughter was in as much doubt about what came out of Rory's mouth as she and William were. She spoke gently. 'But he might have wanted you to believe that so you felt sorry for him. Especially if he knows you're angry with him.'

'You just don't understand, Mum,' Tess mumbled angrily.

'Rory has always been extremely manipulative,' William added. 'And Toby struck me as a decent enough guy, don't you think, Hal? He was very funny, I seem to remember. Very bright. I met him at the odd dinner party. I used to feel sorry for him, actually. Olivia always got so drunk, it was excruciating.'

Hal spoke up. 'He didn't look much like fun when he was kicking Rory in the stomach with his big shiny fucking shoe. But maybe that's just my take on it.'

'You saw it happen?' William shot back, and the car swerved a little onto the noisy markings of the hard shoulder.

'Once, yeah.'

'When? How old were you?'

'About eight.'

'Eight?' Amy wanted to weep. 'That's horrific. Does Olivia know any of this?'

'Maybe,' Hal said, but then added, 'Don't think so.'

'And you didn't tell anyone?' William asked.

'There was a lot of stuff going down in my life too back then, Dad,' Hal said.

Amy calculated that Hal had been eight when his parents divorced, and it seemed that William was reminded of this too. 'Yes, you had a lot on your plate. Sorry, Hal. I wasn't suggesting it was your responsibility. You were only a little boy yourself,' he said, briefly taking his eye off the road to look at his son.

'It was weird, I just kind of forgot it happened,' Hal explained, even though he didn't need to. He had been too young to know what to do about it. 'For years I didn't think about it at all. I've no clue how I'd forget something that bad.'

Amy was unused to Hal revealing this much about himself. She turned around and touched his knee. 'You probably blocked it out because it was too horrible.'

'I was okay,' Hal murmured. 'I just felt bad for Rory, really.'

'Yes,' Amy said. The situation was more complicated than she'd thought.

Slightly opportunistically, William said, 'It seems Rory deserves a chance to turn it around and make an honest life for himself.' He paused, perhaps waiting for Amy to disagree. She didn't know what to say; was outnumbered, and probably in the wrong. He continued. 'But if I do this, you two, I'll have to talk to Olivia about it first. And Rory's got to get away from Logan and stop the dealing. If he doesn't, we'll have no choice but to go to the police. In the meantime, while he sorts himself out, I want neither of you to have anything to do with him. Understand?'

'But we go to school with him!' Hal said.

'That's fine, but no hanging out outside of school. It's my only condition.'

Tess pulled her top lip over her bottom one. 'Olivia won't like it.'

'I'll worry about Olivia,' Amy murmured.

'Hal? Tess? Agreed?' William said.

'I'm totally fine with that,' Hal said, and Tess nodded.

'Good,' William said, squeezing Amy's thigh before nipping over into the fast lane. His blond brow was knitted determinedly. Admittedly, Amy felt a little better for having him carve out a clear path forward and for taking such a big decision out of her hands. It seemed his capacity to contain his emotions was valuable in a crisis. She felt a rush of admiration for him, envying him his ability to be so resolute.

She glanced over her shoulder at Tess and Hal. They were looking at each other, gazes fused, communicating silently. The whole world could have disappeared around them and they wouldn't have noticed.

Outside Amy's window, the rain had turned to a light sleet, neither snow nor rain, neither one thing nor the other. As soon as the flakes landed on the car, they melted away to nothing.

Outside Olivia's house, Amy watched Hal press the code into the gate. He looked back once before disappearing with the envelope of cash. Amy had an urge to slip down in her seat like a criminal in a getaway car. It felt sordid to be there. William turned the radio on. They listened to the tail end of a programme about climate change, which should have put everything into perspective, but didn't.

# FIFTY

William

His first Christmas with Amy at Summerfield House had been magical. The memories of it were like pulling a woolly blanket over himself and snuggling down into its softness. They'd enjoyed chaotic present-opening in the morning room and suffered carols blasting from Tess's new Bluetooth speaker. Amy had been delighted with her diamond earrings – hadn't taken them off since. Hamish had played fetch with balls of wrapping paper and knocked over their seven-foot tree. There'd been frosty walks on Blackdown and hearty roasts in cosy old pubs. Tess had baked mince pies and sticky-taped mistletoe to beams all over the house, insisting he and Amy kiss under it each time. Amy's first-ever turkey had been delicious. The children's laughter around the big round oak kitchen table had been everything he'd ever dreamed of. And it had snowed! Only a light dusting, but still. The house had been at its most beautiful in the snow, like one of those old-fashioned advent calendars.

On Boxing Day, Hal had met Eleanor in London, and from there he'd gone to Somerset for the week. Tess was staying with

Nick in Camden for a few days. Having the house to themselves should have been relaxing, but William had been on tenterhooks waiting for Sophie's reply to his carefully composed email about purchasing the house. She'd finally got back to him on New Year's Eve. Her email had pinged into his inbox while he and Amy were seeing in 2023 by the fire with a brandy in hand, the Hogmanay celebrations blaring from the television. His heart had galloped as he read it to himself. *Let's have lunch and talk about it. I'm in town on 8 Jan. 1 p.m. at Covent Garden Hotel?* she had written. His stomach had dropped. He hadn't wanted to meet her face to face, had promised Amy he wouldn't. Yet here he was, on his way to lunch with her.

He walked over a grey Waterloo Bridge towards Covent Garden. It was a wrench to be shoved into the bustle of the city this morning. Seeing Sophie was a daunting prospect. The wind blew across the twisting water and over London's skyline. Echoes of Avril's utterances in Scarborough swirled through his mind. *He tells me he wants you to be together again. He feels he is to blame. He can't leave until this is fixed.* At the memory, the imaginary blanket of Christmas and its traditions was whipped away, leaving a chill.

When he reached the restaurant, he caught sight of Sophie through the window. His muscles cramped. Stay calm and focused, he told himself. Keep Summerfield House in your sights.

She had applied thick foundation and lipstick but had left her eyes bare, and she looked more vulnerable somehow. Neither of them could hold eye contact for longer than a split second. They caught up superficially, making no reference to their visit to Scarborough in November. She pulled the sleeves of her lavender sweater over her hands, bunching the material into her palms. William occasionally fiddled with something in the pocket of his tweed jacket and nodded politely, starting sentences that she wouldn't let him finish. He couldn't keep up with her nervous talking and nail-biting and was eternally out of his depth with her cleverness and professional integrity.

After their starters, Sophie went outside for a cigarette, during which time William prepared himself in earnest. There was a splash of mud on the hem of his corduroys, which he scratched off. A tiny nod to his other life. When she returned, he asked her direct what she'd thought of his offer on the house.

She responded almost breezily. 'No! Ha. Obviously not.'

He pushed himself back into his seat. 'You won't even think about it?'

'If you'd like me to,' she said absently. She took a sip of water and waved at the waiter. 'Okay, I've thought. And the answer is still no.' She glanced at her wristwatch. It was rare to see a woman wear one these days. There was a little blue gem on the winder, which she used to get the dirt from under her nails.

'But you don't even want to live there yourself! And I do. It's Hal's home. And now I have Amy and her daughter to think about.'

Laughing briefly, she poured the wine. Her attention flitted around the restaurant before returning to him. 'You're obviously just freaking out about what Avril said. And overreacting to it.' The permanent tremor in her hands was obvious as her fingers danced over her ultra-neat but slightly greasy centre parting.

'It's not that,' he said too loudly, attracting a woman's attention from the next table. More quietly, he said, 'I've got the money. You know it's the right thing to do.'

'I'm so sick of everyone telling me what is right,' she sighed, tapping her ring on her glass like Morse code.

'If it hadn't been for me, the whole place would have rotted away!'

She baulked. 'That's a low blow.' She said it under her breath, tracking a woman and her dog's journey past the window.

'Sorry,' he said, pulling back, not wanting to derail things further.

Her main course of salad was in front of her now. She raked at the spiky leaves with her fork and scrutinised them as though they were case files, then put the fork down and picked up a pomegranate seed. 'How's your father these days?' she asked airily, popping the red fruit into her mouth.

'Still alive,' he said, sawing at his steak, thinking of ways he could get them back on track.

'You know, *he* once asked Daddy if he could buy Summerfield House too. Just before he died. For half its market value.'

'What?' William said, appalled. 'Like...' he dropped his voice, 'blackmail?'

'More ambulance-chasing, I imagine. Daddy wasn't too impressed.'

He choked. 'Jesus, sorry. God. That's awful. How embarrassing.'

'I always wondered if it was his toady way of getting one up on Daddy for what he and Mummy did to you.'

He shook his head, gulped at his wine, wiped his mouth with his napkin. 'No, he was absolutely on board with how it all played out.'

She mumbled bitterly, '*More* people who thought they knew what was right for us.'

'What's done is done,' he said, swallowing down a lump of meat that was too big. He'd arrived here so clear-headed, and now there was all this clutter in his mind.

Sophie moved her head forward. Their faces were close. She spoke under her breath. 'But what if we could undo some of it? You know, make amends, like Avril said? What if she's right? What if that's why she's hearing that crying?'

'Are you losing your marbles as well?' he said, feeling like he might lose his own. 'Avril wasn't making any bloody sense with all that baby rubbish. For God's sake.' He went back to his steak, knitting his brow.

'But I realised something when I was talking to her about it later.'

'What's that?' he said miserably.

'That he needs a name.'

William looked up suddenly. His heart hammered. Sophie's eyes had reddened, coloured by an anguished blaze.

'Don't you think?' she asked.

# FIFTY-ONE

## Amy

Amy was looking up and down the Tube train carriage, wondering if she might bump into William. He was also up in London today at various meetings. The likelihood of crossing paths with him was about one in a million. She sat down between a man playing a game on his phone and a woman in a suit whose eyes were closed. Standing next to them was a young mother with a baby. It reminded Amy of the years with Tess in London, struggling with her pram down the stairs and over the gaps. She felt at home suddenly.

Earlier this morning, Pip had picked up her FaceTime call after only half a ring, almost telepathically knowing that Amy needed her. Her red bob had been scraped into a tidy bun on top of her head. She had been 'not working' from home in her pink PJs. Having heard only half the story about the drugs and the money drop, she had declared, 'Stop right there! I'm calling an emergency meeting. You know the drill.'

'I can't. It's the kids' first day back.'

'They're seventeen, they can find their own way home. Let's

go to the big screen in Leicester Square and eat bumper-sized popcorn.'

'Fine. But don't force Jo to come if she's too busy.'

'No deal. Laundrette Lil's fifth cycle of washing can wait,' Pip said. Jo didn't work, from home or from an office, and had once foolishly admitted that on average she put on five washes a day.

'She's not going to like it,' Amy had said.

Now she alighted at Leicester Square and shuffled along with the crowds heading in the direction of the cinema. An image came to her: the pink flush of William's cheeks, the pale green of his eyes and the thick bounce of his blond hair swept to the side. He had been vivid against the snowy heathland behind him. Thinking about him was peaceful and soothing. She loved his face, as familiar to her as one of her own limbs, as though his eyes, his soul belonged to her, would feel part of her for ever, even if she lost him. A shot of ghostly white in the form of Hamish charged across the landscape like a flash of regret. *We should not have given the money to Rory.* She had said it out loud to William. Then that steady hand of his, gloved in scratchy red wool, had been there to help her across an iced puddle.

'We did it for Hal and Tess,' he had reminded her, releasing a cloud of cold breath. And she had leant into him and trusted him to hold her steady.

'I'd get her as far away as possible from both those boys if I were you, my love,' Joanna said. 'The whole thing's horrendous. I can't believe you've had all this going on. You, of all people, who's never even dodged a bus fare.'

As the lights went down and the music built and the trailers started, the world outside seeped away. Sitting in that darkened room in the heart of central London would usually have given

Amy a cosy sense of escapism, but she could only think about what Jo had just said.

'Tess'll be okay. She's too switched on not to be,' Pip said gruffly, counting out six Minstrels. Six was her lucky number. 'Michelle Pfeiffer in *Heat* was okay in the end, right?'

Jo snatched back the chocolates before she got to six. 'It was *Scarface*. And no, she wasn't okay. She turned into a total coke-head!'

Pip threw her arms up. 'But we all secretly wanted to be her.'

Amy chortled guiltily. Pip's lack of judgement was a reprieve. With her friend's blessing, she could be less hard on herself and on William. Her phone pinged. It was her iCalendar, which she kept forgetting to tell William they shared. This one was a reminder for a 1 p.m. reservation at the Covent Garden Hotel. She turned off her phone.

'Remember that silky green number in the club scene?' Jo sighed longingly. 'I always wanted that dress.'

'You know, Neil got kicked out of his secondary school for dealing a bit of weed to his mates,' Pip said.

Jo was aghast. '*What*? How did I not know that?'

Amy *had* known this about Pip's husband. Neil's upbringing was like a fundraiser film for a child abuse charity. But he was now an ambulance driver, and one of the kindest, most by-the-book citizens you were ever likely to meet.

'Because I knew you'd be all judgy.'

'I wouldn't have been!' Jo said. But they knew she would.

'Jo, you think it's wrong that we paid Rory that money, don't you?'

'Sorry,' Jo said in a small voice.

Amy hugged her tub of popcorn. Pip was incredulous. 'Come on, Jo, wouldn't you do the same for Luke and Eve if they got in trouble? If money wasn't an issue? Think about it. If those two gorgeous little scamps made one mistake that could define their whole lives in a really bad way, and you had it in your power to make it all go away and give them one shot to get their shit together, you're telling me you wouldn't take it? I know I would for my three.'

Jo sighed. 'Sorry, but I would still probably go to the police to try to sort it out that way. They have special safeguarding departments now for the kids involved. The dealers need to go to prison so they don't ruin more young people's lives.'

'If I'm honest, that was my first instinct,' Amy said, sighing so hard, pieces of popcorn rustled from the top of the carton onto her lap. 'But William was determined and I got swept up in it.'

Jo leant forward. 'You can still go to the police. It's not too late.'

'Shh, it's about to start,' Pip said.

Jo's words rotated around Amy's head all through the film. It was about a young woman who fell in love with a younger man but realised he wasn't going to solve any of her problems and so left him to find herself instead. The story didn't provide enough distraction. Over and over again Amy asked herself: should she go to the police?

When the credits began to roll, Pip said, 'That was crap.'

'Totally agree,' Amy said. They shuffled out of the row. 'What's wrong with a bit of soppy romance?'

'It's not feminist enough these days,' Pip grumbled.

Outside the cinema, they shouldered the wet, cold rain of Leicester Square.

'Duck pancakes at Ming's?' Pip suggested.

Amy shook her head. 'As yummy as that sounds, I've got to go.'

'Where the hell are you going?' Pip cried.

They huddled in a circle. 'To loiter outside the Covent Garden Hotel,' Amy admitted.

'Drugs?' Pip teased.

Amy snorted. 'Ha, ha. Not funny. No, my phone shares William's iCalendar and the reservation for his lunch meeting popped up. So I'm going to wait for him and surprise him when he comes out. Be romantic, you know? Unlike that film. I think we need to talk.'

'We'll join you,' Joanna said.

'A foursome at a swanky hotel?' Pip chortled. 'I'm in.'

Jo groaned. 'I meant, just wait with her!'

'Seriously, though, thanks. I appreciate the offer, but as much as I love you both, I'll be fine. I'll grab a coffee on Seven Dials and wait for him there. I can't tell you how much you've helped me get things straight in my head. The truth is, by not going to the police, I'm still going along with it. And my mum taught me better.'

Pip wrapped her in a hug. 'She would've been proud. Let us know how it goes. And text us about the hen weekend. I'm polishing up my flip-flops.'

'You won't need them, they provide posh towelling ones.'

'Oh, it's that fancy, is it?'

'They might not even let gobby redheads in,' Amy said.

Heads turned as Pip cackled, 'Cheeky cow! You blonde bimbo.'

'Call us if you need us,' Jo said, giving Amy a kiss and squeezing her hand.

'Thanks for being there for me, you two. Best emergency meeting ever. I needed it.'

Amy rubbed a hole in the steam on the window of the coffee bar and watched the hotel's comings and goings through her own little portal. She sipped her drink, thinking of ways of wording her decision to William. The revolving door spat out mostly arty media types. They wore solid black from head to toe, or clashing blocks of colour in spongy fabrics, or a bohemian mass of prints and flaps.

When a tall, beautiful woman wearing a shabby velvet-collared Crombie and black boots stepped onto the pavement, Amy noticed her immediately. She was the cliché of a scruffy aristocrat. A woman from a bygone era. Her eyes were pale like she'd been crying. There was also something horribly familiar about her face. Amy was staggered and horrified by the coincidence. The next person to appear through the doors was William.

Her coffee cup slipped through her fingers and hot liquid splashed her jeans. She had no idea if it had scalded her thighs, wouldn't have noticed or cared. All her senses were focused on what she was witnessing through the window.

The two of them were tall, slim pillars of old-fashioned refinement, standing opposite each other, too close as they talked. Sophie was nodding, then waved her hand for a cab. William had a sad smile on his face. He looked out of place in his country uniform of Barbour and moleskins. Amy wanted to hurtle across the street and run at them both, scratch Sophie's eyes out and scream at William for breaking his promise, for going behind her back. It would have happened in a film. Instead, she just sat there like a dolt, idiotically watching as a cab drew up and whisked them both away.

Soon the window steamed over and her view was obscured. Or perhaps Sophie Sandeman-Gore had scratched *her* eyes out and she hadn't felt it happening.

# FIFTY-TWO

William

William and Sophie sat in the back of the taxi, crammed at opposite ends of the seat. Cigarette smoke was still heavy around her.

'Where is it you need to be dropped off?' she asked, clicking her phone on and off nervily.

'Umm, just somewhere in Holborn. Kingsway? I can walk over the bridge from there,' he said.

They both knew that he could have ambled through Covent Garden to Waterloo Bridge in less time. He'd wanted just a few more minutes with her, stubbornly clinging to the idea that he might be able to talk her round. Sophie relayed directions to the driver and then clicked off the mic. William's heart kicked out one big beat. She uncrossed and recrossed her legs. Her black tights had a small ladder running up one calf. One black boot bounced up and down in the space between them.

'I'm glad we met,' she said.

'Oh, yes, no problem.' He blushed, suddenly ashamed of the

naivety he'd arrived at the restaurant with. The hope he'd had that she'd sell Summerfield House was slipping from him now.

She cleared her throat, but her voice remained husky. 'He would have been twenty-four this year,' she said, eyes washed out. Pale red seepage from her lipstick stained both corners of her mouth.

'Yes,' he said, feeling wretched.

'You and I are stuck together because of him.'

A wash of grief threatened to drown him. He couldn't talk.

'Whether I sell the house to you or not, he will always be our son,' she continued, swiping tears from her cheeks as she looked out of the window.

Ugh. Christ. It was coming. The agony of it. Tears gathered like needles in his eyeballs. His son's soul filled his whole being. He was lying there next to him again in the yellow room. The baby was wearing Sophie's little sleepsuit with the frog pattern. William could almost touch him. His skin was soft and sweet-smelling like butter icing. His innocence clamping a vice of love around his chest. He held this image in his mind, wanting to bear the unbearable, as though it were still possible to take his place. His brain blacked out just before the crucial, crucifying moment of his passing. The fact that he had not been there to save him was – all over again – too unspeakably horrifying to tolerate. Mind-bending guilt flooded the caverns of loss inside him. He gasped, as though coming up for air, suddenly conscious again of where he was, of the taxi wheels turning underneath them, of life going on as before.

The cab swerved sharply right into Shaftesbury Avenue and Sophie was flung into him. Her hair smelt of dirty pillows. She didn't move away from him as quickly as he would have liked.

He sat forward and switched the mic back on. 'Just up there is fine,' he instructed the driver, needing air.

As the cab changed lanes, heading for the bus stop ahead,

Sophie touched his thigh. The very tips of her long fingers were stubs. Decades of biting them down had deformed them. 'William,' she whispered. 'Don't go yet. I can cancel my afternoon and we can ask him to turn round and take us back to my place.' Her dry red lips were strangely beautiful to him.

'No, no, that's kind. But it's getting on and I need to go home,' he blustered ridiculously. *Home. Amy.* A glimpse of his and Sophie's lovemaking in the apple orchard one summer many moons ago appeared through dark curtains in his mind. It stirred him. He sat back and let her keep her hand there, unable to physically leave her. Being outside amongst people who did not understand the shared pain in their hearts was inconceivable.

'Here okay?' the cab driver asked.

'Sorry, change of plan,' Sophie said into the mic, holding William in her gaze. 'Could we head to Sloane Square? Twenty-three Cadogan Gardens.'

# FIFTY-THREE

## Amy

'How can I believe anything you're saying?' Amy cried, feeling her chest heave with sorrow. She sat down on the window seat. Its thin cushion felt damp through her jeans. She fixated on the curl of the lemon wallpaper by the plug sockets.

'I'm not having an affair with her, Amy, you *have* to believe me.'

'I just don't get why you went behind my back like that,' she repeated. Her accent was as strong as her mother's. She wished she had her by her side shouting in her corner now.

'I couldn't handle the thought of you meeting Sophie. I knew it would be easier without you being there.'

'Because she still has her sights set on you?'

He circled his wrist with his forefinger and thumb, squeezing it like a handcuff. 'Maybe. Yes, I think she might.'

'You said there was nothing between you!'

'Not from my point of view there's not. You must know that in your gut, Amy. You know what you and I have together! But Sophie doesn't care. She never gets the message.'

She felt another sob rise in her chest. 'I want to be able to trust you,' she said.

'You can,' he said gently. 'I only thought I'd have a better chance of buying this house if I saw her and asked her face to face.'

The drawer containing the photograph of Hal in the babygro was right by her feet. 'I want to show you something,' she sniffed, wiping her nose.

The clattering and scraping and rolling of objects in the drawer as she searched for it was deafening. She took everything out: an old screwdriver, a creased tartan scarf, a dog collar, other irrelevant things. Where was it? She yanked the empty drawer out from its rungs and tipped it upside down, staring up at William. 'Where is it?'

'Where's what?' he asked, tears in his voice.

'The photo of Hal.'

'What photo?'

'Of him as a baby in his crib in this very room. The one I showed you.'

'Hal's crib was never in here. He was in the nursery next door. Amy, what's wrong? Why does this matter?' He held his head.

'You're telling me Hal never slept in here as a baby?'

'Never! What's this all about?'

Her jaw slackened. The drawer slipped off her knees. She stared at its emptiness. 'I'm going mad.' Had she made it up? Had the recurring dreams and the photo itself merged into one? She looked around the room. The repeat pattern of the lemon wallpaper had faded; the black beams that cut through it were riddled with wormholes; the windows whistled with faint baby cries. The wardrobe was haunted with remnants of a past she couldn't make sense of.

'This place *is* worth all of this, isn't it?' she asked him.

'Of course it is. One hundred per cent, yes,' he insisted.

She pulled her knees up to her chest. 'I'm trying to understand.'

He pushed the drawer aside and knelt opposite her. 'I'm so sorry I lied. I regret it. But the stakes were so high. She and I have been connected to this house all my adult life. Twenty-four whole years.' He paused and gulped before going on, 'You've no idea what she's like. I wanted to be alone with her to explain that the house has become part of me, that I've brought my son up here, that it's his family home, that it's everything I've ever worked for.' He fiddled with the jewellery in the metal bowl on top of the chest of drawers. The gold and silver made a tinkling noise. 'You've been its missing piece, Amy, and now you're here, it's complete. I'm complete.'

She exhaled all her frustration in one ragged breath. 'Okay, okay. I get it.'

'You do?' he said, searching her face for more than that.

'Yeah, yeah.'

There was a break in their exchange. She sighed, at a loss. The stress was getting to her. 'I need a glass of water.'

William plodded after her like a dopey dog. Her anger had withered into resignation.

When she saw Hal in the kitchen, she wanted to usher him out, protect him from seeing her in this state. 'You're still up?' she asked.

'I couldn't sleep.'

She couldn't help shooting William a dirty look, like it was his fault, which it was. Hamish sniffed him suspiciously.

'Sorry about the shouting,' she said to Hal. But she might as well have said, *Sorry about your father*.

# FIFTY-FOUR

Tess

Their yelling brought back bad memories for Tess. It was how marriages ended.

'He used to argue like that with Mum,' Hal said gloomily, having returned from the kitchen with no food.

'Mine were the same.'

'Let's get out of here.'

'It's eleven thirty!'

'So what? It's not like they'd notice.' Hal pointed in the general direction of the arguing, which had started up again.

'Where would we go?'

'Rory's?'

Neither of them had seen Rory over Christmas. On a group chat, Tess had gleaned that he was out and about again. His flexing had been in overdrive: Nike this, Gucci that; Adidas and Versace labels. In response to each post, she would groan, saddened that he felt he had to show off. On New Year's Eve, he had sent her an emotional message to thank her for 'doing me a solid'. His video was thick with sentiment: he owed her his life and would never forget it. Several times he had brushed his hand across his blond crop, which had grown out a little. He had shyly mumbled into the camera that he missed her, that he'd learned his lesson the hard way, that 2024 was a new start. Tess, although under strict instructions from her mum to never speak to him again, had sent a video message back. She had simply said, 'You're welcome,' and then sent another one reminding him not to be a total dick.

On the bus earlier that morning, she'd caught his eye, but hadn't felt ready to start up a conversation. She still found him dangerously, throbbingly sexy, especially with the new bad-boy scar on his cheek under one of his dazzling blue eyes.

'How was he in economics today?' she asked Hal now over the background din of their respective parents.

'It was okay. He wanted the three of us to hook up.'

'Did he say that?'

'Yup.'

Day-to-day, Rory's name had been the unmentionable in the house. He had become almost like a character in a book on William's shelf, filed away. That was how it felt to Tess, anyway. The creaking old Summerfield House, with its arteries of climbers and its cold leaded window panes and its sun-bleached fabrics, had swallowed up the truth. Nothing like that could happen in a place like this.

'Honestly, I think we should check on him,' Hal said. 'He has nobody.'

'He deserves it.' Even to her own ears it sounded false.

'Those guys had him by the balls. I don't know what I would've done if it was me. Why don't we go over, just for ten minutes, just make sure he's okay.'

Through the walls, her mum's voice began to sound high-pitched and tearful, while William's was loud and sonorous. It was getting right under her skin. Part of her wanted to creep closer to listen, like she had as a younger kid in her first home, to find out what it was about.

Remembering that this never worked out well, she said to Hal, 'Okay, you're right. Ten minutes can't hurt. Let's go.'

She couldn't stand listening to them for a second longer.

As per Rory's instruction, they left their bikes behind the bins and went straight down to the pool house.

A sleeping bag was laid out on a mattress behind one of the sofas. A plastic shopping bag of food sat on the drinks trolley. Rory's Heathside uniform hung from the door of the loo, behind which Tess could see a washbag. There was a hum from a baby fridge. The whole place was a fridge. The electric heater barely touched the cold.

'You're living in here?' Tess asked, flabbergasted.

'Mum won't let me back in the house.'

'Are you kidding me?'

'She doesn't believe I've quit all that... She won't let it go, man. It's doing my head in.'

'*Have* you quit, though?'

'Yes, I swear it. You know I have.' He glanced down at the table. There was a copy of *Waiting for Godot* sitting on top of a pile of play scripts. 'I've been getting back into my acting.'

Tess glared at the huge Georgian house across the lawn. 'It seems a bit mean to keep punishing you like this.'

'She doesn't know what she's doing, she's so drunk most of the time.' He circled his temple with his finger, then lit a cigarette and blew smoke out, leaning back into the leather sofa, pulling his hood over his beanie and zipping his jacket right up. His eyelashes were curled back from his blue eyes. 'School's good these days, though. Banging central heating.' He grinned, but Tess and Hal didn't smile back.

'You told me Logan and his mate had been round, hassling you and your mum,' Hal said.

'Not Logan.'

'Who then?' Tess asked.

'Logan didn't do this to me.' He pointed at his scar. 'Hundred per cent. It was Ralph and some older guy I didn't know. Logan's fucking scared of those nutcases.' He visibly shuddered.

'What's this?' Hal asked, kicking at a second rolled-up sleeping bag.

'A spare.'

'Why do you need a spare?'

'You try sleeping in here. You need the layers.' The look he gave Tess broke her heart. His blue eyes were as defenceless as a baby's.

Hal pulled out his vape, took a hit and eyed Rory from a dark corner.

Tess picked up a copy of a Chekhov play. 'I went on a school trip to see this once.'

'I want to go up to London to see it,' Rory said.

'We should plan it, the three of us,' she said.

He jumped over the sofa and threw his arm around her. 'You still care about me, don't you, Tessie?' he said. Close up, he smelt bad.

She felt heady. She was glad she'd come over. He needed them.

# FIFTY-FIVE

William

Even though it was February, William and Amy were sitting on the bench in the garden dressed in pyjamas and coats. They were enjoying an early-morning cup of black coffee and a chat in the winter sun. William thought how pretty she looked with her red bobble hat pulled down over her forehead and her hair springing out either side of her rosy cheeks. She had slowly begun to thaw out over the weeks since their row about Sophie. He had been relieved she hadn't brought up the sleepsuit and the photograph again.

'Aren't we lucky to be able to look at that view every day?' he said, wanting to remind her of what they were working towards.

'Hmm, yes,' she agreed. There had been a sense that he was on probation, that she was still deciding, still unsure that this was what she wanted.

'Oh! Hang on two secs,' William said, waving his vibrating phone at her. 'It's Sophie.' Amy crossed her fingers at him.

They'd been waiting to hear about their latest offer on the house, impatient to know if she'd reconsidered.

William found privacy in his office. 'Hi. How's it going?' he asked neutrally, mentally crossing all his fingers and toes.

Cutting straight to the point, without so much as a hello, she said, 'You were ever so rude leaving my flat like that.'

He ignored this. 'You got my email?'

Her momentary hesitation felt like a lifetime. 'I wanted to run something past you.'

'Go on,' he said, his heart pounding with nervous excitement.

'I thought we'd hold a little naming ceremony at the house. After you've got your wedding out of the way, of course. I've already talked to Avril about it, and she thinks that's a very Catholic thing to do.'

Her words were a punch to the side of his head. 'There's nothing Catholic about it,' he said, furious with disappointment.

'Not really my main point, William.'

He kicked at the chair leg. 'Fine.'

'Fine about a naming ceremony?'

'Yes. Okay,' He wanted to get her off the phone.

'You sound odd. Are you upset?'

'I'm not upset.' He swept everything off his desk with one furious swipe. How was he ever going to get her out of his life?

'You're being rather chilly with me.'

'I'm not really the type to over-emote, Sophie. Did you expect me to fall about the place wailing and tearing at my clothes?'

'Can we sort out a date then?'

Through a tight jaw, he seethed, 'When? Amy lives here, remember.'

'She goes out occasionally, I imagine?'

'I can't think about this right now.'

'Okay. Fine. I'll send you some dates by email instead. But

we must brainstorm some name ideas. Nothing dreadful like Tarquin or Humphrey, okay?'

Tarquin? Humphrey? James? John? Jesus Christ? Any name was too generic for his son. No name was good enough.

But the moment for rebuke had passed.

'Okay, I'll have a think,' he said, swallowing. 'Have you had a chance to reconsider my offer, though?'

'Not yet,' she said airily.

As he returned to Amy in the main house, he remembered what he'd said to her before Sophie had called. *Aren't we lucky...?* But now he thought, luck has nothing to do with it.

# FIFTY-SIX

## Amy

Amy wrapped herself in a big scarf and cranked up the heater in the car. It was March already, but it was freezing outside. She was finding it hard to imagine the season changing in time for their outdoor wedding in only six weeks.

The drive to Clymping was easy from Haslemere, only forty minutes down deserted B roads, cutting through spectacular countryside. She enjoyed the sense that she was distancing herself from Summerfield House, and was looking forward to reconnecting with Olivia. Although the children appeared to have straightened themselves out, she conceded that she had been preoccupied lately. The Sophie Sandeman-Gore issue had been getting into everything. William's negotiations with her were still unresolved. Sophie seemed to be using the house as a tool to manipulate him and keep him close, albeit in combat. He would brood about her vacillations, incensed that she could hint at accepting their offer one minute and then rescind it the next. Amy had chosen to believe his face-value assurances that Summerfield House was the only reason she was still in his life.

But she couldn't help suspecting there was more to it. The nightmares about baby Hal in the monogrammed sleepsuit continued, driving her quietly mad.

When Olivia had suggested a walk this morning, Amy had jumped at the idea. She hadn't seen Olivia much over recent months. On the one hand, it was as though the whole cash-drop experience had never happened, yet it had come between them. She had missed Olivia's company, wanted back in the loop. It seemed vital to keep abreast of what Rory was up to. All of them had a stake in him staying on the right side of the law. She wanted to prove to herself that they had kept their children safe by paying the dealers off. Perhaps she needed justification.

Amy was the first to arrive. There wasn't a breath of wind. The air was cold but heavy with salt, tasting medicinally healing on her tongue. The sky was icy blue and clear enough for her to spot the white wind turbines near the horizon. She sat on the open boot of the hatchback to change into the boots William had bought her. The smart red elastic on the sides should have made walking easier, but the leather at the heel had refused to soften. However much she enjoyed looking the part in them, she felt the pinch in her toes. She missed her silly pink wellies.

A car horn sounded, and she almost jumped out of her skin. Olivia's Mercedes G-Wagon was speeding towards her along the narrow lane. The side mirror scraped against the flint wall as she parked up. Her black patent Hunter wellies appeared out of the car door before the rest of her. She wore a cinched black puffer and a hot-pink beanie. Her blonde hair was straightened, her cheeks were iridescent, her tan as bottled and expensive as ever.

'Decaf flat white, isn't that right?' she said, thrusting a coffee cup at Amy. On closer inspection, her eyes were weighed down by two neat sacks, like she had been crying or drinking, or both, for weeks.

'My favourite,' Amy said. 'Thank you.'

Olivia's kindness served as a reminder of her many sides. It would be easy to brand her as the mother whose dysfunction had bred a son like Rory, but it would be reductive.

She let out her two Frenchies, who circled Hamish, sniffing his bum and barking at him hoarsely. Then they all trudged left up the pebble incline, passing the unsightly sea defences towards the tumbledown wooden groynes in the distance. The sea was flat and aqua green, which complemented the stunning shock of yellow rapeseed in the adjacent field. Amy took in a lungful of sea air and forgot about the blister forming on her heel. Olivia had been right when she'd suggested they both needed a beach walk to blow the cobwebs out.

'Tell me about the wedding plans. You've been shutting me out,' Olivia said, waving a leather-mittened hand in the air.

Amy stared intently at the steam escaping in thin wisps through her coffee lid. 'Nothing much to tell, really.'

Olivia gave her a sideways glance. 'Trouble in paradise?'

'No, no. It's all good.'

Amy couldn't tell her that she feared Sophie would pull the plug on the whole damn wedding. In fact, she had been worried enough to secretly check cancellation policies with Faye and the caterers and the florist.

'Last-minute nerves are normal,' Olivia said, nudging her.

'Everything's fine, honestly. It's so exciting. You know your idea of a floral archway at the altar – or whatever you call it when it's not in church? The florist showed me pictures of one she did recently. It's amazing. It was such a good idea of yours.'

'Flattery gets you everywhere.' Olivia winked. 'I won't go on prying. I get the hint.'

A desperate call of 'Come here! Come *here*!' sounded from a figure down by the water. A full-sized Dalmatian puppy came bounding up to Hamish, who rolled onto his back submissively. Margot and Mabel began snarling and barking at the larger dog.

'Margot! Mabel! Stop it!' Olivia scolded over the din, clipping them back onto their leads, waiting for the Dalmatian to respond to its owner. 'What were we saying?'

'Er, I've forgotten.' Amy gulped her coffee down too quickly and coughed some up. Steeling herself, she considered how best to bring up Rory, wishing to be delicate about it. Olivia would doubtlessly be for ever embarrassed about the money.

Olivia jumped in first. 'Tell me who's coming. I want a potted history of every single person on the guest list, please.' She slid a thumb under her hat to tidy away an escaped strand of hair.

Hamish shot off to sniff at a rotting fish. Reluctantly Amy did her best to describe her sister, Maggie, and her unconventional boyfriend, who had already booked their hotel stopover on the way down from Tweedbank. And her brother, Danny, and his family, who were flying over from Sydney. Their flights would be costly to cancel, she thought. 'Danny's wife wants to stay in a posh spa hotel with the kids, and I've sent loads of recommendations, but she's changed her mind about a zillion times. Thank God William's dad has made it simple for us. He's going to stay in London at the Garrick with William on the night before the wedding.'

All this was expert sidetracking.

Wearily, with her boots rubbing more than ever, she dutifully answered more questions about their wedding guests. It dawned on her that she was being cowardly, and now complicit, in avoiding the subject of Rory. Like the seagull dive-bombing into the waves nearby, she went in. 'So, how's Rory doing?' she croaked.

Olivia stopped walking and turned to her, dropping her voice despite being miles away from any other human. 'He absolutely swears he's done with all that stuff, and I believe him, I really do.'

Amy exhaled. 'I'm so glad. And he's happier in himself, do you think?'

'So much happier.'

Hamish started barking at a flock of small black and white birds pecking at the pebbles. They flew off in an arrow formation.

'Though he's taken to sleeping in the pool house – strange boy! Probably to get away from me,' Olivia said, snorting.

Amy sipped the cold dregs of her coffee. 'Oh. But you definitely don't think Logan's still—'

'No, no,' Olivia interrupted patronisingly, as though Amy was fussing. 'Definitely not. Ugh.'

'Great,' Amy replied vaguely.

'He's made up with Hal and Tessie, too, I've heard.'

'I didn't know that.' Amy was pained by the news. She had believed Hal and Tess when they'd said they were staying away. Their broken promise didn't bode well. For all Olivia's assurances that Rory had turned a corner, Amy had a bad feeling about it.

The blister on her heel had become raw skin by the time they reached the cars. She realised that her new boots would never fit right. No amount of walking in them would change that. She wanted to hurl them at the flint wall and leave them there.

She charged along the B roads in William's fast car. A nasty headache pounded at her skull, dissolving the benefits of her coastal walk. Familiar misgivings about this new life of hers were coming at her like randomly thrown pebbles. It seemed you could be anywhere in this world, whether it was a sunlounger in St Lucia or a bivvy on Everest, and you couldn't escape yourself. Your regrets were always there, waiting for you in your own head.

# FIFTY-SEVEN

Tess

'Maybe, yes, that's nice,' Tess said to her mum, who was scrolling through dresses before she left for her hen do. She couldn't concentrate on the thumbnail images. Rory was messaging her, hassling her to go over.

For a while now they had been meeting in the shag hut at school – not to shag, but to talk. It was safe there with him, boundaried. She felt less guilty about lying to her mum – technically they were within school hours. He had opened up about Olivia's alcoholism and had confided more stories about his father's violence. He planned to leave home as soon as he turned eighteen. The dream of going to RADA was back on the table. He had set his sights on working hard enough to get a place, and had started studying plays by Pinter and Beckett, often whipping the paperbacks out of his bag to read lines to her. The change in him was marked.

Hal had been seeing more of him again too, bringing him food and lending him cash. The fact that he needed money was a good sign. It meant he wasn't making it from dealing.

His messages kept appearing:

*U coming?*

*Why is hal airing me?*

*Where r u?*

*Tess?*

'This one?' her mum asked.

'Yeah, maybe.'

'More than the other one?'

'Not sure.'

'Tess, the wedding is only three weeks away, you have to choose,' her mum said, in that sighing, victim voice Tess hated. And then her angrier voice. 'Christ's sake! Who *is* that messaging you non-stop?'

'Sorry, it's Noushie. She wants to know what I'm wearing today.'

'I know how she feels!'

'Sorry, look, Mum, please don't worry, I'll find one. I like this pink one. But you've got to go, you're going to be late.'

'But you need to order it today or we won't have time to send it back.'

'Yes, yes, I will. Seriously, you go. I'll buy it and you can pay me back.'

More from Rory:

*Tess?*

*Come over now*

*Need to see you*

*Tess?*

*Tess*

*Tess*

*Stop airing me.*

*Tess???*

*Why r u not calling me back?*

'Sorry, let me just...' she said, picking up her phone, hiding the screen from her mum as she typed.

*Mum is still here coming over when she's gone*

'Ugh!' her mum cried, exasperated. 'Okay. I give up. Wear a Juicy tracksuit for all I care.' She stomped out.

When Tess heard the car crunch over the gravel, she hollered, 'Hal! Let's go!' She texted Rory, heart racing: *Coming.*

Hal leant on the door frame, watching her fix her hair in the mirror.

'Rory said we might head down to Portsmouth,' she said.

'Yeah, cool.'

'We can take the bikes.'

'In that skirt?'

She cocked her hip jauntily at him. 'Too short?'

'For Rory?'

'For biking, *idiot*.' She brushed past him and out of the bathroom and he followed her down the stairs.

'You obviously know he's still into you,' he said.

'Too bad. I'm not into him.'

She grabbed her North Face from the boot room. The weather had been changeable. Day-to-day the seasons had been switching from winter to spring and back again. April showers could show up in either. Today was spring-like, along with her mood. There was a sense that they were emerging from winter boredom into the more colourful, fun months of the year. Just like the daffodils, she was coming out. Or maybe even out-out, if she was lucky. If they caught the train to Portsmouth, they could have some beers on the beach and a paddle in the sea. There was sometimes a good crowd down there. The three of them could be together again like old times.

Outside the pool house there were stacks of old pizza boxes. Tess could smell weed through the double doors. Instinctively she looked over her shoulder at the main house. It loomed above them, oppressive and majestic. She imagined ladies in Empire-line dresses and ringlets taking turns across the terrace.

The blue tarpaulin at the kitchen window flapped and marred the image.

She could hear the dogs barking and hesitated before opening the pool house door. 'Shall we check on Margot and Mabel first?' she asked.

Before Hal could reply, one of the doors opened a crack, and to her horror, Logan's skinny form appeared in the gap. Shock moved through her like the sensation before throwing up. She wanted to run away.

His scowl turned into a sneering half-grin. 'Oh, it's you.' The way his eyes swivelled slowly to look at them suggested he was high. 'All right, Tess,' he said. 'Hal, bruv.' He offered his fist to Hal for a bump, but Hal didn't respond. He looked as blindsided by Logan's appearance as Tess was. Logan wiped sweat from the black fluff on his upper lip. Behind him, Rory was man-sprawling on the leather sofa, talking on his phone.

The air was acrid with drugs, body odour and lethargy. Dirty clothes were slung about. Disgusting mess everywhere. Old pizza boxes encrusted with ketchup. An empty mayonnaise bottle. Some mini scales. Cling film. A foil-wrapped pipe. A jar of instant coffee. The television from the house had been positioned between the two sofas. The CGI image of two men with machine guns was frozen on the screen.

Tess was still deciding what to do when Rory swooped in to encircle her waist. 'You look hot.' He snuffled into her ear. His sweat smelt sweet and sharp. She ducked from his kiss.

His phone rang and he answered. 'ACE... What you after?'

Her heart sank. She remembered him telling her that ACE was the name of the drug line.

'White or brown?... Yeah, three for two... All right, cool, see you on the bench in five.' He put his hood up. 'Stay here, yeah.

I'll be back. Just heading to the rec.' He disappeared across the lawn.

'Hal, let's go,' Tess said.

'One game?' Logan held the controller up.

Hal shook his head. 'Nah, it's okay. We're out of here.'

Logan grabbed his upper arm. There was a discernible flicker of pain. He wasn't giving Hal any choice in the matter. 'One game, bruv,' he repeated.

'Okay,' Hal said, glancing apologetically at Tess. She understood. Logan was frightening. Rage surged through her. They had trusted Rory, and now they were here in this vile place. When she thought back to his tortured confessions in the shag hut and how she had lapped it up, she felt the heat build in her cheeks.

Rory came back, out of breath, edgy. He sat down, panting, straightening the heavy silver chain around his neck. His right bicep had been marked with a new tattoo, which she hadn't noticed under his uniform at school. His head was freshly shaved into an aggressive skin fade. There was a greying edge to his white T-shirt and stains down his sweatpants.

'Want some?' He handed her a litre bottle half full of orange liquid. The thin plastic cracked and warped in his grip.

'What's in it?' she asked.

'Lucozade and lean.'

She made a face. 'No thanks.'

'Suit yourself.' He popped the cap off a bottle of Sol and offered it to her. She turned that down too, sat at the opposite end of the settee from him, perched on the arm, waiting for the game to finish, panicking, hoping Logan would let them go.

A text came through on Rory's phone. He got up and said something into Logan's ear. They turned the music up on the speaker. Tess looked over at Hal, suggesting wordlessly that it was their opportunity to leave. He nodded, but the mood in the room had changed.

Everything began happening quickly. There was a knock on the door. Logan held a flick knife behind his back as he approached it. A skinny kid no older than fourteen, with sparse black chin hair and stone-washed jeans, stepped across the threshold. An older girl, blonde, was glued to his side, showing off her tiny waist in low cut-off jeans. There were some hellos and then an exchange of something between palms. The pair didn't stay.

Tess gaped at Rory. Hal's eyes flicked up to hers, but they were unreadable.

She stood up and said firmly, 'No, sorry, we have to go now.'

'Okay, but wait,' Rory said. 'Come with me a sec, Tessie. Just one sec, that's all, I swear it.' He pulled her hand and guided her to the toilet. They both squeezed inside. She crossed her arms and glared. 'Tess,' he whispered urgently, 'don't make trouble with Logan, okay? Just stay for a bit. Please. If you go, Hal will go, and I need him to be here. I need you. Please. Just an hour or so.'

She was caught between fear for him and fear for herself. 'Why are you still seeing Logan? Seriously? Are you that dumb?' she hissed.

'He's only going to be here a few more weeks. That's all, I swear it.'

'He's *staying* here?'

'Just for a bit.'

'Does Hal know?'

'Don't tell him. Hal's been good to me, man. He brings shit into school for me. I've got no money. Every fucking penny is going to Logan and his olders.' He stabbed his forefinger aggressively towards the door.

'Jesus Christ, Rory.' Her throat closed.

'I know, I know.'

There was a bang on the door. It was Logan. 'Oi, lovebirds. We got a visitor.'

Rory's blue eyes sharpened with terror. 'Shit. He's here.'

'Who is?'

'Ralph. One of the olders. You met him at Summerfield House, remember?' He pulled her out of the bathroom.

Ralph's eyes were magnified by his Versace glasses as they snaked their way up her bare legs. Rory draped his arm over her shoulders, weighing her down with his belligerent fear. Hal was sitting very still on the settee.

Tess felt her leg muscles tighten. She knew it was now or never. They had to get out of there.

'We've gotta get back, haven't we, Hal?' she said, trying to keep the quiver from her voice.

'Yup,' Hal said, standing up.

This time Rory didn't object. He made a show of kissing her on the lips, which turned her stomach. 'Laters, babe,' he said, sounding like a total dick.

To get to the door, she had to pass by Ralph. He sucked his teeth and trailed his podgy white fingers up the back of her thigh, then before she had a chance to stop him, he had pushed them suddenly into her knickers. She twisted around and hissed, '*Don't. Please.*' Tears blurred everything. Her hands shook as she undid the latch on the door. Hal had been distracted by saying goodbye to Rory and would not have seen what had happened. He nudged her in the small of her back, urging her outside. Rescuing her too late.

'Seeing as you said *please*,' Ralph snorted after her. 'I'll come over to your place next time, yeah?'

Tess and Hal grabbed their bikes from the grass, wheeling them forward before they'd even swung their legs over the bars. As she pedalled, Tess was hurting where Ralph's fingers had pressed.

# FIFTY-EIGHT

Amy

Her friends were in a circle in the jacuzzi. Amy very much wanted them to get along with each other.

'The point comes when you have to let them go,' Olivia said loudly over the trundle of the bubbles, sipping from her plastic flute. She was wearing a pair of very strange blue-tinted sunglasses. Amy couldn't see her eyes properly.

'You think?' Joanna said. Her long dark hair was plaited into an expert French braid, accentuating her high forehead. Her cheeks had turned a sugary-sweet pink in the heat of the jacuzzi.

'Jo, you'll be making Luke macaroni cheese with a special crusty topping until he's fifty,' Pip teased, winking at her friend. 'Poor Eve, on the other hand, will be out on her ear by her eighteenth birthday.'

Jo chuckled. 'But Eve is more capable than Luke!' She was quite used to Pip's ribbing. Nobody else could get away with it. Somehow Pip was also getting away with the old-lady swimsuit she was wearing. Having left hers at home, she'd grabbed one from a local Tesco superstore at the last minute. It had a pointy padded chest and a lurid purple flower pattern, which, quite implausibly, complemented her fiery red hair.

Olivia adjusted her delicate gold chain so that the green pendant dangled into her cleavage. 'How old are yours again?'

Jo grinned proudly. 'Luke is Rory's age and Eve is ten.'

'Mine are eight, ten and sixteen,' Pip said. The absence of names was notable, Amy thought.

'Oh, still young.' Olivia nodded at Pip, cocking her head to the side. 'Do you have help?'

'Aside from the iPad, you mean?' Pip joked.

Olivia didn't smile. 'You're *so* good. I don't know what I would have done without help when Rory was that age. He was such a terror. We had our Filly until he was thirteen.'

Joanna looked puzzled. 'Filly?'

'Our Filipino. It didn't work out in the end. I'd agreed to pay for her son to come over from Manila and had started all the paperwork, but Toby changed his mind. Just like that.'

Marte said, 'I'm not being racist or anything, but I hear they're always wanting their relatives to come over. What you need is a couple. From Eastern Europe. It's the only way forward.'

Amy was horrified, wanted to die a thousand deaths. She couldn't even look at the shock she knew would be hanging from Pip and Jo's dropped jaws.

'Oh yes, a *couple*. Essential,' Pip said.

'What do you mean by a couple?' Jo asked.

'You know, a married couple. Ours are Piotr and Agata. They're Polish. She's the housekeeper and he's the gardener. But they're like family to us now. I don't know what I'd do without them. I think they worked for some other parents at our school before they came to us – Agata was mistreated, I heard. Do you remember the Huxleys, Olivia?'

Olivia nodded. 'They had that amazing *Grand Designs* house with the copper roof, didn't they? Didn't it burn down?'

'Hmm. Some kind of insurance fraud. Anyway, Piotr and Agata will literally turn their hand to anything. So hard-working. I'll never forget the time Agata had to deal with Oscar's worms when we were in London.' Marte snorted.

Nobody wanted to ask.

'Some teenagers never rebel,' Amy said quickly, trying to get the conversation back on track. Seeing her newer friends through the eyes of her old mates was an uncomfortable experience. Their faults were magnified. Either she'd become inured to their prejudices and privilege, or she'd been too forgiving of them. Trying to get through it for now, she began wittering. 'My brother's elder daughter didn't push boundaries at all. She was as good as gold all the way through. She and her mum just never fought.'

'According to whom?' Marte asked brusquely, flattening her white widow's peak into a high, dry ponytail.

'My sister-in-law,' Amy said. 'Abby, she's called.'

'Abby's a liar then,' Marte said.

'*Unimaginable* that a mum could enjoy looking after her own kids,' Pip said, shaking her head and emptying her glass.

'Ha!' Amy laughed nervously, keen to defuse the pop of open hostility between the two women. 'Honestly, some people are just made for motherhood.'

'And we're not, because we get help?' Marte said archly.

Pip opened her mouth, no doubt ready for another comeback, but Amy coughed and continued in a chivvying tone, 'Thank God we're all through the baby phase! There's this poor baby next door to us who cries all the time, and it reminds me of how hard it all was.'

'Which side?' Olivia asked. 'Not David and Lou. They have teens, don't they?'

'No, the family on the other side, in the bungalow.'

'The Martins bought that bungalow. But they've never had any children.'

'They haven't?'

'No. I know them quite well.'

Goosebumps ran up Amy's arms. 'You're sure?'

'One hundred per cent. She's at least sixty now anyway. I had a chat with her on the high street the other day.'

'Maybe they've got family staying or something,' she said vaguely. A flash of her recurring dream seared across her vision, dizzying her.

Olivia sighed. 'To be honest, I'd kill to rewind to the baby phase. Rory's current phase is challenging to say the least.'

Paula piped up. 'You think *you* lot have problems. Oscar's going through his *sex* phase.' She shrugged one shoulder and knocked back her champagne. They all spluttered. 'I'm serious.' She let out a restrained little giggle, as if to say, *C'est la vie*.

But Olivia continued on her jag. '*I'm* serious too, Paula. If Rory doesn't show some bloody respect and stop taking everything for granted, then he has to go.'

'Wow,' Pip murmured.

Amy hoped Olivia hadn't heard.

Paula frowned. 'What do you mean, hon? You want him to "go" in what way?'

'My son, my *darling* son, is taking the bloody piss again and I'm not having it,' Olivia explained.

Amy was alarmed to hear this. 'The last time we spoke,' she said cautiously, 'you thought he'd settled down a bit.' What had changed since their walk by the sea? Had Olivia faced up to facts about Rory? Or had Rory's antics escalated? She wanted to ask all these questions but knew she would have to be cautious in front of the others.

Olivia raised her blue sunglasses and stuck them on her head. 'I never know what he's *doing* in there.'

'In where?' Jo asked.

'The pool house.'

'Oh, of course, the pool house,' Pip said, cutting a fine line between banter and combat.

'But,' Olivia whispered, too drunk to notice, 'guess. What. I. Did?'

Uh-oh, Amy thought, here goes. What the hell has she done?

'I installed a CCTV camera. You know the ones? That connect to your phone?' From behind her, Olivia reached for her iPhone, which had been glued to her side all day. The rest of them had put theirs in their lockers, as per the rules. 'See?' She showed Amy the screen, where a grainy image of the double doors to the pool house was visible.

'And Rory doesn't know?' Amy asked, flabbergasted.

She chuckled. 'The installation guy hid it in the guttering.'

'The perfect spot for it, I always say,' Pip said. Amy kicked her under the bubbles.

'If I catch him up to no good, he's OUT,' Olivia said, raising her voice, flinging her arm wide and pointing outside. A spray of water hit Amy's face. There was a nervous titter from Marte.

'But what do you think he's up to in there, sweetie?' Paula asked.

Olivia put her glasses back over her swimming eyes. 'Never you mind.'

'Have you seen anything that looks wrong?' Amy asked.

'A few people coming and going,' Olivia offered enigmatically.

Amy wanted to ask if Logan had been coming and going but knew she couldn't. 'Anyone you're worried about?'

'Ha! I saw your two today. Let me rewind it a bit.'

'You saw Tess and Hal? Today? At your place?'

'Yes. Look at them. So lovely that the three of them are friends again.'

There, unmistakably caught on camera, was footage of Tess

and Hal emerging from the pool house. Although the images weren't sharp enough to pick out their expressions, Amy could interpret that they were in a rush to leave. There was something wrong, it was plain to her. Tess's body language wasn't right. She felt the world go still. 'When was that?' she asked urgently.

'Umm. A couple of hours or so ago?' Olivia checked. 'It says here 15.02.'

'Sorry, I've just got to make a call.' Without caring how it might look to the others, Amy shot out of the jacuzzi and ran to her locker to find her phone.

# FIFTY-NINE

William

'Hi, William. It's me,' Amy said in hushed tones.

'Hi, darling. Everything okay?'

'Are the kids there? They're not answering their phones!'

William looked over at Tess and Hal, who were stretched out in front of the telly, gripped by an old Denzel Washington thriller he'd recommended. They each had a huge bowl of popcorn on their lap. Hal threw a piece of popcorn into Hamish's mouth.

'Tess? Hal?' he asked them, holding out the phone. 'Mum-stroke-Amy wants to know you're here.'

They grunted a mixture of 'Yeah, why?' and 'Hi, Mum.'

He put the phone back to his ear. 'Looks like they're here.'

'Thank God!' Amy cried.

'Why, what's up?' he asked her. 'Wait, let me go outside.'

He left the kids in the den and stepped into the garden through the French windows in the kitchen. The grass was damp through his socks. The evening sun was lost to the horizon, leaving a pretty glow in the sky. While he listened to Amy's frantic version of what he already knew, he admired the South Downs, digging his heels into the ground. He was determined to look at that view from this exact vantage point until his dying day.

'It's okay. I know they snuck over to Rory's. They didn't mention anything about the camera thingy, though.'

'How did you find out?'

'They were in a strange mood when they got home, and I smelt a rat and harangued them until they confessed. I was like the Gestapo.'

She wanted full details.

'Okay, so Tess ran upstairs in tears, poor thing. She was in a terrible state, and Hal and I followed her up. I sat on the bed and she just came out with it. Basically, to cut a long story short, they've been meeting up with Rory quite a bit recently, I'm afraid. Tess believed he wanted to change, but today they found out he's still kicking about with Logan.'

'Wow. I had no idea. Butter wouldn't bloody melt.'

'I know, and she was very sheepish about lying to you. But I don't think we need to worry about it now. They were both spooked. Tess said she never wanted to see him again. Which is reassuring, don't you think?'

'Hmm. Yes.'

'Please don't worry,' he said. 'They're fine.' They had to be fine. His decision to give Rory the money had to be fine. 'How's it going there?'

Amy sighed. 'Oh, you know, okay, I guess. Olivia is drinking too much.'

'Is it any wonder Rory behaves like he does?'

'No, it really isn't,' she said, and then, 'I just want to come home.'

'No, no. We're all fine.'

'I can't tell you how relieved I am about that.'

'Now, you go and enjoy yourself.'

'Are you sure?'

'Amy, it's your hen do! Let your hair down. I've got this.'

'Okay.' There was a pause. 'By the way, the Martins in the bungalow next door don't have a baby.'

'Why did you think they had?'

'I hear it crying all the time.'

His heart stopped beating. He cleared his throat. 'I never hear it.'

'It must be some kind of sound travelling weirdly from another house or something.'

'That does happen,' he said, feeling sick. 'Now go and have some champagne.'

'I need it. Love you,' she said.

'Love you too.'

When he went into the den to watch the rest of the film, Hal looked up at him. In that split second, as William held his son's gaze, his firstborn's soul appeared to him, blinking back from Hal's face. The same almond-shaped eyes, the same long fan of lashes, the same devotion, crystal clear, as though his baby were nestled in his arms now. The dawning triggered a roil of grief almost too painful to take. Hal had his dead brother's eyes. How had William not been able to see it until now?

# SIXTY

## Hal

Leaning on his elbow, Hal watched Tess as she stirred. The duvet shifted, revealing her bra. Her lovely arms were flung above her head and her full mouth muttered something unintelligible. Hamish was stretched out alongside her. He was snoring, lying on his back, legs akimbo, showing the world his hairy balls.

The two of them were a pair. Defenceless. Trusting.

Hal scratched Hamish's tummy before nudging him to the bottom of the bed so that he could pull the duvet up over Tess. Her mussed dark fringe fell away from her forehead. Her shoulders were hunched cosily around her ears. She was lovely.

By falling asleep in their underwear in his bed with her wrapped in his arms, they had perhaps overstepped. With any other scantily clad beautiful girl, he would have been stirred to try more on, but he wouldn't have dreamed of it with Tess. He had sensed that she had been exceptionally vulnerable last night.

Rory had let them down. He was in too deep himself to be a

decent friend to them. It shouldn't have shocked Hal, but it did. Fatally so. On a personal level, he could handle Rory's bad treatment, having endured years of it. The pattern was familiar: they fought and made up, fought and made up, fought and… and then Hal forgave. Last night, however, Rory had taken it too far, pushed the limits of what was okay. He had tricked Hal into believing they were going to hang out as a threesome, just like old times, when in truth he had only wanted to use them as a buffer. The atmosphere had been thick with menace. Ralph and Logan had been intimidating. Putting Tess in danger with scum like that to protect himself had been out of order. The bad taste of it was still in Hal's mouth this morning.

He should have said all this to Rory's face last night. For Tess's sake, if not his own. But he hadn't had the chance. Given a few more minutes, he hoped he might have been the one to stand up. He liked to think so. His father believed he was upstanding enough to be his best man at his wedding in two weeks' time.

All the same, if he was honest with himself, he knew he would've sat there at Rory's like a dick all night and dug them deeper into the shit. For Hal, passivity, low-profiling it, always seemed safer. It made him as bad as Rory. That was the problem. He and Rory were peas in a pod. Two morally bankrupt kids, one of whom was simply more honest about it than the other.

# SIXTY-ONE

Amy

They were hauling the golden chairs out into the bluebell wood. The kids and Olivia had helped. It was a long procession of laughter and excitement, hindered only by Hamish's excited zigzagging across their path. The sun had come out for them. Lisa, the florist, had used ribbon to tie the cascades of wildflower bouquets to the trees at the edge of the clearing.

Amy, in her curlers and dressing gown, felt her nerves thrumming through her. The carpet of blue was vivid in the dappled light. Later, she would step into this scene as the bride. With the snap of twigs under her feet and the rustle of animals in the undergrowth and the call of birds announcing their role in the upcoming nuptials, she felt cocooned. Her doubts receded. The bricks and mortar of Summerfield House itself faded into the background. This natural world was as much hers as it was anyone's. While Sophie Sandeman-Gore might legally be able to claim ownership of its boundaries, no landowner alive would have jurisdiction over this wild patch of countryside, or over Amy's bliss today.

She thought of poor William at the Garrick with his dad. His sense of duty towards him and his need to stick to tradition was honourable, but Amy wished he had stayed at Summerfield House. In bed the previous morning, as they'd slotted together under the sheets and talked about his trip to London, his whole body had tensed up. It had been like spooning with an actual spoon. When he got out of bed to pack, he moved with an almost arthritic stiffness. The dread seemed to have attacked his joints.

Tess's hand slipped into hers. 'This is magical, Mum.'

Feeling a hiccup of love, Amy turned to her daughter and held her face. 'Thank you, sweetheart. I wouldn't have been able to do it without you.'

'Love you. Today's going to be perfect,' Tess said. The delicate strap of her cami fell off her shoulder. When Amy readjusted it, she was reminded of Tess pushing up those long-gone purple spectacles.

How her daughter had been transformed from that geeky, feisty teen. Gone were the glasses, the straggly hair and the bobbly M&S Christmas jammies she'd worn all year round. Her skin was bronzed with expensive tanning product; her dark fringe was blunt and well cut and glossy; her long eyelashes were permanently curled upwards around her big brown eyes. Everything about her was smoothed out, groomed, flawless, like a new doll fresh out of the box. Even her demeanour, how she talked and smiled, was well managed. Gone was the rampant reading for fun, the let-it-all-out moonwalks in her socks, the loony swear-word alternatives. She could be regularly overheard dropping the F-bomb with her friends; only moved her body to music when she went on a run to get fit; only read books to improve her English lit grades.

With a small shiver, Amy wondered if these changes were part of growing up, of becoming a woman, or whether they were too manufactured, too controlled. Having money made it easy to make the outside perfect, effortlessly hiding the disharmony inside, and achieving and excelling at smothering all sorts of insecurities.

Tess had been frighteningly efficient on the wedding front. Terrifyingly so. She'd even printed out a 'One Week To Go' tick-list from the internet, stuck it on the fridge and galvanised Amy every morning with little reminders. *Have you confirmed final details with the caterers, Mum? Have you paid Faye the full amount yet? Have you written your vows for the registrar? What time are we meeting Uncle Danny and Auntie Abby at the Park House Hotel? Have you reminded William to collect the suits? Have you booked the taxis to take everyone home?* Et cetera, et cetera, et cetera.

A little scared of her, Amy had obeyed her and completed her tasks. Whenever she could, she'd hurry out the back door with her boots on and Hamish by her side to explore the expanse of countryside. She'd got into the habit of rambling for miles, getting lost, taking wrong turns, finding her way back, smiling inside. It was all she wanted to do with her time. Everything else beyond this unruly solitude was an intrusion. The secret routes were off the beaten tracks and into the wilds, where she might not see another human for hours. The heathland often reminded her of Scotland. She couldn't believe that she and William were going to be up there together tomorrow.

'Which room has the best light for Auntie Maggie, d'you think?' Tess asked now.

Maggie was due to arrive any minute. She had offered to do Amy's hair and make-up as a wedding gift, which Amy had been delighted about.

'Not sure. She'll tell us.'

As they wove back through the woods to the house, Hamish charged ahead barking, having heard visitors before his humans had.

'That must be them now.' Amy was apprehensive about the

reception she'd get from her sister and her partner, Damian. During the pandemic, her relationship with Maggie had been limited to FaceTime. Meeting William had swallowed her time further. An emotional distance she'd never imagined possible had come between them, and she'd felt it more than ever over the last few video calls.

Damian's grey van skidded around the circular drive. The wheels were raised, and the tinted windows and chrome VW sign were wrapped in matt black. The exhaust noise echoed across Blackdown. Damian jumped down from the passenger seat almost before the engine was off and enveloped Amy in his arms, bending his tattooed knees to give her a proper hug. 'All right, mate,' he said, adding a tighter squeeze.

'So good to see you,' she said, feeling choked up. Before he let go, she sucked in his smell of engine oil and aftershave. Having raced motocross bikes in his youth, he was now a bike mechanic with an unconventional lifestyle. He loved his freedom and his tinkering in the garage. He picked up work where he could and found jobs to pay the bills rather than to own bigger and better things.

'Sis!' Maggie leapt down from the heights of the van with an excited little jump. She had tonged her blue hair and had a nose stud Amy hadn't seen before. A tear wobbled down Amy's cheek. Maggie wiped it away and said in her soft, scuffed Liverpudlian tones, 'I've brought a truck-load of make-up, but you don't need a scrap. You look bloody gorgeous, sis.'

'It's been too long.' These were Amy's people, and she had neglected them. She was self-conscious and embarrassed by the splendour of Summerfield House, but it appeared her sister hadn't noticed or didn't care.

Maggie and Damian spotted Tess and went straight in with the hugs. 'Look at you!' Maggie cried. 'All growed up!'

Introductions were made to Hal and Olivia.

Olivia hugged Maggie as though she were her own sister. 'I've heard so much about you!' she said.

'And I've heard so much about you too!' Maggie replied, which wasn't true. Oddly, whenever they spoke, Amy had not wanted to bring Olivia up.

Olivia blinked slowly. 'Okay then, I promised I'd help Faye with the cake table. See you in a bit. *So* lovely to meet you. Your hair is so cool, by the way.'

When she had gone, Maggie asked, with a half-cocked smile, 'Was she messin'?'

'No, she means it, honest,' Amy said, her Northern accent slipping back in. 'You'll get used to her, won't she, Tess?'

'Oh yes, absolutely you will!' Tess said. 'She's just—' Her phone rang in her hand and she looked at it, frowned, pressed ignore. It went again immediately. 'Sorry about this.' She silenced it, but it kept vibrating.

'Go on, get it, babe! He sounds keen!' Maggie laughed, winking at Amy.

'Sorry. I'm so sorry. Maybe I should,' Tess said, stepping away to answer it. Hal flopped his hair and loped after her.

'She sounds like the Queen!' Maggie whispered, nudging Amy.

Amy knew what she meant. Tess's accent had changed. 'I guess she needed to fit in.'

'I don't blame her. Look at this place.' Maggie whistled.

'Hmm, we're so lucky,' Amy said cryptically, eyeing suspiciously the house she had once gazed upon in wonder.

'So how are *you* fitting in here, sis?' Maggie asked.

Amy paused before she answered. 'I think I'll feel better when we're actually married.'

'Yeah, too right. Put a bloody ring on it. Come on, I want to see your dress.'

The dress! It had been the first thing Amy had seen as she'd opened her eyes this morning, hanging from the door of the very wardrobe that had once secreted those disturbing mementos from Sophie Sandeman-Gore's past. The heirloom seemed to have its clutches on Amy's wedding dress for now, but not for long. As soon as they owned this house – which Sophie had promised would happen after the wedding – Sophie's furniture was going. Every single piece of her would be removed. Amy didn't care what William thought of that.

# SIXTY-TWO

Hal

Hal was proud to be in his suit and standing by the ribboned tree at the entrance to the field. Dutifully he bent to greet the guests as they pulled up in their cars. He advised them on where to park and then asked them to follow the ribbons through the woods to the house on foot.

'Hal! How did you get so tall?' This was from the wife of an old friend of his dad's, whose name Hal couldn't remember.

His phone vibrated in his pocket. Rory had been ringing on a loop, with only a few minutes' breather between each call. Hal checked the caller ID. Amy, Olivia and Tess needed him to be in contact at all times to ensure the day ran smoothly. It rang out again. He gritted his teeth, would not be dragged into this. Rory only had himself to blame for where he was at. His dad and Amy's wedding day was Hal's sole focus today.

'So good of you to come.' He smiled at more guests. 'Just up there would be great.'

A black Mercedes pulled up next, and a woman wearing strange lace gloves pressed her window down. She hesitated, ignoring where he was ushering her. A queue of cars was building behind her. She ran her pale eyes slowly and carefully over his face, locked onto his gaze. There was a strong smell of cigarettes and stale perfume through the open window. When her red lips pulled back into a smile, her teeth were a little crooked, but somehow it didn't spoil her arresting beauty. The quirk perhaps even added to it.

'Are you Hal?' she asked him finally in a husky voice.

'Yes. Hello.'

'You have your brother's eyes,' she breathed.

He furrowed his brow. 'Sorry, I don't have a brother,' he returned politely.

'My mistake.' Absent-mindedly she fingered the veil of an elegant black hat that lay on the passenger seat next to a packet of cigarettes. 'I'm an old school friend of your father's.' Hal thought he detected tears glistening in the rim of one eye. As she drove off, he felt the hairs rise on the back of his neck. What a strange woman, he thought.

His phone vibrated. This time he answered it. 'Rory. For fuck's sake,' he hissed, putting on a smile for the wedding guests and continuing to wave them through. 'Stop fucking calling.'

'Mate, Hal, you have to believe me this time. I'm gonna get *shanked*. I'm gonna die. They're coming for me.' Rory was barely audible, hoarse, tearful perhaps, but gabbling as though he didn't have time to draw breath. 'Don't hang up. Hear me out. Ralph and Logan have turned up at Oak Hills with machetes. They've got into the house and are going through all Mum's jewellery and crap, turning over the whole fucking place, slashing the curtains and sofas. Ralph says if I don't pay up, he'll kill me. And he will. I swear it. He will fucking do it. For real, Hal. This isn't a game.'

Hal's teeth started to chatter. Having seen the cold, hateful stare behind Ralph's bottle-thick eyewear, he believed he was capable of it. But he didn't know what he could do for Rory. 'You have to call the police,' he said shakily.

'You know I can't do that! I need to get away from here, bro. Can I hide at Summerfield House?'

'You are not going to ruin Dad's day. Not a fucking chance.' Even as he said it, Hal felt guilty. Could he be this cold?

'Nobody will ever find out. I could hide in the outbuildings. Remember when we used to play dead soldiers there? I'll keep quiet, I swear. Make sure I'm not seen.'

'No, Rory. Not this time. I'm sorry,' Hal said. As he hung up, his palms were slick with sweat.

When the next call came in, he groaned and checked his screen. He was relieved to see Tess's name flash up.

'Your dad and Grandpa Ru are here!' she said excitedly.

'Who's going to stand in for me here?'

'I'm coming to take over. Pip's late and keeps calling for directions, but I said I'd wait for her there. There can't be many more to come, can there? The tent's full already, and Olivia said she's going to start rounding them up soon and get them seated.'

He checked the time on his phone and his heart raced forward a few beats. 'Jesus. It's almost time.'

'I know! Eeek! You boys need to take your positions under the flower arch soonish.'

'Yup. Okay. Coming.'

He hung up. His conversation with Rory ran through his mind as he hurried past the ambling guests. They were dressed in bright colours and hats. He might check the outbuildings later. He knew Rory well enough to know he would ignore his pleas to stay away. It would be easy to hate him for it, but he couldn't. After all, Summerfield House was Rory's home from home. It had been somewhere to find respite; a haven from everything bad in his life.

He saw his father and Grandpa Ru shuffling about together awkwardly on the gravel outside the front door. As he approached them, their faces lit up nervously. Hamish jumped up, leaving dusty paw prints and blond fur on his lapels.

'Don't muddy the threads, Hamish,' he said, giving the dog a scratch in his favourite spot.

Instead of saying hello or telling him how much he'd grown or how he'd missed him, Grandpa Ru went straight in with 'Want some Dutch courage, my boy?' He shook Hal's left hand while shoving a silver flask into his other. Hal had never needed booze more. 'That'll put hairs on your chest,' Grandpa said, snorting through his beaky, broken-veined nose and grinning wickedly. 'And this is for later,' he added, slipping a cellophane-wrapped cigar into Hal's pocket with a shaky hand.

'Thanks,' Hal said, taking a sip, and then another, and another, until his dad wrestled the flask out of his hand.

'That's quite enough, young man.' William chortled before taking some himself. Then he brought out the little black ring box. He fiddled with it for a moment before thrusting it at Hal. 'I'm trusting you with this now, Hal. All my happiness is in your hands,' he said, squeezing his left shoulder.

Grandpa Ru nodded seriously, as though Hal had become the grandson he had always wanted. Within this circle of men, Hal belonged. Unlike Rory, he was lucky to have them love him, keep him on the straight and narrow, forgive him. The weight of his dad's paternal trust rested proudly on his shoulders. These two men were his kin, and he would do everything he could to honour that today.

Having pocketed the ring box, he patted Hamish's flank, feeling bashful. But the dog's ears pricked up suddenly and he dashed off at full pelt in the general direction of the outbuildings. Hal guessed whose scent he'd picked up on, and secretly hoped he would guard him.

# SIXTY-THREE

Tess

The air was cool on Tess's back. The ruching of material at the base of her spine was so low the elastic of her underwear would sometimes show. She quickly adjusted the halter neck, redoing the bow, enjoying the sensation of the satin ties slipping about on her skin.

'We're here!' Pip cried through the car window. 'Only a few wrong turns. But if you *do* insist on living in the back of bloody beyond...' She pulled on the handbrake and jumped out of the car, encircling Tess in a hug. 'You look too bloody beautiful in that slip of a dress. You remind me of what an old frump I am!'

Tess laughed joyfully, flattered by Pip, who was her favourite of her mum's friends. 'Don't be silly, Pip! You look amazing.' And she did. She was like a flame in her red suit. 'You've got to hurry, though. Make sure Mum can see you near the front, or she'll panic.'

She watched her park up, get out and brush her husband's crumpled suit down with a hairbrush. Then they charged off through the woods hand in hand.

Held back by the last-minute stragglers, Tess began to get restive, dying to head back to her mum. Her heart sank when a black hatchback sped into the field, revving over the uneven ground. Vape smoke poured out of one of its windows. She knew the guest list back to front and couldn't think who this might be. The car came to a stop diagonally across two other cars. The engine continued to purr. Had they taken a wrong turn? She lifted her hem and made her way over the bumpy ground to investigate, tiptoeing so that her kitten heels didn't sink into the soil. A blue flower from her hair fell at her feet. She picked it up and wove it back into place in the ribbon of her tiara.

As soon as she got close enough to see who was in the car, her guts cramped up with fear. The driver's-side door opened, and without a second's thought, she turned and ran. She dropped her phone, scrabbled for it. It slowed her down, as did her shoes. She kicked them off and fled in bare feet, hardly noticing the sharpness of the ground cutting into her soles. She tried to use her phone, but her hands were shaking hard as she scrolled for Hal's number. Her ankle twisted on the rocky path and her heaving breath burned her windpipe. As she tore past the second ribbon in the woods, she felt a hard forearm snake around her waist, bending her in the middle, winding her, stopping her feet from taking her anywhere. He yanked the phone from her hand. She thrashed about, scratching and twisting, but his strength was brutish and unyielding.

Her ear-splitting screams of terror would not be heard. They were too far from the house. By the time he had bundled her into the car and tied her hands, she had given up and flopped on her side in the back seat. Her cheek was soon soaked in a patch of her own tears.

# SIXTY-FOUR

Amy

Brides were meant to be late. It was tradition, and William loved tradition. Either way, Amy refused to get into her dress without Tess there. It was now half past four, half an hour after the ceremony had been scheduled to begin. It had been an hour since Tess had dashed off to greet Pip. Amy had called and texted her repeatedly over the last fifteen minutes, but there had been radio silence. She sat down, stood up, paced, stood still, checked her phone, tried calling again, nervously sipping her way through too much champagne.

Convinced there would be a logical explanation for Tess's lateness, she came up with some scenarios. There'd been a mishap she'd not wanted Amy to know about – Hamish had gobbled the wedding cake, Hal had lost the ring, one of the guests had fainted. There were all sorts of things that could have gone wrong.

A message arrived from Olivia:

*Everything okay? Need any help? X*

*All good. Just waiting for Tess xxx*

It seemed Olivia – who had been instrumental in the smooth running of the day so far – wasn't aware of any calamity. This should have been a good thing. But if everything was in order logistically, where the hell was Tess?

Amy redid her dressing gown tie and swallowed more champagne. A glass stood ready for Tess. On tiptoes, she peered out of the high window. She could see into the tent in the back garden where the guests had been drinking their two allocated glasses of bubbly before being herded down to the bluebell wood.

It was a modern, oat-coloured undulating tent without sides, set back from the kitchen windows. A local farmer – the one who had kindly lent them the field for parking – had also dropped off four hay bales for the guests to sit on. Olivia had brought some cushions and throws to scatter about. Now there were only two little boys in bow ties and knee-length blue shorts left. She watched and smiled as they scampered about, launching themselves off the bales. A forgotten scarf lay on a table. Teenage waitresses were collecting glasses. Other than that, the space was empty.

By now, the guests would be shuffling about on their gilt chairs in the woods, craning their necks behind them, waiting to see her approach. The sun was low. Its soupy glow would be setting the bluebells on fire. William would be standing by the magnificent floral archway up front, perhaps mumbling funny, nervy asides to Hal. They had looked so handsome in their suits. She imagined him scratching his eyebrow, stealing glances at his wristwatch, squinting into the trees, hoping to catch his first glimpse of her through the branches. She longed to be holding his gaze as she walked towards him and into their future together. But her excitement was beginning to tip into a knee-jiggling concern about Tess's whereabouts.

Reminders of what had gone on with Rory filtered into her thoughts. What if he had shown up to spite them and had distracted Tess, lured her away from her duties with his hypnotic blue eyes? The mere idea of him being anywhere near her on a day like today was enough to prompt action.

She began shoving on her jeans, feeling a little woozy after all the champagne. There was a knock on the door and her heart soared. 'Tess!' she cried, hopping over on one leg. 'Oh. Pip. Jo.' Crushing disappointment was mixed with gratitude for her friends' timely arrival.

'We just thought we'd check on you. Is everything okay?' Jo asked gently. Her long dark hair was curled and the sky-blue fascinator brought out her eyes.

But Pip, in red, said, 'William looks like he's got a poker up his arse, love, and the guests are getting hangry. What's the hold-up?'

'Thank God you're here,' she said, and went on to explain.

# SIXTY-FIVE

William

The guests in front of William had become a colourful blurry blob. While he waited for Amy to appear through the thicket of trees, he caught the eye of so-and-so or waved at such-and-such. Mostly his hands were clasped behind his back and his smile was fixed. He tried to focus on enjoying the string quartet that was playing, but his impatience for her to arrive overwhelmed him.

The celebrant, an older woman with a comfortable face, looked at her watch. William fingered the ring box Hal had slipped into his pocket before nipping off for a quick pee in the bushes. He had joked that he didn't trust himself to keep it safe. Fifteen minutes had passed since then. Somehow William had failed to notice the time fly by. His throat constricted. He felt instantly furious, thinking how depressingly predictable it would be of Hal to disappear at the crucial moment.

He reassured the celebrant, 'He'll be back any minute now.'

'It's lucky she's a little late,' she said in a soothing voice. It was the first out-loud mention of the real problem here, and

William felt the slap of it. The time read 4.45. Amy was never, ever late. What could possibly have held her up?

He and Maggie locked gazes. Doubt flickered in her eyes. Hamish yelped. Pip and Jo's empty seats acted as portents. He felt the burn of humiliation. Everyone would be concerned for him. Everyone would be thinking what he was thinking: she was having last-minute doubts; she'd seen through him; he wasn't worthy; he wasn't good enough for her; he was worse than average, a total nobody; who could blame her?

A few minutes later, he saw a latecomer appear through the trees and take her place in the back row. She was rangier than most and sported white lace gloves and a pillbox hat with a thick veil, like a fifties film star at a funeral. None of her features were clear. The rows of guests between them obscured a better view of her. But it didn't take long for him to twig. The way she moved gave her away: how she tilted her head to the side and nervously fiddled with one of her pearl earrings. His brain refused to catch up with what he saw. He preferred to believe his eyes were playing tricks on him. Then she pulled up her veil to reveal her high cheekbones, her dry red lips, her pale eyes. Her identity was undeniable. And his insides collapsed.

# SIXTY-SIX

Amy

'Oh gosh, it's stuffy in here,' Olivia said, opening the bedroom window.

She wore a floor-length floral dress with floppy bows tied to the shoulders. Gold flecks in the material caught the light. Her golden hair and skin were glowing. Despite everything Amy knew about her, she felt jealous of her. A feeling she wasn't proud of. Her clean, shiny beauty hid a multitude of sins and was utterly impossible to compete with, even as the bride.

Amy grabbed her jeans from the bed again. 'Pip and Jo have gone looking for her. They wouldn't let me go myself, but I think I should.'

'There's no point, sweetheart.'

'Why?'

'The thing is, Hal's gone AWOL too.' Olivia looked down at her phone. 'I collared Jo's husband, knowing he's a whizz with tech, and we did some detective work with those location apps on their phones.'

'And?'

'And I'm afraid we saw her little avatar hovering at home.'

'Here?'

'Sorry, no, my home.'

'Oak Hills?'

'Yes.'

'With Rory? Now?'

'I'm afraid Rory finally admitted it. He said she was very upset but safe, and not to worry.'

'But that doesn't make sense! She—' Amy broke off. 'What about Hal?'

'Yes, he's there too. I'm so sorry, Amy.'

'But she said... I don't get it... Unless she...' Unless she hadn't been telling her the truth. Had Amy's maternal bias blinded her? Was she as much in denial about Tess as Olivia had been about Rory? Had Tess been harbouring conflicting feelings all along? 'But why is she there?'

'I got the impression that the boys were consoling her, that she needed a bit of time to pull herself together.' Olivia tugged at her earring and glanced up into the corner of the room. 'I think she's been struggling with the idea of you remarrying.'

Amy was appalled. 'No!'

'I don't think she's been as honest with you as you think.' Olivia was oozing with smugness: the ultimate payback for all the times Amy had judged her for buying into Rory's lies. 'When teenagers get wrapped up in their own dramas, they can be devious little so-and-sos. But we can't let them ruin our lives just because things aren't going their way, can we?'

'What do you know?'

'Um.' She cocked her head to the side. 'Apparently the wedding was causing quite a few arguments between you and William?'

'I guess so,' Amy admitted. Though they weren't about the wedding, she thought, and glanced at the drawer of the wardrobe. *Something old...*

'And sometimes she wished it wasn't going ahead.'

'She felt that strongly?'

'She *really* didn't want you to know. And I didn't feel it was my place to say anything.'

It was a twist Amy could not have predicted. She flushed behind her thick make-up. 'I wish I'd known she felt like that,' she said miserably. Guilt rolled through her. She had not spared enough time to look beyond Tess's polished new smile.

'Oh hon, they can be so self-centred. It's almost like they can't help it. And it makes them so reckless. And *sneaky*. You know I found mini scales in Rory's pocket the other day? While he looked me straight in the eye and swore on his life he wasn't dealing any more! Then he disappeared for three whole days.'

Amy swallowed her pride to say, 'I feel terrible. Will you try calling her? I've tried a million times, but she might talk to you.'

'Maybe I could text her. Say that you're not angry with her. Say we just want to know she's okay and ask her if she wants me to pick her up from Oak Hills. No questions asked. Would that help, do you think?'

'Yes, do that.' Amy perched on the window seat and waited while Olivia composed a text.

'Okay. Done,' Olivia said, pouring some champagne into the glass reserved for Tess. Amy felt annoyed with her for taking Tess's glass. Unfairly, of course.

A text pinged through. 'Here we go,' Olivia said, reading it.

Braced for some home truths, Amy closed her eyes. 'What does it say?' She tasted blood and realised she'd been gnawing at the inside of her cheek.

Olivia read Tess's words out. '"Don't come. I'm fine. Tell Mum I'm sorry. Leaving now. Meet her there."'

Amy felt hopeful again. 'Does she mean she's meeting me in the woods instead?'

'I guess so. No more waiting about, Amy. You've got to put yourself first for once in your life. This is your wedding day.'

Olivia pulled out a folded tissue from her clutch and delicately patted at Amy's escaped tears. 'All your friends and family are out there waiting for you. And poor darling William has been getting paler by the minute.'

Amy's mind wandered back to memories of her gloriously aspirational, self-righteous mother, who had shown her love through criticism, ear clips and strict rules. She would have cheered on Olivia's no-nonsense approach.

'Okay,' she sighed.

When Pip and Jo returned a few seconds later, Olivia immediately showed them the text. Jo shot her one of her withering looks, reserved only for her least favourite people, and said, 'She never would have done something like this before.'

All four women knew what she meant by 'before'. *Before they came here and met the likes of you, Olivia*, blaming her for Rory's influence on Tess.

'Righto,' Pip said. 'Come on, love. It's time to get into your dress and get your arse down that aisle. And have a gulp of champers.'

As though in a dream, Amy downed another glass of champagne and watched Olivia unzip the dress from its bag and hold it out for her, like a mother to her child. She gingerly dipped her toes into the puddle of material.

As Pip and Jo went back to join the guests, Olivia buttoned her up. The tightness of the bodice pushed Amy's worry and hurt deep inside her. Its constriction, all the way up to the base of her skull, was welcome, almost as though the fabric had known she'd need its structure to support her today.

'Oh my God,' Olivia breathed, handing her the bouquet of red roses. 'Literal perfection.'

When Amy stared at herself in the wardrobe mirror, she saw the woman her mother would have wanted her to be. Her freckles were airbrushed and her hair was straightened. The dress gave her an elongated, aristocratic neckline. Her poised appearance encapsulated her mother's dreams for her. From the outside, she was the cliché of a self-assured, wealthy Surrey housewife. She lived in an old manor house with real beams; prepared her husband beautiful evening meals with organic meat; sent her daughter to private school; went to coffee mornings at houses as big as hotels; drove a BMW (soon to be an electric Mercedes); was a member of a health club; walked the dog like it was a day job and pretended to want a day job she didn't need.

Yet she couldn't marry up this image in the mirror with the woman she was inside: still the same Amy, with little confidence in herself. She had never cared like her mother had about appearances or postcodes or accents, and wanted nothing more than a simple life of family and love and laughter. She could never be Olivia. Or Eleanor. Or Sophie Sandeman-Gore. She had never wanted to be. But was she looking more and more like them, *becoming* more and more like them by default. While she had judged Tess for changing, she too had been corrupted in subtle, seemingly innocuous ways. Would she soon be shutting secrets away to fester in the old wardrobe drawers? Over the last year, had the influences around her insidiously altered her priorities and her aspirations? And did she like what she saw now? Was she okay with it?

# SIXTY-SEVEN

Hal

Hal's breathing was rapid as he gripped the steering wheel and sped through the lanes. His eyes were peeled for police cars, nervous he'd be caught as an unchaperoned learner driver. His fear dampened the armpits of his suit.

The message he had received from Rory earlier burned his eyelids every time he blinked.

*They've got her im sorry my fault sorry they want money i don't have*

He parked up on the grass verge a few houses down from Oak Hills and made the remainder of the way on foot. Trickles of cold sweat ran down his back. Every now and again he tapped his pocket absent-mindedly before remembering he'd had the foresight to give the ring box to his dad before he left, just in case. *Just in case.*

A long-ago image came to him of his father standing on the driveway of Summerfield House, waving goodbye as Hal was driven away on the school run by his mum. Every day, without fail, his father had stood there grinning like a halfwit until he was gone. At the time, Hal had liked to believe he'd remained there all day, in the same spot by the stone birdbath, with one arm raised, eternally waving. The thought of this used to fortify him throughout his day at school, bolstering him when confronted by a mean kid in the playground or a strict teacher who had it in for him.

And so it was now.

His father would be waiting for him at the floral altar, muttering expletives under his breath. He'd be angry he wasn't by his side, perhaps keen to despair about him with Amy, if only she'd walk down that bloody aisle. He had given Rory that money to protect Hal, proving his love was unconditional. It was that simple. William would do anything for his son. And this core knowledge gave Hal the courage to go for Tess, to bring her back home to Summerfield House. To their newly formed family, which he valued more than he had ever imagined possible.

It didn't mean he wasn't scared. He was fucking terrified. The men who might have hold of Tess were dangerous. Machete and handgun kind of dangerous. Out of Hal's league dangerous. Still, he was compelled to confront them. He would not let anything happen to her.

# SIXTY-EIGHT

## Amy

Amy heard the string quartet through the trees. *Here comes the bride. Here comes the bride. Here comes the bride.* The material of her veil fluttered lightly over her features. Through it, the sunset-lit woodland was gauzy, filtered, more beautiful than ever. The lace of her train rustled behind her through the bluebells.

As her footstep cracked twigs, announcing her arrival, a man in the back row twisted around. There was an intake of breath. Word spread quickly. Mutters of 'Oh my goodness!' and 'Wow!' and 'Stunning!' Phones were held up.

The aisle between the two banks of chairs had been cleared and delineated by pink ribbons tied to stakes. Amy clutched her bouquet and traced her eyes along the rows of guests. Tess didn't seem to be there. Could this really be true? Could she go ahead without her? *You've got to put yourself first for once in your life. This is your wedding day,* Olivia had said. As she got closer, William's face appeared at the end of the aisle. He was framed by the archway of flowers, which was a burst of happy colours behind him. He swept his crop of blond hair to the side, neatening it behind his ears. Everything around them receded. His green eyes became beacons of love and security and she was drawn to them. Her feet glided as though on solid air. *You've got to put yourself first.*

A squirrel scurried up a tree. A woodpecker's beak knocked on wood. Hamish barked. But the vacuum of Tess was like a hole in the atmosphere. William's smile faded, as though reading her doubts. Then his eyes darted to his left, anxiously, briefly, breaking the spell between them. Amy glanced over to where he was looking. There, standing close enough to reach out and touch, was Sophie Sandeman-Gore.

She experienced a violent shudder. It couldn't be real. She'd conjured the ghost of the house. She tried to hold her head up higher and blank out the vision. Uncontrollable trembling broke out through her limbs. Her knees buckled slightly, but somehow her legs kept working to move on past this spectre. She glanced over one more time, hoping to see the horrible vision of Sophie gone. But there she was in front of her; entitled to be on her own land. Amy baulked.

Noting her hesitation, Sophie pulled the corners of her red lips into a smile that was both benign and slightly strained. It was the smile of a queen who was weary of glad-handing all day, who was humouring her loyal, dumb subjects. One dumb subject – Amy. Who was Amy trying to kid? This was Sophie's house. Sophie's land. Sophie's rarefied air. She owned it all. Including William. And she would never let go. They'd been naive.

Imagining Sophie's black stiletto pinning her train to the forest floor, holding her back, Amy faltered, pausing halfway down the aisle. A glimmer of fear crossed William's face, a tiny shake of his head, the glint of tears not yet shed. His feelings were for ever contained, rusting away at his joints under his armour of good manners and responsibility and tradition. It struck Amy that she'd been loved by him but had never truly understood him. The real ties that bound him to Summerfield House were a mystery still. The place had a grip on him that went beyond logic, beyond the obvious beauty and its rambling grounds. Darker and more compelling was the history of whispered secrets and cries and rows between him and Sophie. A little club that Amy had been excluded from and had tried not to mind about. Stupidly, she had clung to the idea of today. A beautiful wedding day that rose above Sophie's game-playing like a castle in the clouds.

Yet here she was to spoil it. How pathetic Amy must seem to her. Tess's instincts to call this day out as a sham had proved spot on.

Crushed and humiliated, Amy hiked the hem of her wedding dress, turned on her heel and fled the wrong way up the aisle of bluebells, leaving William behind her.

# SIXTY-NINE

## Hal

Rory was huddled in the corner of the outhouse behind Pete's sit-on mower. A handgun was balanced on top of his knees. He stared at it, finishing off his explanation of what had gone wrong. '...then it just sort of became the plan that Oak Hills was like our stash house, you know? I mean, who would suspect all that shit was buried under the hydrangeas, right? So Logan and I hid loads of it. We had like twenty G-packs of white and brown. But then some fucking crackhead found out about it and ran off with it one night. And now we're fucked.'

Hal listened, but his attention was on the gun.

'Is that real?' he breathed.

Rory aimed it at him. 'Yup. A Glock nine-millimetre. I could take your head off with it.'

He sounded tough, but his eyes were red and swollen from crying.

'You have to stop this and go to the police.'

'If I go to the police, Hal, I'm a dead man walking.' He

sniffed, wiping snot with the back of his hand. 'D'you understand? My life is nothing to them.' He let out a sob and covered his face, mumbling into his hands. 'If I'd known what it would be like, I would never have got involved. I swear it. A thousand per cent. I never thought it would be me, you know? I genuinely thought I had it covered. But I'm in too deep now.'

Hal had never seen him so distraught or so frightened. 'Amy'll catch on soon enough and they'll call the police anyway,' he reminded him, almost in tears himself.

'She won't yet. Mum said she fell for the whole story about Tess being upset and shit.'

'What?' Hal was flabbergasted, had had no idea. 'You got your mum to lie to Amy?'

Rory's jaw tightened around his words to control its juddering. 'Jesus, Hal. If Amy knew the truth, she'd have flipped out. We had to think of *something*. It gives us time to get this shit sorted.'

'But the police'll know what to do. They must've done this a million times.'

'There's no way to fucking stop these guys! They're murderers. Get that into your fucking brain. All they care about is their fucking money. And if I don't give it to them, they'll kill her. And me and Mum and fucking you. They won't stop until they get paid. And they know we paid up last time.' He snapped his fingers. 'Just like that.'

'But Dad won't pay up again.'

Taking up the handgun, Rory laughed, waved it about a little manically. 'And then blap-blap,' he said, putting it to his temple.

'Rory, don't,' Hal said.

It wasn't the first time he'd seen Rory holding a gun. Most country boys had aimed a shotgun at a few clay pigeons or a tin can in a field at some point in time. But he and Rory had learned in a less orthodox setting at their mate Oscar's 2022 New Year's Eve party on his hundred-acre estate in Chiddingfold. Oscar's dad, Jared, who'd been inebriated on aged whisky from his cellar, had unlocked his arsenal of weapons and set up target practice in the paddock. Under his drunken sergeant-major-like instruction, Hal, Rory and six other boys had been shown how to fire every type of gun you could imagine. He'd never forget the frenzied excitement in Rory's eyes that night at his first experience of the kickback.

'We have to find the money,' he said now, thinking, thinking, thinking. 'What about your dad?'

'He won't give me a fucking penny. He doesn't give a shit about me.' Rory dropped the hand holding the gun into his lap.

Hal sat down cross-legged next to him. 'There has to be something we can do,' he said desperately.

Rory thought for a moment. 'You know, Dad has loads of Rolexes in his watch box.'

'Yeah,' Hal said, nodding slowly, locking eyes with him. 'You mean, you could steal one of them?'

'Or two.'

'Don't get greedy.'

'Well, he fucking owes me, man.' Rory wiped his snotty nose again.

'Yeah, I guess he does,' Hal agreed. It wasn't a bad idea. If there was a way Rory's dad could finally help his son, it was this. Hal thought of his own dad now, feeling horrible about letting him down. His wedding was in tatters. But the immediate danger to Tess overrode all that. They didn't have time to think about anything else.

He went straight to the logistics of the plan. 'You can catch the train up to London.' He checked his phone app and looked up train times. 'Want me to drive you to the station?'

Rory brushed a hand over his blond head. 'What? Now?'

'Yeah, now, dickhead. And I might need that,' Hal said,

nodding at the gun. Rory handed it to him, sheepish now. 'Got your phone?' Hal added, yanking Rory up by his limp wrist. 'You can make the 18.02. Just make sure you don't miss the last train home, which is at 23.45 and gets in at... 01.02. I'll collect you from the station and we can take it from there.'

# SEVENTY

William

William was hiding in his garden office. Not much came up when he vomited, but he felt wretched. He stayed by the toilet for a bit with his tall frame curled over the bowl. His hair flopped into his eyes. When his knees began to hurt, he picked himself up and washed his face, staring at his greenish complexion in the mirror.

There was a rap on the loo door. 'William?'

He froze.

'Are you all right in there?'

If he didn't make a sound, she might go away. Before he had a chance to lock the door, though, Sophie opened it. Her face provoked a surge of rage.

'Get out,' he seethed, flinging his arm out to point at the door.

Sophie jumped aside nervily, as though he might hit her. He shoved past.

'If you yell like that, someone will hear us. And everyone's already terribly worked up about everything.' She sounded jittery, breathy. Her long fingers, mottled purple under the white gloves, plucked at her black veil. She looked around the space furtively. Outside, the apple trees were plump with flowers, mocking him with their joyful pink.

Mechanically, he said, 'You promised you'd stay away. Just for today.'

She used a tissue from her clutch bag to wipe a smear of lipstick from the corner of her mouth and discarded it in the bin. It was stained red like cartoon blood. Her colourless lashes fluttered back down over her eyes. 'Sorry,' she whispered, hanging her head. 'I'm so sorry. I didn't intend to come, but I couldn't stay away and now I've ruined it for you. You didn't deserve that out there from her. You really don't deserve any of this shit. This is all my fault. Everything is my fault.' She wiped a finger under each eye.

He was unmoved. 'Yes, it was your fault.' The silence that fell between them was noxious. He had a casual thought that he might kill her.

'You know, before Mummy died,' she sniffed tearily, 'this renovation obsessed her. It's protected land, and she couldn't get planning permission for the conversion and resorted to all sorts of dodgy backhanders with the council. In the end, she got what she wanted, and Avril's son came over from the Alps to build it. Did you know that? It's why it's Alpine in style.'

He did not know this. He did not care, didn't know why she was telling him. He sat on his chair and pressed his hands to his ears. He felt nausea roll through him. He had to keep it all tamped down, having learned that this was the done thing after a tragedy, that this was how one coped with trauma. He would adopt his father's way, stitch up his pain and turn his mind from the unthinkable to a subject he could control.

From the corner of his eye, he saw Sophie's fingers quivering over the small painting of an apple blossom tree. Annie Sandeman-Gore's black initials were inscribed in the right-hand corner. William had always found it difficult to imagine Annie sitting here painting. Her heavy grey bob and rod-straight back and waxy, well-preserved face had suited the kind of woman who ran a well-oiled household, hosted charity lunches and wore pearls to cocktail parties. She hadn't had the demeanour of an artist. But they'd all been changed by what had happened.

'Mummy would come here to paint in those final days. I would find her asleep on the chair sometimes, and I would think she had...' She broke off. 'I've got her portfolio at home. She did dozens of similar paintings and pencil sketches – studies of apples and blossom, some of the branches, others of the whole orchard in the distance.' Sophie unwound the cords of the roman blinds. The white linen unfolded and collapsed to the floor. The light changed. 'I'm telling you all this for a reason,' she said, locking the door. 'Because I've got something to show you.'

# SEVENTY-ONE

Hal

Rory was stretched out along the back seat of the car. Most of the guests had gone, but as Hal moved off, he caught a flash of white in his rear-view mirror. He came to a slow stop, turned the engine and lights off and held his breath.

'Stay down, okay?' he whispered. 'I've just seen Amy.'

She was jogging towards the house from the woods, a streak of white, clutching something to her chest. As the security light on the garages flashed on, her face was illuminated, contorted in a mad agony. The sight of the torn, muddy lace of her dress raised the hair on his arms. Her beauty and her fear scared him.

'Looks like she knows Tess is in trouble.' He gulped back tears, shaken, beginning to regret their plan, wanting to follow her into the safety of the house. His resolve quickly returned and he continued on. He pulled through the gates, took a left out of the main entrance towards the station.

'You have to call your dad,' Rory said.

'Why? We don't need his money now.' The thought of facing his dad after abandoning him at the altar was agonising.

'I already told you. You have to stop them calling the police.'

'But how? What do I say?'

'You have to tell him Tess got cold feet about going down the aisle and is so fucked up about everything she's legged it back to her dad's in London, and that I'm going to get her or something. Crank up the guilt, man. Parents always think they're to blame for why their kids fuck things up.'

There was a burst of drill music. It was Rory's TikTok feed. Hal glanced over his shoulder, catching a boy on Rory's screen flexing cash, trainers, watches, cars. Given their current predicament, he couldn't stomach it. 'Jesus, turn that off,' he said, angry at this casualness. It appeared the blubbering, guilt-ridden, regretful Rory had been put away.

'It's all on you now, man. If you can't persuade your dad and Amy not to call the police, we might as well forget the watches and say goodbye to Tess,' Rory said.

White-hot anger shot through Hal. It amazed him that Rory could so easily shirk his responsibility for what was happening. For a minute back there, he had felt sorry for him. Stand up, the real Rory Clark! Who are you? Which is your true self? The whimpering victim or the unapologetic sociopath? Hal counted down from ten, reminding himself to keep a lid on his frustration.

'I'll talk to Dad,' he promised with a clunk of dread.

He deposited Rory on the train. The carriage doors closed on him. Rory slumped in a window seat, popped his hood up and bit at his thumbnail.

Hal made his way back over the railway bridge to his car.

Daunted by the task ahead, he pictured an aerial view of the radius he needed to cover to find Tess. The mass of trees, the tangle of dark, quiet hidden lanes spread out for miles.

# SEVENTY-TWO

William

The dying light struggled through the blinds, lending William's study an other-worldly quality. Time seemed suspended. Without knowing why, William was helping Sophie push his desk right up against the bookshelves. It left an expanse of carpet stretching out before them. 'What are we doing?' he asked her.

'Do you have a knife or some scissors, anything sharp?' She was already rifling through his drawers, finding a penknife. She went to one corner of the room, slid the blade under the carpet, ripped it up and then rolled it back with a series of grunts.

The ground seemed to shift under his feet. Before him was a breathtaking latticework of hand-painted apple blossom neatly contained within an inlaid square of nine flagstones. It was a painstaking work of art. A labour of love. A shrine?

'What is this?' he rasped. A column of terror slotted over him, like a claustrophobic tunnel of his own making. A trapped sob grew in his chest, lumpy and painful. There was no room for that swell of feeling, no room.

'You know Mummy told us that he'd been cremated and that she'd scattered his ashes in the sea at Bute?'

He nodded.

'It was a lie.' She dropped her gaze to their feet.

He swallowed fear down his papery gullet. 'No, no, no. He can't be...' He looked down.

'He's buried here, William.'

The dawning of it scorched William's heart.

'What? No!' he cried, letting out a small moan, comprehending now why he had felt connected to this space. He took a jerky step forward and put one knee down, then the other, feeling the knobbles of his joints grind into the tiles. A violent urge to heave up the painted tiles and scrabble under the earth came over him. A need to hold his baby son tight in his arms once again, as though he might be able to hug the collection of tiny bones and bring him back to life. Just one more time he wanted to feel him alive; to marvel at his squirming, fleshy little body and his fists punching the air, face scrunched, hair thick and black. The yearning was unendurable.

'Why didn't you tell me?' he said, gulping back decades of emotion.

'I didn't know myself until recently. Avril told me.'

'Avril?'

'She's the only one left alive who knew the full story.' She sighed. 'According to her, my parents fought over what to do with his body at first. Daddy thought they should make their own funeral pyre. Do it that way. You know, to eliminate the risk of him being discovered later on. But Mummy couldn't bear the thought.' She swallowed hard, put her hand to her forehead. 'So they preserved him for a few weeks while they decided.'

'What? How?' he rasped.

She looked away from him. 'In the chest freezer in the old barn that was here before it was converted?'

The absurdity and indignity of it hit him like a punch. He

shook his head. 'I can't believe we let that happen. How did we not know all this? Why didn't we ask more questions?'

'We were sixteen! We were traumatised, we thought the grown-ups knew best. And after you broke the tiles, you were literally frogmarched off the grounds. What choice did you have? You had to accept what they told you. You had to move on and put it behind you.'

'We should have known the truth.'

'Knowing Daddy, he didn't trust us with the information. Unlawful burial carries a prison sentence. He never trusted your father either. Avril told me your dad threatened to go to the police at one point, which was why they ended up paying him off.'

'Blood money to keep our baby's little life a secret.' His voice broke. 'Our baby,' he repeated in a murmur, placing both palms flat on the tiles, holding a roar of pain at bay.

'Think about it. You've been here with him always,' she said. She folded herself up, her back a C shape and her knees curled into her chest, like the embryo that had grown inside her.

The memory of her screams rattled through his brain. He went back in time, was sitting on the floor outside the bedroom with his forehead digging into his knees. Annie had not allowed him into the room to see the birth. At one stage, his father had come along the panelled corridor in his red brushed-cotton trousers, holding a glass of wine. William had been absurdly relieved to see him. But Rupert had only stopped briefly on his way to bed. He had winced at the animalistic noises from behind the door and remarked on how William's mother had been silent as the night when she had given birth to him. As William had waited for his baby to be born, he had never wanted his quiet, kind mother more in his life.

When he saw his son for the first time, his heart had been flooded with a love so intense, he had wondered whether he would ever be able to look at anything or anyone else again.

Those beautiful eyes, almond-shaped and violet, had blinked up at him, trying to find focus, vulnerable and trusting. They had become the centre of his whole universe. Never could he have conceived in his worst nightmares that the sweet pink lids would close over them for the last time and shut away a part of him for ever.

'It's magnificent, isn't it?' Sophie moved her fingers over the painted blossom like she was brushing soil from a headstone.

William's breath caught in his chest. He pressed his temples, squeezed his eyes shut. Sophie nestled her wet face into his neck. Her pale, dirty hair irritated his nose, but he allowed her to stay there and patted her shoulder methodically, which was all he could manage.

He rested his head back, was able to breathe better, and stared at the skylights, dark now. There was a click as she opened her clutch bag and unfolded a photograph of their baby son in a crib in the yellow room. He felt the strange presence of the three of them together again. He gazed at the image greedily. He could see why Amy had mistaken him for Hal. They were so alike. 'How did you get hold of this?'

'The other week, when you were out, I swung by to look for my old babygro in that horrible old wardrobe. I wanted it for the naming ceremony. And I stumbled on this.'

'So that's where it went.'

She folded the photograph away again. 'Mummy always said it was better that he wasn't named.' She chewed the nail on her forefinger, continuing in a whisper, like she was in church, 'Because we would connect with him less, or something.'

He came back angrily, 'She thought he was less of a human being because he didn't have a name?'

'She was from the generation that really believed you could put stuff away like that.' Sophie turned onto her back with her knees bent. Her eyes shone. 'I'm like her, though, you know. I can switch off, just like that.' She clicked her fingers, so much louder than their voices, and it jarred.

'Well. Sometimes it's the only way to survive,' he murmured, rubbing his hands up and down his long thighs.

'I feel for you. You've been an innocent bystander in all this.'

'You were just as much a victim of what happened.'

'It was worse for you, though. Mummy handled it appallingly. She was ghastly to you. Cutting you out of my life like that, and then paying your dad off and shipping Avril up north like she was some criminal. It was brutal the way they covered the whole thing up and expected us never to speak of it again.' She reached out a hand and placed it on his knee. 'And we needed each other.'

'I never blamed your parents at the time,' he said, feeling strange about that now.

'Except when you went nuts and smacked your fist into the tile.'

'No. That was after an argument with Dad when he said that I'd forget...' The memory snagged. 'How could anyone forget about losing...' He broke off, gathered himself, 'Anyway, my outburst had nothing to do with your parents. They did everything they could to make things better.'

'I always assumed you hated them. How funny,' she said, but she wasn't smiling.

'You can't judge them for throwing money at it. Thank God they did. Where would we be now without their money?'

'I'd probably be rotting away in some women's prison.'

'You don't go to prison for sudden infant death syndrome,' he reminded her gently.

Abruptly she sat up on her haunches, stretched her hair back from her forehead, appearing scared suddenly. 'But I'm to blame,' she said, blanching.

He held his breath, sat back guardedly. A mercurial slide of hot liquid filled his veins. 'It was a horrible tragedy, Sophie. You can't hold onto the guilt for ever.'

She hesitated, sipped air through her slightly parted lips. 'Yes, horrible,' she whispered hoarsely. 'Quite horrible.'

After some time in silence, William's phone rang. The noise was almost shocking. When he saw the caller ID, his heart lurched. 'It's Hal. I have to get this.'

# SEVENTY-THREE

Hal

Hal's armpits had been hot with fear and shame as the phone rang. He imagined how furious his father would be after his disappearing act. His dad's voice filled the car.

'Hal! Where the hell did you go?' Despite his cross tone, Hal detected relief too.

He clicked on the indicator and turned left onto Courts Mount Road. His eyes were peeled for a black four-door hatchback.

'Hal? You still there?' His dad's voice echoed from the car speaker and reverberated through Hal's heart.

'Dad. Can you listen without reacting?'

A car bibbed its horn at another car. It was nothing to do with him, but his dad cottoned on fast. 'Are you in the car?'

'Yes.'

'Hal! You could lose your—'

Hal stopped him. 'Please. Can you just listen to me for a minute?'

A pause. He heard the clicking of shoes on a hard floor and

then the squeak of a door. 'Okay,' his dad said finally. 'I'm alone now. What's going on?'

Hal was braced to spin the lie that Rory had concocted about Tess: that she'd got cold feet about going down the aisle with her mum and had run back to her dad's in London, and that Rory was heading off there now. These were the lines he needed to spout. Rory would have regurgitated them artfully. But they wouldn't come out of Hal's mouth.

'In case Amy gets it into her head that she wants to report Tess missing, you have to stop her. Just until you've heard from me again.'

'She's not home yet?' his dad shot back.

Hal passed the builders' yard and took a left on Midhurst Road. Then a right down Scotland Lane, along the narrow section, waiting in a gap while a car passed him.

'You didn't know?'

'After everything... I... I've been... I haven't been into the house yet,' his dad stammered. The humiliation of being left at the altar.

'I understand,' Hal said, moving quickly on. 'Sorry, Dad, but Tess didn't show up in the end. So I'm going to get her, but I need some time, and I need you to trust me.' He craned his neck as he slowed down outside Oak Hills. There were no cars in the driveway. No lights on in the house. He carried on driving. 'Can you trust me?'

'That depends.'

'It can't depend on anything.'

'I don't want you putting yourself in danger.'

'I know what I'm doing.'

There was a pause. 'Do you?'

'What I do know is that it'll do more harm than good if the police are involved. Do you fully get what I'm saying? You have to do this for Tess.'

The car almost came to a standstill as he waited for his dad's response.

'Yes. Okay. I'll do what I can my end.'

Hal exhaled with relief, pressing down on the gas. 'Thanks. Thanks, Dad,' he breathed. *I love you.*

'Keep me updated. And stay safe,' were his dad's parting words.

His father was forever waving and grinning to the younger Hal from the driveway of Summerfield House. This gave Hal more courage than the gun in the glove box ever could. He planned to make his dad proud and walk into the kitchen of Summerfield House with Tess by his side.

He pulled out the gun, rested it on the seat and continued his hunt for the black hatchback, methodically combing the lanes he'd grown up in. His knowledge of the area was an advantage over the men who had her. This was his stamping ground, his neighbourhood, not theirs. He knew every lay-by, every road, every hidey-hole a novice might try lurking in. He was determined to outsmart them.

# SEVENTY-FOUR

Tess

The car windows had steamed up white against the night outside. The digital clock read 19:46. Tess had been lying across the back seat of the now stationary car for what seemed like hours. Terror had quickened her heart into a permanent gallop. Her breathing was shallow, almost like a pant. She was trying not to move a muscle or risk making a sound to attract their attention in the front.

From the darkness outside, an owl hooted as though calling out to her. The bass from the car's speakers pounded through her limbs.

Ralph and Logan talked under their breath. The backs of their heads were dark silhouettes. The phone rang every few minutes. Their patois was impossible to decipher. After the latest call, Ralph sucked his teeth. He looked back at her from the driver's side. 'Your boy was doin' good, then he fucked it.'

Tess stopped breathing. Her skin was tight with fury and dried tears. She glared into his eyes, smeary and distorted by his metal-framed glasses, and said nothing.

Ralph reached to pull one of her crossed arms away from her chest. 'Man's gonna get shaved, bitch.' She clamped it there tighter and bit his hand like an animal. Her fear ripped into his muscle. 'You fuckin' ho!' he roared, nursing his thumb. 'She needs gagging, bruv.'

Tess retched at the taste of chemical sweat in her mouth.

Logan turned to her. His eyes were black and wide and scared, like he didn't want to be there any more than she did. 'Relax, yeah?' he urged.

'Maybe, while we waitin', he let me drill his bitch, tho, yeah?' Ralph said, crawling his hand over her hip.

Her muscles seized. She had a scream in her chest, too dangerous to let out. Nobody would hear her where they were. Wherever that was, parked up miles somewhere down a deserted lane. Through the fogged windows, she could see the moon behind the trees.

And then she caught the glare of headlights and the sound of a car approaching out of nowhere, illuminating the branches overhead.

'Stay the fuck down,' Ralph whispered, pressing a handgun into her thigh.

The car's beam lit up his glasses and created long, spiky shadows of his hair on the roof. She dared to hope that someone had found her. The vehicle's disappearance and the return of the dark left her reeling.

They ignored her for a while, carried on talking, sucked on some roll-ups. A cold stiffness set into her joints.

Then the call they'd been waiting for came in.

'Is him,' Ralph said, sucking his teeth and answering. 'What's goin' on?' He paused to listen. Tess couldn't hear what was said on the other end. 'Yeah... yeah... Good, yeah...' He snorted, hung up and threw the phone on the dash. 'Man's blubbin' all over the place. Flexing some Rolex, bruv. Worth twenty Ps. Fucking pussy.'

They both started laughing and slapping the dashboard triumphantly, jumping about in their seats, whooping manically, waving the gun about. They turned on a drill track loud, not caring this time whose attention they might attract. A bottle of something strong was downed. They lit a joint. The reason for their celebration was lost on her.

She shut her eyes tight, but the tears leaked out anyway.

After a while, Ralph turned around to her and flashed a slick, nasty grin. 'Time to get down, baby.' Terror tore through her.

# SEVENTY-FIVE

William

'Drink this. It'll calm your nerves,' Olivia said, presenting Amy with a tumbler of whisky, rubbing her back.

Amy glared at it like it was poison. 'I don't need a drink. I need to sober up so I can drive,' she said through clenched teeth. She cut a ragged figure slumped on the kitchen stool. The stunning vision of her earlier as she had walked towards William through the bluebells was ravaged and ripped. He wished she'd changed out of the dress. It was a grim reminder of their ruined day.

She picked up her phone again.

Olivia shot William a look. Unlike Amy, she was still immaculate in her golden dress. Her elegant presentation was ill-suited to the anguish of the room. Behind her, Pip and Jo were at the round table, conferring in whispers. Their feathery, colourful hats were in front of them. Faintly ridiculous now.

William paced up and down at the window. Hamish followed him nervously, knowing something was up. Apple blossom branches threaded their way through his mind, clawing at the past. After Hal had called, Sophie had understood the urgency of the situation and had let William go, said she would make her own way to her car. That had been three quarters of an hour ago.

Amy's phone went. 'It's Maggie,' she said, snatching it up. Maggie and Damian had been the only ones sober enough to drive and had gone out in the van to Rory's to see if they could find Tess.

Her face fell as she listened to her sister's news. She hung up, put her phone on the countertop. 'They're going to drive around for a bit. Check the rec and then the high street.' She looked at William. 'It's almost eight. When did the police say they'd be here again?'

*Can you trust me?... It'll do more harm than good if the police are involved... I know what I'm doing.* Hal had said all this down the phone to him and he had listened. His decision had been instinctual. He'd pushed aside the many years of frayed relations between them and dug out what he knew about Hal's character. He had always been a clever, sensible boy. Loyal and brave. Laughing when he fell; sympathetic to others when they were hurt. This was the Hal he knew before Rory. Before the divorce. Before William had fucked him up.

'The officer I spoke to said they were having an extremely busy night, and because she's only been missing a couple of hours, it's not top of the pile,' he replied. The truth was, he hadn't called the police. He wondered if lies were like that: once you started with one, you couldn't stop. Each lie protected the one before it, the truth less and less easy to grasp with every new story. Maybe this was how liars started believing their own untruths.

'A busy night? What the hell?' Amy cried. 'This is my daughter!'

William blanched. 'I know, I know.'

Was it plausible that there'd be any delay from a Home

Counties police force at the mention of a missing kid? What did he know about police procedure? What did any of them know about any of this? They were all blindfolded, feeling around, trying to do what they thought was best for their children.

Her eyes blazed with fury. She blamed him for this. 'I think I'll call them myself,' she said defiantly.

He flinched. But it was Olivia who rushed towards her, only just stopping short of grabbing the phone off her. 'There's no need.'

Amy grimaced at her. 'Tess going missing isn't a *need*?'

'I've told you, she's heading up to her dad's.'

'You've told me Rory's story about her going to her dad's, but I can't get hold of Nick. And quite honestly, I don't buy it. I know Tess, and it doesn't sound right.'

'You can't call them,' Olivia reiterated. It dawned on William that she was in the know about something.

'Watch me.' Amy clicked on her home screen, but Olivia prised the device out of her hand.

'What the hell?' Amy was agog. Hearing her changed tone of voice, Hamish jumped up, placed his paws on her knees. Her hand shot out towards Olivia. 'Can I have my phone back, please? Or shall I just use Pip's?'

William held his breath, checked his watch. It had been almost an hour since he'd spoken to Hal. The longest hour of his life. Olivia gave the phone up and leant back into the kitchen units. Amy was now flanked by Pip and Jo and had Hamish at her feet. The formidable group eyed William and Olivia, suspicious.

Pip wrinkled her nose and cocked her head to the side. 'Why don't you want her to call the police?'

William was focused on Amy, who was pressing the first 9 into her screen. *Beep*.

His heart stopped. If Hal was to be believed, she risked

setting off a cataclysmic chain of events that could endanger both their children.

'Stop!' Olivia cried before she had time to dial the next digit.

Amy paused, glancing up. Her finger hovered.

'Put it down, Amy, please,' Olivia begged. 'I'll explain everything.'

# SEVENTY-SIX

Amy

As Amy listened to Olivia, William inched closer and gripped her hand. Pip and Jo had retreated to the kitchen table. What Olivia was relaying was horrific, hard to compute, worse than anything in Amy's nightmares.

'They've got Tess? Like a ransom?' she asked again, still unable to take it in. Her extremities had gone ice-cold and yet her head was thumping hot.

'Yes, I'm so sorry.' Olivia reached out to touch her, but Amy pulled back. Olivia looked hurt. 'But now you understand why we can't call the police.'

William choked. 'If I'd known what Hal was planning, I never would have... He asked me to trust him, and I wanted to... I don't know why, but I thought... I don't know what I was thinking, I just never imagined...' He couldn't finish his sentence.

Amy had tugged her hand out of his.

'Hal went out looking for Tess himself,' Olivia explained.

William's head fell into his palms.

'And you say they knew the two men?' Amy asked.

Olivia nodded. 'Rory said they did.'

'It might be a scare tactic,' Jo said optimistically.

'I'm sure it is,' Olivia said, but a small twitch in her brow suggested otherwise. 'Rory wouldn't tell me where he was getting the money from.' She tutted. 'But he swore he had it and that he'd be able to pay them tonight, and then they'd let her go. They just want their money, that's all.'

'That's *all*?' Amy said.

'Sorry, I didn't mean it that way,' Olivia murmured, biting her lip. 'I'm as worried about Rory as you are about Tess. As I am sure William is about Hal.'

Amy thought about Maggie and Damian, who were searching for Tess, and felt her heart swell with gratitude. They'd been uninterested in waiting for the police to get their act together, and Amy now felt the same.

'We have to go out looking for her. I'm sober enough now.' As she said it, she looked down at herself, caught by the fact that she was still in her dress. It was her wedding night. They should have been dancing now, eating cake, laughing and chatting with their guests, high on love, excited about their drive to Scotland. How had it come to this?

'Hal took the BMW,' William said.

'We've got my old banger,' Jo said. 'I can drive.'

'Neil and Ted went home in our car,' Pip explained.

'Okay. You guys go together in Jo's, then. I'll take the Mini,' Amy said. She would have to risk getting pulled over for being over the limit. 'Rupert can stay here in case someone shows up.'

William nodded. 'I'll come with you.'

'No!' Amy blurted. His mouth fell open. She covered it up with logic. 'You go with Jo and Pip. They don't know the area.'

'Oh. Right. Yes. Of course.'

Being alone with him in the car would have been explosive.

. . .

William and Olivia followed Amy out into the hall. Amy tried to stem her tears. 'This is all our fault,' she said. Barely able to see straight, she sifted haphazardly through the bowl for the car key.

'No, sweetie,' Olivia said, placing a hand on her back.

'If we'd gone to the police last time, Tess wouldn't be in this situation,' Amy said, swiping an escaped tear.

William looked down at his feet. 'We did what we thought was right at the time.'

'What *you* thought was right!' she yelled, anger gargling in her throat. She looked away, unable to bear his guilt, unable to bear her own.

Jo appeared and jangled her own key. 'Okay, let's get going, William.'

Amy was relieved when they left.

Olivia said, 'Don't be too hard on him. It's thanks to him that Rory wasn't stabbed in the head multiple times.'

Amy couldn't hold back her fury. 'And it's thanks to Rory that Tess has been bundled into a fucking car and held at ransom!' she hissed, feeling the tears now spill onto her cheeks.

Olivia's blue eyes blinked slowly. In a voice that a reception teacher might use to a four-year-old, she said, 'Denial isn't helpful, Amy. *All* our kids have played a part in this.' She put her hand into the bowl and brought out the key.

'How do you figure that?' Amy spluttered, grabbing it from her.

'Well, I didn't want to have to say it, but it's a bit of a coincidence that Logan came onto the scene at just the same time Tess moved here. And suddenly they're all good friends?'

Amy frowned, wiped her nose with a tissue she'd found in her sleeve and threw her a look of utter disbelief. 'What the hell?'

'Well, did they know each other before or not?' Olivia said plainly.

Amy actually laughed. 'Are you seriously suggesting that Tess introduced Logan to Rory?'

Olivia blinked. 'How else would he meet someone like that? There has to be some connection.'

'Just in case you hadn't noticed,' Amy snorted, 'London's quite a big place.'

Olivia put up a palm. 'Okay, fair enough, maybe Tess didn't *know* Logan exactly, but they're from similar backgrounds, aren't they?'

'By "background", what do you mean?' Amy asked, using her fingers as speech marks, dropping the key. She left it there between them on the black and white tiles.

'I'm not being a snob, Amy, I'm just being realistic. They'd have similar references. And when they met here, they might have recognised something in each other, you know? Found common ground.'

'And corrupted Rory?'

'I'm just saying, it would explain the timing of all this.'

Amy clutched her head. 'Oh my fucking God.'

Olivia flicked her hair. 'You can't blame me for saying it out loud.'

'You really don't get it, do you?' Amy swiped the key up from the floor.

'There's no point edging round the issue, though, is there?' Olivia added, crossing her arms, rubbing a hand back and forth nervously over one cashmere elbow. Olivia's elbows were so sharp, she would be forever barging through the crowds to get Rory ahead. She wouldn't notice how she gouged the flesh of others in the process. Beyond the gates of her beautiful home, she didn't care. Amy had been seduced by her. But she'd had enough.

'Get the hell out,' she seethed.

Olivia gasped. 'Amy? Just because—'

'I mean it. Get the hell out of my house!'

Olivia hugged her handbag into her middle protectively and arched an eyebrow. '*Your* house, is it?' Then she turned and strode towards the front door, slamming it on her way out.

The hall fell deathly quiet.

Amy crawled through the lanes looking for her missing daughter. She was tense, rueful, tormented by all the mistakes she'd made that had led her to this horror.

Jo had been right that day in London. Amy should have gone to the police and exposed Rory for what he was. But she'd lost her confidence, had been softened by Rory's sob story and persuaded by William's money, shrinking behind his stiff-upper-lip approach towards the matter. The money had given them a force field.

She was driving past a series of magnificent homes. The modern architecture of glass and steel. The timeless charm of seventeenth-century beams. And everything in between, nestled exclusively into manicured yet rambling gardens. High-end security lights were hidden behind hedges, blinding anyone who dared walk past; electric gates were controlled by secret codes to keep everyone out. These homes were a picture post-card from a destination miles away from ordinariness. *Wish you were here?* Amy once had.

These people thought they were living the dream. Like William, they appreciated what they had materially with a kind of zealous gratitude and an aching need to hold on tightly. The echo of *Aren't we lucky?* drifted on the breeze, but what they meant was *Aren't we clever?* They wanted their kids to be the best at everything and they wanted the best for their kids. Like the slogan on the Heathside Heights school bus: *We Are Prepared For Greater Things!* Greater than average. Greater than *you*.

William's knee-jerk response to Rory's problem had been to

sort it out himself, privately. He'd had the luxury of instant access to cash, had been able to drop the money and move on. It was only natural that he'd want to protect his own from the stigma of a scandal. The nasty transaction had barely touched the sides of their lives, greasing the path back to decency and normality. It would have been a source of pride to William to have provided such a cushion for his son's best friend. *Aren't I clever?*

Putting aside the fact that it had not been *right*. Not in the moral sense. Forgetting how wrong it had been to put money into the hands of violent drug dealers and perpetuate the exploitation and brutalisation of other people's children. But who had time to think about those other kids? Who cared about right and wrong when your own children needed protection from such a dirty business?

Amy cared now. Cared desperately. By sending out the wrong message, they had allowed the bullies to win and come back stronger. The gang had learned that people like them were cowardly and dishonest and greedy. They had guessed they would not go to the police. They had spotted a weak link and had stolen Tess away. Tess was the cost of their cover-up. Tess's kidnap was the direct result of Amy's own weak, immoral choices. And she hated herself for it.

# SEVENTY-SEVEN

Hal

When Hal saw the black hatchback, a calm descended upon him. He put all his fear in a box on a shelf in his mind and continued along the pitch-black dead-end lane. Knowing there was a second lay-by further up where he could park, he had driven past the vehicle without slowing down. If he had drawn up next to them, they would have had time to speed off. Instead, he would approach on foot.

He knew these woods well, and wove through the trees stealthily. His mouth and throat were dry. His heart throbbed through his bones. He reached the base of a vast oak on the brow of a slope to the sunken lane and looked down upon the roof of the parked car below. Over the music that blasted from the speakers, he heard muffled yelling from Tess.

They would not be able to hear him as he skidded down the tree's tentacled roots, green and slippery with moss, stumbling down the bank. He gathered himself and approached the rear of the car. When he reached for Rory's handgun from the back of his trousers, his hands shook too much to hold it straight in front of him. He could see two men either side of the rear doors. It appeared to be Logan on the right-hand side, bent into the passenger seats. Ralph was at the left-hand door, positioning himself between Tess's legs. In the midst of this horrifying scene, it was the sight of her bare, muddy feet that pinched at Hal's heart, almost derailing him.

But he remained steadfast and took a step closer, watching Ralph fumbling with his flies, trying to pull one side of his jeans down with one hand as Tess's heels kicked out at his face and groin.

'Get the fuck off her!' Hal bellowed, announcing himself, sounding different, possessed by a voice he didn't know he had. He held the gun up.

Ralph's eyes were huge and oblong, inhuman behind his metal-rimmed glasses. He squinted at Hal through the murky light. Tess managed to scramble out of the car. Ralph grabbed at her ankles, catching one, roaring, 'Logan, man! Get da strap!'

But Logan didn't obey the instruction to reach for a gun. He put his hands straight up. 'Easy, man. Easy.'

Tess wriggled free of Ralph's grip on her ankle and darted forward a few paces before hesitating and glancing back. Hal yelled, 'RUN, TESS!' while moving the gun from one man's face to the other.

In his peripheral vision, he could see her veering right and clawing her way up the bank. He hoped she'd find her way home. As the crow flew, it would take her over an hour. At least she'd known not to stay on the lane, where they would be able to catch her if it all went wrong.

Assured that she was away, he refocused on his own survival. So far, he was in control. The two of them were trapped by the invisible beam of his trembling 9mm. He had no idea whether he was capable of using it. Self-doubt must have flickered across his expression, and Ralph took advantage of his momentary hesitation, ducking into the car and bringing out a handgun. Hal didn't have time to think; he pressed the trigger. Its bite forced the gun out of his hand and onto the road. Ralph writhed on the ground, clutching his thigh and howling. As Hal scrabbled for his weapon, his phone fell out of his pocket and skittered across the tarmac, stopping at Logan's feet.

Logan stamped on the handset, wild-eyed, fumbling with his own shooter. 'I don't wanna do this, bruv, but I've got no choice.'

In that split second, leaving nothing to chance, Hal aimed his gun and pulled the trigger one more time.

# SEVENTY-EIGHT

William

'It's almost ten o'clock now and we're getting nowhere!' Amy was distraught. 'She could be anywhere!'

'We'll go back out,' Jo suggested.

'No, Jo. It's time to call the police, and I don't care what any of you think about that.' Amy glared at William, challenging him. The fear she was outwardly expressing about Tess, he too felt about Hal. Didn't she know this? Couldn't she understand that his decision *not* to call the police was because of how much he loved *both* their children? Why couldn't she see this?

'But remember what Olivia told us,' he said.

He had believed Olivia's stories from Rory about the demise of snitches. She had heard of one boy who had been stabbed three times in the head; another had been shot in the street; another had been macheted. Moreover, he would never forget how Hal had sounded on the phone earlier. His certainty about the right course of action had been impossible to dismiss, as though their roles as father and son had been reversed.

He glanced at his own father, who was sitting quietly at the kitchen table with his hands placed on his knees. He was still wearing his waistcoat and shirt, but his blue silk tie had been removed. He wasn't moving a muscle, wouldn't look at anyone, as though his presence – or his disapproval – could go unnoticed. William found his silence more vexing than any recriminations he might have.

'I don't give a flying shit what Olivia said!' Amy yelled at him. 'I'm doing what we should have done months ago!' She pressed the phone to her ear and waited. He lurched forward to stop her.

Out of nowhere, Rupert moved like lightning towards William and grabbed his wrist. 'Son, let her call the police. It's the right thing to do. We both know how it turns out when you don't.'

William was agog. There was so much more to this statement than anyone else in the room could ever fathom. It didn't make sense. Rupert had happily taken a fat bribe off the Sandeman-Gores and had lived a good life in Portugal with the money. Was that such a bad result? By managing the situation under the radar of the law, Annie and Thomas had upheld their good name, kept Thomas's political career on track and protected Sophie and William's futures.

*One doesn't air one's dirty laundry in public, does one?* Annie had said.

For three decades, William had lived in what he believed to be a dignified and private manner. Annie's words had directly informed his decision to give Rory the two thousand pounds and pay their way out of the problem. Had it not been the best method of handling the situation?

Now, his father's sudden interjection was like an admission of regret. The implication was that he and the Sandeman-Gores had made a mistake back in 1990. It sent shock waves through William, spearing him with uncertainty and a seepage of shame.

He twisted out of his father's cold, arthritic pincer grip and retreated to the window seat, rubbing at his wrist, nursing his self-loathing. *Your mother would be rolling in her grave.* He was shaken to the core by his father's implication. It was triggering intrusive memories from back then. The confluence of the present and the past, the echoes of one inside the other, racked his chest and made it hard for him to breathe.

He listened to Amy explain the situation to the officer on the phone. It had only been a few hours, but this wasn't a normal situation, she insisted. There were county lines gangs involved. They hadn't been paid. They'd taken her daughter. Her teenage stepson had gone out looking for them. A third teenager was missing. The third teenager was to blame, she said.

William's feelings slid towards a worse anguish. This call to the police offered no respite. His mobile was glued to his hand as he waited to hear from Hal. Why hadn't he phoned? Could this happen to a father twice? Could life be that cruel? He couldn't lose two sons. He wouldn't survive it.

He paced along the windows, staring out at the night-soaked garden, occasionally catching sight of his own ghostly reflection. *We both know how it turns out when you don't*, his father had said. To what was he referring? Hadn't William made a success of his life? Hadn't he shown his father and the Sandeman-Gores that he had been able to move on as they had wanted him to? He had spent his whole adult life cultivating ways of keeping the secret of his firstborn at bay. Even from his own psyche. He'd developed strategies of banishing it from his conscious mind, backing off from potential friendships, turning memories off like light switches and building emotional walls that would make therapists weep in defeat. In one way, his father had been right. He had been able to forget. After decades of keeping it hidden, he had enough expertise to write a self-help bestseller on *How to Bury Trauma and F**king Do It Anyway*. Christ! Shouldn't his dad be bloody proud?

He checked his phone for the umpteenth time, tried calling Hal again. It went straight to voicemail. His reflection in the window blurred as his eyes refocused on the beyond. On Annie's odd chalet-style mausoleum, where the tiny bones of his baby were buried.

Shattering his remembrances, the boot room door flew open.

# SEVENTY-NINE

## Amy

Amy swivelled around, falling off her stool, and gulped in air until it burned her chest, barely able to believe her eyes. '*Tess?*'

'Mum!' Tess cried.

Amy let out a yelp and stumbled towards her. 'Oh my God! Tess!' She enveloped her daughter, covered her with kisses, told her over and over how much she loved her. She clasped Tess's face, held her head there, looked her up and down, inspecting every inch of her.

The flesh and blood of her was overwhelming. It was true: she was really there.

The others gathered around the two of them with their own gasps of relief. The collective joy bubbled over for a few minutes. Rivers of tears were shed. Desperate, grateful, loving hugs were shared.

Amy thanked every star in the sky for granting her this wish. The dark pacts she had made with the devil to take her life and spare her daughter's shrivelled into obscurity. They had been the pleas of a desperate mother, and they were no longer relevant. Tess was safe and well in her arms. Or maybe not so well. She noticed the dirt and the blood and the rips in her pink satin dress. Later, she would ask those horrible questions.

'You're freezing. Come on, let's get you by the Aga and get a hot chocolate inside you,' she said, gripping Tess's hand, spilling more tears, hugging her some more. 'Oh my God, thank God you're safe.'

Only then did she turn to look at William, and she could tell that his heart was still in darkness. His eyes were consumed with fear. While she had her child back, he did not. She said urgently to Tess, 'Where's Hal, sweetheart?'

Tess's bloodshot eyes darted over to William, and she sobbed, 'Hal was the one who found me. He saved my life! But I left him there! I just left him!'

William came closer. 'It's okay, sweetheart. Shh, shh. Where is he now, Tess? Where can I find him?'

# EIGHTY

Hal

The train station was quiet. A few taxis and a huddle of teens were the only signs of life. Hal had slid right down in the front seat. He was traumatised, could barely think straight. The image of Logan and Ralph writhing on the potholed tarmac strobed in slow motion on a loop in his mind; his phone lying in the lane, smashed by Logan's foot.

He had left this vile scene behind and scaled the muddy bank like an animal, sprinting away through the trees. The sense that they were right behind him, grabbing at him through the dark, had spurred him on to run faster than he'd thought possible.

Once he was back in the car and driving away, he had retched several times and trembled violently until his teeth were chattering. He couldn't go home. There were too many unknowns. What if Logan and Ralph's injuries were minor enough for them to drive, and they recovered and tracked him down? What if they were dead? What if Hal was now a murderer?

He needed to wait for Rory, warn him.

His thighs shook uncontrollably. He doubted he would ever be able to stand again. Fear for Rory plagued him. Payback for what Hal had done to Ralph and Logan would be a typical show of power from the men further up the chain.

What had he done?

When the train screeched into the station, Hal didn't dare sit up to scour the crowds. He hoped Rory would see the car parked up near the ticket machine. His heart raced as he listened to a passenger's high heels clip-clopping along the blue pedestrian path to her car. He pictured Tess's bare, dirty feet and his throat closed. They would be torn to shreds by the undergrowth on her long run home.

How he longed to know how she was doing. He hoped she was safe within the walls of Summerfield House, being fussed over by Amy, by her family and friends. But there would be anxiety etched on his father's face...

The conjuring of this happy scene was interrupted by a tap on the window. The intrusion sent him jumping out of his seat and his heart pumping in his chest. He blinked, not trusting what he saw. For a second, he thought his imaginings of Summerfield House had infiltrated his reality. His father couldn't really be there on the other side of this window.

Then William spoke. 'Hal, it's me, Dad. Open up.'

Hal couldn't open the car door fast enough. He felt like a little kid again, catapulting into his dad after a tough day at school, holding him so tightly it hurt. The sobs came thick and fast. William's soothing voice echoed through his chest. Hal was in his dad's arms at last. 'Did Tess make it home?' he cried.

'She's safe,' his father reassured him. 'Thanks to you, she's by the Aga with hot cocoa and Hamish licking her face off.'

They laughed briefly, but his dad was crying. They were both crying. 'My brave boy,' he spluttered. 'It's going to be okay. I'm here now.'

Then Hal remembered why he had been waiting. 'Rory's meant to be on this train. Is he here?' He pulled away from his dad, fear rushing back in. The station had emptied around them.

'I'm afraid we've just heard some bad news, Hal,' his dad said gravely. His voice became small, as though far away. 'Rory has been injured in a knife attack. He was found lying on the pavement outside his dad's London house. He's in a bad way. They don't know if he'll pull through.' And the world fell still.

When they returned to the house, there were two police officers standing at the kitchen island. They just needed to ask Hal some questions about a phone they'd found at the scene. He wasn't in any trouble.

# EIGHTY-ONE

## Amy

It was barely morning. Amy was throwing clothes into a suitcase, tears rolling down her face. William was trotting after her like a loyal, nervous puppy dog, following her from wardrobe to dresser to bathroom and back to the bed.

The rest of the household would be slumbering after a tumultuous night. Maggie and Damian had stayed in the top room. Rupert had slept in a pull-out in the morning room. Jo and Pip had pulled blankets over themselves in the TV den and watched *Friends*. Hal, after talking to the police, had collapsed in his own bed and was asleep before William had even crept out of his room. Amy felt terrible about taking Tess away from him. But her mind was made up. She'd woken Tess half an hour ago and asked her to pack a few of her things.

'You're leaving?' William breathed incredulously. He had already explained that he had seen Sophie only seconds before Amy herself appeared at the clearing, that he had been as shocked to find her there as she had been. But she couldn't listen to his excuses any more.

'Jo's offered to put us up for a few weeks.'

'What about Scotland? Why can't we work things out up there? The house is beautiful and it's too late to cancel it, so we might as well...' He broke off.

'It wouldn't feel right.'

In bed last night, she'd played over in her mind the events of their wedding night. She'd been unable to hang onto her feelings of relief. The cosiness of knowing the kids were tucked up safely and that William was by her side again, albeit not as her husband, had offered up less and less comfort. His breathing had kept her wide awake.

'But Hal and Tess are safe now,' William said. 'Everything's okay!'

'Rory's not safe! He's lying in St George's with three stab wounds to his chest. He could *die*!' she cried.

'I know. I'm desperately worried for him. But you can't blame me for that.'

She hissed under her breath, 'You stood there in the kitchen last night and allowed Hal to lie through his teeth to the police. He didn't even admit he'd been there.'

He brushed his hair off his forehead. 'What the hell was I supposed to do? Was I meant to leap in and tell them he'd shot two men and left them there on the roadside? Especially as they seemed to believe him when he said he'd lent his phone to Tess, and Tess corroborated that. Anyway, they said their injuries were minor and that they'd make a full recovery. Why would the police need to know it was anything other than gang infighting?'

'What if Logan identifies him?'

'Hal was adamant he wouldn't say anything. There's too much at stake further up the line. Snitches aren't treated well in prison.'

'Either way, you should have insisted Hal tell the police the truth. Whatever the outcome.'

'Telling the truth would have ruined his life!'

'William! It's ruined already! His life changed the moment he pulled that trigger, but he can't take it back and you can't pretend it didn't happen!'

'You're okay about him going to prison?'

She threw her trainers into the open suitcase. She felt so tired. 'Jesus. He's a middle-class kid with no previous, and he was saving a girl from being raped by two armed drug dealers, for Christ's sake. With your resources, you could buy him the best lawyer in the country and he'd no doubt walk free.'

'Walk free? To what? He'd be labelled a criminal, stigmatised for the rest of his life. No decent university would take a student who was recently mixed up in county lines. The press would probably get hold of it as well. All his hopes and dreams, gone, in one fell swoop.'

'All *your* hopes and dreams, William. Perhaps Hal has others. Maybe Oxford isn't good enough for him.'

William pleaded with her to understand, dropping his voice even lower. 'Logan and that other dealer would've ended up in trouble with the police someday anyway. So what's the difference?'

Reeling at his prejudices, she spluttered, 'Why is it impossible to imagine that Logan – who is a seventeen-year-old *kid*, by the way – could turn his life around given the right help?'

'Kids who get into that stuff don't tend to get out of it, that's all I meant.'

'On the other hand, you believed Rory deserved a second chance?'

'No, I'm just saying it's more likely he'll get out of that world.'

'Firstly, do you even know what Logan's mum and dad are like? How do you know they're not loving, caring parents who're tearing their hair out right now? How do you know what kind of kid he was before he was groomed by those gangs?'

He tugged at the corner of a pillow on their bed, straightening it. 'I don't.'

'Whereas you know *exactly* what Rory's family is like. His mum's a raging alcoholic – and, quite frankly, mentally unstable – and his dad beat him to a pulp for most of his childhood. From where I'm standing, that kid doesn't have great prospects either. What do you reckon?'

'But what do you expect me to do about that? You want me to deprive Hal of what he has, just to make it fairer?'

Amy was soaked in disappointment, deflated by him. 'You haven't learned a bloody thing from any of this, have you? Literally nothing.'

'What do you mean?'

'I'm talking about the *truth*, William. Honesty. Decency. Right and wrong. Doesn't that stand for anything?'

He puffed out his chest and stood stiff and wide-legged. 'I would do anything for my son!'

She let her hands flop by her sides. 'Then show him how to be a decent human being. Show him that he is not above the law. That he has to take responsibility for his actions. Show him how to be a *true* hero. He's got what it takes to do that, if only you'd let him. I mean, look at what he did for Tess. He's an amazing and courageous young man. Believe in him, William. Expect better.'

'I absolutely expect the very best for him!' he bellowed, losing his temper for the first time since they'd been together. 'That's what I stand for! I stand for providing the best for my family! I stand for loyalty and decent values! I stand for my family's good name! And if it's the last thing I do, I'll make sure our dirty laundry isn't washed in public. That's what I stand for,' he added, 'and if you don't stand for the same things, then we have a problem.'

She looked away from him and zipped up her bag. 'Yes, William. We do have a problem.'

Over the months of living at Summerfield House, she had learned fast, adapted, tried to make this alien life her own. She had changed for him: sold her flat, left her London life behind, her good friends, her job, and had even uprooted her daughter. She hadn't minded. It had all been for love. And she had found a rhythm and contentedness in the countryside. Yet he had changed so little for her. During moments of tension, when she'd doubted his integrity and his honesty, doubted *herself*, she had been the one to concede, to compromise and to forgive. Rather than finding the confidence to speak up, find some middle ground between them, she had given ever more ground, had edged closer and closer towards what he wanted. She had almost given him all her money, even. It was impossible to get any nearer without stepping over a line and losing herself entirely.

The bad example they'd set had had near-devastating consequences for their own children. Olivia was living out that very reality right now. If William couldn't recognise that they were in part to blame, it was impossible to see how they'd recover from it. Bridging the gap was going to take a monumental shift on his part. Last night, when he had allowed Hal to lie to the police, he had proven he was incapable of it.

In the face of so much change around them, his intransigence, his incapacity for compromise, his inability to open up or form close friendships struck her now as deeply dysfunctional. A survival mechanism, perhaps. But what was he surviving? Had the death of his mother at such a young age shut him down, arrested his development? Probably. Tragically. Though Amy didn't know for sure. He was indeed impenetrable, as Eleanor had apparently once remarked.

She picked up her bag, preparing to walk out.

'You can't leave,' he said, almost inaudibly. He took a step back. His pale green eyes were so washed out they were almost colourless. He'd slept in his clothes. They were rumpled. His grey waistcoat was buttoned up wrongly. Her heart ripped in two. If she had made it down the aisle yesterday, she might have tenderly rebuttoned it. The congregation would have chuckled affectionately, charmed by a sweet moment that marked the beginning of her caring for him as his wife.

'I *can* leave,' she said. 'But you can't. Can you?'

He opened his mouth, closed it. Then breathed, 'But you don't know why I can't.'

'*Why*, William? Please tell me why,' she begged.

*Dare to know.*

He sat heavily on the window seat. 'You know that photo you found? The one of the baby you thought was Hal?'

'Yes?'

'It wasn't Hal.'

She stood very still, put her bag back down on the bed. She'd known there was something he had been keeping from her. Deep down, she'd always known. 'Who was it, William?' she asked quietly.

'He was my firstborn son.' And he began to speak, the banks finally breaking.

The unfolding of his tragedy was like a tidal wave, leaving her short of breath. The story unravelled from William's lips, but it seemed to her that it was his baby son who was relaying the details of his short life to her, as though pressing his existence onto her, filling the room, making himself as important to Amy as he had been to William. Tears rolled down her cheeks as she listened, sitting on the edge of the bed as though she might need to bolt from the room, unable to hear any more. By the end, she was sore-eyed and distraught.

She couldn't believe what William had been through nor what he had kept from her. She needed time to absorb this new reality. He had harboured a secret so dark and devastating, she felt she was looking upon an entirely different man from the one she had so innocently fallen in love with. In one way, her admiration and sympathy for him was greater than ever, for surviving one of the worst traumas any human could experience: the loss of a child. Throughout every excruciating twist, he'd thought he could manage the unmanageable. Her heart went out to him. But in her other guise, as the duped partner, she knew she couldn't pick up these pieces for him now, not when he had chosen to shut her out for so long.

Through a barely controlled sob, she stammered, 'I'm so sorry, William.' She tried to stem the tears spilling from her eyes as she looked up at his anguished, haggard face. 'I'm so sorry you've been through this. The pain you've experienced is literally... unimaginable. I'm so sorry for you. I'm so sorry for you.'

He fell before her, laid his head on her lap. 'Now you know why I can never leave this house.'

A wave of profound sadness swamped her. She rested her hand on his head and stroked it briefly, feeling desperate about what she had to do.

'And now I know why I can never stay,' she said, the terrible words catching in her throat.

Still in tears, she slipped out from under the weight of him, grabbed her bag and propelled herself out of the door, leaving the broken shards of her heart in a trail behind her.

William stayed in the yellow room while Amy and Tess climbed into the back of Jo's car. Maggie came down in her nightie to hug them goodbye while Damian packed their things upstairs.

Amy said to her sister, 'If you see him before you leave... I mean, if you two talk at all before you leave, just tell him... tell him I love him, won't you?'

'Oh pet, are you sure about this?' Maggie asked.

'Yes. One hundred per cent.' Amy embraced her again so that she couldn't see her tormented face.

'Come and visit us in Scotland soon,' Maggie said, and Amy promised she would.

As they drove away, with Pip reassuring them that this was the right thing to do, Amy turned back to take in the receding vision of the house. In the morning light, half of it was illuminated and warmed by the sun, and the other half was in shadow. The heads of the pink roses that scaled its walls fell forward heavily. The oak door was blackened with age but still solid. The leaded diamonds on the windows were elegant bars keeping the occupants in, separating them off. Protecting them from nothing.

A tiny baby was not at rest there. She had heard his cries herself.

# EIGHTY-TWO

William

Hal had taken only a couple of days off school. William felt it was better that he return to his routine as soon as possible. It showed everyone that Rory's demise was not Hal's too. The headmaster of Heathside Heights had made a point of making sure he had the emotional support he needed after the shock of Rory's attack. Everyone was understanding; none of them understood. Hal's and Tess's involvement might have been a whisper on the wind, but there weren't any facts. Exactly how William had wanted it.

Every day he worked in the spare room where he'd set up his office. His chalet office was locked. He never went near it. Each afternoon Hal came home from school and went straight to his room. He came down for supper at seven and William quizzed him on his lessons and his homework. Hal ate very little of what Mercy cooked for them. But thank God for Mercy! William had extended her hours and increased her pay. In turn, she took care of them and the house. They didn't talk about anything but the weather and shopping lists. As it should be.

Weeks passed by like this. Months passed by like this. Life passed him by.

He had nothing left for anything else. Amy's tear-stained freckles had stripped him bare. He did not feel pain. Neither did he feel any pleasure. The last time had been when Amy had walked towards him through the bluebells. He'd been eager as a boy to pull up her veil and see her face and take her hands in his, yet this joy had been out of his reach. Permitting himself love at those depths had been wrong. He ought to have carried with him at all times the aide-memoire of his shameful past. Happiness wasn't on the cards for him.

Hal was his only reason to get up in the morning.

Then, like a vulture swooping in on a dead carcass, Sophie had called in on him one afternoon in May. He made them coffee. His tasted too bitter to drink.

'How's the boy, Rory, doing?' she asked in her husky voice, shaking her head, replacing a strand of hair into her barrette. Unlike him, she looked well rested.

'He's made a full recovery,' he mumbled, numb to her false concern.

'I hear they moved to Somerset.'

'So you know anyway.'

'I keep my ear to the ground.' She sipped her coffee and let out a long exhale. 'Wow. It's good to be back.'

'It's *so* good to have you,' he said, his voice dripping with sarcasm.

'Oh, darling. Don't be like that. I'm a fact of your life.'

She was indeed a fact of his life. She was perhaps all he had now. Not forgetting his father, who occasionally visited from Portugal. They were the people who'd made him who he was. People like him. People like us.

'It's all too late now.' He was beyond caring.

There was silence between them.

'What Amy did to you was unforgivable. But you'll get on and it'll feel better soon.'

Irritation rushed up inside him. 'You sound just like your mum.'

She pursed her lips, but they twitched into a smile. 'I'll take that as a compliment.'

He turned away to put his cup in the dishwasher.

She said, 'Oh William. You can't mope about with me now. I've had a lovely idea for the naming ceremony.'

# EIGHTY-THREE

Tess

It was June half-term. Tess and Hal were at the counter of Juice It Up. She glanced at him as he squinted at the menu board. His cheeks were hollow. His hands, resting on the counter, were skeletal. His jeans were hanging loose from the bones of his hips.

'Order the Zone,' Tess suggested. 'It'll bulk you up.'

'What're you saying?'

'More meat on a sparrow's ankle, as my gran would've said.'

He managed half a grin and ordered the protein smoothie. She ordered her regular and they ambled towards Riddlesdown Common. It was a sunny day, which she was glad about.

'So this is your hood,' he said.

'Yup,' she replied, but the noisy streets of the city made her jumpy these days.

'I bet you don't miss Haslemere.'

'No bloody way.'

'One for the swear box.'

She laughed. They continued on without talking for a bit. She was thinking about Rory. 'Have you heard how he's doing?'

'You know that after he got out of hospital, Olivia sold Oak Hills and they moved to Somerset, don't you?'

'Yeah, Mum told me that much. I just haven't heard anything since.'

'Some boarding school down there took him, I think.'

'They must be desperate.'

He snorted. 'Or kind-hearted and forgiving.'

'Yeah, right. More like they needed the fees really badly.'

'Olivia calls Mum sometimes. I think she's met someone. And Rory's doing okay.'

'No consequences, then?'

There was a sticky silence, and she remembered that for Hal there had been none either. The bubble of wealth continued to protect him. She was glad of it, considering what he had done for her. But envy laced through her as she pictured his mapped-out life in the beauty of Summerfield House versus her own uncertain future in Jo's attic room, sharing a bed with her mum.

'I wonder what'll happen to Logan,' he said absently, as though reading her mind.

'Mum did some digging and found out. The police have put him in some kind of witness protection programme. They said he'd been groomed by that gang from the age of ten. But a police officer helped him get out of it.'

'For real?'

'Yup. He'll probably have a chance of a normal life now.'

'A normal life,' he muttered. 'Do you even know what that would feel like?' he asked, turning to her as though he expected a real answer.

'I've no clue.'

The weight of what they'd been through together slowed her down for a minute. Catching her breath, she hoped she wasn't going to have one of her panic attacks in front of him. Hal stopped and waited for her. A concerned frown formed on his brow, as though he understood what was going through her head. Around them the traffic was a distant hum. She focused on the calming noises: the giggle of a child on a scooter and the birds singing in the trees.

Her love of nature was one topic she regularly returned to in her therapy sessions. Together she and her psychotherapist had identified that green spaces helped her to process her trauma. It was why she walked with her mum on the common every day, sharing news of her day and how she was feeling about everything. They would discuss where they should live and would scroll through Rightmove on their phones. Tess never wanted these walks to end. The thought of going back through the hard London streets to Jo's house – with its one inadequate lock – was always a struggle. Nightmares about Ralph breaking in to finish the job plagued her every night. Her screams would wake Eve or Luke one floor down. But her mum would shuffle up next to her and stroke her forehead until she fell asleep again. In the cold light of day, she knew Ralph was on remand in Feltham, but at night she felt his presence nearby, and wondered if she would for the rest of her life.

Jo and Ted had been kind, insisted they stay for as long as they needed. It had already been too long. As much as possible they tried to stay out of their hosts' way. Their only escape was their bedroom, the spare room in the eaves, which was too small for two adults to stand up in. They had to share the double bed and keep their clothes in their suitcases underneath. The only surface for Tess's schoolbooks was the chest of drawers under the skylight, which was crowded with the spider plants that Ted cultivated.

There was no respite for her at her new school either. The atmosphere was edgy. There was knife-detection security at the entrance, prison-like lines painted along the corridors to separate the flows of children, and daily visits from a police van. Tess kept her head down, got by, but her heart wasn't in it. More than anything, she missed having friends, even longed for a chat with Anoushka and Tilly. They sometimes FaceTimed, but more often they aired her.

Malena was at the outstanding Catholic sixth-form college nearby, where Tess would have gone had she stayed at Kenmore High. It had strict admission criteria, taking only children from three specific feeder schools. Occasionally they would meet up and share a Nando's, but their wildly different experiences had left them with little in common. Tess found it impossible to talk about her life at Summerfield House, which felt like a dream that had morphed into a nightmare.

She said to Hal now, 'You know, Mum said rare orchids grow round here.'

'No way.'

'It's hard to believe, right?'

'Most of life these days has become hard to believe,' he said glumly.

Her legs felt wobbly. They found a bench and stayed there for a while. He put his arm around her when she cried. He didn't need to ask her why.

An elderly couple pottered past. They smiled at them tenderly, as though they recognised young love. 'We were like you two once,' the woman said.

'We're just brother and sister,' Hal said politely. He squeezed Tess and kissed her forehead.

Brother and sister. This was true, and it gave her a sense of belonging. She felt at home with Hal in a soulful way. This awkward boy had become her unlikely brother. He had been there at her worst point and had saved her from even worse. And she missed him every single day.

'How's your dad doing?' she asked.

'Good. Yeah. Mercy is full-time now. And he's bought an electric Porsche.'

'Mid-life crisis?' she teased.

He didn't smile. 'How's your mum?'

'Great. She got her old job back and she's doing an evening course in kitchen design. We're looking at apartments round here. Jo and Ted have been amazing.'

'That's good.' He removed his arm from her shoulders, taking a short sip from his smoothie, which she noticed was still full.

'Yeah,' she said under her breath.

They looked at each other and Tess guffawed. 'We're so full of shit! Mum's *sooo* not fine!'

Hal chuckled sheepishly. 'Dad fucking hates that car. It gives him backache. He is so fucking miserable, even Mercy took me aside and suggested he get some help.'

'Mercy?' Tess was agog. 'It really must be bad.'

'It's like he's totally shut down.'

'That must be awful for you,' she said, scanning his hollowed-out face.

'I wish they'd get back together.' Shyly Hal peered at her from under his lank flop of hair.

She was taken aback. Her mum talked about William endlessly and passionately, sometimes like a stuck record, but it was usually in negative terms.

'I wish they would too,' she said, truthfully. Despite his faults, it was obvious her mum still loved him.

But she suspected Hal wanted their parents to make another go of it for his own sake. She felt sad for him. His thinness was alarming. From an outsider's point of view, he might look either anorexic or ill. Tess suspected it was post-traumatic stress. What he had done for her that night seemed to have eaten him away, and she felt a stab of guilt. Despite the recent challenges, she was unbelievably lucky to have her mum looking after her. And to have Pip and Jo with their bear hugs and cheese straws on tap. To have her therapist to talk to and cry with every week. Everyone around her was in tune with what she needed emotionally, which made all the difference. She was so much more fortunate than Hal. Of the two of them, *she* was the privileged one. Before now, she had never fully appreciated this.

# EIGHTY-FOUR

William

The tips of William's trainers were lined up behind a seam of grouting. This was where he wanted them to stay. The apple blossom exploded before them like a mess of feeling he was tentative about stepping into. Sophie was kneeling at his feet with her small black paintbrush, expertly drawing the beginnings of an italic 'T'.

Nervously he watched her painstaking efforts. Despite agreeing to this, he was suddenly worried that it would unleash something scary in him. Or the opposite. It might be inadequate, anticlimactic, not provide the closure he'd hoped for. He couldn't seem to imagine how it would feel to see it come to fruition.

The 'h' and the 'o' were painted already.

The 'm' was feathery light with Sophie's brush. Incomplete, like his son's existence.

She wrote the 'a'.

He couldn't rest as he watched. He drilled his thumb knuckles into his thighs to still his quivering hands.

The 's' was scribed with a flourish.

She plopped the brush into the murky glass of water and stood up slowly, tilted her head to peruse her beautiful calligraphy.

'Thomas,' she whispered.

It was the name of her father and now their dead son. The sound of it winded him. He couldn't breathe for a second. His baby's soul engulfed him.

His tiny presence had once been larger than life. Every hope and dream of William's had been tied up in those minute fingers and toes. Little Thomas had never learned how to say 'Daddy', but he had known his daddy. He had lived almost his entire life in his daddy's arms. William had held him, watched him suck eagerly on those little bottles, seen his zest for life. He had known him deeply, as well as you could know any other living being. In his arms, his son had been a little personality already. A sweet, determined, feisty boy. William had traced every inch of his velvety skin with his fingers and had loved who he was already, and who he would be.

Yet nobody else in the world had known him. His beautiful boy had become a dreadful whispered secret. How could that be? How could they have hidden his life away? How had he denied him a funeral? A eulogy? A congregation of mourners? A family celebrating his days alive and the intense joy those had brought into William's heart?

As William stood by Sophie, he could not fathom how he had let this happen.

Baby Thomas's searching, blinking almond eyes were inside him now, open, filling him with unending love and with the truth of his existence.

'Why did we keep him a secret?' he said.

'What?'

Louder this time. 'I said, why did we keep him a secret?'

'William,' Sophie whined disapprovingly.

'I want an answer. I want to know why.' He was nearly shouting. He would not let it go.

'You know why,' she said under her breath, glancing at the door. 'To protect us. To allow us a normal life.'

He said what he had never before dared to think. 'That morning, you were already awake when I came in, weren't you?'

'I don't remember.'

'You had your eyes closed, but I could tell by your breathing that you were pretending.'

'Why would I do that?'

'You knew he was dead. You waited until I found him.'

'No,' she whispered, covering her face.

'You told me that you felt to blame for his death, and I assumed it was only natural to feel guilty about what had happened. Anyone would. I felt illogically guilty too, for not being in the room when he was struggling.' He faltered. 'But you were trying to tell me something more than that, weren't you? You were telling me something I didn't want to hear.'

She lowered her hands. Her eyes were red. 'I let him cry himself out. Every mother has let their baby cry too long!'

William's head filled with blood and he wondered if her long fingers were around his throat. But they weren't, they were wrapped around her own, like a bony necklace.

His voice became a low, menacing growl, like a dog's before it bit. 'When you were letting him "cry out", did you know he was under the covers?'

Her nails scratched at her skin. She shook her head. 'I don't know.'

'I think you do, Sophie.'

Her eyes leaked guilt. Her lips turned blue, as though the life force was draining out of her before his very eyes. He didn't need to hear her answer.

The violent desire to lurch at her reared up inside him. She had shredded the truth, tossed it into the air and left the broken pieces spinning around his head. He couldn't make sense of it, couldn't put it back together in his mind. Didn't want to believe it. The reality of her culpability versus what he had previously understood as a tragic accident seesawed in his thoughts. One version crashing to the ground as untrue while the other elevated itself, upheld as fact. Then *boom*, it switched and the other was aloft. Amy's words came into his head like a battle cry: *I'm talking about the truth, William. Honesty. Decency. Right and wrong. Doesn't that stand for anything?*

Those words gave him power, and he held himself back from Sophie.

'I don't need you to say it,' he murmured.

He was walking away from her, out into the hot summer sun. He shielded his eyes as he strode through the orchard, powerful and determined for the first time in his life. Without delay, without a second's more deliberation or prevarication, he drove out of Summerfield House, towards the police station.

This was where he would become the man he'd been too scared to be.

This was the day he would finally tell the truth.

The truth was that Thomas Hargreaves had been born on 19 November 1990 and had died on 20 December 1990 by suffocation.

It was the truth that he had been running from all his adult life. He didn't yet know where that truth would take him or what the consequences of it would be, but he didn't care. All that mattered to him was that Thomas, his son, be counted.

# EIGHTY-FIVE

## 20 DECEMBER 1990

Me, Thomas

My mother put on loud music and twirled me around the green room. The walls were spinning. My new eyes couldn't keep up. Her skin got hot, her body vibrated, and I sensed her joy. I was feeling warm and safe, thinking life was going to be good if it carried on like this. If I hadn't been too young to giggle or gurgle, I would have. Hiccuping and lolling about on her shoulder was more my thing, and burping sick onto a little towel embroidered with two green apples. Mum gave me a kiss when I did that, like I'd done something she was proud of.

The happy dancing time didn't last. When night-time came, she was scratchy and fractious. I had been a handful all day. My complaining was too much for her. Her frowns and lip-biting and sighs caused bubbles of worry in my belly. When she picked me up, I would cry louder.

Before bed, my father came in to change my nappy. He blew raspberries onto my tummy. I weed into his face and he laughed his head off. I loved gazing into his eyes. They were the definition of loving. Looking at him calmed me down.

After my milk, I couldn't get a burp up, which made me cross. But she didn't understand. Her pretty eyes reddened and narrowed and her mouth contorted, and she shouted at me for the first and the last time.

'OH MY GOD. *Shut the FUCK UP!*' she screeched, and she slung me onto the sheets. I shouted back at her and kicked out my heels and curled my toes, incandescent with rage.

I wished we had been able to kiss and make up before the end.

The eiderdown quilt was goose down and patterned with little red roses. Its warmth and weight muffled my grating screams and pinned my mother's limbs to the mattress. The tiny, squirming mound of me was there at her feet, but she wasn't helping me. I wanted her to hear me as I punched into that eiderdown and sucked in its heavy cotton. But she didn't. The thickness of it must've smothered my crying. Because if she'd heard me, she would have taken it off my face.

Instead, her eyes were wide and fixed on nothing in the dark, waiting for me to stop, punishing me. I had rejected her, so she was rejecting me. That's all. That's all it was.

Wah, wah, wah, I went on and on. *Make it stop!* my mother screamed in her head.

My father was asleep a few rooms away. If she had woken him, she feared he'd view her as a failure. Better he did not find out that the mother of his child was unfit for the job.

Finally my mewling sounds abated. My feet and fists stopped jerking about, too exhausted to fight any more. The air fell still. For my mother, the relief was like death itself. Part of me wondered whether I chose to leave her, as though I sensed she couldn't cope with me any longer.

She slept. She dreamed of a giant baby in the corner of a stripped-bare room like a squat. This baby was grubby and quiet and menacing. Like me, he had learned that crying got him nowhere.

The dawn light crept in. My mother and I lay motionless.

When my father came in to say good morning, my mother closed her tired, tired eyes and played dead. Inside, she *was* dead. What she had done – or failed to do – that night had been the silent slaughtering of two souls. Mine and hers. Yet she was not cognisant of this. She knew only of the escalating panic in my father as he searched for his son. His purpled, lifeless son. But I would never open my eyes to gaze on him lovingly again.

And now they had named me, six feet above where I had been laid to rest. The truth of my demise was out. I could leave my parents in peace now. My soul drifted from my little makeshift tomb, rising to swirl around their heads, further on up to eddy above the roofs and trees.

The grounds of Summerfield House would find quietness at long last.

*I love you, Mum and Dad. Thank you.*

# EIGHTY-SIX

Amy

The estate agent was also called Sophie, which rankled with Amy and tempered her enthusiasm for the flat they were viewing.

'It's got double-glazing throughout,' Sophie enthused.

There were two windows. One in the bedroom and one in the front room. Both were grimy, offering a soft-focus view across the double-laned traffic to the GP hub of the Purley War Memorial Hospital. Along one wall there was what you might call a kitchen, which faced a sofa, where Sophie had suggested they put their own sofa bed to double as a second bedroom.

'It's a lot smaller than our last place,' Amy said dolefully, longing to step across the comforting threshold of number 7 again, wanting to erase the last year completely.

Sophie shoved her paisley-print Alice band forward a little, making a bigger quiff of her hair at the front. 'Prices have gone crazy over the last couple of years. Most go to sealed bids.'

'Not this one?' Amy asked, wondering what was wrong with it – other than the obvious.

'The vendor wants a quick sale.'

'It's a lot better than the other places we've seen. And we've got to imagine it cleaned up and with our own furniture. We can make it cosy, right?' Amy said, trying to make the best of it.

'Hmm,' Tess said, nodding. It was clear she wanted to cry. So did Amy.

Worse than ending up back at square one, here they were at minus square one, with less space than number 7. When she imagined pottering around the kitchen of Summerfield House, which was double the size of the flat they stood in now, she realised she had begun to take it for granted. Aspects of it had begun to annoy her. She had wished the curtains were different; had been irritated by the stiffness of the cutlery drawer; had thought the downlighters too bright. How easy it was to be spoiled, to become dissatisfied with what you had.

They trudged down the stairwell that smelt of dead things and outside onto the street, passing an old man sitting by his window on a kitchen chair. He had a large paunch and no teeth, but he grinned a beautiful gummy smile from ear to ear and waved in a friendly way before taking another puff of his cigarette. Sophie waved back. 'Hello, Tony. How's it going?'

'Can't complain,' he said, winking at them.

Can't complain, Amy thought. Couldn't he? Could *she*?

They said goodbye to Tony and then to Sophie, telling her they'd think about it, promising they'd get back to her this afternoon. Or they'd miss out, she warned.

Amy and Tess sat at the bus stop. A young man sat next to them. He wore tortoiseshell glasses and carried a black leather portfolio and a glass coffee cup with a red plastic top. He did a double take at Tess, who didn't notice his admiring glance. She looked as beautiful and as glum as a girl could be.

'I'm sorry,' Amy said. She had failed her daughter. 'It won't be too bad.'

'Mum, honestly, I'm fine with it,' Tess replied earnestly,

pulling out her best smile, which fell short of happy by about a thousand miles.

'You can have the main bedroom.'

'No! Mum, you have to have that.'

'No way. It's non-negotiable. You've got your A levels next year.'

On the way home to Jo's place, Amy silently mulled over how she might earn more. If they were to stay in Purley, or anywhere near London, buying a two-bed was unaffordable. Renting was the next option, but it would burn through their cash in no time. Before long they'd have no money left and would have to move anyway. They were so lucky to have the money to buy anywhere.

Can't complain, she thought.

Her heart thudded like a big drum when the cinematic image of William's tall, loping form filled her mind. His kind eyes and flyaway blond hair and shy halfway-there smile were painful to think about still. Suppressing her love for that face of his would be a lifelong battle. She questioned the hypocrisy of this. Here she was, resolving to shove him away into the recesses of her mind, disallowing her feelings. It was exactly what she had accused him of. Now she contemplated a whole life of denying how much she loved him. It was one way of surviving it.

Before dinner, which Tess was cooking tonight, Amy went upstairs for a shower. She stood in the bathtub with the duck-patterned shower curtain clinging to her legs and cried. The water cascaded over her face until she decided she had stood there long enough. She turned off the tap, along with her self-pity.

Wrapped in her towel, she sat on the bed with her wet feet dripping onto the clothes in her suitcase. Going down for dinner tonight was going to be hard. She didn't know how she would put a brave face on it. Maybe she could just sit here all night and see what happened. Given time, the bad feelings might go away. A chill set in across her arms. Her hair dried in fluffy clumps. The bad feelings weren't going anywhere. When she heard the thud-thud of footsteps up the stairs, she tried to rally herself, picked up her phone as a foil.

'Mum? Your pasta's going cold. You okay?' Tess said, hovering at the doorway.

'Oh yes, sorry! I had a few work emails to finish.'

Tess didn't question her and closed the door, perhaps scared to come closer, which Amy didn't blame her for. Now that the phone was in her palm, she clicked into Instagram, lost for anything better to do. She scrolled through the pretty photographs of other people's lives. For a while, not one shot represented what she wanted – fancy lifestyles had lost their appeal – until her eyes feasted upon a reel of an ordinary-looking woman and her dog. They were walking along an empty beach in Scotland. The space around them caught Amy's breath. In the three-second film, the woman had stopped to lean into the wind that came off the sea in strong gusts. The spaniel's long ears were plastered to the sides of his head. He was howling and the woman was throwing her arms out with wild abandon. It represented happiness to Amy.

She tried to scroll on and forget it, but she returned to that one post multiple times. Each time she replayed it, she was overcome by a very specific yearning to feel like that woman. In her heart, she was already her. She had rejected a life that was bound by string and had flung her arms out to feel the freedom of that choice. The only regret was that William hadn't been confident enough to do the same. *Confidence is good, but overconfidence always sinks the ship.* William's overconfidence hid the real man. He'd been taught to cheat the system, jump the rungs, fast-track success. All the while, he skipped the slow, hard graft of becoming himself, of facing up to his fears, experiencing failure and finding his own truth.

Tess had lit candles. Everyone was in a chatty mood. Eve mentioned Jamie in her English class – apparently for the third time – and they teased her about it. Ted joked about polishing his shotgun, which made them laugh. But Amy couldn't engage. She was waiting for a lull in the banter.

'The flat we saw today was hideous,' she declared, having finally found her window.

'Oh no!' Jo cried.

'It was filthy and right opposite the hospital and it didn't even have a proper kitchen or a second bedroom.'

'Have you got more viewings planned?' Ted asked nervously.

'Nope. That's the best we're going to get around here.'

Jo laughed. 'Right, okay. I'll get budgeting for that extension then.'

'No! Sorry, Jo. I didn't mean to freak you out. We're not going to be outstaying our welcome here much longer, I promise. Because I have a plan.' Amy paused. 'I haven't even discussed it with Tess. So Tess, please do say if you hate the idea.'

'Go on,' Tess said, obviously intrigued.

'I was thinking we could move nearer to my sister. In Scotland somewhere,' Amy said, biting her lip but forging on. 'We'd be able to find a little house, even. The schools and universities are amazing. And the countryside is gorgeous. It would be a brand-new start for both of us. Away from everything that's happened. We would be able to live better there. And I mean *live* rather than just exist.'

All eyes were on Tess.

'I'm not anti the idea, weirdly,' Tess said.

At this, Amy couldn't rein in her new-found enthusiasm. 'I honestly think it's the solution. I miss the countryside so much. Don't you?' Tess nodded. 'But we can't go back to Surrey, for obvious reasons, and we have connections in Scotland. And it's only a train ride away from you guys.' She looked to Jo.

'A bloody long train ride,' Jo said grumpily.

'But it makes sense, right?'

'It doesn't sound totally insane,' Ted conceded.

'Admittedly, it's a bit of a wild card,' Amy said, pinching her thumb and forefinger together and wincing. 'But after the year we've had, maybe going large on an adventure is just the thing to do.'

'I'm up for it, Mum,' Tess said. 'Anything but that depressing flat we saw today!' she added.

Her big, happy, genuine smile said it all. For the first time in a long time, Amy felt hope swell in her chest.

# EIGHTY-SEVEN

William

William's bones were tired as he trudged away from the dug-out, defunct chalet office. He hardly had enough energy to push open the French windows to the main house. Mercy immediately zipped her anorak up over her sweatshirt, which said *I Need You* across the front, and reached for her handbag.

'They're gone, I think,' he sighed. 'Wait a second.' He found some cash. 'Thank you. For all the extra hours. I don't know what I would have done without you over these past few weeks.'

Her smile was kind. 'It's nothing,' she said. This was untrue. Hosting the various police officers tramping through the house had not been easy on either of them. William couldn't yet think straight about what it had been like to see the men dig down below the blossom tiles under his office to shed sunlight on his son's remains. His baby bones had been embedded in the soil like a delicate, precious fossil. What he had gone through in that moment as he'd vomited his guts out onto the Sandeman-Gores' hallowed ground would take many lifetimes to get over.

The hours being questioned by the police had been equally

traumatic. He'd been forced to rake up every last detail of what had happened and had feared for his future. However, it was Sophie who had been charged with neglect and gross negligence manslaughter, although not with the unlawful burial of her baby's body. Avril had taken the blame for that, convincing the police that both William and Sophie had been ignorant of the cover-up. Due to her age and ill health – and the suspicion that she had been at the mercy of what her employers had dictated – their lawyers predicted she would be spared incarceration. As, they suspected, would Sophie, who might get a suspended sentence, depending on how the trial panned out next year.

The lawyers remained cautiously optimistic. Avril would be a key witness. Her testimony should prove that Sophie, at only sixteen, had not been in control of the decision to hide Thomas's life and death. Whether or not she had knowingly left the covers on his face was impossible to prove. They expected that the late Annie Sandeman-Gore and the late Thomas Sandeman-Gore Senior would be found as the guilty parties. William was okay about that. He'd come to the conclusion that Sophie had suffered enough.

'Eleanor called. Hal will be home at seven,' Mercy said, bustling about. 'I've made a lasagne. Put it in for forty-five minutes at a hundred and eighty degrees. Not that he'll eat it.' She tsked.

'Whyever not? It's his favourite.'

She raised both eyebrows at him. 'I'll see you tomorrow.'

Tomorrow? There was a tomorrow? He didn't know what that would bring or whether he'd get there. He buried his face in Hamish's fur. For now, all he could think about was resting his eyes on Hal's face. Hal had been on holiday with Eleanor and the pilot in Corfu, and oblivious to what had happened here. The anticipation of seeing him was the only incentive to remain upright. It felt like he had been away for months, but it had only been three weeks. Three of the hardest, longest weeks.

He reheated the lasagne. Then he laid the table and waited for Hal to arrive. When he heard the taxi on the drive, his heart fluttered. He put the steaming dish on a mat in the middle of the table and headed for the door. They collided with each other in the hall.

Suddenly William understood what Mercy had been trying to tell him. The shock of Hal's weight loss hit him with blunt force. He wondered if he had gasped out loud – hoped he had not. Hal pulled his lips into a smile. The corners of his mouth were red raw, like the beginnings of malnutrition. He allowed William to hug his bony frame, giving him a moment to rearrange his features and catch his breath. His mind raced. Hal had tipped from thin, which William had previously put down to stress, to dangerously underweight. How had he not noticed before? How had this happened so fast?

Feeling panicky, he had an urge to shovel the whole tray of lasagne into Hal's mouth. Then he contemplated bundling him into the car and taking him straight to A&E. Logically, he knew nothing could be done tonight, but the urgency of his son's state gripped him, had flipped a switch inside him. It dawned on him that while he had been force-feeding him his foolish values over these past months, Hal had been embarking on a quiet ongoing campaign of rejecting them. He had turned himself inside out, exposing an internal agony for all to see. William had been too wrapped up in his own grief to notice his gradual decline. He realised he had been getting away with nothing.

'Come and sit down. Have some lasagne,' he said pathetically.

He reached for the serving spoon, breaking through the cheesy crust, dolloping a portion on his son's plate. Hal stared at the steam rising, but the pile of food went untouched. They caught up in superficial ways. Hal talked at an unusual rate to distract from what he wasn't putting in his mouth, but he shared little of any value. Every forkful that William ate further highlighted Hal's not eating.

'Just have a few mouthfuls, maybe,' William cajoled.

Hal toyed with the food. The lasagne congealed on his plate.

William was only able to get through half of his before putting his fork down and giving up himself. Hal's skeletal appearance was like a grotesque reflection of his mistakes as a father, a generational echo of festering secrets and repressed feelings, and it was gut-wrenching. This was Hal's hunger strike. He was making himself ill from their keeping of secrets: both William's and his own.

Humbled and terrified, William stood up to clear their plates, questioning whether to act on instinct. The shackles of his upbringing, of his class, of his indoctrinations were tight around his ankles.

Bravely he turned to face his son and asked him to remain seated.

'I've got something to tell you, Hal,' he began, dry-throated.

Hal's stricken expression almost floored him. William was not ready, would never be ready, but morning would come soon, and Hal would see for himself the dismantled chalet office.

As William paced along the bank of windows, he fumbled backwards and forwards in time and told Hal about the police, and the secret past of Summerfield House, and the baby brother he'd never met. And it felt like free-falling.

# EIGHTY-EIGHT

## SIX MONTHS LATER

Amy

Amy unpacked the shopping. She had become careful about making a thorough list before she went to the supermarket these days. If she forgot the butter, it was a strenuous drive in her old Land Rover along a single-lane track to the shop in Balmaha to get more.

A couple of orange lentils escaped. She decanted the whole lot from the packet into the glass jar and put it back on the open shelf. Dhal was on the menu for Hal's last meal with them tonight. He liked it with yoghurt and fresh coriander. Over the five days he'd been there, she'd cooked him only his favourite meals. Already his appetite had started to improve, helped by the hikes that Tess had dragged him on with Meggie, their scruffy rescue mutt.

When Tess had first suggested he visit them on his way to look at Glasgow University, Amy had been sceptical, nervous of how to be around him. The simple fact of his closeness to William was unsettling. Nevertheless, Tess had been dead set on it and Hal had flown up here on his own to stay the week. And it had whizzed by.

Later that evening, when Hal and Tess came to eat their steaming bowls of dhal, Amy noticed they were shuffling about edgily, in a jumpy mood. There was a conspiratorial air between the two of them. Amy didn't like what it brought up in her, reminding her of kept secrets of the past.

Towards the end of the meal, when Hal shared the latest on his court case, she wondered whether this had been the source of their agitation.

'I'm very impressed with you, you know. For coming clean to the police. That took real guts,' she said, subtly passing comment on the failings of his father.

'You know, Dad was the one who made me go to the police,' he told her. 'I would never have done it otherwise.'

Her heart thumped. She hadn't known this. 'Is that right?' she replied casually, bowled over by the revelation.

'He was relentless, going on and on about honesty and decency and lecturing me all the time about right and wrong. It wasn't like him at all.' He shrugged, half grinning at Amy.

Without missing a beat, she said, 'I'm glad he was listening to me after all,' and mopped up her dhal with the last of her naan to stop the tremor in her fingers.

'I wanted to tell you...' Hal broke off, looking shyly at Tess, who nodded at him to go on. 'I just wanted to say that it was the right thing to do. You know? It's a real weight lifted. And my barrister thinks it's going to be okay. He can argue I was using reasonable force to protect myself... and others.' He rubbed the back of his neck. 'Also, there's my age. And the information I gave them on Ralph will help. As long as I don't leg it to South America or anything.'

Amy immediately understood the significance of what he

was telling her; not so much about the fact that he would avoid going to prison, but about his father's advice to him. She would not allow herself to fully absorb the reality of such a shift in William; could barely believe in it. While he lived under the roof of Summerfield House, he would be for ever stuck in the past. Caged by tradition, he would die its prisoner. She told herself this as they finished up their food.

However, it seemed that Hal and Tess had more up their sleeves. It soon became clear why they had been in a strange mood.

'Mum, William's going to collect Hal from here tomorrow. On the way to Glasgow,' Tess said, stacking their bowls.

'But it's not on the way!' Amy exclaimed, before glancing guiltily at Hal. Their tiny row of old cottages on the edge of Loch Lomond was not on the way to anywhere, and certainly not to Glasgow University. Sounding less hysterical, she added, 'As I said, I'm more than happy to take you, Hal. It's crazy for him to come all this way.'

'We can't change it now, sorry,' Tess said, standing up with the plates and sounding very adult about it. Amy couldn't find a way to argue back.

Twenty-four hours after hearing the news of William's visit, Amy was still trembling, and her skin was cold. They were to see each other any minute now after eleven months and three days of no contact. The thought of facing him after all this time had turned her happy little world upside down. She had been doing well without him, had almost managed to forget how it had felt to be in love. Her life was full enough without the complexities of heartbreak to dwell upon.

She was proud of everything she had achieved. Her position at a local joinery company near Balloch had morphed into a design job. Two days a week she was allowed to work from home. She drew her kitchens at a small oak desk at a window on the landing upstairs, Meggie curled at her feet. It was a happy place with its view over the water. On calm days, she might nip out for a lunchtime swim. On rainy days, she met friends at the café for an egg sandwich and a warming pot of tea. Every day, she walked, exploring the shores of Loch Lomond or climbing Conic Hill and its surrounds.

Tess was happy too. When she wasn't out with her boyfriend, Matt, she'd stay in and make hot chocolate, pull her knees up under the tartan blanket and gossip with Amy into the early hours by the fire. Admittedly, most of the time she was out with Matt. They'd met in their English class at their sixth-form college. He was a mountain climber and wore fleeces and drove her to college in a camper van that broke down all the time. According to Tess, he was perfect. They had both gained provisional places at Edinburgh University. Matt was going to study archaeology and Tess was going to study English literature. They'd got it all worked out.

Amy had got her life all worked out, too. And William did not figure in it.

She shredded the kale for the stew and drained the beans, referring to the recipe more often than usual. Her nerves were frayed.

When she spied his grey Porsche pulling up in front of the cottages, her flip-flopping heart sank to her toes. A Porsche? What a cliché, she thought. Then big blond Hamish bolted through the back seats and scrambled onto his lap and licked his face. William clambered out of the low sporty seat with him. The ungainliness of it made her chuckle. She checked herself. She would not be smiling at him much today.

Having rearranged his long limbs and straightened his green crew-neck sweater and clipped Hamish onto his lead, he stood for a while with his back to the terrace and stared out at the view over the loch. Hamish sat quietly by his side. Today the water was glassy, reflecting the occasional cloud in the sky. Amy could have sworn she saw his shoulders drop.

When he knocked on the door, she whipped off her apron and hung back in the kitchen, letting Hal and Tess welcome him into the front room. He had to stoop slightly to get in. Hamish bounded up at each one of them, licking and yelping and howling his excitement. Amy buried her face in his fur to smell the outdoors on him. Tears prickled in her eyes. Old Meggie sniffed at Hamish's backside and then at William's knee, very cautiously, before retreating into her basket.

It was crowded with the dogs and the four of them inside. Amy's palms became clammy. She and William couldn't look each other in the eye for more than a split second. But then, when he came forward to kiss her on the cheek, she was warmed by him and could have stayed there for ever. He smelt of old oak trees and freshly cut flowers and laundered cotton. The soft graze from his beard left a welcome tingling on her skin. Absently she put her hand to her cheek as though treasuring it. Looking at his face was like coming home. He'd cut his hair. It suited him. No longer would he need to sweep it off his forehead. Thinking back, she realised this had been like a nervous tic of his.

She began heating up the bean and kale stew.

Soon, over their steaming plates, the conversation between the four of them flowed as though no time had passed. There was a lot to catch up on. It reminded her of how they had eaten and chatted together at the big round table at Summerfield House every evening after school. Here they were at a small square table, but there was little material difference in terms of how it felt. The reasons why they had fallen apart were impossible to grasp.

'I never thought I'd see the day that Tess enjoyed a bowl of mushy beans and greens,' William teased.

'Don't worry, I still eat peanut butter straight out of the jar,' she laughed.

'Oh good. You know how little I like change.'

'God, yes,' Tess guffawed.

He leant back into his chair. 'But I'll have you know, I've been embracing lots of change lately too, haven't I, Hal?'

Hal cleared his throat and looked down at his shoes. 'Yup. He's a different man,' he said, but Amy couldn't tell if his tone was shy or mocking. Tess shot him a questioning glance.

Amy said, 'Oh?'

'Go on, tell them,' Hal said.

William put all ten fingers on the edge of the table and said, 'I've moved out of Summerfield House.'

Amy felt her cheeks burn. 'That must have been very hard,' she said, genuinely heartbroken for him.

Processing what it meant for them, she got up to open the back window, put the kettle on, rummaged through the boxes of tea bags in the cupboard to find the Darjeeling. She had bought William's favourite tea unconsciously many months ago, like a habit she couldn't break.

The box fell out onto the floor. He picked it up and handed it to her and they soaked in each other's features for as long as was polite.

'I've got lots to talk to you about, if you'll let me,' he said.

Both clung to the box as they slowly stood up.

'I think that's our cue to leave, Hal,' Tess said. 'Matt's going to be down at the pub, if you fancy a pint?'

When their grown-up children had left, Amy and William floundered around like actual children. Neither one of them could start the conversation they needed to have. Hamish snored under the table. Small talk about the kids or their jobs took over again. The *lots to talk about* had become nothing, and time was running out. She was eager to hear of the months lost between them, but couldn't summon up the courage to ask him.

When she was washing up their mugs, feeling depressed about the awkwardness between them, she had an idea.

'Let's go for a swim in the loch.'

'But it's freezing outside!'

'Exactly.' She wanted to feel something, she wanted him to feel something. She wanted to shake them up again and knock the last eleven months out of them.

'I'm not good with cold water.'

'But you're embracing change, right?'

'Oh dear. I said that, didn't I.'

She put her hands on her hips. 'Well then?'

'Okay. In the spirit of the new me,' he said regretfully.

'Great,' she said, inhaling sharply. 'I'll go and find Hal's swimmers.'

As they peeled off their warm clothes and contemplated the chilly brown water lapping at their toes, Amy decided she had been mad to suggest this. Her skin was mottled after the long winter. She was shy of it in front of William.

'Come on,' she said, laughing at him as he stood shivering in Hal's trunks, which were a little too snug.

Stripped down, almost as naked as the day they were born, the two of them were the same, just flesh and blood and full of self-doubt, like everyone else and as good as none.

'Is this some form of punishment?' he asked, hopping from one foot to the other at the edge of the loch. Hamish barked at the water.

The thought hadn't occurred to her, but she liked it as an idea. 'I guess you do deserve it.'

'No question about that,' he chortled.

'Ignore all the rules and do it quickly, okay? Like ripping off a plaster.'

She anticipated how her heart would seize up and beat so

fast panic would set in. She'd feel vulnerable and weakened, cracked open, left wondering if she could withstand the pain of exposure. Then she'd harness her breath and overcome her anxiety and swim.

Grabbing William's hand, she confidently waded in. Hamish followed and then shot back to the safety of the shore again to sniff about.

Together, clasping onto one another, Amy and William picked up the pace and ran screaming and laughing into the freezing-cold water. Before they dived in, their eyes met, and Amy saw colours dancing in his irises, pitched greener than she had ever seen them. It looked to her as though many tears had flowed through them, cleansing them, shining them up to see a world anew, unfiltered and unfettered by secrets and shame. He was stripped down, exposed and brave, and she had never loved him more.

After resurfacing, he swam a speedy breaststroke towards her and whooped, gasping, exhilarated and thrilled, 'Woo-hoo! Oh my God, my heart's stopped! This was your plan all along, wasn't it? To kill me off!'

But from the look of his smile, she knew that she'd done just the opposite.

# A LETTER FROM CLARE

Dear Readers,

Thank you for reading *The Wedding Night*. If you have enjoyed it, please do keep in touch by clicking on the sign-up link below, where you'll hear about what I'm working on next.

*www.bookouture.com/clare-boyd*

I loved the process of writing this book. Perhaps because I'm fascinated by teenagers. They get a bad rap, but they're amazing. They're going through so many extraordinary changes as they begin to separate from their parents or carers to become their own people. And they do it with such passion.

But it's a precarious time as a parent or carer. You never know what they're doing behind your back. In *The Wedding Night*, the teens become products of their environment. Hal learns to be as secretive as his dad. Tess loses herself to Rory. Rory thinks money will solve all his problems. Because of the lies their parents are telling themselves, the children make bad choices and end up in very real danger.

County lines drug gangs tend to target and groom vulnerable children just like Rory. His dysfunctional home life leaves him susceptible to Logan's wiles. Gangs are known to recruit 'clean skins' from middle-class backgrounds who don't have criminal records and are therefore off the police radar. Right across the social spectrum, from the privileged to the underprivileged, kids of any age or background can be enticed by the cash incentives and comradeship promised by offenders. As an aside, it's worth remembering that every recreational drug taken casually at a party will have child exploitation at its source.

Anyone affected by the issues raised in this book can contact two incredible charities: Pace (Parents Against Child Exploitation), which supports parents and carers whose children are being exploited; and WiSE (What is Sexual Exploitation), which helps children and young people to stay safe in their relationships.

On a much lighter note, please do follow me on social media to hear hot-off-the-press news of my upcoming books.

Again, I can't thank you enough for reading *The Wedding Night*. Please do leave a review if you liked it!

With very best wishes,

Clare

facebook.com/clare.boyd.14

twitter.com/ClareBoydClark

instagram.com/claresboyd

# ACKNOWLEDGEMENTS

Thanks, as always, go to Broo Doherty and Jessie Botterill. Writing books wouldn't be half as much fun without you. And I'd like to thank Jayne Osborne, who is a very welcome new addition to the publishing dream team.

I want to say a big thank you to Maria Edwards, a child vulnerability adviser, who put me in touch with the brilliant PC Matt Bryant. Matt is passionately dedicated to helping the young victims of county lines drugs gangs in his role as a SPOT (single point of contact) on the child exploitation team in Surrey and Sussex. I have no doubt that he and his colleagues have saved many young lives. He works closely with the charities Pace and WiSE mentioned above. I'm so grateful to him for his help in the shaping of the county lines story strand. Any inaccuracies or errors I may have made are mine alone.

Printed in Great Britain
by Amazon

24741656R00229